# Other books by Fred Patten

Best in Show: Fifteen Years of Outstanding Furry Fiction (2003)
Reprinted as:
Furry! The World's Best Anthropomorphic Fiction! (2006)

Watching Anime, Reading Manga:
25 Years of Essays and Reviews (2004)

Already Among Us; An Anthropomorphic Anthology (2012)

The Ursa Major Awards Anthology:
A Tenth Anniversary Celebration (2012)

What Happens Next: An Anthology of Sequels (2013)

Five Fortunes (2014)

Funny Animals and More: From Anime to Zoomorphics (2014)

# Anthropomorphic Aliens
## An Interstellar Anthology

*Edited by Fred Patten*

# Anthropomorphic Aliens
## An Interstellar Anthology

Production copyright FurPlanet Productions © 2014
Cover artwork copyright © 2014 by Roz Gibson

**Published by FurPlanet Productions**
Dallas, Texas
www.FurPlanet.com

ISBN 978-1-61450-192-3

Printed in the United States of America
First Edition Trade Paperback July 2014

Dedicated to: **Poul Anderson & Gordon R. Dickson**

The creators of the Hokas—the first furry aliens that I met, in my early teens.

I had encountered intelligent aliens before them, such as the Venerians and Martians in Robert A. Heinlein's *Space Cadet* and *Red Planet,* and Tweel the Martian in Stanley G. Weinbaum's "A Martian Odyssey", but none that really stood out as characters rather than as part of the exotic alien backgrounds. The Hokas were my introduction to charismatic non-humans that I really hoped that we would find when humanity develops space travel.

So here's to the Hokas, and all of their galactic brethren! May there be lots of them.

# Table of Contents

# Introduction

## by Fred Patten

Science fiction has been a popular genre for over a hundred years, going back to Jules Verne's, H. G. Wells' and Edgar Rice Burroughs' novels. The first dedicated s-f magazine was Hugo Gernsback's *Amazing Stories* that started in April 1926. Before then the popular term for s-f stories was "scientific romances" or "scientific fiction". Gernsback coined the awkward "scientifiction" in his first issue, but it was almost immediately shortened by s-f's fans into "science fiction", with or without a hyphen. By a decade later, "science fiction" was almost universally in use.

Early science fiction included many interplanetary and interstellar aliens, but in almost all cases, these were just background or supporting characters to the heroic human spacemen. The first alien to really stand out as an individual was the birdlike Martian Tweel in Stanley G. Weinbaum's "A Martian Odyssey", in *Wonder Stories*, July 1934. "We are v-r-r-riends! Ouch!" But the friendly Tweel, even though it is the most memorable character in the story, is little more than a very weird alien described by the castaway spaceman Dick Jarvis. "A Martian Odyssey" is basically the s-f equivalent of an adventure tale of a 19th-century American or European explorer discovering an unknown African or Amazonian or Australian tribe, and being befriended by a helpful exotic native.

It was around 1950 that non-monster inhuman aliens started to become memorable characters in their own right. The oldest story in *Anthropomorphic Aliens* is L. Sprague de Camp's humorous "The Inspector's Teeth" (*Astounding Science Fiction*, April 1950), in which an extrasolar Osirian who looks like a human-sized tyrannosaur or velociraptor wants to enroll in one of Earth's famous colleges. Hithafea is the only alien surrounded by adolescent and early-20s human students—can you imagine a velociraptor enthusiastically joining a college fraternity? ("The Inspector's Teeth" is set in 2054; an example of early s-f authors' optimism as to how soon humanity would develop interstellar travel.) As s-f matured during the last half of the 20th century, the aliens (and uplifted or genetically altered anthropomorphic Earth animals) gradually stopped being supporting characters and became the main protagonists to human supporting characters.

Here are eleven stories reprinted from magazines and books from 1950 to 2013 that feature memorable "furries" of the future, from aliens to uplifted animals, in an interstellar civilization.

P.S.: Rereading all of these stories has revealed that there has been no standardization of the spelling of "furry" and "Furry", and "furries" and "furrys" up to now. We have chosen to use "furry" and "furries" throughout *Anthropomorphic Aliens*, even when it has required changing the spelling in some stories.

The WebFed stories by Ken Pick are set in a galactic nation of human and alien equality. Humans, the foxlike Thalendri, the otterlike Rylii Selkies, the savage predatory avian Skreeln, the saurian Larant, and other sapients all share the same interstellar civilization. There are also the Artificials; in this case, genetically-created lifeforms made to look like Terran "funny animals", most prominently the sexy rabbit-women made for pornographic purposes.

"Mask of the Ferret" features an Artificial of a different kind in a "death on a spaceship" plot. The Free Trader Coventry, on a eight-day FTL journey from Calafia to Alorya, has a mixed-species crew and passengers; the latter including a Human Roman Catholic priest, a Human dowager and her young daughter, a Selkie travel-writer, and Jill Noir, a Human-sized ferret who deliberately looks like a funny-animal chain-smoking 17th-century pirate captain to get attention. Something starts killing them all on their first day. Who among the Humans and aliens will figure out how to save the survivors?

# Mask of the Ferret

## by Ken Pick and C. Alan Loewen

*"My argument is not that we create because that is in our nature. My argument is that unlike God, we're not willing to die for our handiwork."*
—*The Travel Diaries of Father Heidler*

Free Trader Coventry
Catalina Highport, Calafia
Pacifica System, the Grey Zone

Space on interstellar craft is always at a premium so the room to work was tight, even for a Thalendri. Yet with practiced ease, Nuyann squeezed his slim paravulpine body through the access hatch and slid inside, seven-eighths of his weight vanishing as ship gravity gave way to Catalina's one-eighth gee. The enclosed air was stale with the odor of hot electronics, old plastics, and lubricants; Nuyann fought the urge to sneeze.

*Leave it to* Humandri *to design a ship they can't repair themselves,* he thought as he braced himself in the tight low-gee accessway, massaging the tools and parts out of his tote-vest. Nuyann had enjoyed his status as chief engineer aboard the *Coventry* for almost two years now, but even two years was not enough time to understand all the reasoning and actions of the primarily-Human crew. If it weren't for the two Thalendri and the one Rylii aboard, the slickskins would never have survived the political and social intricacies of the Grey Zone.

The ship groaned, the pressure bulkhead massaging his back with a shudder that ended with a jolt. The sharp metal-on-metal sounds of a freight container being secured in the hold set his vulpine ears twitching,

15

then silence. A moment later, the shuddering resumed as the next container slid into place on the other side of the bulkhead.

This time, they'd be running nearly full; forty-two standard containers, common-carrier shipments filled out with spec-trade goods, bound from Califia System to the main-trunk Web connection at Alorya. Load, undock, boost out, FTL insertion, FTL emergence, boost in, dock, unload, repeat—the routine of a small-trader in the halo of minor worlds and systems between WebFed and the New Suns Nebula, where traffic was too sparse for the big main-route merchies. This time, complicated with five passengers and an avionics grid that decided to go *keshi* at the last minute.

"Nuyann?" a human voice crackled over his intercom. "We're done here. See you forward."

"I just have to replace this panel, Lewis," Nuyann yipped back into the shoulder-mounted intercom. "Ten minutes tops. Tell the Captain for me."

The Thalendri continued his work, gekkering over the manufacturer of cheap electronics that would fry just when the need for them was most critical. Behind him, the crew left on other important pre-lift tasks leaving him in peace.

He had the last circuit panel almost in place when he froze, ears and tail twitching. A noise, a sound, so subtle that his fox-like ears had almost missed it.

"*Wowowow?*" he called. "Anybody there?" No answer; just the crackling and popping of normal thermal stress. Instinctively, he tongued his nosepad, trying to catch some scent. Captain, Lewis, Williams, Sayers, Melai, *nim*-Chokonnu, traces of the last batch of passengers and stevedores—nothing out of the ordinary....

Then it hit—a wave of para-adrenalin that stood his fur on end. Something was in there with him—without sound, without scent, but there. A predator, like some sort of invisible *gildarr*, stalking him, closing for the kill.

And he was trapped—wedged into the tight accessway. Any second the great clawed paw of a *gildarr* would reach in and dig him out in pieces; or the toothy maw of a para-serp would slither in…

Senses heightened by dread, Nuyann felt the presence as *it* inexorably moved closer to where he lay paralyzed in the accessway. Trapped in a burrow. At any moment, *it* would seize him and his fear whispered of unthinkable horror.

"NUYANN!" a voice crackled through his intercom.

Nuyann screamed, a shrill piercing *yelp* that reverberated in the narrow crawlway even while a tiny rational part of his brain assured him the voice was nothing but Captain Carroll and that the presence had already left as quickly as shadows when a light is turned on.

"Nuyann!" the voice cried again, but this time through both intercom and accessway, heavy with concern. "You alright in there?"

The Thalendri gulped in air as fought to keep his emotions under control. "Yes," he said, his voice reduced to a squeal. "You just startled me."

The captain's face appeared at the accessway hatch. "Lewis said you'd be done in ten. Not asleep in there are you?"

"My ten minutes aren't up yet," Nuyann said. "I'm almost finished."

"Nuyann," the captain said calmly, "That was half an hour ago. I think you've lost track of time."

\* \* \*

In her undress uniform with rank-striped sleeves, Merchant Captain Third-class Louise Carroll made her way through the entry airlock into the pressurized boarding tunnel where it was ship's tradition to greet oncoming passengers along with the *Coventry's* stewardess. At Nuyann's panicked request, she had stayed with him, "standing guard" just outside the accessway entry, until the panel had been replaced. Despite his protests that all was well, the captain had tactfully avoided pointing out the large wet spot in the crotch of his coveralls. She could hardly believe that her calling out Nuyann's name would have scared him to that degree, but time was of the essence, and she would pursue the matter later with Melanai, his girlfriend as well as shipmate.

Carroll found Melanai, the ship's stewardess, in the small reception alcove in the boarding tunnel waiting patiently for the captain to grant permission to allow the passengers on board. Carroll thought it best not to mention the incident with Nuyann at present. Passengers could be a handful and Melanai had other problems.

Melanai's name was para-human, a recurring fashion among Thalendri. Her main responsibility was to make sure the passengers were reasonably comfortable throughout the voyage, and she did her job not only efficiently, but with the trademark elegance of a Thalendri.

Though humanity's xenophobic tendencies were still present in their racial memory, the bottom line was the vast majority of humans liked Thalendri. The fear of what was different had been replaced by memories of Reynard the Fox and other tales and amusements of human childhood. Xenobiologists had a field day arguing how an alien race could so accurately mimic an anthropomorphic version of Terry foxes, but regardless, the Thalendri reaped the rewards of the coincidence and everybody was happy.

"Are we ready for our guests?" Carroll asked.

"Yes, Captain," the sharp-uniformed vixen replied. "We have five passengers. Three *Humandri*, one *Rylii*, and another."

The captain arched her eyebrow in question. "Please tell me we're not taking a Skreeln." Involuntarily she shuddered. Those great flightless birds-of-prey from N'kree had bad reputations as ship's passengers—at least aboard non-Skreeln ships. Like any warlike society, their social skills were highly ritualistic. It was a five-minute ceremony of bowing and greeting and invitations and hospitality offerings just to enter a ship, and the captain hated the lengthy rites.

"No," Melanai said. "An Artificial."

Melanai carefully observed the captain, watching her facial features tighten in an amazing passage of emotions from repugnance to anger to frustration to very reluctant acceptance. In spite of the captain's feelings, even in the Zone there were laws that had to be obeyed. If a passenger had the money, they were given a ticket. To refuse for any reason could result in loss of the license needed to carry passengers and carrying passengers was good money even if you had to carry genetically-created lifeforms.

"Of course, it's female," the captain said, gritting her teeth.

"Yes," Melanai said.

"And it's a porn star."

"No. Some sort of Courier."

"I'm surprised." the captain said and then sighed. "Sometimes humanity disgusts me."

The Thalendri put her silken hand on the captain's arm. "*Mirai*, please remember that we create Artificials too."

"I know," Carroll said, "but you treat them like real people, give them full rights and all sorts of legal protection. We use ours for wanker-toys. What's the base-template?"

Melanai checked her smartpad. "Ferret," she said. "I'm unfamiliar with the species."

"It's an Earth animal," the captain said. "A pet."

The Thalendri again checked her smartpad. "They're waiting."

Captain Carroll sighed. "Crack the hatch," she said. "Let's greet the guests."

Melanai prided herself in knowing the psychology of many species that formed WebFed and its surrounding territories. It didn't matter whether her guests were the ritualistic Skreeln, the telepathic M'Kranthi, the saurian Larant, or any of the other species that formed the interstellar community. She could effectively interact with each one, no mean feat for a Thalendri.

Captain Carroll knew this all too well; which is why Melanai was one of the best-paid ship's stewardesses in the entire Grey Zone—at least outside corporate liveries.

The pressure doors at the far end of the boarding tunnel spun open. The first guests were a human woman and her daughter in Califian casual wear. The woman was obviously distracted by the hustle-and-bustle of preparing for the trip to Alorya, and she tugged her eight-year old daughter after her as if she were merely another piece of baggage.

"Mrs. Naomi Goodrich?" the Thalendri asked in her soft yipping voice. "Welcome aboard the *Coventrai*. I am Melanai, your stewardess for the journey. May I introduce Captainess Louise Carroll?"

The woman blinked at them owlishly. Far back in her eyes, Melanai could see awareness gathering as synapses started firing into recognizable patterns.

"Oh, yes," the woman said. "I'm sorry. I'm not much for space travel. Where's my stateroom?"

"I'll be happy to show you," Melanai purred. She bent down to stare eye-to-eye with the human child. "And you must be Winter."

The girl stared at the fox-like alien with an open mouth, a little frightened and yet mostly enchanted. Melanai wondered if she were the first Thalendri the child had seen close-up and prepared for the indignity of being petted.

"Come, Winter," the mother said.

The next passenger was a Selkie whom Melanai introduced to the Captain as Mr. Pitter. Definitely not a Selkie name, which meant he was travelling obviously incognito—not unusual for the small musteloids.

If Thalendri served as the cosmos' equivalent to Terry foxes, Rylii/ Selkies were the equivalent of Terry otters: small and agile, with slick fur that made them glisten in the light. Pitter was a three-tone-blue Littorial, with dark blue-grey head and tail and large, blue eyes, nude except for a wide utility tote-belt and a cloth Gatsby cap.

He bowed low toward Captain Carroll, chirping in the Selkie tradition. Standing, his head was level with the Captain's abdomen. "I'm looking forward to the trip, Captain," he chittered, his small front teeth glistening as his lips pulled back in a parody of a human grin. "I'm a freelance travel-writer, and I do hope we'll have an opportunity to talk while FTL. I get all my ideas from fascinating people I meet."

Melanai was secretly pleased to see the Captain smile in response and assure the Selkie that she looked forward to a small chat.

Assured that his luggage was waiting for him in his stateroom, the Selkie moved gracefully down the hallway.

The next guest was an elderly Human, tall and gaunt, but with a smile on his face, in not-quite-casual wear except for a black shirt with a Roman collar. "Father Eric Heidler," he said, shaking the Captain's hand before Melanai had a chance to introduce him. "Roman Catholic Church, Old Earth. My friends call me Eric."

"And friends call me Melanai. Welcome aboard the *Coventrai*," the Thalendri said, offering her hand in an attempt to regain some modicum of control. The priest took her hand and smiled.

"I just arrived in the Zone two weeks ago," he said, "and I've not had an opportunity to talk to any Thalendri yet. I hope you'll offer me an opportunity to rectify that situation?"

Melanai nodded her head and gave the priest the location and number of his stateroom.

The captain waited until Father Heidler was well out of earshot. "How delightful," she muttered. "I'm going to be cornered by a writer-wannabe, and you're going to be converted. Now where is our last passenger? She's going to be late in five minutes."

Twenty-five minutes later, Melanai watched Captain Carroll run through the fascinating human transition from frustration to annoyance to anger. In five more minutes, the passenger could be classed as a no-show, but the half-hour allowed a passenger to be late directly impacted the port's launch schedules.

Exactly with one minute to spare, the final passenger arrived, nonchalantly strolling down the boarding tunnel. Melanai smelled the Artifical well before she saw her. The creature reeked of benga—cheap rush-blends, instead of the fragrant taste-blends she and Nuyann liked to do occasionally.

"Captainess Carroll, please meet Jill Noir."

The Captain stared despite her professionalism. The construct only stood up to the captain's chin, but despite her short stature, she could easily turn heads due to her overwhelming uniqueness.

Black, intelligent eyes peered out of a furry, muzzled face, an anthropomorphic ferret from a child's fairy-tale story with a large pink nosepad and a dark-brown mask stretching around her eyes. The face was framed by a long cascade of jet-black curls, an outrageous addition to her frilled costume and long, black tailcoat that reminded the captain of childhood stories of fairies and pirate captains. Not really wanting to do so, she sneaked a look at the creature's left hand.

Instead of the half-expected sharp hook, the creature had a hand, chocolate-furred and claw-tipped, with the source of her incense-burner odor—a benga cigarette at the end of an ivory-tipped holder.

"I'm sorry," Melanai said, "but smoking is restricted to your stateroom. You'll have to extinguish your bengastick before boarding."

With a graceful move, the ferret lifted cigarette holder to muzzle and took two long deep inhales that made Melanai wince before simply pinching out the end of the bengastick, ignoring what had to be some discomfort to her fingertips from the burning embers.

It blew a column of grey smoke towards the overhead, then faced the human and vixen. "Satisfied?"

"I will be staying in my room throughout most of the trip," it continued with a slight lisp. "I trust that I have a solo stateroom as contracted?"

"Of course," Melanai said, the picture of an effective stewardess. "We hope you will enjoy your passage."

"And my baggage?"

"Stowed and confirmed. In our LCL area, at the forward end of the hold."

The creature moved on, ignoring to shake the captain's hand or even address her. The Captain simply stared and shook her head.

"*Tahai ari*, Captainess?" Melanai asked.

Carroll sighed and shook her head. "I swear the reason you're the stewardess and I'm the captain is because I could never do your job."

Melanai gave the equivalent of a Thalendri smile. "That's why I earn the *shildri*."

\* \* \*

Jill Noir detoured from the fore-and-aft corridor through the passenger wardroom enjoying the impact she had on her fellow passengers. The human woman with her child simply stared. The one Selkie even stared though he tried hard to pretend he was reading a news chit. The remaining human went back to his private thoughts after nothing more than a casual glance.

A few moments later, the ship's stewardess appeared and escorted them to their staterooms.

Jill sighed with relief to see she had been given Cabin 4, a lucky number for her. A short corridor flanked by stowage lockers and "facilities" opened onto a compartment with built-in sofa/bunk, video-wall, a small smartdesk and minimal table space; all small enough to climb around in Zero-G if internal gravity failed.

She stowed her luggage in the locker, then carefully removed her wig and sat it on a collapsible headstand she pulled from her carry-ons.

Without it, she looked even more animal-like and Jill detested seeing herself in a mirror without her wig in place.

She stripped off her coat, ruffled shirt, thigh-boots, and cauda-breeches and sighed with pleasure at the coolness. To make herself even more comfortable, Jill found the cabin's environmental controls and dropped the ambient temperature by five degrees.

She caught a glimpse of herself in the small vanity mirror in the lavatory alcove, and her lips pulled back in an involuntary snarl. Naked, she was nothing more than a large, soulless animal, a mocking blend of human and animal traits; a human woman costumed in the fur, tail and head of a Terry ferret, owned by her creators. Well she would show them. They had trained her too well. She may have no rights or no soul, but she had the mind of a ... the mind of a...

The message light on the video wall and smartdesk began to blink, signaling an incoming message, most likely the standard video on what to do in case of an emergency.

The blinking light caught her attention, blinking on and off with a hypnotic effect. *Shinything!* She stared at it with a weird fascination as an uncontrollable urge started to well up within her, an urge to touch the light, pry it out of the wall, worry it with her teeth. *Dook dook dook dook...*

Suddenly, Jill shook her head savagely. "NO!"

She went into the lavatory and stood over the sink, her fur bristled in concentration. A few moments later, she began to gag until she vomited up a small plastic capsule big enough to fit in the palm of her hand. Rinsing it off and drying it well, she unscrewed the capsule and poured the contents into her hand, a handful of tiny yellow pills. She sighed with relief and popped one in her mouth.

The ferret buried inside her would now remain buried for at least another six hours.

She stretched out on the bunk at the far end of the stateroom, careful to avoid her thrown clothing. There would a few hours until the *Coventry* could launch and pull far enough out to initiate FTL insertion but she had enough time for the luxury of a stretch.

Lazily, she yawned, revealing a full set of mustelid teeth. Jill knew the item she was couriering was safe in the hold and deep within it was buried the real article she had been told to deliver, the article that was going to buy her freedom and help her escape once and for all from her owners.

It would be her first act of thievery and if her plans for the rest of her life went well, it would only be the first theft of many more to come.

\* \* \*

"Catalina Control to *Coventry*—" the voice crackled over the bridge speakers. "You are cleared for lift."

Captain Carroll sat back in her command chair, while Lewis and Nuyann finished the last of their checklists.

"Acknowledged." Looking to port, she got confirmation from Lewis at the navigation/co-pilot console, then to starboard for the same from Nuyann at the Engineering station. "All right, cast us off."

The ship shuddered faintly as the boarding tunnels detached; faint echoing booms came from aft as the umbilicals blew loose and retracted. "Nuyann, how are we?"

"Full internal power, all *ari*... Aetherics online and ready to lift."

"Then let's go." The Captain reached forward for the pilot's controls, keyed in her intercom. On the holo-HUD before her, a wireframe tunnel marked the departure route from the port into deep space. "Catalina Control, this is *Coventry*. We are lifting now."

Drive fields strengthened, then the *Coventry's* eighty-meter length lifted from the landing bay. Perimeter walls fell away as she rose, revealing Catalina's cratered surface, like pockmarked Portland Cement stretching to a close-in horizon that fell away and curved to become a well-cratered moon.

Before them stretched Calafia's ring-bisected crescent, city lights sparkling at occasional intervals on the world's dark side. Caroll kept the *Cov's* pip centered in the wireframe display, as the wireframe tunnel widened into a funnel, then pulled back to a system display.

"*Coventry*, you are clear of port space. *Bon voyage*."

"Acknowledged. See you next time round."

Drive fields rippled, biased. With maneuvering thrust, Carroll slowly pivoted the ship away from the world and its orange main sun, then cut in full power. A ghost of acceleration came through the compensators as the *Cov* began her boost to FTL Insertion point, angling out from the world and sun and off the ecliptic, away from the gravity wells and dust and debris that could interfere with Insertion.

Engaging the autopilot, the Captain relaxed back in her command chair as the *Coventry* boosted out at her full two gees. The ship's crew may be small, but its training served them well. Chokonnu, the Selkie, served as ship's medic and the humans Lewis, Williams, and Sayers—New Anglian expats like herself—served the remaining roles as navigator, assistant engineer and jack-of-all trades and master of some.

Together, Human and non-human, they made a close-knit community where the company was comfortable and the pay was sufficient.

Again, Carroll skimmed over the passenger roster and scowled. Docking fees and fuel prices ran high in the backwaters of the Zone so transporting passengers were an economic necessity, but not the most enjoyable part of captaining a spaceship. Cargo didn't make many demands or throw up in the staterooms.

A priest, a woman and her young daughter, a churp-and-slurp, and a man-made monster, filling four of the eight passenger cabins. Only half-full, but Carroll wasn't going to begrudge the loss of income, a tradeoff for some additional peace and quiet.

She looked again at the name of Jill Noir. When a child, Carroll had actually owned a ferret, but this creature on her ship was a travesty, a caricature of the hyperactive goof of a mustelid she grew up with. It didn't even have the musky smell of a ferret, but the reek of benga rush-blends.

"Smells like an incense burner," the captain muttered.

"Sorry, Captain?" Lewis asked. "Did you say something?"

"Nothing," she replied. "How long until we can Insert?"

"Checking." An overlay appeared on the display, with a projected course path intersecting. "ETI is sixteen hours and twenty-three minutes."

\* \* \*

The priest had not yet retired to his stateroom. He knew that during the eight days' trip he would soon tire of the cramped quarters so for the present he enjoyed the slightly larger space of the passenger wardroom, starboard of the corridor.

Through the millennia, the Roman Catholic Church had proven itself to be a successful survivor. With the advent of space travel, many aspects of Christendom had faded away, splintering and dissipating, unable to cope with the realities of First Contact and the influx of alien technology and paradigms. Some of the splinters had gone into deep denial; others had taken the "Islamic Approach", fighting any and all change with blood and terror, triggering no-fault persecutions from secular governments. However, the Catholic Church had foreseen the strong possibility they were not alone in the cosmos and as far back as the 20th Century (Gregorian Calendar) had formed a statement of purpose and action if sentient alien life did exist.

And now there were new challenges to face, some far more deadly and evil than those 20th century visionaries had imagined.

Alone in the wardroom, Heidler pulled out his smartpad, configured the datasystem for keyboard mode, and began to type.

Vicar-General Choi:

Carcosa Artifact definitely stolen by its courier. Now aboard free-trader Coventry, R2-500 type, New Anglian Registry G-TDRFAB, bound for Alorya System NOT repeat NOT Changorr. ETA Alorya Prime in approximately eight days (FSC 575-205). I will continue to follow and be alert for an opportunity, but I will not move unless there is almost absolute certainty of success.

Make any other chasers aware the courier is a construct armed with natural teeth and claws with the obvious agility and power to use them.

Heidler

Heidler double-encrypted the message, attached his expense card ID for payment, saved it to a chit and paged the stewardess. He gave her the chit and requested it be sent. "Will you be able to relay this back to Califia?" he asked. "It needs to go out by tachyon-cable before we Insert."

Assured by the Thalendri stewardess that it was possible, he settled back into his chair, rubbing his left hand.

Though not as tactile as his original hand, his new one was actually composed of organic plastics with interesting claws of its own. A simple mental thought, a deliberate flexing of muscles, and each fingertip would shoot out a sharp plastic hypodermic needle armed with a fascinating choice of drugs and chemicals.

Heidler abhorred violence, but if the courier refused to give up the artifact he was prepared to put her out of action.

\* \* \*

To an eight-year old child, the Coventry exuded mystery and wonder. Winter had read enough about starflight to know what FTL engines did; how they kicked the ship up into "another dimension" and let it fall back somewhere else. Yet, FTL physics aside, the best treat of the trip were her fellow passengers; upright talking foxes and otters, or at least the alien equivalents, and the strange creature her mother had called a ferret. Curious, Winter had looked up the reference in her portable school smartpad and the pictures showed a small four-legged furred animal still existing on Old Earth, a world she had never seen and never expected to.

She asked her mother why the ferrets in the pictures walked on four legs and the ferret they had seen on board walked on two, but her mother hushed her into silence. "I don't want to talk about that creature," her mother said impatiently, "And I don't want you to have anything to do with it while we're on board ship. You have your 'pad and you have your lessons. They'll keep you busy enough."

Winter had sighed and kept quiet, yet she had been thinking.

An hour later, the message light began blinking on the video screen. It was at least several more hours before the *Coventry* would get out far enough for Insertion, and the clock they followed said it was time for the afternoon meal.

Winter's mother gave her child a thorough inspection, pronounced her decent enough to represent humanity amongst the alien savages and with a quick command to behave, they entered the dining compartment opposite the wardroom, where a table had already been prepared for the five passengers.

The elderly man in the Roman collar already sat at the table unconsciously rubbing his left hand. He smiled warmly at the mother and daughter and actually stood up from his seat as they approached.

The Selkie took that moment to exit his stateroom and join them and Winter caught herself just in time to stop herself before she giggled. The creature stood just a little taller than herself and the quick, inquisitive twitch of his nosepad delighted the little girl no end.

"Good afternoon," the Selkie chirped to the three humans, "Mr. Pitter," He bowed low to the group.

There was an uncomfortable moment of silence. Courtesy dictated the lady introduce herself first, but she simply motioned for her daughter to sit next to her and maintained a stony stare at the table setting.

"Father Eric Heidler," the man said quickly, to smooth over the social *faux pas*, and he bowed in response. Pitter *churped* in return and to Winter's great delight and her mother's chagrin, took the seat across from her.

Mrs. Goodrich nodded at the priest. "Mrs. Naomi Goodrich and this is my daughter, Winter."

"The pleasure is mine," Heidler said to them both, fighting a growing annoyance with the woman's obvious xenophobia.

The priest and the Selkie took their seats and Winter eagerly waited for the next episode to take place in this new delightful Wonderland.

The Thalendri stewardess appeared and Winter stared openly. Though she had been raised on Califia, only on board the *Coventry* had she been allowed so close to these wonderful creatures, ignoring her mother's comments about non-humans.

"*Yip!* Again, my name is Melanai. As the ship's stewardess my pleasure is to attend to your needs while you are our guests. I'm assuming introductions have been made? *Ari.*" The Thalendri shot a glance at the closed door of Stateroom 4, her ears flicking down in irritation. "One of our guests may have lost track of time or maybe took a quick nap. Excuse me …"

At that moment, the door suddenly slid open and Jill made her grand appearance.

Once again, the construct was clothed in a lace and brocade suit remindingWinter of the old movies she had seen of the old swashbucklers of the Spanish Main. She looked in awe at the curly wig and even craned her neck to see if, like the movie pirates, the creature wore a long sword. Aside from the fantastic costume, the first thing Winter noticed about the newcomer was her aroma, a thick, cloying scent of burned spice with an underlying whiff of musk.

Father Heidler and Pitter stood as the new guest joined them at the table and took a seat with a small flourish. Winter's mother sniffed audibly.

"And what's for lunch?" the creature asked.

Melanai went to the galley dumbwaiter in the aft bulkhead and opened a small cabinet with stacked trays. With individual names printed on the foil wrappers, the stewardess peeled off the covers; immediately the contents began to steam, throwing off tantalizing smells. "We're having Terry Coq-au-vin, with a special order of Thanandree-biocompatible sushi for *Mir* Pitter. Please be careful as they are hot." The stewardess added, "In future, please check your cabin monitors to make your choices from the daily menu."

While the trays were being served, Winter stared at the ferret-woman until she had caught her attention.

"I'm Winter Goodrich," she said, ignoring the sudden sharp intake of breath from her mother. "And this is my mother. Is this your first trip, too?"

The response was a stare and though the face remained impassive, the eyes displayed a more puzzled reaction as if pondering her answer.

"Jill Noir," the construct said. "The last name means 'black' in Thermidorian. And yes, this is my first time that I will experience FTL." Jill turned to her plate and began picking at her food, avoiding eye contact.

Melanai broke the silence. "I want to take a moment to go over ship procedures with you before we go FTL—which should be in about six hours."

"Our FTL engines are Second-manifold Nightflames, with the FTL speed of most packet liners. We've made the Califia-to-Alorya run several times since I came aboard." The vixen thought for a moment, translating her next sentence in her mind. "Every time, we've taken about eight days— one day out to Insertion, six FTL, and one day in after Emergence."

Winter was fascinated. Her parents had come to Califia when she was only an infant. Now, she and her mother travelled to join her father at his new position in one of the sky-cities of Alorya and the concept of FTL travel was fascinating.

"Will we feel anything when the ship Inserts?' Winter asked.

Her mother tried to hush her, but Melanai raised her furred hand. "Yes, we'll all feel strange for a moment at the transition. Captainess Carroll will give us plenty of advance warning. When the *Coventrai* actually goes FTL, you will most likely feel a little strange for a fleeting moment. Everything will flash blue emitting a harmless form of Cerenkov radiation and then we'll be on our way.

"During Insertion, we will all be together in the wardroom across the way. Afterwards, you are welcome to amuse yourselves any way you wish. All we ask is that you remain in the passenger area, do not harass the crew, and be thoughtful of other's desires and privacy.

"Meals will be held here three times a day. Please be on time. Any questions?"

Winter raised her hand immediately.

"My dear," her mother said with growing impatience, "I'm sure the stewardess doesn't want to be bothered right now."

"No bother, *Mirai Goodrichai*," Melanai said. "Let me answer her question."

Winter looked apprehensively at her mother and then back at the stewardess. "Well," she said, "Can I see the bridge sometime?"

Melanai smiled. "In order to see the bridge, Captainess Carroll has to offer a special invitation and I'll see what I can do. However, just a reminder. The upper deck is the bridge and crews' quarters and is off-limits to all passengers, along with the cargo holds and engine rooms."

Jill, still picking at her food with a fork looked up. "I would like to check on my cargo during the trip. It is very valuable and very delicate."

Melanai's ears flicked. "I'll see what I can do," she said.

Father Heidler had attacked his meal with gusto and his tray lay almost empty. "I'm curious, Ms. Noir. If I may ask, what is your vocation?" he said with a pleasant smile.

Jill paused for a moment before replying. "I'm a dealer in antiques. Self-employed."

"Fascinating," Mr. Pitter interrupted. "It's obvious you're an Artificial. When did you pay off your production contract and become independent?"

The change that came over Jill was frightening. For a moment, the animal inside her came to full awakening and an immediate silence born of shock filled the room.

*I'm going to see a Selkie die*, Father Heidler thought, but in a flash, the wave of emotion on the construct's face disappeared as she regained control.

The Selkie stuttered out an apology, expressing how sorry he had evidently breached some etiquette, but Jill brushed his apology off. "I'm used to questions about my status," she said with a levity that rang hollow. "To answer your question, I fulfilled my contract some years ago and am now a legally-free agent."

Father Heidler smiled grimly as he picked at his dinner. He knew the construct lied and he wondered what game she played.

"What's for pudding?" Winter chimed in.

* * *

Checklists echoed through the bridge as Captain Caroll aligned the HUD pipper on Alorya's star; theoretically a ship could Insert FTL in any attitude, but aligning the ship bow-on to the destination eased the process a bit—at least in most captains' minds. Engaging autopilot to hold attitude, she released the controls and leaned back.

"We're aligned. All right, people. You know the drill." Carroll smiled, sighed and stretched in her command chair. She enjoyed the smoothness with which her crew operated. FTL Insertion was a complex procedure inherent with some danger, but the crew made it look as though they were simply taking a stroll through a park. "Engineering?"

"Capacitors at full," Nuyann said, his vulpine form hunched over his console. "*Ari*, ready to go."

"Confirm capacitors at full. Ten percent overage, stable and waiting," Williams chimed in over the engine-room intercom.

"Navigation?" the captain asked. Lewis had the trickiest part; any anomaly in the process, even a microsecond out-of-sync current surge, could throw them wildly off-course instead of dropping them cleanly into Alorya System.

"Checking…" the navigator said, followed by over a minute of silence as the Nav systems ran through simulation after simulation. "Fab… fab… and Ab-Fab; we have a solution." With a flourish, he flipped his interlock switch. "Ready to Insert."

Carroll keyed the intercom. "This is your captain. We are ready for FTL Insertion. Melanai?"

Melanai's voice routed through the bridge speakers. "Passengers are all in the passenger wardroom, Captainess. All hatches secured. We're ready."

Carroll leaned forward, lifted a safety cover on her console, revealing the large red button that would trigger Insertion. *Looks just like the "self-destruct" button on all the adventure videos—the one that blows up the ship with you in it.* She readied her hand by the button, checked again with Lewis and Nuyann, then sounded the bell. "Coming up on Insertion—"

On the lower deck, Melanai and the passengers sat ready for transition.

"—in five... four... three... two... one—Now!" Her hand came down on the red button.

The entire cosmos flashed an intense blue for an instant; the four on the bridge jerked against their seat harnesses as their nervous systems spasmed from the transition—a sudden, sharp jolt like when struggling to stay awake.

Then everything was back to normal, with one exception. The stars had streaked into lines instead of points; one end at their positions at Insertion, the other where they would be at Emergence. One streak—the phantom image of Alorya's sun—extended from dead ahead to a large bright red spot to starboard; astern, two similar streaks to a vanishing point ghosted Califia's sun and its red dwarf companion.

"Lewis, how are we?"

A moment passed as the navigator took fixes on the stretched stars. This was the worst time; when they'd find out if they were off-course, with no way to correct until they Emerged.

Lewis relaxed. "Clean Insertion, Second Manifold, no problems. ETE Alorya in..." Another pause while the figures came through. "...150 hours, give or take ten."

At the engineering console, Nuyann began powering down. From now until Emergence, they would coast on APU only.

"Good job, people," Carroll said. "Very good job."

The captain could feel the tension flow out of the atmosphere of the bridge. As the old cliché went, space travel was long periods of overwhelming repetitive tedium punctuated with moments of sheer terror. Now solidly FTL, the ship's course was predetermined and nothing was to be done except standard ship maintenance, lots of Terry coffee or Web *takfa* and the occasional book or video.

Suddenly, Nuyann sprang to his feet, spun around and looked toward the rear of the ship, ears down and tail tucking between his legs. Even with his alien features, Carroll could see growing concern on his face.

"Nuyann, what's the matter?"

The Captain turned to look just as the intercom chimed from the passenger wardroom. "Captain," Melanai's voice yipped over the tiny speaker. "The passengers are fine, but I think we should have the cargo hold checked."

The Captain knew Thalendri well enough to recognize the concern in the stewardess's voice.

"Captainess," Nuyann said, his ears flattening and voice rising in panic, "Do you hear that?"

"No," the Captain replied. "Hear what?"

Then suddenly, she did hear something. A sound had finally entered the frequency range of her ears, and it was pouring up the hallway from the cargo hold.

"Is there a passenger in the hold?" the Captain asked, getting to her feet.

The sound grew and it was more than a sound. It was a scream. No. It was a bestial howl, an echoing snarl of rage from some horrific creature escaped from some lunatic's nightmare.

"What the bloody hell is that?" Carroll whispered.

Sayers turned to his console and called up a security diagram of the ship. "Captain," he said. "Nothing shows on the sensors. No life signs whatsoever."

The console screen showed a diagram of the *Coventry*, red dots showing the presence of the bridge crew upper deck forward, the passengers on the lower deck forward, and Williams alone in Engineering aft. However, the hold amidships showed nothing.

"Could we have heard something structural?" Carroll asked. *Or one of the cargoes had a little "extra" they didn't tell us about?*

Sayers' hands flew over his console; low-light camera feeds windowed up on the screen—hold hatches, corrugated metal walls of freight containers, the restraint webbing of the LCL area, loose debris floating in Zero-G. "Air pressure holding, internal gravity off, life-support minimal. Ambient temperature is five above freezing. Hold temperature seems a bit low, but everything else is F.A.B."

\* \* \*

In the passenger wardroom, Melanai spoke calmly to Mrs. Goodrich, assuring her that the strange noise was nothing to be concerned about. The stewardess' biggest concern was to make sure the woman's panic didn't spread to the other passengers. However, aside from the woman's young daughter, the Selkie, the human priest and the construct all remained outwardly calm though curious.

"I'm going to sue!" the woman babbled, near tears. She clutched at her child. "I was told this journey was safe!"

"*Mirai Goodrichai,*" the Thalendri explained, "the Captainess is going to find out what the noise was in a few moments and I assure you the chances are that everything is going to be fine. There are no alarms and no calls from the Captainess to take safety precautions. We'll find out what that noise was in a moment."

"Are we FTL now?" Winter asked. Pale, she still remained calmer than her mother.

"Yes," Melanai said. "That blue flash you saw that came from everywhere was Insertion. From here on, physics does all the rest. In about six days, we'll come out on the other side safe and sound."

* * *

"Nuyann—get aft and find out the source of that noise." The Captain rubbed her temples in frustration. Though the problem would probably be turn out to be minimal, malfunctions and problems in FTL had a tendency to become lethal if not properly looked after.

Nuyann's hands flew over his console; camera-feed windows brightened as the hold lights came on. "I'm bringing the hold life-support up to full. Give me about thirty minutes."

Williams' voice came over the intercom. "Okay, boss. You're the chief engineer. Lead the way."

Nuyann looked shaken. "I didn't like that sound. Sounded like..." The Thalendri's voice trailed off as he realized the rest stared at him. "Never mind. I'll get aft." The paravulpine left the bridge for Engineering, hatch hissing shut behind him.

The ship's sensors had reported that Engineering remained secure and sound, with only the APU active and the main engines cooling down. Nuyann and Williams ran diagnostics and scans with no problems presenting themselves.

Nuyann hit the intercom. "Captain. *Tantulari* back here. Is the cargo hold ready to enter?"

The Captain's voice came back with a faint electronic hiss. "Sayers says there's a chill in the air, but life support is up completely; hold gravity at half a gee. Sayers has also completed a limited visual scan of the exterior. There's nothing showing up on the external cameras so there's no need for an EVA."

On the lower Engineering deck, Williams opened the hatch to the cargo hold; a wave of cold air billowed in as Nuyann joined him with a pair of data-sticks.

"Wish I had fur," Williams said.

"Blame evolution," Nuyann retorted, then hesitated before the open hatch and tongued his nosepad, sniffing for whatever *had* to be in the hold. Nothing—only the usual scents and a lot of cold. Ears tucked, he cautiously stepped through the hatch, feeling half his weight disappear.

The *Coventry's* hold held forty-two cargo containers loaded with goods for Alorya. Stacked two deep on either side of a cleared access lane, each one represented a flat transport fee or spec-trade goods; a near-full load of forty-two meant a mildly-profitable run.

Aside from the long access corridor overhead connecting the upper deck to Engineering, there were four other exits—the two large airlocks port and starboard for loading and unloading, a forward hatch leading past the LCL area into the lifeboat bays and passenger deck, and a companionway beside it to the crew quarters on the upper deck.

"All the hatches seem fine," Williams said.

"That noise may have been a pressurized blow-out from one of the pallets," Nuyann said. "You check the lower rows and I'll check the uppers."

Williams nodded in agreement, and the two slowly worked their way forward down the corrugated walls of containers, stopping and checking each lading chip with their data-sticks. All on-manifest, all secured, no sign of any rupture.

The *Coventry* had a capacity of fifty standard containers; with forty-two loaded, the walls of corrugated metal and hold-downs broke into occasional gaps amidships and forward.

"Nothing so far," Williams called to Nuyann up through one of the gaps. "I'll check the LCL area for the passenger baggage. Want to bet a can of shaving cream decided to go?"

Nuyann heard him go forward, to the extreme forward end of the hold, where the LCL area held passenger baggage and miscellaneous stores behind restraint nets.

"Alloa!" Williams called a few minutes later. "I may have found something here in the passenger area behind the netting."

"Coming!" Nuyann called.

Then, a strangled gurgle that set the Thalendri's fur bristling and tail tucking.

"Williams? *Wowowow?*"

The gurgle grew, faltered, came back louder. Nuyann flew down the catwalk towards the companionway, the cramped way becoming narrower by the microsecond. The *gildarr* was coming, the invisible, unscentable one from the accessway—

"WILLIAMS!"

The gurgle choked into a moan, then cut off as Nuyann got to the open area at the forward end of the hold, fur bristling and hands shaking, *something* invisible just behind him ready to strike.

He looked down into the LCL area, a whiff of human urine burning his nostrils. His assistant engineer lay collapsed on the deck, curled up in a semi-fetal position in front of the passenger baggage area. The netting that separated the passenger's cargo from the commercial had been pulled back. A passenger's container—basically an oversized bread box with a latch—had been opened. Brightly colored clothes had spilled out of it.

Yelping, Nuyann made it down the companionway to the prostrate form and checked for a pulse. There was none.

\* \* \*

Captain Carroll sat impatiently by the ship's intercom waiting for a report. She jumped when Nuyann's panicked voice yelped through the speaker.

"Medical emergency—LCL area, cargo hold!" he barked. "Williams is down!"

The Captain hit the Respond key, "Chokonnu! Medical Emergency, LCL Area! We're on our way. Sayers! You have the con!"

Carroll sprinted for the aft hatch, picking up Chokonnu about halfway through the crew quarters. Nuyann's sudden scream—a shrieking *YELP!* like a dog smashed under a vehicle's wheels—made them run faster.

Faster than the Captain, the Selkie medic arrived first, bouncing down the companionway on all fours, medpack banging on the rungs. At the base of the steps, Nuyann laid bucking and jerking in a *grand mal* seizure, his eyes rolled back, muzzle foaming.

Concerned that whatever felled the two engineers may be environmental, the small musteloid held his breath, grabbed Nuyann under the shoulders and pulled him through the lower-deck hatch, getting it shut just as the Captain arrived.

Nuyann lay on the deck between the passenger airlock and the lifeboat bay, his limbs still trembling. The Thalendri whined.

"I've got to get Williams," Carroll said. "Lewis will be here in a moment to help you get Nuyann into sickbay."

Nuyann's eyes snapped open. "*GILDARR!—Ie, NIMSHUUTH!*" he gasped. "Eating my mind!"

"Nuyann," Carroll said. She wanted to be gentle with the stricken Thalendri, but Williams was still in the hold. "What happened? Where's Williams?"

"Dead," the Thalendri gasped. "He's dead! *Nimshuuth* killed him— In the passenger lockers—Stay out!" Then his body started bucking in another seizure, and didn't stop until Chokonnu's injector hissed into him.

\* \* \*

In the passengers' wardroom, Melanai had restored some semblance of peace. Mrs. Goodrich had calmed down and the rest made the decision to retire to their rooms for an early night.

The Thalendri stewardess sighed in relief. Ever since that strange sound that seemed to emanate from the ship itself, she had been getting a slight headache and the pain was growing, like something grinding away inside her skull. *Get up to sickbay, down some pentazocines...*

"Are you well?"

Melanai turned to see the human priest staring at her while she rubbed her temples, her ears drooping. "*Ari*, Holyfather, thank you for asking."

The priest looked about the wardroom as if looking for something. "I've noticed a growing headache and a feeling of nervousness. It's very slight." *And kind of familiar, but from where?*

Melanai looked at him in alarm. Maybe she should have asked the other passengers. "Not slight to me..." Then she winced, her fang-tips showing. "Growing worse."

"Interesting." *Then it isn't just me. Thalendri have lower pain thresholds than humans; she would feel it first, whatever it is...* "Forgive a strange question, but please walk over here and tell me if you feel the same?"

Intrigued by Father Heidler's request, Melanai walked with him to the forward tip of the passenger deck.

"*Murr...*" the vixen purred, her ears starting to perk up. "Better over here."

"That confirms my own subjective feelings," the priest replied. "Whatever's causing our symptoms is coming from the rear. Is the cargo hold on the other side of that sealed door?"

"Yes, after the reception airlocks and lifeboat bay," Melanai said, "Excuse me, but I'd better check on the passengers and talk to the captainess."

The staterooms of the priest himself and the Selkie passenger were at the forward end of the passenger corridor and as she went to knock on Mr. Pitter's door, she suddenly stumbled and had to grab for a table to keep from falling.

"Allow me," said a voice behind her. She felt Father Heidler's strong hands grasp her shoulders and lead her back away from the rear of the compartment.

Gasping, the stewardess clung to the priest as she caught her breath. "How…? That feeling—Growing stronger—The passengers! Don't you feel—like something gnawing inside?"

"Yes, I feel it," the priest said, "but it appears to affect you more strongly. I'll go check on the passengers. Catch your breath and then notify the Captain."

Now he recognized the feeling. As part of his training, he'd been familiarized with psionics, up to and including psi-attacks. A Larant telepath—a man-sized, sand-and-spinach theropod dinosaur—had probed him, teaching him to recognize the symptoms and sensations of feeling someone else's mind literally *push* into his. Except this wasn't a pushing, it was a grinding, like something trying to cut its way in with power tools.

Steeling himself as best he could, he made his way to Mr. Pitter's stateroom. The closer he walked toward the door, the more he walked into a mass of acidic gel that ate at his mental defenses. A psi attack was supposed to feel—had felt in the demonstrations—like a blow to the head, except from the inside out. This was like a power-grinder, *tearing* at his neurons in a cascade of sparks.

Decades of spiritual discipline augmented with his mental training in seminary allowed him to concentrate, but he could feel even these stopgap mental shields slowly crumbling. Mentally, he went through the Rosary, the repetition of Our Fathers and Hail Marys pushing the grinder away from his head.

No response to the chime; he opened the door to find the Selkie collapsed shivering on the floor, staring at nothing and drooling. *Petit mal—that confirms it.* Though Father Heidler had a few years on him, he picked up the Selkie and carried him back outside.

The stewardess had already gone up the ladder to the upper deck. The priest laid the Selkie down on the deck as far forward as he could go, gritted his teeth for another plunge into the power-grinder and went to the stateroom of Mrs. Goodrich and her daughter.

Like Mr. Pitter, Mrs. Goodrich lay unconscious on the floor, her daughter laying protectively across her mother, whimpering in delirium. Father Heidler stared in amazement. Whatever attacked the adults had evidently less of an impact on the child.

He carried the girl to safety first and then returned to drag the woman back to a safer area. By the time he reached the ladder, Winter lay with her eyes open.

"Mommy?" she whispered.

"She'll be fine," Father Heidler said, praying he wasn't lying. "She just needs to rest. You lay next to her and let her sleep."

The priest caught his breath, centered his mind and walked back into the mental battle. He groaned. Whatever it was grew stronger. Surely, he thought, the Carcosa Artifact lay behind all of this.

The priest didn't bother with the chime for Jill Noir's room—Number 4, the farthest aft. He opened the door without knocking and stopped in surprise.

The construct had ripped the bed to shreds. Anything loose had been scattered along the floor along with a handful of bright yellow pills and scattered smoking accessories. A sharp *"Dook!"* came from the bathroom, followed by a gekkering sound like an angered Thalendri, but deeper and different.

The sound from the bathroom paused and Jill suddenly staggered into the doorway, her clothing hanging off her in ragged tatters, her tail boofed out, her ferret head bare. *So she was wearing a wig...*

"Out!" she ordered, her voice almost a wail. "Get out!" The struggle she endured to hold on to her mind lay clear in her dark eyes.

"Miss Noir," the priest said, "We're under some form of psionic attack. You'll feel better if you come out and go toward the front of the ship."

His warning came too late. He watched in horror as the last semblance of sentience drained from the construct's eyes. It blinked at him once, glanced around the room with sharp, quick movements, and then saw him as if for the first time. It lunged.

Backpedaling, Father Heidler slammed the stateroom door in the construct's face and backed away while whatever Jill Noir had become scrabbled at the door.

The grinding wheel sent another shower of sparks from his neurons and he almost succumbed. The power grew stronger by the minute.

Leaving the construct in God's hands, the priest went to check on the rest of the passenger's. The Selkie and Mrs. Goodrich still lay unconscious, but Winter lay across her mother weeping quietly.

The priest touched the little girl gently on the shoulder. "Winter," he said gently, "Everything's going to be fine. You must be brave just a little longer."

He grabbed Mr. Pitter, grateful at how small and light the creature felt in his arms. He stuffed the limp form into the dumbwaiter.

Climbing up the ladder, he opened the door and looked out into the crew's wardroom.

"Hello?" he called. "It's Father Heidler."

A human crewman appeared out of a hallway leading aft, panic on his face.

"I need some help," he said.

*　*　*

It took a few minutes, but they were able to get Mr. Pitter, Mrs. Goodrich and her daughter to the upper deck. The oversized dumbwaiter to the galley helped with the Selkie and the little girl. The crewman—Father Heidler learned his name was Sayers—used a fireman's carry to get the limp form of Mrs. Goodrich up the ladder. The priest sighed in relief as the Selkie and the woman began to show signs of regaining consciousness.

"Is this all the passengers?" Sayers asked. "Anyone still down there?"

Father Heidler shook his head. "There's another passenger, Miss Noir, a construct, but whatever attack we're under has made her totally feral. We can't help her without getting injured or worse. And the crew?"

The priest watched the emotions play over the crewman's face. "We have several down," he said.

"Dead?"

Sayers shook his head. "We've lost Williams. The Captain's trapped back in Engineering. The rest collapsed by the hatch to the cargo hold, lower deck."

Father Heidler paused for a moment in thought. "Look," he said, "I think I know what's going on; the construct brought something on board. Can I talk to the Captain in some way?"

"There's the ship's intercom system. That panel over on the wall."

*　*　*

Captain Carroll swore as she paced back in forth in Engineering. Her crew lay on the deck at the other end of the hold, but any attempt to go forward and she felt her brain being ripped apart. Somehow, there had to be some type of shielding she could use to protect herself. A spacesuit had already been tried and discarded—she'd tried a dead run forward down the access corridor, only to come crawling back to safety.

The intercom buzzed. "Captain?" a strange voice said, "This is Father Eric Heidler. Are you there?"

Carroll hit the intercom. "Where's my crewman?" she shouted. "Is Sayers there?"

"Yes, Captain, he's here. He's moving Mrs.Goodrich over to the far bulkhead."

The captain groaned. In her anxiety for her own crew, she had forgotten about the payload. When Melanai joined them in the hallway, she collapsed along with the others before she had relayed any information.

"Captain?"

Carroll hit the button. "Still here, Father. Get the passengers to someplace safe. My crew will try to sort the problem."

"Sayers here, Captain. The passengers have been affected. Mrs Goodrich and Mr Pitter seem to be recovering, but slowly, the girl's not as bad. There's another still on the lower deck. The Priest says she seems to have gone insane."

"The construct?"

There was a short pause. "Father Heidler says it's the construct. And Captain, he says he knows what the problem is."

Captain Carroll sighed. "With all due respect," she said, knowing the priest was surely overhearing the conversation, "This is not a matter of faith and we're not going to sort it with a few prayers."

There was another period of silence on the intercom. This time, it was Father Heidler's voice.

"I agree with you, Captain. We're dealing with a psionic phenomenon caused by a relic the construct brought aboard the ship. It's in the cargo hold."

The Captain felt her anger and frustration growing. "You'd best tell me what you know."

"I'll make it short and sweet," the priest replied. "The Church has been collecting archaeological specimens from this region of space that we call the Carcosa Artifacts.

"There was an ancient civilization—sometime between the Old Ones and the Cluster Alliance—that had also made the discovery of FTL Manifolds. However, being homebodies, they weren't all that interested in travel. They thought the Manifolds were their equivalent of the afterlife and they composed a religion around it.

"The Church has been studying them for a long time. We have been purchasing artifacts as we find them to piece together the Carcosan theology. We were purchasing this one, but the construct stole it and I've been following her to get it back and see who else is interested in these artifacts."

The Captain's voice came back, cold as liquid helium. "You mean to tell me you allowed this artifact on my ship to put my crew and passengers in danger?"

"No, ma'am. No Carcosa Artifact has ever acted like this when exposed to the Manifolds. As far as we could tell, they were all 'dead' from sheer age. This is something completely unexpected."

"So, please tell me you know how to deal with it."

The Captain could hear the finality in the priest's voice. "No. I don't. We'll have to solve the problem together, but I know this. It's some form of psionic attack, and the area of effect is growing."

"Bloody Hell." If it was psionic, shielding would be useless. There was nothing aboard the *Cov* that they could use to bodge up a psi-shield.

The Captain looked down the corridor toward the crew compartments, her brow furrowed in thought. She stepped through the hatch and immediately jumped back with a gasp of pain. She had been able to get partway down the corridor before, but now the mind-ripping started almost at the engine room bulkhead. Before long, she'd be backed right up against the reactor bulkheads and out the aft airlock.

\* \* \*

"I have a theory, Captain."

"Talk."

"I believe the artifact is getting its power from the higher brain functions of the people on the *Coventry*. That is the logical explanation as to why the little girl, Winter was not so strongly affected and why the construct has gone feral. It also explains why you and I have some limited endurance."

The Captain snorted in derision. "You're saying you and I are dimwits?"

"No. I'm saying your primal anger at the circumstances gave you enough strength to fight your way into Engineering when the rest of your crew succumbed. My training in spiritual and mental disciplines is my own personal form of protection."

"Captain?" Sayers cut in. "I'm on the bridge. We're showing something in the hold."

"Yes?"

"Well, something must be wrong, Ma'am. The sensors indicate a small source of Cerenkov radiation coming from the LCL area—passenger baggage."

"Did you hear that, Father?" Carroll asked.

"Yes, I did. That pretty much confirms it"

"What does this artifact look like?"

"It's a small orb, about fifty millimeters across. Captain, I have an idea."

"Yes?"

"I'm expendable. I can't get to your people in the hallway, but there's another entrance to the hold up here in the crew wardroom. I think I can hold it together long enough to get a visual of what's going on. The answer may be as simple as blowing it out the airlock."

"Blowing an airlock is not simple," came the immediate retort.

Father Heidler smiled. "Well, what do you think of my idea of looking into the cargo hold?"

"If you think you can resist the attack better than my crewman, I hate to say it, but at least we'll get a better understanding of what's going on. However, have Sayers tie a tether around you in case you collapse."

"Good idea. I'll get back to you in a moment."

The priest checked in quickly on Mr. Pitter and Mrs. Goodrich, both sleeping in the tiny sickbay. When they had recovered from the attack, they both complained of severe headaches, bordering on what Sayers said described a cluster migraine. He had given them medicine from the sickbay and sedated them. The little girl slept peacefully on a pallet next to her mother.

Sayers met him outside the sickbay. He held a rope in his hand made of some tough synthetic.

"I'll need a few moments to gather my wits," Father Heidler said, "Before I open that door. The area of effect has expanded by at least another meter. I can't go out on the stair landing for long."

While Father Heidler stilled his mind, Sayers made an impromptu halter around the priest's shoulders and upper chest.

"What didn't you tell the Captain?" Sayers stepped around to face the priest. "Why would the Vatican be interested in some alien artifacts?"

"Not 'the Vatican', my order; we've been the Church's 'Intelligence Service' since we branched off from the Jesuits." He considered a moment, then continued.

"I told your Captain the truth, but not all of it. As far as we can reconstruct, the Manifolds weren't just the afterlife to the Carcosans, they were the 'spirit world'—including 'making magick' by dealing with *things* in the Manifolds, outside our reality. One theory—looks like it's true—is the Artifacts were some sort of psionic quantum tap to those *things*." A *Thing of Power* for "Materialist Magicians"…

Sayers looked up from where he was securing the knots. "'The Manifolds are the gate through which the realities meet—not necessarily ours'—Lados Nightflame, the scaly who invented the drive." He met the priest's quizzical reaction with a sheepish shrug. "Err... I dabbled with Kluuthism when I was younger."

Father Heidler smiled. *God's revelation to the Larant, according to their biology and psychology, as the Way of the White Prophet was to the Kthymri and the Eternal Dance to the Thalendri...* "God manifested in science and knowledge, with exploration and discovery as sacraments and our universe an island of fractal order with a Crawling Chaos outside trying to break in?"

Sayers nodded and tightened the final knots.

"Then you have some idea. Science is a wonderful tool, but not an end in itself." *Maybe the Larant have more general revelation coming...* "It deals with measurements and facts, but not what we know as good and evil. Despite how we try to redefine them away." *Like we've done again and again for almost three millennia since St John died and general revelation ended. At least for humans.*

His voice hardened. "And the Carcosa Artifacts are evil. Whatever they tap is not only abstract power, but a predator, actively seeking prey. 'Like a roaring lion, seeking whoever he may devour'—we know that now. The Church has scientist-priests of her own; as scientists they classify and analyze, but as priests they understand that an inanimate object can be much, much more in the cosmic scheme."

"The Church has stood against evil for thousands of years." *Even when we almost succumbed from the inside.* "When we went out to the stars, we took our age-old mandate with us."

"And you? Are you one of those scientist-priests?"

"No. My story is my own." As if on cue, phantom pain twinged in his cyborged limb, from the left hand down the forearm. "Right now, reality is that my faith is probably the best weapon we have to save everyone aboard this ship."

He closed his eyes and stood silent for a long moment. A very long moment, while the pressure inside Sayers' head grew; the crewman was about to grab and shake the priest when he opened his eyes and said, "It's time."

Focusing his mind, Father Heidler walked toward the door. A meter and a half from the door, the grinder started ripping. An involuntary groan escaped his lips; mental acid tore at his brain as he groped for the hatch release into the hold.

Behind him, Sayers fed out the tether line.

His hands began to involuntarily shake and his legs quiver, then the portal slid open and he lurched out onto the companionway.

Below him, he saw the limp form of a crewman sprawled across the floor and made a quick and silent prayer for the dead. Next to the body, synthetic-canvas webbing lay across the alcove that formed the passengers' baggage area. The air radiated a cerulean aura, beautiful and deadly, its source an open passenger's container.

He felt his mind go. With a cry of agony he hurled himself back into the wardroom, Sayers pulling on the tether with all his strength.

When the priest was finally able to stand again, his limbs continued to tremble.

He stumbled to the intercom. "Captain."

"Are you all right?"

"It's the artifact. The source is coming from a container in the passengers' cargo alcove. If we blew the airlock, all we would probably lose is air."

"I'm not having any results here either. I haven't discovered anything that would shield us from the effects, but I've not given up yet."

The priest slumped at a table, his mind unable to think. He dimly remembered the construct downstairs and felt a wave of compassion for the creature.

"I'd better check on the passenger downstairs," he said to Sayers.

"She may not be alive."

The priest shrugged. "She may be worse than dead. But I have to try and help her."

Father Heidler pressed his left hand hard in several spots. His pharmacological armory was limited, but if the construct was unconscious, he had the capability of putting her in a true sleep simply by touching her. That, of course, was assuming the artifact's area of effect hadn't grown to the point where he was denied access to the passenger wardroom.

He trembled as he walked to the access ladder, feeling the artifact grinding away at his mind. He opened the hatch, but a sudden intuition made him get on his knees and look down into the compartment below before he put his feet on the rungs.

He looked down into utter destruction, perfumed with ferret musk and poop. Jill Noir crouched naked across the compartment, a man-sized mustelid.

She had something in her hand that sparkled, a glittering object the construct chewed in a frenzied preoccupation. *She's a biter. Great.*

With a quick jerk, she looked up to see Father Heidler's head. Heidler managed to slam the hatch closed just in time. He couldn't believe the construct could move with such amazing speed.

Ten minutes later, he contacted the Captain with an idea.

\* \* \*

"You're crazy," Sayers said.

"Crazy as a ferret," the priest said grimly. "It's the only idea I have."

He made sure the door to the sickbay was locked and with a grunt of exertion, he endured the agony of the artifact long enough to open the door to the cargo hold.

"Ready?" he called.

"Ready," Sayers answered.

Quickly, he opened the hatch to the passengers' wardroom praying he wouldn't be staring into the construct's face on the ladder. The ladder was empty.

Father Heidler ran back into the bridge. Sayers slammed the hatch behind him.

Together, they watched the sensors.

A red dot showed the Captain in Engineering. Dots clustered around the cargo hold door in the Engineering corridor represented the still living, but comatose forms of Melanai, Chokonnu and Nuyann.

Three passengers lay in the sickbay behind locked doors. In the cargo bay, a blue dot pulsed.

Sayers and Father Heidler watched the red dot representing Jill Noir moving around the passengers' wardroom.

"Look at her move!" Sayers said.

"She's fast," Father Heidler said in agreement.

"She found the open hatch to the upper deck."

Together, they watched the dot as it wandered about the crews' wardroom. The ferret had found all sorts of new toys to activate the creature's natural curiosity.

"When is she going to find the hatch to the cargo hold?" Sayers asked.

"Be patient," the priest replied.

They only had to wait ten minutes longer.

"How can she get so close to that *thing* in there and still be conscious?" Sayers asked.

Father Heidler smiled grimly. "Trust me. She *is* unconscious. What is left is the animal part of her. Poor Saint Francis. How heartbroken he would have been to discover that animals lack higher brain functions."

"There she goes," Sayers said excitedly, pointing to the sensor screen. The red dot had moved toward the artifact. "How's she going to get the artifact out of the container?"

"Oh, just leave that up to a ferret. If they see a sparkly, they'll find a way to get it."

Another five minutes, and the ferret and the artifact had moved into the center of the room.

Sayers hit the intercom. "Captain," he said excitedly, "It worked. The construct has the artifact out of the passengers' cargo alcove."

"Ab-Fab," the Captain said in reply. "Father Heidler, go and seal the hatches and we'll blow the lock."

The priest hit the intercom button. "Captain, you can't blow the construct out of the airlock with the artifact."

The reply came back quickly. "You yourself said the creature was dangerous. You can't get it out of the hold without putting yourself in danger. It'll be on you before you shut the door. If you can't do it, Sayers will shut the door for you. There'll be no blood on your hands."

Father Heidler felt himself growing angry. "First, there will be blood on my hands because I'm giving assent to a plan that will result in the death of what is, or was, and maybe can be again, a fellow sentient. Secondly, Sayers can't get that close. He'll succumb. The strength of that artifact is growing stronger by the second. It's like a vampire. It killed your first crewman in its first hunger, but now it's simply feeding and using your crew as food."

"Sayers?" the Captain said. "Get ready to blow the lock."

Sayers looked at the priest and shrugged. His fingers danced over several keypads and warning chimes started going off on the bridge; from a distance aft came the dull thuds of closing pressure hatches. "Done, ma'am," he said. "Cargo hold's sealed off and ready to blow."

"Father Heidler," the Captain said, "If we let this effect spread any farther, we'll have to abandon ship. While FTL—and God knows where we'll Emerge if we leave the *Cov*. We have enough reserve air to repressurise the hold, but not the amount we'll lose if any hatches are open to the quarters. And if we get explosive decompression into the quarters, everyone in Sickbay and what's left of my crew below decks will be right in the midst of it. Your call. Kill the construct or kill us all."

The priest gritted his teeth in anger. "Let me try to get her out."

Patiently, he waited.

"How, priest?" the Captain asked.

"I'll go down and get her—lure her out of the hold. If you have a spare headset, you can listen in and I'll tell you when we're clear."

Sayers looked up from his console. "Sounds like it'd work, Captain. I can monitor him from here, and blow the lock on his signal."

The Captain's voice crackled back. "If this takes too long, Father, Sayers will have to blow the lock on *my* signal. I can't jeopardize the ship and everyone else aboard for two passengers."

"I understand." Father Heidler took the headset Sayers handed him and fitted it on. "Captain, I'm going now."

"Good," came the reply. "Nobody will judge you."

"Yes," Father Heidler replied. "Nobody will judge me."

Quickly, the priest moved down the corridor, past Sickbay and the galley/wardroom, toward the hatch to the cargo hold, the energies of the artifact grinding away at his brain with each step aft. This time, instead of the standard Rosary—he'd worked through the Sorrowful Mysteries, and the situation didn't mesh well with the Glorious—he was using something a bit more apropos: Saint Faustina's Chaplet.

*Eternal Father, I offer you the Body and Blood, Soul and Divinity of Your deeply beloved Son, Our Lord Jesus Christ, in atonement for our sins and those of the world. For the sake of His sorrowful Passion, have mercy on us and on all the worlds...*

The hatch opened as he reached it. With a groan, he went through the portal and stepped out onto the companionway landing. Below him, what had been Jill Noir stared with rapt attention at the cyan-glowing ball pulsing in her paws, its surface already scarred by the construct's teeth.

*For the sake of His sorrowful Passion, have mercy on us and on all the worlds...*

"Hey!" Father Heidler yelled. The construct looked up with a jerk of her head.

The priest reached into his shirt and brought out the gold crucifix that hung on a chain around his neck. He swung it back and forth, the bright light in the cargo bay making it glisten. "See the sparkly," he called through gritted teeth. "Come and get the sparkly."

*For the sake of His sorrowful Passion, have mercy on us and on all the worlds...*

The giant ferret followed the sparkling crucifix, quivering in a weasel war dance. "DOOK?"

He swung the crucifix around, letting it jingle on the railing, as the power-grinder worked away inside his head. "Sparkly..."

*For the sake of His sorrowful Passion, have mercy on us and on all the worlds...*

Jill dropped the artifact and sped up the steps, a brown blur.

Father Heidler leaped back and as the construct sped up the stairs he threw his crucifix forward towards the bridge. Jill was on it before it hit the floor.

*For the sake of His sorrowful Passion, have mercy on us and on all the worlds…*

With a cry of relief, the priest yelled "WE'RE CLEAR! BLOW IT!" into the headset mike. The blast of alarms, the flash of warning beacons, and the hatch quantumed shut with a metallic THUD! Then the pneumatic locks hissed and they were safe.

*For the sake of His sorrowful Passion, have mercy on us and on all the worlds…*

Another set of alarms sounded—the four sharp pulses of depressurization alarms echoing through the bulkhead, competing with the screeching shower of sparks inside his head. He faltered, tore off the headset, grabbed for the Zero-G handholds to keep from collapsing. Another depressurization klaxon blasted through the crew deck; in the ear-ringing silence between the pulses came an inhuman cry, half-wail, half-snarl—a ferret in pain from the blaring alarms.

*For the sake of His sorrowful Passion…*

Fifty kilos of fur and fury hit the priest from behind, smashing him against the closed hatch and onto the deck.

Landing on his left arm, he tried to spin around to use his cyborg hand to inject a strong sedative into Jill's body, but the construct was simply too fast.

He felt mustelid teeth rip into his throat, going for the bright shiny white spot at the front of his Roman collar; his nostrils filled with the overpowering scent of musk followed by that of blood.

"Lord!" he cried and then knew no more.

\* \* \*

Father Heidler awoke to the feeling of fire in his throat. Finished with his head, the power-grinder had moved down a bit and started up again. He opened his eyes in the bright light of a starport sickbay.

A nurse entered his field of vision—a Thalendri vixen, in green-trimmed white, urgently yipping something he didn't understand.

Carefully, the priest attempted a tentative swallow and immediately regretted the action. Tears of pain came to his eyes.

The nurse swiveled her ears and made an adjustment to Father Heidler's IV tube. Within seconds, a painless sleep overtook him.

When he woke up later, his throat felt somewhat better, but was suddenly aware of other pain in his abdomen and chest.

Again, a nurse—this one human, in white—entered his field of vision.

"Don't talk," she said. "You're on Alorya Prime. You've been frozen and thawed and you've had extensive surgery on your throat."

He opened his mouth, but the nurse quickly put her hand over it.

"No!" she ordered. "The doctor spent hours reconstructing your larynx and vocal cords. If you try to speak, I'll knock you out instead."

Wisely, Father Heidler kept his mouth shut.

* * *

Three days later, he had his first visitor.

"I guess I should thank you," Captain Carroll said, "for saving my ship and those on board, but I do have to say that your being here in hospital is your own fault."

Father Heidler cocked an eyebrow, tapped something onto a smartpad and gave it to the Captain.

"Okay," the Captain nodded. "Here's the story. It was a good half-hour after we blew that bloody artifact out of the airlock before the construct had enough of her brains back to let Sayers off the bridge and me into the wardroom.

"You had been ripped to shreds; I still can't believe we managed to shovel you into our only med berth and freeze you down before you died on us.

"The rest of the crew woke up an hour later, but we had to sedate them for days. The migraines were devastating.

"We lost Williams, but thankfully everybody else has recovered enough that they've been able to get on with their lives except for Mrs. Goodrich and her lawyers. I think I'm going to have to stay out in the Grey Zone from now on."

Father Heidler took the smartpad back and tapped in some more text. The Captain looked at the pad and shrugged.

"The ferret's 'nicked up'—in prison. Smuggling a dangerous artifact. Other stuff. We'll never see her again. Alorya's a cluster of sky-cities; they don't have the luxury of going out of their way for a dangerous construct and her owners have denied any ownership. She'd have been better off if you'd blown her out the airlock."

* * *

A month later, Jill Noir sat in a small outdoor cafe partway up the endcap of Alorya Prime, fur shining in the ruddy sunlight coming through the light-pipe array at the spin-core. Too hot in the sky-city for her full costume, she had finally given herself permission to strip down to what was considered decent—a Thalendri-style top and sheer slacks. And her wig—after what had happened, she was never going bareheaded again. Ignoring the stares from the other patrons of the cafe, she fingered the small chain and medallion that had arrived in the mail when she sat in prison.

The medallion sparkled in the sunlight and she fought an urge to nibble on it. Inscribed on the medallion were the words *The Order of Saint Dismas* along with a bas-relief of a human face.

She took a puff on the cigarette holder clamped in her mustelid muzzle and once again read the letter that had come with the medallion.

Dear Ms Noir:

I hope you will accept our offer to pay your bail and Weregild. I do believe my order will be able to reduce your charge and penalty and gainful employment with my organization may open doors that will benefit us both in the long run.

The Order of Saint Dismas is in need of couriers and especially someone of your unique talents. I am certain you will find the job description and perks to your liking.

Rev. Eric Heidler, O.S.D.

Jill took another long drag on the bengastick, the heady rush-blend in her lungs stifling the ferret within. A few wheels and deals on the Underside after her release and she had enough funds to buy a ticket off-world, well into the WebFed proper where she could lose herself in an environment far friendlier to constructs. *Where I'm not an animal.*

She preferred being a fugitive and it would be a cold day in that priest's version of hell before she ever worked for anybody else but herself. *He can have me when I feed the maggots; until then, I'm free and I'm going for as much as I can.*

She toyed with the idea of hocking the medallion, but it did sparkle so. She put it around her neck and slipped it into her frilly top.

\* \* \*

An endcap terrace away in the concave cityscape, the older human in a Roman collar watched Jill through the open-air "window" of a small restaurant. Casually, he sipped his tea—a WebFed herbal blend, including the same type of leaf the ferret-woman was smoking, sweetened down with Terry honey.

A meter-tall Selkie—a sand-and-white Inlander, with musteloid features almost as sharp as Jill's—came up to his table and waited impatiently.

Still unable to talk, Father Heidler smiled and motioned for his companion to join him, tapping voder setup codes into his smartpad.

The Selkie took his seat and looked around nervously, fidgeting like a ferret as he pulled out and started up a pocket cybertranslator. "The Artificial you told me to tail—here's what I found. She's shipping out this evening—for the Thalendri homeworld—aboard a monohull bulk-freighter, the *Greatwings Pride*. Forty-fifty days—counting stops."

Father Heidler nodded and smiled his appreciation. "Good job," came a synthesized voice from his smartpad, in Sentic. "Any more details?"

"The ship's purser told me she's denning with another Artificial—something called a "rabbit" coming out from Changorr System. Said one was enough and he was miffed that he had to take care of two of them on the trip. Said he bunked them together because they both breathed smoke."

Father Heidler smiled again and casually slipped the Selkie a wallet. With a look of relief, the Selkie grabbed it and disappeared into the crowd.

The priest looked down across the endcap and watched Jill pay her bill. Before she disappeared into the crowd, he raised his teacup to her in an impromptu toast.

*The Order of Saint Dismas will see you again,* he thought to himself as he saluted her. *We don't make empty investments. Until later, my little thief.*

Father Heidler smiled, drained his cup and with his smartpad's voice called for the bill.

L. Sprague de Camp's Viagens Interplanetarias *novels and short stories were set between the mid-21st and the 22nd centuries, when humans developed interstellar travel and spread throughout the galaxy. De Camp postulated that Brazil had become the social and economic leader of Terra (Earth), with Viagens Interplanetarias ("Interplanetary Tours") as the biggest commercial space-travel company. This enabled de Camp to write short and long stories set on different planets inhabited by a large variety of primitive or advanced aliens, with plots ranging from humorous to serious. A favorite theme was an average Terran space tourist getting lost on a planet, and having a colorful adventure amidst exotic customs that he had to figure out. Among his most-used planets were the worlds of the stars Tau Ceti (Krishna and Vishnu), Procyon (Isis, Osiris, and Thoth), Epsilon Eridani (Kukulkan and Thor), and Lalande 21185 (Ormazd), to use their Terran-assigned names.*

*While some of de Camp's other worlds feature furrier or more centauroid inhabitants,* Anthropomorphic Aliens *presents a dinosaur-like Osirian in one of the shortest and funniest stories of the series.*

# The Inspector's Teeth

## by L. Sprague de Camp

A.D. 2054-2088

World Manager Chagas sat waiting for the Osirian ambassador, mentally practicing the brisk handshake and the glassy smile. Across the conference table the First Assistant to the Manager, Wu, chain-smoked. while the Minister of External Affairs, Evans, filed his nails. Although the faint rasp annoyed Chagas, he gave no sign, imperturbability being one of the qualities for which he was paid. The indirect lighting threw soft highlights from the silver skullcaps covering the shaven crania of the three.

Chagas said; "I shall be glad when I can let my hair grow again like a civilized man."

"My dear Chagas," said Wu, "with the hair you have, I don't see what difference it makes."

Evans put away his nail file and said; "Gentlemen, when I was a kid a century ago, I wondered what it would be like to be on the inside of a great historical moment. Now I'm in on one, I find it queer I'm the same old Jefferson Evans, and not Napoleon or Caesar." He looked at his nails. "Wish we knew more Osirian psychology…" Wu said; "Don't start that Neo-Paretan nonsense again about Osirians being guided by sentiments, so we need only know which one to play on, like pressing a button. Osirians are rational people; would have to be to invent space travel independently of us. Therefore they will be guided by their economic interests alone."

"Neo-Marxist tapioca!" snapped Evans. "Sure, they're rational, but also sentimental and capricious like us. There's no contradiction-"

"But there is!" said Wu excitedly. "Environment makes the man, and not the contrary."

"Do not start that, I beg," said Chagas. "This is too important to get your systems full of adrenaline over theory. Thank God I am a plain man who tries to do his duty and does not worry about sociological theories. If he takes our terms, the Althing will ratify the treaty and we shall have an Interplanetary Council to keep peace. If he insists on the terms we privately think he is entitled to, the Althing will not ratify. Then we shall have separate sovereignties, and it will be the history of our poor Earth all over again."

"You borrow trouble, chief," said Wu, "There are no serious disputes between our system and the Procyonic. Even if there were, there is no economic advantage to a war at such distance, even though Osirians have a capitalistic economy like Evans' country…"

"Who said wars are always fought for economic advantage?" said Evans. "Ever hear of the Crusades? Or the war that was fought over one pig?"

Wu said; "You mean the war some sentimental historian without grasp of social and economic factors thought was fought for a pig-"

"Stop it!" said Chagas.

"Okay," said Evans. "But I'll bet you a drink, Wu, that the Osirian takes our offer as it stands."

"You are on," said Wu.

A bell chimed, bringing the men to their feet.

As the Osirian came in, they advanced with outstretched hands, uttering polite platitudes. The Osirian set down his bulging briefcase and shook their hands. He looked like a small dinosaur, a head taller than a man—one of the little ones that ran about on its hind legs with its tail stuck out behind to balance. A complex pattern of red-and-gold paint decorated his scales.

The Osirian took the backless chair that had been provided for him. "A kreat pleashure, chentlemen," he said slowly, in an accent they could barely understand. This was natural, considering the difference between his vocal organs and theirs. "I half stuttiet the offer of the Worlt Fetteration and have reched my tecishion."

Chagas gave him a meaningless diplomatic smile. "Well, sir?"

The ambassador, whose face was not built for smiles, flicked his forked tongue out and back. With irritating deliberation he began ticking off points on his claws.

"On one hant, I know political conditions in the Solar System and on Earth in particular. Hence I know why you hat to ask me the things you dit. On the other, my people will not like some of these things. They will consitter many of your demands unchust. I could go ofer the grunts of opchection one py one. Howeffer, since you alretty know these opchections, I can make my point better py tellink you a little story."

Wu and Evans exchanged a quick glance of impatience.

The forked tongue flicked out again. "This is a true story, of the old tays when the mesonic drive had first enabled you to fly to other stars and put your system in touch with ours. Pefore there was talk apout galactic government, and before you leart to guart against our little hypnotic powers with those pretty silfer hats. When a younk Sha'akhfa, or as you say an Osirian, hat come to your Earth to seek wisdom…"

\* \* \*

When Herbert Lengyel, a junior, proposed that they bid Hithafea, the Osirian freshman, the Iota Gamma Omicron's council was thrown into turmoil. Herb persisted, glasses flashing.

"He's got everything! He's got money, and he's smart and good-natured, and good company, and full of college spirit. Look how he got elected yell-leader when he'd been here only a few weeks! Of course it would be easier if he looked less like a fugitive from the reptile house in the zoo, but we're civilized people and should judge by the personality inside-"

"Just a minute!" John Fitzgerald, being a three-letter man and a senior, threw much weight in the council. "We got too many queer types in this fraternity already."

He looked hard at Lengyel, though Herb, who would have liked to have punched his handsome face, was merely a sober and serious student instead of a rah-rah boy. Fitzgerald went on.

"Who wants the Iotas to be a haven for all the campus freaks? Next thing you'll find a thing like a bug, a praying mantis a couple meters high sitting in your chair, and you'll be told that's the new pledge from Mars—"

"Another thing," said Lengyel, "We have an anti discrimination clause in our charter. So we can't bar this man—this student, I should say—"

"Oh yes we can," said Fitzgerald, stifling a yawn, "That refers only to the races of mankind; it don't apply to nonhuman beings. We're still a club of gentlemen—get that, gentle-men—and Hithafea ain't no man."

"Principle's the same," said Lengyel. "Why d'you think Atlantic's one of the few universities left with fraternities? Because the frats have upheld the democratic traditions and avoided snobbery and discrimination. Now—"

"Nuts!" said Fitzgerald, "It isn't discriminatory to pick folks you think will be congenial. It wouldn't be so bad if Herb had merely proposed some guy from Krishna, where they look more or less human—"

"There aren't any Krishnans at Atlantic this year," muttered Lengyel.

"—but no, he has to foist a shuddery scaly reptile—"

"John's got a phobia against snakes," said Lengyel

"So does every normal person—"

"Nuts to you, Brother Fitzgerald. It's merely a neurosis, implanted by—"

"You're both getting away from the subject," said Brother Brown, president of the chapter.

They went on like that for some time until a vote was called for. Since Fitzgerald blackballed Hithafea, Lengyel blackballed Fitzgerald's younger brother.

"Hey!" cried Fitzgerald, "You can't do that!"

"Says who?" said Lengyel. "I just don't like the young lout."

After further wrangling, each withdrew his veto against the other's protegé.

On his way out, Fitzgerald punched Lengyel in the solar plexus with a thumb the size of a broomstick end and said; "You're taking Alice to the game tomorrow for me, see? And be sure you give her back in the same condition as you got her!"

"Okay, Stinker," said Lengyel, and went to his room to study. Although they did not like each other, they managed to get along. Lengyel secretly admired Fitzgerald for being the perfect movie idea of Joe College, while Fitzgerald secretly envied Lengyel's brains. It amused Fitzgerald to turn over his coed to Lengyel because he regarded Herb as a harmless Gloop who wouldn't dare try to make time with her himself.

Next day, the last Saturday of the 2054 football season, Atlantic played Yale on the home field. Herb Lengyel led Alice Holm into the stands. As usual, when he got near her his tongue got glued to the roof of his mouth. So he studied the pink card he found thumbtacked to the bleacher seat in front of him. On this were listed, by number, the things he was supposed to do with a big square of cardboard, orange on one side and black on the other, when the cheerleader gave the command, in order to present a letter, number, or picture to the opposite side of the stadium.

He finally said, "D'I tell you we decided to bid Hithafea? Speak it not in Gath, though; it's confidential."

"I won't," said Alice, looking very blonde and lovely. "Does that mean that when John takes me to your dances Hithafea will ask to dance with me?"

"Not if you don't want him to. I don't know if he dances."

"I'll try not to shudder. Are you sure he didn't use his mysterious hypnotic powers to make you propose him?"

"Fooey! Professor Kantor in psych says all this talk about the hypnotic powers of the Osirians is bunk. If a man's a naturally good hypnotic subject he'll be hypnotizable, otherwise not. There aren't any mysterious rays the Osirians shoot from their eyes."

"Well," said Alice, "Professor Peterson doesn't agree. He thinks there's something to it, even though nobody has been able to figure out how it works—Oh, here they come. Hithafea makes a divine yell-leader, doesn't he?"

Although the adjective was perhaps not well chosen, the sight of Hithafea, flanked by three pretty coeds on each side, and prancing and waving his megaphone, was certainly unforgettable. It was made even more so by the fact that he was wearing an orange sweater with a big black A on the chest and a freshman beanie on his head. His locomotive-whistle voice rose above the general uproar.

"Atlantic! A-T-L-A-N..."

At the end of each yell Hithafea flung out his arms with talons spread and leaped three meters into the air on his birdlike legs. He got much more kick out of the rooters' reaction to his yell-leading than the players did, since they were playing football. Hithafea himself had hopes of going out for intercollegiate athletics, preferably track, until the coach had broken it to him as gently as possible that nobody would compete against a being who could broad jump twelve meters without drawing a deep breath.

As both teams were strong that year, the score at the end of the first quarter still stood 0-0. Yale completed a pass and it looked as if the receiver were in the clear until John Fitzgerald, the biggest of the fourteen right tackles of the Atlantic varsity, nailed him. Hithafea screamed;

"Fitzcheralt! Rah, rah, rah, Fitzcheralt!"

A drunken Yale senior, returning to his seat after visiting the gentleman's room under the stands, got turned around and showed up on the grass strip in front of the Atlantic side of the stadium. There he tramped up and down and bumped into people and fell over the chairs of the Atlantic band and made a general nuisance of himself.

At last Hithafea, observing that everybody else was too much interested in the game to abate this nuisance, caught the man by the shoulder and turned him around. The man looked up at Hithafea and shrieked; "I got 'em! I got 'em!" and tried to break away.

He might as well have saved his trouble; the Sha'akhfi freshman held him firmly by both shoulders and hissed something at him. Then he let him go.

Instead of running away, the man threw off his hat with its little blue feather, his furry overcoat, his coat and vest and shirt and pants. Despite the cold he ran out onto the field in his underwear, hugging his bottle under one arm and pretending it was a football.

Before he was finally taken away, the man had caused Yale to be penalized for having twelve men on the field during a play. Luckily the Yale rooters were too far away on the other side of the stadium to understand what was happening, or there might have been a riot. As it was, they were pretty indignant when they found out later, feeling that somebody pulled a fast one on them. Especially as the game ended 21-20 in favor of Atlantic.

\* \* \*

After the game Hithafea went to his mailbox in the Administration Building. All the other frosh were eagerly pushing around the pigeonholes to get theirs, for this was the day when fraternity bids were distributed. When Hithafea softly hissed, "Excuse me, please," they made plenty of room for him.

He took three little white envelopes from his box and scooted for his room in the freshman dorm. He burst into the room to find his roommate, Frank Hodiak, studying his one bid. Hithafea sat down on his bed with his tail curling up against the wall and opened his envelopes, slitting them neatly along the edge with his claws.

"Frank!" he cried. "They want me!"

"Hey," said Hodiak, "whats the matter with you? You're drooling on the rug! Are you sick?"

"No, I am cryink."

"What?"

"Sure. This is the way we Sha'akhfi cry."

"And why are you crying?"

"Pecause I am so happy! I am ofercome with emotion!"

"Well, for goodness; sake," said Hodiak unfeelingly, "go cry in the sink then. I see you got three. Which you gonna take?"

"I think the Iota Gamma Omicrons."

"Why? Some of the others got more prestige."

"I do not care. I am takink them anyway, for sentimental reasons."

"Don't tell me a cold-blooded reptile like you is sentimental!"

"Sure, All we Sha'akhfi are. You think we are not pecause we do not show our feelinks in our faces."

"Well," persisted Hodiak, "what are these sentimental reasons, huh?"

"First,", Hithafea counted on his claws, "pecause Herp Lengyel iss one. He was the first man on the campus to treat me like a fellow beink. Second, pecause the kreat de Câmara was an Iota when he attendet Atlantic many years ako."

"Who's this guy de Câmara?"

"Dit you neffer know? My, some of you echucated Earthmen are iknorant of your own history! He was one of the great space pioneers, the founder of the Viagens Interplanetarias, and the first Earthman to set foor on Osiris."

"Oh, Another Brazzy, eh?"

"Yes. It was de Câmara who brought the false teeth of our Chief Inspector Ficèsaqha back to Earth from Osiris, and gave them to Atlantic when they presented him with an honorary degree. Pefore I leat yells at a game, I go up to the museum and gaze upon the teeth. Their sentimental associations inspire me. I am very sentimental apout Senhor de Câmara, although some of our people claim he stole those teeth and other thinks when he left our planet."

At the first pledge meeting, Hithafea squatted down humbly among his fellow pledges, who looked at him with traces of distaste or apprehension. When the prospective members' duties had been explained to them, Fitzgerald and a couple of the other brothers undertook to have a little fun of the sadistic sort associated with initiations. They brought out a couple of wooden paddles, like ping-pong racquets but heavier, and fired nonsensical questions at the freshmen. Those who failed to answer glibly were paddled for their ignorance, whereas those who answered glibly were paddled for being fresh.

By and by Hithafea said, "Will nopody pattle me?"

"Why, Monster?" said Fitzgerald, "D'you wanna be?"

"Of course! It's part of peink a pletch. It would preak my heart if I were not pattled the same as the others."

The brothers looked at each other with expressions of bafflement. Brother Brown, indicating Hithafea's streamlined stern, asked, "How the hell can we? I mean, where's his—uh—I mean, where shall we hit him?"

"Oh, anywhere!" said Hithafea.

Brother Brown, looking a bit unhappy about the whole thing, hauled off with his paddle and whacked Hithafea's scaly haunch. He hit again and again, until Hithafea said, "I do not efen feel it. Are you sure you're not goink easy on me on purpose? It would wound my feelinks if you dit."

Brown shook his head. "Might as well shoot an elephant with a peashooter. You try, John."

Fitzgerald swung his massive arm and dealt Hithafea a swat that broke the paddle. He wrung his hand, looked at the other brothers, and said, "Guess we'll have to consider you constructively paddled, Hithafea. Let's go on to business."

The other pledges grinned, evidently glad to escape any further beating. As the brothers had been made to feel a little foolish, the fun seemed to have gone out of the paddling for the time being. The brothers sternly commanded the pledges to show up at the house the following night for the Thanksgiving dance, to do the serving and messwork. Moreover they were told to bring three cats each to the next pledge meeting the following week.

Hithafea as usual showed up an hour early for his duties at the dance, wearing a black bow tie around his scaly neck in deference to the formality of the occasion. John Fitzgerald, of course, brought Alice Holm, while Herbert Lengyel came stag and hovered uneasily, trying by an air of bored superiority to mask the fact that he would have liked to bring her himself.

When Hithafea stalked in bearing a tray of refreshments, some of the girls, who were not Atlantic coeds and so had never seen him before, shrieked. Alice, mastering her initial revulsion, said, "Are you dancing, Hithafea?"

Hithafea said, "Alas, Miss Holm, I could not!"

"Oh, I bet you dance divinely!"

"It's not that. At home on Osiris I perform the fertility tance with the pest of them. Put look at my tail! I should neet the whole floor to myself, I fear. You have no idea how much trouple a tail is in a worlt where peinks do not normally have them. Every time I try to go through a swingink door—"

"Let's dance, Alice," said Fitzgerald abruptly, "And you, Monster, get to work!"

Alice said, "Why John, I think you're jealous of poor Hithafea. I found him sweet!"

"Me jealous of a slithery reptile? Ha!" sneered Fitzgerald as they spun away in the gymnastic measures of the Zulu.

\* \* \*

At the next pledge meeting, a great yowling arose when the pledges showed up with three cats apiece, for which they had raided alleys and their friend's houses and the city pound. Brother Brown said, "Where's Hithafea? The Monster's not usually late—"

The doorbell rang. When one of the pledges opened it he looked out, then leaped back with the alacrity if not the grace of a startled fawn, meanwhile making a froglike noise in his throat. There on the doorstep stood Hithafea with a full-grown lioness on a leash. The cats frantically raced off to other parts of the fraternity house or climbed curtains and mantelpieces. The brothers looked as if they would have done likewise if they had not been afraid of losing face before the pledges.

"Goot evenink," said Hithafea. "This is Tootsie. I rented her. I thought if I prought one cat bik enough it would do for the three I was tolt to pring. You like her, I trust?"

"A character," said Fitzgerald, "Not only a monster, but a character."

"Do I get pattled?" said Hithafea hopefully.

"Paddling you," said Fitzgerald, "is like beating a rhinoceros with a flyswatter." And he set to work with a little extra vim on the fundaments of the other pledges.

When the pledge meeting was over, the brothers went into conference. Brother Broderick said, "I think we'll have to give 'em something more original to do for the next time. Specially Hithafea here. S'pose we tell him to bring—ah—how about that set of false teeth belonging to that guy—that emperor or whatever he was of Osiris, in the museum?"

Hithafea said, "You mean the teeth of our great Chief Inspector, Ficèsaqha?"

"Yeah, Inspector Fish—well, you pronounce it, but that's what I mean."

"That will be a kreat honor," said Hithafea. "Pefore we go, Mr. Fitzcherald, may I speak with you alone for a moment?"

Fitzgerald frowned and said, "Okay, Monster, but hurry it up. I got a date." He followed the Sha'akhfa out, and the other brothers heard Hithafea hissing something to him in the corridor.

Then Hithafea stuck his head in the doorway and said, "Mr. Lengyel, may I speak to you, now?" And the same thing happened to Lengyel.

The other brothers did not listen to the conversation between Lengyel and Hithafea because they were more interested in what was happening in the parlor. John Fitzgerald came through, all slicked up in his best clothes, and the lioness tackled him and tried to wrestle with him. The more he tried to get away the more vigorously she wrestled. He finally gave up and lay on his back while Tootsie sat on his chest and licked his face. As having your face licked by a lion is something like having it gone over with coarse sandpaper, Fitzgerald was somewhat the worse for wear by the time Hithafea came back into the room and pulled his pet off.

"I am fery sorry," he told them, "She is playful."

The night before the next pledge meeting, shadows moved in the shrubbery around the museum. The front door opened and a shadow came out—unmistakably that of a big broad-shouldered man. The shadow looked about, then back into the darkness whence it had come. Sounds came from the darkness. The shadow trotted swiftly down the front steps and whispered, "Here!"

Another shadow rose from among the shrubs; not that of a man, but something out of the Mesozoic. The human shadow tossed a package to the reptilian shadow just as the museum's watchman appeared in the doorway and shouted, "Hey, you!"

The human shadow ran like the wind, while the reptilian shadow faded into the bushes. The watchman yelled again, blew on a police whistle, and ran after the human shadow, but gave up, puffing, after a while. The quarry had disappeared.

"Be goddamned," muttered the watchman. "Gotta get the cops on this one. Let's see, who came in late this afternoon, just before closing? There was that little Italian-looking girl, and that red haired professor, and that big football-type guy…"

Frank Hodiak found his roommate packing his few simple belongings, and asked, "Where are you going?"

"I am gettink retty to leave for the Christmas vacation." said Hithafea. "I got permissions to leafe a few tays aheat of the rest." He shut his small suitcase with a snap and said, "Goot-pye, Frank. It is nice to have known you."

"Good-bye? Are you going right now?"

"Yes."

"You sound as if you weren't coming back!"

"Perhaps. Some tay. Sahcikhthasèf, as we say on Osiris."

Hodiak said, "Say, what's that funny-looking package you put in your—"

But before he finished, Hithafea was gone.

When the next pledge meeting was called, Hithafea, hitherto the outstanding eager beaver among the pledges, was absent. They called the dormitory and got in touch with Frank Hodiak, who said that Hithafea had shoved off hours previously.

The other curious fact was that John Fitzgerald had his right wrist bandaged. When the brothers asked him why, he said, "Damn'f I know! I just found myself in my room with a cut on my wrist, and no idea how it got there."

The meeting was well underway and the paddles were descending, when the doorbell rang. Two men came in, one of the campus cops and a regular municipal policeman.

The former said, "Is John Fitzgerald here?"

"Yeah," said Fitzgerald. "I'm him."

"Get your coat and hat and come with us."

"Whaffor?"

"We wanna ask you a few questions about the disappearance of an exhibit from the museum."

"I don't know anything about it. Run along and peddle your papers."

That was the wrong line to take, because the city cop brought out a piece of paper with a lot of fancy printing on it and said, "Okay, here's a warrant. You're pinched. Come—" and he took Fitzgerald by the arm.

Fitzgerald cut loose with a swing that ended, splush, on the cop's face, so that the policeman fell down on his back and lay there, moving a little and moaning. The other brothers got excited and seized both cops and threw them out the front door and bumpety-bump down the stone steps of the fraternity house. Then they went back to their pledge meeting.

In five minutes four radio patrol cars stopped in front of the frat house and a dozen cops rushed in.

The brothers, so belligerent a few minutes before, got out of the way at the sight of the clubs and blackjacks. Hands reached out of blue-clad sleeves toward Fitzgerald. He hit another cop and knocked him down, and then the hands fastened onto all his limbs and held him fast. When he persisted in struggling, a cop hit him on the head with a blackjack and he stopped.

When he came to and calmed down, on the way to the police station, he asked, "What the hell is this all about? I tell you, I never stole nothing from a museum in my whole life!"

"Oh yes you did," said a cop. "It was the false teeth of one of them things from another planet. O'Riley, I think they call it. You was seen going into the museum around closing time, and you left your fingerprints all over the glass case when you busted it. Boy, this time we'll sure throw the book at you! Damn college kids, think they're better than other folks..."

Next day Herbert Lengyel got a letter,

Dear Herb,

When you read this I shall be enroute to Osiris with the teeth of Chief Inspector Ficèsaqha, one of our greatest heroes. I managed to get a berth on a ship leaving for Pluto, whence I shall proceed to my own system on an Osirian interstellar liner.

When Fitzgerald suggested I steal the teeth, the temptation to recover this relic, originally stolen by de Câmara, was irresistible. Not being an experienced burglar, I hypnotized Fitzgerald into doing the deed for me. Thus I killed three birds with one stone, as you Earthmen say. I got the teeth; I got even with Fitzgerald for his insults; and I got him in Dutch to give you a clear field with Miss Holm.

I tell you this so you can save him from being expelled, as I do not think he deserves so harsh a penalty. I also gave you Osirian hypnosis to remove some of your inhibitions, so you shall be able to handle your end of the project.

I regret not having finished my course at Atlantic and not being finally initiated into Iota Gamma Omicron. However, my people will honor me for this deed, as we admire the refined sentiments.

Fraternally,
Hithafea

Lengyel put the letter away and looked at himself in the mirror. He now understood why he had felt so light, daring, and self-confident the last few hours. Not like his old self at all. He grinned, brushed back his hair, and started for the house phone to call Alice.

*　*　*

"So, chentlemen," said Hithafea, "now you unterstant why I have decidet to sign your agreement as it stants. I shall perhaps be criticized for giffink in to you too easily. But you see, I am soft-heartet apout your planet, and nowhere have I peen taking in and mate to feel at home as I was py the Iota Gamma Omicron fraternity many years ago."

The ambassador began to gather up his papers. "Have you a memorantum of this meetink for me to initial? Goot." Hithafea signed, using his claw for a pen. "Then we can have a formal signink next week, eh? With cameras and speeches? Some tay if you feel like erecting a monument to the founders of the Interplanetary Council, you might erect it to Mr. Herbert Lengyel."

Evans said, "Sir, I'm told you Osirians like our Earthly alcoholic drinks. Would you care to step down to the Federation bar…"

"I am so sorry, not this time. Next time, yes. Now I must catch an airplane to Baltimore, U. S. A."

"What are you doing there?" said Chagas.

"Why, Atlantic University is giving me an honoary degree. How I shall balance one of those funny hats with the tassel on my crest I do not yet know. But that was another reason I agreet to your terms. You see, we are a sentimental race. What is the matter with Mr. Wu? He looks sick."

Chagas said, "He has been watching his lifelong philosophy crumble to bits, that is all. Come, we will see you to your aircraft."

As Wu pulled himself together and rose with the rest, Evans grinned wryly at him, saying, "After we've dropped the ambassador, I think I'll make it a champagne cocktail!"

"Specialist" is set in a galaxy populated entirely by aliens—including humans. All intelligences are parts of a whole, and naturally get along fine with each other—except Earth, which is in a galactic backwater. Humans evolved in isolation, and were forced to take on the attributes of the other intelligences. As a result, all humans are naturally incomplete. It is this incompleteness that subconsciously causes doubt, stress, fear, disagreements, and wars.

A galactic Ship is caught in a photon storm. There is one fatality; the Pusher, the specialist who propels the Ship at faster-than-light speeds. Without a Pusher, everyone in the Crew will be dead of old age before the Ship reaches the nearest galactic planet. Their only hope is to find an undiscovered planet of Pushers and persuade one of them to join their brotherhood. They do find such a planet—but when the Crew approach their proto-Pusher, he screams in panic and runs away.

How can the Crew get the unknowing Pusher to recognize them as his brothers, his natural family, instead of as a group of individual monsters? And learn to Push?

# Specialist

## by Robert Sheckley

The photon storm struck without warning, pouncing upon the Ship from behind a bank of giant red stars. Eye barely had time to flash a last second warning through Talker before it was upon them.

It was Talker's third journey into deep space, and his first light-pressure storm. He felt a sudden pang of fear as the Ship yawed violently, caught the force of the wave front and careened end for end. Then the fear was gone, replaced by a strong pulse of excitement.

Why should he be afraid, he asked himself—hadn't he been trained for just this sort of emergency?

He had been talking to Feeder when the storm hit, but he cut off the conversation abruptly. He hoped Feeder would be all right. It was the youngster's first deep space trip.

The wire like filaments that made up most of Talker's body were extended throughout the Ship. Quickly he withdrew all except the ones linking him to Eye, Engine, and the Walls. This was strictly their job now. The rest of the Crew would have to shift for themselves until the storm was over.

Eye had flattened his disk like body against a Wall, and had one seeing organ extended outside the Ship. For greater concentration, the rest of his seeing organs were collapsed, clustered against his body.

Through Eye's seeing organ, Talker watched the storm. He translated Eye's purely visual image into a direction for Engine, who shoved the Ship around to meet the waves.

At appreciably the same time, Talker translated direction into velocity for the Walls who stiffened to meet the shocks.

The coordination was swift and sure—Eye measuring the waves, Talker relaying the messages to Engine and Walls, Engine driving the ship nose-first into the waves, and Walls bracing to meet the shock.

Talker forgot any fear he might have had in the swiftly functioning teamwork. He had no time to think. As the Ship's communication system, he had to translate and flash his messages at top speed, coordinating information and directing action.

In a matter of minutes, the storm was over.

"All right," Talker said. "Let's see if there was any damage." His filaments had become tangled during the storm, but he untwisted and extended them through the Ship, plugging everyone into circuit. "Engine?"

"I'm fine," Engine said. The tremendous old fellow had dampened his plates during the storm, easing down the atomic explosions in his stomach. No storm could catch an experienced spacer like Engine unaware.

"Walls?"

The Walls reported one by one, and this took a long time. There were almost a thousand of them, thin, rectangular fellows making up the entire skin of the Ship. Naturally, they had reinforced their edges during the storm, giving the whole Ship resiliency. But one or two were dented badly.

Doctor announced that he was all right. He removed Talker's filament from his head, taking himself out of circuit, and went to work on the dented Walls. Made mostly of hands, Doctor had clung to an Accumulator during the storm.

"Let's go a little faster now," Talker said, remembering that there still was the problem of determining where they were. He opened the circuit to the four Accumulators. "How are you?" he asked.

There was no answer. The Accumulators were asleep.

They had had their receptors open during the storm and were bloated on energy. Talker twitched his filaments around them, but they didn't stir.

"Let me," Feeder said. Feeder had taken quite a beating before planting his suction cups to a Wall, but his cockiness was intact. He was the only member of the Crew who never needed Doctor's attention; his body was quite capable of repairing itself.

He scuttled across the floor on a dozen or so tentacles, and booted the nearest Accumulator. The big, conical storage unit opened one eye, then closed it again. Feeder kicked him again, getting no response. He reached for the Accumulator's safety valve and drained off some energy.

"Stop that," the Accumulator said.

"Then wake up and report," Talker told him.

The Accumulators said testily that they were all right, as any fool could see. They had been anchored to the floor during the storm.

The rest of the inspection went quickly. Thinker was fine, and Eye was ecstatic over the beauty of the storm. There was only one casualty.

Pusher was dead. Bipedal, he didn't have the stability of the rest of the Crew. The storm had caught him in the middle of a floor, thrown him against a stiffened Wall, and broken several of his important bones. He was beyond Doctor's skill to repair.

They were silent for a while. It was always serious when a part of the Ship died. The Ship was a cooperative unit, composed entirely of the Crew. The loss of any member was a blow to all the rest.

It was especially serious now. They had just delivered a cargo to a port several thousand light-years from Galactic Center. There was no telling where they might be. Eye crawled to a Wall and extended a seeing organ outside. The Walls let it through, then sealed around it. Eye's organ pushed out, far enough from the Ship so he could view the entire sphere of stars. The picture traveled through Talker, who gave it to Thinker.

Thinker lay in one corner of the room, a great shapeless blob of protoplasm. Within him were all the memories of his space-going ancestors. He considered the picture, compared it rapidly with others stored in his cells, and said, "No galactic planets within reach."

Talker automatically translated for everyone. It was what they had feared.

Eye, with Thinker's help, calculated that they were several hundred light-years off their course, on the galactic periphery.

Every Crew member knew what that meant. Without a Pusher to boost the Ship to a multiple of the speed of light, they would never get home. The trip back, without a Pusher, would take longer than most of their lifetimes.

"What would you suggest?" Talker asked Thinker.

This was too vague a question for the literal-minded Thinker. He asked to have it rephrased.

"What would be our best line of action," Talker asked, "to get back to a galactic planet?"

Thinker needed several minutes to go through all the possibilities stored in his cells. In the meantime, Doctor had patched the Walls and was asking to be given something to eat.

"In a little while we'll all eat," Talker said, twitching his tendrils nervously. Even though he was the second youngest Crew member—only Feeder was younger—the responsibility was largely on him. This was still an emergency; he had to coordinate information and direct action.

One of the Walls suggested that they get good and drunk. This unrealistic solution was vetoed at once. It was typical of the Walls' attitude, however. They were fine workers and good shipmates, but happy-go-lucky fellows at best. When they returned to their home planets, they would probably blow all their wages on a spree. "Loss of the Ship's Pusher cripples the Ship for sustained faster-than-light speeds," Thinker began without preamble. "The nearest galactic planet is four hundred and five light-years off."

Talker translated all this instantly along his wave- packet body.

"Two courses of action are open. First, the Ship can proceed to the nearest galactic planet under atomic power from Engine. This will take approximately two hundred years. Engine might still be alive at this time, although no one else will.

"Second, locate a primitive planet in this region, upon which are latent Pushers. Find one and train him. Have him push the Ship back to galactic territory."

Thinker was silent, having given all the possibilities he could find in the memories of his ancestors. They held a quick vote and decided upon Thinker's second alternative. There was no choice, really. It was the only one which offered them any hope of getting back to their homes.

"All right," Talker said. "Let's eat. I think we all deserve it."

The body of the dead Pusher was shoved into the mouth of Engine, who consumed it at once, breaking down the atoms to energy. Engine was the only member of the Crew who lived on atomic energy.

For the rest, Feeder dashed up and loaded himself from the nearest Accumulator. Then he transformed the food within him into the substances each member ate. His body chemistry changed, altered, adapted, making the different foods for the Crew.

Eye lived entirely on a complex chlorophyll chitin. Feeder reproduced this for him, then went over to give Talker his hydrocarbons, and the Walls their chlorine compound. For Doctor he made a facsimile of a silicate fruit that grew on Doctor's native planet.

Finally, feeding was over and the Ship back in order, The Accumulators were stacked in a corner, blissfully sleeping again. Eye was extending his vision as far as he could, shaping his main seeing organ for high-powered telescopic reception. Even in this emergency, Eye couldn't resist making verses. He announced that he was at work on a new narrative poem, called Peripheral Glow. No one wanted to hear it, so Eye fed it to Thinker, who stored everything, good or bad, right or wrong.

Engine never slept. Filled to the brim on Pusher, he shoved the Ship along at several times the speed of light. The Walls were arguing among themselves about who had been the drunkest during their last leave.

Talker decided to make himself comfortable. He released his hold on the Walls and swung in the air, his small round body suspended by his crisscrossed network of filaments.

He thought briefly about Pusher. It was strange. Pusher had been everyone's friend and now he was forgotten.

That wasn't because of indifference; it was because the Ship was a unit. The loss of a member was regretted, but the important thing was for the unit to go on.

The Ship raced through the suns of the periphery.

Thinker laid out a search spiral, calculating their odds of finding a Pusher planet at roughly four to one. In a week they found a planet of primitive Walls. Dropping low, they could see the leathery, rectangular fellows basking in the sun, crawling over rocks, stretching themselves thin in order to float in the breeze.

All the Ship's Walls heaved a sigh of nostalgia. It was just like home.

The Walls on the planet hadn't been contacted by a galactic team yet, and were still unaware of their great destiny to join in the vast Cooperation of the Galaxy. There were plenty of dead worlds in the spiral, and worlds too young to bear life. They found a planet of Talkers. The Talkers had extended .their spidery communication lines across half a continent.

Talker looked at them eagerly through Eye. A wave of self-pity washed over him. He remembered home, his family, his friends. He thought of the tree he was going to buy when he got back.

For a moment, Talker wondered what he was doing here, part of a Ship in a far corner of the Galaxy.

He shrugged off the mood. They were bound to find a Pusher planet, if they looked long enough.

At least, he hoped so.

There was a long stretch of arid worlds as the Ship speeded through the unexplored periphery. Then a planetful of primeval Engines, swimming in a radio- active ocean.

"This is rich territory," Feeder said to Talker. "Galactic should send a Contact party here."

"They probably will, after we get back," Talker said.

They were good friends, above and beyond the all-enveloping friendship of the Crew. It wasn't only because they were the youngest Crew members, although that had something to do with it. They both had the same kind of functions and that made for a certain rapport. Talker translated languages; Feeder transformed foods. Also, they looked somewhat alike. Talker was a central core with radiating filaments; Feeder was a central core with radiating tentacles.

Talker thought that Feeder was the next most aware being on the Ship. He was never really able to understand how some of the others carried on the processes of consciousness.

More suns, more planets. Engine started to overheat. Usually, Engine was used only for taking off and landing, and for fine maneuvering in a planetary group. Now he had been running continuously for weeks, both over and under the speed of light. The strain was telling on him

Feeder, with Doctor's help, rigged a cooling system for him. It was crude, but it had to suffice. Feeder rearranged nitrogen, oxygen and hydrogen atoms to make a coolant for the system. Doctor diagnosed a long rest for Engine. He said that the gallant old fellow couldn't stand the strain for more than a week.

The search continued, with the Crew's spirits gradually dropping. They all realized that Pushers were rather rare in the Galaxy, as compared to the fertile Walls and Engines.

The Walls were getting pock-marked from interstellar dust. They complained that they would need a full beauty treatment when they got home. Talker assured them that the company would pay for it.

Even Eye was getting bloodshot from staring into space so continuously.

They dipped over another planet. Its characteristics were flashed to Thinker, who mulled over them.

Closer, and they could make out the forms.

Pushers! Primitive Pushers!

They zoomed back into space to make plans. Feeder produced twenty-three different kinds of intoxicants for a celebration.

The Ship wasn't fit to function for three days.

"Everyone ready now?" Talker asked, a bit fuzzily. He had a hangover that burned all along his nerve ends.

What a drunk he had thrown! He had a vague recollection of embracing Engine, and inviting him to share his tree when they got home.

He shuddered at the idea.

The rest of the Crew were pretty shaky, too. The Walls were letting air leak into space; they were just too wobbly to seal their edges properly. Doctor had passed out.

But the worst off was Feeder. Since his system could adapt to any type of fuel except atomic, he had been sampling every batch he made, whether it was unbalanced iodine, pure oxygen or a supercharged ester. He was really miserable. His tentacles, usually a healthy aqua, were shot through with orange streaks. His system was working furiously, purging itself of everything, and Feeder was suffering the effects of the purge.

The only sober ones were Thinker and Engine. Thinker didn't drink, which was unusual for a spacer, though typical of Thinker, and Engine couldn't.

They listened while Thinker reeled off some astounding facts. From Eye's pictures of the planet's surface, Thinker had detected the presence of metallic construction. He put forth the alarming suggestion that these Pushers had constructed a mechanical civilization.

"That's impossible," three of the Walls said flatly, and most of the Crew were inclined to agree with them. All the metal they had ever seen had been buried in the ground or lying around in worthless oxidized chunks.

"Do you mean that they make things out of metal?" Talker demanded. "Out of just plain dead metal? What could they make?"

"They couldn't make anything," Feeder said positively. "It would break down constantly. I mean metal doesn't know when it's weakening."

But it seemed to be true. Eye magnified his pictures, and everyone could see that the Pushers had made vast shelters, vehicles, and other articles from inanimate material.

The reason for this was not readily apparent, but it wasn't a good sign. However, the really hard part was over. The Pusher planet had been found. All that remained was the relatively easy job of convincing a native Pusher.

That shouldn't be too difficult. Talker knew that cooperation was the keystone of the Galaxy, even among primitive peoples.

The Crew decided not to land in a populated region. Of course, there was no reason not to expect a friendly greeting, but it was the job of a Contact Team to get in touch with them as a race. All they wanted was an individual.

Accordingly, they picked out a sparsely populated landmass, drifting in while that side of the planet was dark. They were able to locate a solitary Pusher almost at once.

Eye adapted his vision to see in the dark, and they followed the Pusher's movements. He lay down, after a while, beside a small fire. Thinker told them that this was a well-known resting habit of Pushers.

Just before dawn, the Walls opened, and Feeder, Talker and Doctor came out.

Feeder dashed forward and tapped the creature on the shoulder. Talker followed with a communication tendril. The Pusher opened his seeing organs, blinked them, and made a movement with his eating organ. Then he leaped to his feet and started to run. The three Crew members were amazed. The Pusher hadn't even waited to find out what the three of them wanted!

Talker extended a filament rapidly, and caught the Pusher, fifty feet away, by a limb. The Pusher fell.

"Treat him gently," Feeder said. "He might be startled by our appearance." He twitched his tendrils at the idea of a Pusher—one of the strangest sights in the Galaxy, with his multiple organs—being startled at someone else's appearance. Feeder and Doctor scurried to the fallen Pusher, picked him up and carried him back to the Ship.

The Walls sealed again. They released the Pusher and prepared to talk. As soon as he was free, the Pusher sprang to his limbs and ran at the place where the Walls had sealed. He pounded against them frantically, his eating organ open and vibrating,

"Stop that," the Wall said. He bulged, and the Pusher tumbled to the floor. Instantly, he jumped up, and started to run forward.

"Stop him," Talker said. "He might hurt himself."

One of the Accumulators woke up enough to roll into the Pusher's path. The Pusher fell, got up again, and ran on.

Talker had his filaments in the front of the Ship also, and he caught the Pusher in the bow. The Pusher started to tear at his tendrils, and Talker let go hastily.

"Plug him into the communication system!" Feeder shouted. "Maybe we can reason with him!"

Talker advanced a filament toward the Pusher's head, waving it in the universal sign of communication, but the Pusher continued his amazing behavior, jumping out of the way. He had a piece of metal in his hand and he was waving it frantically.

"What do you think he's going to do with that?" Feeder asked. The Pusher started to attack the side of the Ship, pounding at one of the Walls. The Wall stiffened instinctively and the metal snapped.

"Leave him alone," Talker said. "Give him a chance to calm down."

Talker consulted with Thinker, but they couldn't decide what to do about the Pusher. He wouldn't accept communication. Every time Talker extended a filament, the Pusher showed all the signs of violent panic. Temporarily, it was an impasse.

Thinker vetoed the plan of finding another Pusher on the planet. He considered this Pusher's behavior typical; nothing would be gained by approaching another. Also, a planet was supposed to be contacted only by a Contact Team.

If they couldn't communicate with this Pusher, they never would with another on the planet.

"I think I know what the trouble is," Eye said. He crawled up on an Accumulator. "These Pushers have evolved a mechanical civilization.

Consider for a minute how they went about it. They developed the use of their fingers, like Doctor, to shape metal. They utilized their seeing organs, like myself. And probably countless other organs." He paused for effect.

"These Pushers have become unspecialized!"

They argued over it for several hours. The Walls maintained that no intelligent creature could be unspecialized. It was unknown in the Galaxy. But the evidence was before them. The Pusher cities, their vehicles ... This Pusher, exemplifying the rest, seemed capable of a multitude of things.

He was able to do everything except Push!

Thinker supplied a partial explanation. "This is not a primitive planet. It is relatively old and should have been in the Cooperation thousands of years ago. Since it was not, the Pushers upon it were robbed of their birthright. Their ability, their specialty was to Push, but there was nothing to Push. Naturally, they have developed a deviant culture.

"Exactly what this culture is, we can only guess. But on the basis of the evidence, there is reason to believe that these Pushers are uncooperative.'"

Thinker had a habit of uttering the most shattering statement in the quietest possible way.

"It is entirely possible," Thinker went on inexorably, "that these Pushers will have nothing to do with us. In which case, our chances are approximately 283 to one against finding another Pusher planet."

"We can't be sure he won't cooperate," Talker said, "until we get him into communication." He found it almost impossible to believe that any intelligent creature would refuse to cooperate willingly.

"But how?" Feeder asked. They decided upon a course of action. Doctor walked slowly up to the Pusher, who backed away from him. In the meantime, Talker extended a filament outside the Ship, around, and in again, behind the Pusher. The Pusher backed against a Wall and Talker shoved the filament through the Pusher's head; into the communication socket in the center of his brain.

The Pusher collapsed.

When he came to, Feeder and Doctor had to hold the Pusher's limbs, or he would have ripped out the communication line. Talker exercised his skill in learning the Pusher's language.

It wasn't too hard. All Pusher languages were of the same family, and this was no exception. Talker was able to catch enough surface thoughts to form a pattern.

He tried to communicate with the Pusher.

The Pusher was silent.

"I think he needs food," Feeder said. They remembered that it had been almost two days since they had taken the Pusher on board. Feeder worked up some standard Pusher food and offered it:

"My God! A steak!" the Pusher said.

The Crew cheered along Talker's communication circuits. The Pusher had said his first words!

Talker examined the words and searched his memory. He knew about two hundred Pusher languages and many more simple variations. He found that this Pusher was speaking a cross between two Pusher tongues.

After the Pusher had eaten, he looked around. Talker caught his thoughts and broadcast them to the Crew.

The Pusher had a queer way of looking at the Ship. He saw it as a riot of colors. The walls undulated. In front of him was something resembling a gigantic spider, colored black and green, with his web running all over the Ship and into the heads of all the creatures. He saw Eye as a strange, naked little animal, something between a skinned rabbit and an egg yolk—whatever those things were.

Talker was fascinated by the new perspective the Pusher's mind gave him. He had never seen things that way before. But now that the Pusher was pointing it out, Eye was a pretty funny looking creature.

They settled down to communication.

"What in hell are you things?" the Pusher asked, much calmer now than he had been during the two days. "Why did you grab me? Have I gone nuts?"

"No," Talker said, "you are not psychotic. We are a galactic trading ship. We were blown off course by a storm and our Pusher was killed."

"Well, what does that have to do with me?"

"We would like you to join our crew," Talker said, "To be our new Pusher."

The Pusher thought it over after the situation was explained to him. Talker could catch the feeling of conflict in the Pusher's thoughts. He hadn't decided whether to accept this as a real situation or not. Finally, the Pusher decided that he wasn't crazy.

"Look, boys," he said, "I don't know what you are or how this makes sense. I have to get out of here. I'm on a furlough, and if I don't get back soon, the U. S. Army's going to be very interested."

Talker asked the Pusher to give him more information about 'army,' and he fed it to Thinker.

"These Pushers engage in personal combat," was Thinker's conclusion.

"But why?" Talker asked. Sadly he admitted to himself that Thinker might have been right; the Pusher didn't show many signs of willingness to cooperate.

"I'd like to help you lads out," Pusher said, "but I don't know where you get the idea that I could push anything this size. You'd need a whole division of tanks just to budge it."

"Do you approve of these wars?" Talker asked, getting a suggestion from Thinker.

"Nobody likes war—not those who have to do the dying at least."

"Then why do you fight them?"

The Pusher made a gesture with his eating organ, which Eye picked up and sent to Thinker. "It's kill or be killed. You guys know what war is, don't you?"

"We don't have any wars," Talker said.

"You're lucky," the Pusher said bitterly. "We do. Plenty of them."

"Of course," Talker said. He had the full explanation from Thinker now. "Would you like to end them?"

"Of course I would."

"Then come with us. Be our Pusher."

The Pusher stood tip and walked up to an Accumulator. He sat down on it and doubled the ends of his upper limbs.

"How the hell can I stop all wars?" the Pusher demanded. "Even if I went to the big shots and told them—"

"You won't have to," Talker said. "All you have to do is come with us. Push us to our base. Galactic will send a Contact Team to your planet. That will end your wars."

"The hell you say," The Pusher replied. "You boys are stranded here, huh? Good enough. No monsters are going to take over Earth."

Bewildered, Talker tried to understand the reasoning. Had he said something wrong? Was it possible that the Pusher didn't understand him?

"I thought you wanted to end wars," Talker said.

"Sure I do. But I don't want anyone making us stop. I'm no traitor. I'd rather fight."

"No one will make you stop. You will just stop because there will be no further need for fighting."

"Do you know why we're fighting?"

"It's obvious."

"Yeah? What's your explanation?"

"You Pushers have been separated from the main stream of the Galaxy," Talker explained. "You have your specialty—pushing—but nothing to Push. Accordingly, you have no real jobs. You play with things, metal, inanimate objects, but find no real satisfaction. Robbed of your true vocation, you fight from sheer frustration.

"Once you find your place in the galactic Cooperation—and I assure you that it is an important place—your fighting will stop. Why should you fight, which is an unnatural occupation, when you can Push? Also, your mechanical civilization will end, since there will be no need for it."

The Pusher shook his head in what Talker guessed was a gesture of confusion. "What is this pushing?"

Talker told him as best he could. Since the job was out of his scope, he had only a general idea of what a Pusher did.

"You mean to say that that is what every Earthman should be doing?"

"Of course," Talker said. "It is your great specialty."

The Pusher thought about it for several minutes. "I think you want a physicist or a mentalist or something. I could never do anything like that. I'm a junior architect. And besides—well, it's difficult to explain."

But Talker had already caught Pusher's objection. He saw a Pusher female in his thoughts. No, two, three. And he caught a feeling of loneliness, strangeness. The Pusher was filled with doubts. He was afraid.

"When we reach galactic," Talker said, hoping it was the right thing, "you can meet other Pushers. Pusher females, too. All you Pushers look alike, so you should become friends with them. As far as loneliness in the Ship goes—it just doesn't exist. You don't understand the Cooperation yet. No one is lonely in the Cooperation."

The Pusher was still considering the idea of there being other Pushers. Talker couldn't understand why he was so startled at that. The Galaxy was filled with Pushers; Feeders, Talkers, and many other species, endlessly duplicated.

"I can't believe that anybody could end all war," Pusher said. "How do I know you're not lying?"

Talker felt as if he had been struck in the core. Thinker must have been right when he said these Pushers would be uncooperative. Was this going to be the end of Talker's career? Were he and the rest of the Crew going to spend the rest of their lives in space, because of the stupidity of a bunch of Pushers?

Even thinking this, Talker was able to feel sorry for the Pusher. It must be terrible, he thought. Doubting, uncertain, never trusting anyone. If these Pushers didn't find their place in the Galaxy, they would exterminate themselves. Their place in the Cooperation was long overdue.

"What can I do to convince you?" Talker asked.

In despair, he opened all the circuits to the Pusher. He let the Pusher see Engine's good-natured gruffness, the devil-may-care humor of the

Walls; he showed him Eye's poetic attempts, and Feeder's cocky good nature. He opened his own mind and showed the Pusher a picture of his home planet, his family, the tree he was planning to buy when he got home.

The pictures told the story of all of them, from different planets, representing different ethics, united by a common bond-the galactic Cooperation.

The Pusher watched it all in silence.

After a while, he shook his head. The thought accompanying the gesture was uncertain, weak, but negative.

Talker told the Walls to open. They did, and the Pusher stared in amazement. "You may leave," Talker said. "Just remove the communication line and go."

"What will you do?"

"We will look for another Pusher planet."

"Where? Mars? Venus?"

"We don't know. All we can do is hope there is another in this region."

The Pusher looked at the opening, then back at the Crew. He hesitated and his face screwed up in a grimace of indecision.

"All that you showed me was true?"

No answer was necessary.

"All right," the Pusher said suddenly. "I'll go. I'm a damned fool, but I'll go. If this means what you say—it must mean what you say!"

Talker saw that the agony of the Pusher's decision had forced him out of contact with reality. He believed that he was in a dream, where decisions are easy and unimportant.

"There's just one little trouble," Pusher said with the lightness of hysteria. "Boys, I'll be damned if I know how to Push. You said something about faster-than-light? I can't even run the mile in an hour."

"Of course you can Push," Talker assured him, hoping he was right. He knew what a Pusher's abilities were but this one…

"Just try it."

"Sure," Pusher agreed. "I'll probably wake up out of this, anyhow."

They sealed the ship for takeoff while Pusher talked to himself.

"Funny," Pusher said. "I thought a camping trip would be a nice way to spend a furlough and all I do is get nightmares!" ·

Engine boosted the Ship into the air. The Walls were sealed and Eye was guiding them away from the planet. "We're in open space now," Talker said. Listening to Pusher, he hoped his mind hadn't cracked. "Eye and Thinker will give a direction, I'll transmit it to you, and you Push along it."

"You're crazy," Pusher mumbled. "You must have the wrong planet. I wish you nightmares would go away."

"You're in the Cooperation now," Talker said desperately. "There's the direction. Push!"

The Pusher didn't do anything for a moment. He was slowly emerging from his fantasy, realizing that he wasn't in a dream, after all. He felt the Cooperation. Eye to Thinker, Thinker to Talker, Talker to Pusher, all inter-coordinated with Walls, and with each other.

"What is this?" Pusher asked. He felt the oneness of the Ship, the great warmth, the closeness achieved only in the Cooperation.

He Pushed.

Nothing happened.

"Try again," Talker begged.

Pusher searched his mind... He found a deep well of doubt and fear. Staring into it, he saw his own tortured face.

Thinker illuminated it for him.

Pushers had lived with this doubt and fear for centuries. Pushers had fought through fear, killed through doubt.

That was where the Pusher organ was!

Human—specialist—Pusher—he entered fully into the Crew, merged with them, threw mental arms around the shoulders of Thinker and Talker.

Suddenly, the Ship shot forward at eight times the speed of light. It continued to accelerate.

"Point of Focus" begins, "Federation Emissary Holis Bork was a confident man—and, if he felt a twinge of curious uneasiness at his first glimpse of Mellidan VII, it was not because he doubted his own capabilities, or the value of the Federation's name as a civilizing force." The reader has to get into the story a bit to discover that Holis Bork is a representative of the all-powerful aliens, and the humans are the underdogs—or upstarts.

This story is typical of the s-f of the mid-20th century. Aliens were no longer just supporting characters. Sometimes the stories were from their viewpoint. But the humans still always triumphed in the end.

"Point of Focus" can also be seen as representative of young and vigorous America (the obviously American Terrans), and the emerging independent African, Caribbean, South American, Asiatic, and Oceanic nations (the Mellidani, led by the Terrans), versus the still gigantic cultures of the old, tired, and ossified European powers. But without analyzing the story too much, this features three species; notably the non-human Federation leaders and the exotic Mellidani.

# Point of Focus

## by Robert Silverberg

Federation Emissary Holis Bork was a confident man—and, if he felt a twinge of curious uneasiness at his first glimpse of Mellidan VII, it was not because he doubted his own capabilities, or the value of the Federation's name as a civilizing force.

No, he told himself that it was something subtler and deeper that twinged him, as the warship spiraled down about the unfederated planet.

Emissary Bork worried about that subliminal reaction through most of the landing period. He sat broodingly with his eyes fixed; the members of his staff gave him a wide berth. It was, he saw, the deference due to a Federation Emissary so obviously deep in creative thinking. The others were clustered at the far end of the observation deck, staring down at the fog-shrouded yellow-green ball that was soon to be the newest addition to the far-flung Federation. Bork listened to them.

Vyn Kumagon was saying, "Look at that place! The atmosphere blankets it like so much soup."

"I wonder what it's like to breathe chlorine?" asked Hu Sdreen. "And to give off carbon tetrachloride instead of $CO_2$?"

"To them it's all the same," Kumagon snapped.

Emissary Bork looked away. He had the answer! he knew what was troubling him.

Mellidan VII was *different*. The peoples of the worlds of the Federation, and even the four non-Federated worlds of the Sol system, shared one seemingly universal characteristic: they breathed oxygen, gave off carbon dioxide. And the Mellidani? A chlorine-carbon tetrachloride cycle which worked well for them—but was strange, *different*. And that difference troubled Federation Emissary Bork on a deep, shadowy, half-grasped plane of thought.

He shook his mind clear and nudged the speaker panel at his wrist. "How long till landing?"

"We enter final orbit in thirty-nine minutes," Control Center told him. "Contact's been made with the Mellidani and they're guiding us in."

Bork leaned back in the comforting webfoam network and twined his twelve tapering fingers calmly together. He was not worried. Despite Mellidan VII's alienness, there would be no problems. In minutes, the landing would be effected, and past experience told him it would be but a matter of time before the Federation had annexed its four hundred eighty-sixth world.

* * *

Later, Bork stood by the rear screens, looking down at the planet as the Federation ship whistled downward through the murky green atmosphere. *To civilize is our mission*, he thought. *To offer the benefits—*

It was four years Galactic since a Federation survey ship had first touched down on Mellidan VII. It had been strictly an accidental planetfall. The prelim scouts had thoroughly established that there was little point in bothering to search a chlorine world orbiting a white dwarf sun for oxygen-type life. That was easily understood.

What was not so easily understood was the possibility of a non-oxygen metabolism. Statistics lay against it; the four hundred eighty-five worlds of the Federation all operated on an oxynitrogen atmosphere and a respiration-photosynthesis cycle that endlessly recirculated oxygen and carbon dioxide. The four inhabited worlds of the unfederated system of Sol were similarly constituted. It was a rule to which no exceptions had been found.

But then the scoutship of Dos Nollibar, cruising out of Vronik XII, came tumbling down into the chlorinated soup of Mellidan VII's atmosphere, three ultrones in its warp—drive fused beyond repair. It took six weeks for a rescue ship to locate and remove the eleven Federation scouts—and by that time, Chief Scout Dos Nollibar and his men had discovered and made contact with the Mellidani.

Standing at the screen watching his ship thunder down into the thick green shroud of the planet, Emissary Bork cast an inward eye back over Nollibar's scout report-a last-minute refresher, as it were.

"—*inhabitants roughly humanoid in external structure, though probably nearly solid internally. This is subject to later verification when a specimen is available for complete examination.*"

"—*main constituents of atmosphere: hydrogen, chlorine, nitrogen, helium. Smaller quantities of other gases. No oxygen. This mixture is, of course, unbreathable by all forms of Federation life.*"

"—*mean temperature 260 Absolute. Animal life gives off carbon tetrachloride as respiratory waste; this is broken down by plants to chlorine and complex hydrocarbons. Inhabitants consume plants, smaller animal life, drink hydrochloric acid—*"

"—*seat of planetary government apparently located not far from our landing-point, unless aliens have deliberately misled or we have misunderstood. Naturally most of our data is highly tentative in nature, subject to confirmation after this world is enrolled in the Federation and available for further study.*"

Which was Bork's job.

For four years, ever since Nollibar had filed his report, Bork had readied himself for the task of bringing Mellidan VII into the Federation. Nollibar had returned with recorded samples of the language, and a few months of phoneme analysis had been sufficient to work out a rough conversion-equation to Federation, good enough for Bork to learn and speak.

There would undoubtedly be a promotion in this for him: to Subgalactic Overchief, perhaps, or Third Warden. Of the ten emissaries whose task it was to bring newly discovered planets into the Federation, it was he the First Warden had chosen for this job. That was significant, Bork thought: on no other world would the Emissary be forced to forego direct face-to-face contact with the leaders of the species to be absorbed. Here, on the other hand—

Bork sensed a presence behind him. He turned.

It was Vyn Kumagon, Adjutant in Charge of Communications. Bork had no way of knowing how long Kumagon had been peering over his shoulder; he resented the intrusion on an Emissary's privacy.

And Kumagon's green eyes were faintly slitted—the mark of Gyralin blood somewhere in his heritage. As a pure-bred Vengol of the Federation's First Planet, Bork felt vague contempt for his assistant. "Yes?" he said, mildly but with undertones of scorn.

Kumagon's slitted eyes fixed sharply on the Emissary's. "Sir, the Mellidani have beamed us for some advice."

"Eh?"

"They'd like to know how close to the Terran dome we want to land, sir."

Bork barely repressed a gasp. "*What* Terran dome?"

"They said the Terrans established a base here several months ago. Sir? Are you well? You—"

"Tell them," Bork said heavily, "that we wish to land no closer than five miles from the Terran dome, and no farther than ten. Can you translate that into their equivalents?"

"Yes, sir."

"Then transmit it." Bork choked back a strangled cry of rage. Someone, he thought, had blundered in the home office. That Terrans should be allowed to land on a world being groomed for Federation entry—!

Why, it was unthinkable!

\* \* \*

The planet was the most forbidding-looking Bork had ever seen, and he had seen a great many. With screens turned to maximal periphery, he could stand in the snout of the ship and look out on Mellidan VII as if he stood outside. It was hardly a pleasant sight.

The land was utterly flat. Long stretches of barren gray-brown soil extended in every direction, sweeping upward into tiny hillocks far toward the horizon. Soil implied the presence of bacteria: anaerobic bacteria, of course, needing no oxygen.

There were seas, too, shimmering shallow pools of carbon tetrachloride that had precipitated out of the atmosphere. Plants grew in these ponds: ugly squishy plants that looked like hordes of gray bladders strung on thick hairy ropes. They lay flat against the bright surface of the carbon tetrachloride pond, drifting. As Bork watched, a Mellidani appeared, wading knee-deep, gathering the bladders, slinging them over his blocky round shoulders. He was a farmer, no doubt.

At this distance it was difficult to tell much about the alien, except that his body was segmented crustacean fashion, humanoid otherwise; his skin looked thick, waxy, leathery. Chief Scout Nollibar had postulated some member of the paraffin series as the chief constituent of Mellidam protoplasm; he was probably right.

Clouds of gaseous chlorine hung thick overhead, draping the sky with a yellow-green blanket. Somewhere directly above burned the sun Mellidan: a white dwarf of ferocious intensity, its heat negated by the planet's distance from it and by the swath of chlorine that was the atmosphere's main component. One other distinct feature made up the view as Bork saw it. Some eight miles directly westward, the violet-hued arc of a plastic-extrusion habitation dome rose from the bare plain. Bork had seen such domes before—more than forty years before, when he had served as a member of the last mission to Terra.

He had been only a Fifth Attaché then, though soon afterward he had begun the rapid climb that would bring him to the rank of Federation Emissary. On that occasion, the Emissary had been old Morvil Brek, who had added twelve worlds to the Federation during his distinguished career. Brek had been named to make the fifth attempt to enroll the Sol system.

The mission had been a failure; the Terran government had emphatically rejected any offer to federate, and Emissary Brek then declared the system nonfederated for good, in a bitter little speech which fell short of making its intended effect of altering the Terran decision. The Galactics had departed and, on the outward trip, Bork had seen the violet domes on the snowswept plains of Sol IX, where the Terrans had established an encampment.

He scowled. Terrans on Mellidan VII? Why? Why? "Contact has been made with the Mellidani leaders, sir," Kumagon said gently. Bork drew his eyes from the Terran dome. It seemed to him he could almost see the Terrans moving about within it, pale-skinned, ten-fingered, almost repellently hairy men with that damned sly expression always on their faces—

Just imagination. He sighed.

"Transfer the line up here," Bork said to his Adjutant. "I'll talk to them from my chair."

\* \* \*

Bork sprawled in a leisure-loving way into the intricate reticulations of the webfoam chair; he nudged a stud at its base and the chair began to quiver gently, massaging him, easing the stress-and-fatigue poisons from his muscles. After a moment, the communicator screen lit up, breaking into the wide-periphery view of the landscape.

Three Mellidani faced him squarely. They were chalk white and without hair: their eyes were set deep in their round skulls, ringed with massive orbital ridges, veiled from time to time by fast-flickering nictitating membranes, while their mouths, if mouths they were, were but thin lipless slits. Three nostrils formed a squat triangle midway between eyes and mouth, while cupped processes jutting from the sides of the head seemed to equate with ears. Bork was not surprised at this superficial resemblance to the standard humanoid type; there is a certain most efficient pattern of construction for an erect humanoid biped, and virtually all such life adheres to it.

The Emissary said, "I greet you in the name of the Federation of Worlds. My name is Holis Bork; my title, 'Emissary'.»

The centermost of the aliens moved his lipless mouth; words came forth. The linguistic pattern, too, adhered to norms. "I am Leader this month. My name is unimportant. What does your Federation want with us?"

It was the expected quasi-belligerent response. Twenty years of Emissary duties had reduced the operation to a series of conditioned reflexes, so far as Bork was concerned. Stimulus A produced response B, which was dealt with by means of technique C.

He said, "The Federation is composed of four hundred eighty-five worlds scattered throughout some thirty thousand light-years. Its capital and First Planet is Vengo in the Darkir system; its member peoples live in unmatched unity."

"Current Federation population is twenty-seven billion. Membership in the Federation will guarantee you free and equal rights, full representation, and the complete benefits of a Galactic civilization that has been in existence for eleven thousand years."

He paused triumphantly with soundless fanfare. The array of statistics was calculated to arouse a feeling of awe and lead naturally to the next group of response-leads. The Federation's psychometrists had perfected this technique over millennia.

But the Mellidani Leader's reaction jarred Bork. The alien said, "Why is it that the Terrans do not belong to the Federation?"

Bork had been ready with the next concept-group; he had already begun to bring forth the second phase of his argument when the impact of the Mellidani's sudden irrelevant question slammed into his nervous system and set the neat circuitry of his mind oscillating wildly.

It was a dizzy moment. But Bork had his nerves under control almost instantly, and a moment later had formulated a new pat reply he hoped would cover the new situation.

"The Terrans," he said, "did not choose to enter the Federation—thereby demonstrating that they lack the wisdom and maturity of a truly Galactic-minded race."

It was impossible to tell what emotions were in play behind the alien's almost inflexible features. Bork found himself trembling; he docketed a mental note to have a neural overhaul when he returned to Vengo.

The alien said, "You imply by this that the Federation worlds are superior to the Terran worlds. In what way?" Again Bork's nerves were jolted. The interview was taking a very unpredictable pattern indeed. *Damn* those Terrans, he thought. And double-damn Security for allowing them to get a foothold here with an Emissary on his way! Sweat dribbled down the Emissary's olive-green skin.

His military collar was probably drooping by now. He rooted in his mind for some sequence of arguments that would answer the stubborn alien's question, and at length came up with: "The Federation worlds are superior in that they have complete homogeneity of thought, feeling, and purpose. We have a common ground for intellectual endeavor and for commercial traffic. We share laws, works of art, ways of thinking. The Earthmen have deliberately placed themselves beyond the pale of this communion—cut themselves off from every other civilized world of the galaxy."

"They have not cut themselves off from us. They came here quite willingly and have lived here during three Leaderships."

*Damn the Terrans! Damn damn damn—*

"They mean to corrupt you," Bork said desperately. "To lead you away from the right path. They are malicious: unable to enter Galactic society themselves through their own antisocial tendencies, they try now to drag an innocent world into the same quagmire, the same—"

Bork stopped suddenly. His hands were shaking; his body was bathed in perspiration. He realized gloomily that for the first time in his career he had no notion whatever of the next line of thought to pursue.

Promotion, glory, past achievements-all down the sink because of failure now, here? He swallowed hard.

"We'll continue our discussions tomorrow," he said hoarsely. "I would not keep you from your daily work."

"Very well. Tomorrow the man at my left will be Leader. Address your words then to him."

In the state he was in, Bork had little further interest in protocol. He broke the contact hastily and sank back in the cradle of webfoam, tense, sweat-drenched.

The pouch of his tunic yielded three green-gold pellets: metabolic compensators. Bork gobbled them hurriedly, and, as his body returned to normal equilibrium, sank back to brood over the ignominious course of the interview.

\* \* \*

Naturally, Bork thought, the conversation had been monitored and recorded. That meant that Vyn Kumagon and six or seven technicians had been eye-witness to the Emissary's fumbling handling of the first interview—and, with the interview already permanently locked into a cellular recorder, there would be many more eavesdroppers, a long chain of them between here and Vengo and the First Warden.

Bork knew he had to redeem himself.

High faith had been placed in him—but who could have anticipated a Terran counter-propaganda force on Mellidan VII? It had shattered his calm.

He would have to rethink his approach.

Undeniably, the Terrans were here. And undeniably they had made overtures of some sort toward the aliens. Of what sort? That was the missing datum. The keystone of all possible speculations was missing: the purpose of the Terrans.

Did they have some strategic use in mind for Mellidan VII? That seemed improbable, in view of the world's forbidding nature. No Terran colony could survive here without the protection of a dome. Unless, he thought coldly, they meant to take over the planet and convert it into a new Earth, as they had done with Sol II, Sol IV, and one of the moons of Sol VI. That would mean the death or deportation of the Mellidani, but would the Terrans worry long over that?

But—why would they pick an inhabited world for such a project, when there yet remained a dead planet in their own system? Bork forced himself to reject the colonization plan as implausible under any circumstances.

Perhaps Terra had some yet unknown economic need that Mellidan VII met. Perhaps—

Bork's head ached. Speculation was not easy for him. After a while he rose and went below to seek sleep.

*   *   *

There was a fixed routine for the assimilation of worlds into the Federation. It was a routine developed over thousands of years—ever since Vengo spread out to absorb its three sister worlds, eleven thousand years Galactic before, and the Federation was born. The routine customarily was successful.

Growth had been slow, at first. Two solar systems the first millennium, yielding five inhabited worlds. Then three systems the second millennium, with four worlds. Eleven worlds the next, seventeen the next—

Until four hundred eighty-five worlds had been folded into the protective warmth of the Federation, nineteen during Bork's own lifetime. Only four worlds had ever refused to come in: the four Terran worlds, approached five times without success over the preceding two centuries. And now, Mellidan VII showed signs of recalcitrance. Bork resolved to use the age-old phrases and persuasion techniques until the Mellidani were unable to resist.

Violence, of course was shunned; the Federation had outgrown that millennia ago, But there were other methods. When the Mellidani trio returned on the following day for their meeting with Bork, the Emissary was ready for them, nerves soothed, mind primed and alert. Today, he noticed, the order had indeed been shuffled. The monthly changeover in planetary leadership had taken place.

Bork said, "Yesterday we were discussing the advantages of Federation membership for your world. You suggested that you might be more sympathetic to the Terrans than you are to us. Would you care to tell me just what guarantees the Terrans have made to you?"

"None."

"But—"

"The Terrans have warned us against entering your Federation. They say your promises are false, that you will deceive us and swallow us up in your hugeness."

Bork stiffened. "Did they ask you to sign any sort of treaty with them?"

"No. None whatever."

"Then what have they been doing here since they landed?" Bork demanded, exasperated.

"Taking measurements of our planet, making scientific studies, exploring and learning. They have also been telling us somewhat about your Federation and warning us against you."

"They have no right to poison your minds against us! We came here in good faith to demonstrate to you how it was to your advantage to join the Federation."

"And the Terrans came in good faith to tell us the opposite," returned the alien implacably. Bork had a sudden sense of the unfleshliness of the creature, of its strange hydrocarbon chemistry and its chlorine-breathing lungs. It seemed to him that the stiff white face of the Mellidam was a mask that hid only other masks within.

"Whom should we believe?" the alien asked. "You—or the Terrans?"

Bork moistened tension-parched lips. "The Earthmen clearly lie. We have brought with us films and charts of Galactic progress; The Federation is plainly preferable to the rootless, companionless life the Terrans have chosen. Be reasonable, friends. Should you cut yourself off from the main current of Galactic life by refusing to join the Federation? You're intelligent; I can see that immediately. Why withdraw? If you decline to Federate, it will become impossible for you to have cultural or commercial interchange with any of the Federated worlds. You—" ·

"Answer this question, please," said the Mellidani abruptly. "Why is this Federation of yours necessary?"

"What?"

"Why can't we have these contacts *without* joining?"

"Why—because—"

Bork gasped like a creature jerked suddenly from its natural element. This sudden nerve-shattering question had thrust itself between his ribs like a keen blade.

He realized he had no answer to the alien's question. No glib catchphrases rose to his lips. He sputtered inanely, reddened, and finally took recourse in the same tactic of retreat he had employed the day before.

"This is a question that requires further study. I'll take it up with you tomorrow at this time."

The Mellidani faded from the glowing screen. Emissary Bork made contact with Adjutant Kumagon and said, "Get in touch with the Terrans. There has to be an immediate conference with them."

"At once," Kumagon said.

Bork scowled. The Adjutant seemed almost pleased. Was that the shadow of a smile flickering on the man's lips?

\* \* \*

Later that day a hatch near the firing tubes of the Federation ship pivoted open and the shining beetle-like shape of a landcar dropped through, its treads striking the barren Mellidani soil and carrying it swiftly away. Aboard were Emissary Holis Bork and two aides: Fifth Attaché Hu Sdreen and Third Attaché Brui Dirrib. The landcar sped across the ground, through the shallow pools of precipitated carbon tetrachloride, through the low-hanging thick murk of the sky, and minutes later arrived at the violet-hued Terran habitation dome.

There, a hatch swung open, admitting the car to an air lock. The hatch sealed with a hiss; a second lock irised open, and air—oxynitrogen air—coursed in. Several Terrans were waiting as Bork and his aides stepped from the landcar.

Bork felt uneasy in their presence. They were trim, lean, efficient-looking men, all clad more or less alike. One, older than the rest, came forward and lifted his hand in a formal Federation salute, which Bork automatically returned.

"I'm Major-General Gambrell," the Terran said, speaking fluent Federation. The second mission to Terra had educated the natives in the Galactic tongue, and they had never forgotten it. "I'm in charge here for the time being," Gambrell said. "Suppose you come on up to my office and we can talk this thing over.

Gambrell led the way up a neat row of low metal houses, and entered one several stories high; Bork followed him, signaling the aides to remain outside. When they were within, Gambrell seated himself behind a battered wooden desk, fished in his pocket, and produced a cigarette pack. He offered it to Bork.

"Care to have a smoke?"

"Sorry," the Emissary said, repressing his disgust. "We don't induige."

"Of course. I forgot." Gambrell smiled apologetically. "You don't mind if I smoke, do you?"

Bork shrugged. "Not at all."

Gambrell flicked the igniting capsule at the cigarette's tip, waited a moment, then puffed at the other end. He looked utterly relaxed. Bork was sharply tuned for this meeting; every nerve was tight-strung.

The Earthman said, "All right. Just why have you requested this meeting, Emissary Bork?"

"You know our purpose here on Mellidan VII?" Bork asked.

"Certainly. You're here to enroll the Mellidani in your Federation."

Bork nodded. "Our aim is clear to you, then. But why are *you* here, Major-General Gambrell? Why has Earth established this outpost?"

The Earthman ran one hand lightly through the close-cropped thatch of graying hair that covered most of his scalp. Bork thought of the vestigial topknot that was *his* only heritage from the past, and smiled smugly. After a moment Gambrell said, "We're here to keep Mellidan VII from joining the Federation. Is that clear enough?"

"It is," Bork said tightly. "May I ask what you hope to gain by this deliberate interference? I suppose you plan to use Mellidan VII as some sort of military base, no doubt."

"No."

Bork had gained flexibility during the past few days. He shot an instant rejoinder at the Earthman: "In that case you must have some commercial purpose in mind. What?"

The Earthman shook his head. "Let me be perfectly honest with you, Emissary Bork. *We don't have any actual use for Mellidan VII.* It's just too damn alien a world for oxygen-breathers to use without conversion."

Bork frowned. "You have *no use* for Mellidan VII? But—then—that means you came here solely for the purpose of—of—"

"Right. Of keeping it out of the Federation's hands."

The man's arrogance stunned Bork. That Earth should wantonly block a Federation mission for no reason at all—

"This is a very serious matter," Bork said:

"I know. More serious than you yourself think, Emissary Bork. Look here: suppose you tell me why the Federation wants Mellidan VII, now?"

Bork glared at the infuriatingly calm Earthman. "We want it because—because—"

He stopped. The question paralleled the ones the Mellidani Leader had asked. It produced the same visceral reaction. These basic questions hit deep, he thought. And there were no ready answers for them.

Gambrell said smoothly, "I see you're in difficulties. Here's an answer for you: *you want it simply because it's there*. Because for eleven thousand years you've Federated every planet you could, swallowed it up in your benevolent arms, thoroughly homogenized its culture into yours and blotted out any minor differences that might have existed. You don't see any reason to stop now. But you don't have any possible use for this world, do you? You can't trade with it, you can't colonize here, you can't turn it into a vacation resort. For the first time in your considerable history you've run up against an inhabited world that's *utterly useless* as Federation stock. But you're trying to Federate it anyway."

"We—"

"Keep quiet," said the Earthman sharply. "Don't try to argue, because you don't know how to argue. Or to think. Vengo's ruled the roost so long you've reduced every cerebral process to a set of conditioned reflexes. And when you strike an exception to a pattern, you just steamroll right on ahead. You find a planet, so you offer it a place in the Federation and proceed to digest it alive. What function does this Federation of yours serve, anyway?"

Bork was on solid ground here. "It serves as a unifying force that holds together the disparate worlds of the galaxy, bringing order out of confusion."

"Okay. I'll buy that statement even if it does come rolling out of you automatically." The Earthman hunched forward and his eyes fixed coldly on Bork's. "The Federation's so big and complex that it hasn't yet learned that it died three thousand years ago. Its function atrophied, dried up, vanished. *F'oosh!* The galaxy is orderly; trade routes are established, patterns of cultural contact built, war forgotten… There's no longer any need for a benevolent tyranny operating out of Vengo that makes sure the whole thing doesn't come apart. But still you go on, bringing the joys of Federation from planet to planet, as if the same chaotic situation prevails now that prevailed in those barbaric days when your warlord ancestors first came down out of Vengo to conquer the universe."

Bork sat very quietly. He was thinking: *the Terran is insane. The things he says have no meaning. The Federation dead? Nonsense!*

"I knew the Earthmen were fools, but I didn't think they were morons as well," the Emissary said out loud, lightly. "Anyone can see that the Federation is alive and healthy, and will be for eternity to come."

"Federations don't last that long. They don't even last *half* an eternity. And yours died millennia ago. It's like some great beast whose nervous system is so slow to react it takes hours to realize that it's dead. Well, the Federation will last a couple of thousand years more, on its accumulated momentum. But it's dead now."

Bork rose. "I can't spend any further time on this kind of foolish talking," he said wearily. "I'll have to get back to my base." He fingered the glittering platinum ornaments on his stiff green jacket. "And I don't intend to give up trying to Federate the Mellidani, despite your obstructions."

Gambrell chuckled in an oddly offensive manner. "Keep at it, then. Keep on mouthing clichés and giving them hollow arguments that fall to flinders when you poke at the roots. We've warned the Mellidani. Besides, they can think for themselves, and aren't impressed easily by big words and gilded phrases. They won't be suckers for your routine."

Bork was very quiet for a long moment, staring stonily at the Earthman, trying to see behind those ice-cool gray eyes. At length he said, "Is this all just petty spite on your part? Why are you doing this, Gambrell? If you Terrans don't want to enter the Federation, why don't you keep off by yourselves and stop meddling with our activities?"

"Because the Mellidani represent something unique in the galaxy," Gambrell said. "And because *we* see their value, even if you don't. Do you know what would happen if you Federated the Mellidani? Within a century you'd have to exterminate them or expel them from the Federation. They're *alien*, Bork. Totally and absolutely and unchangeably alien. They don't breathe the same kind of atmosphere you do. They don't digest the same foods. Their lungs don't work on the principles yours do. Neither do their brains."

"What does this—"

Gambrell cut him off and continued unstoppably. "They're a cosmic fluke, Bork. They don't conform to the oxygen-carbon pattern of life, and they might very well be the only race in the universe that doesn't. We can't afford to let the Federation come in here and destroy them And you *will* destroy them, because they're different and the Federation can't abide differences that can't be smoothed out by a little deportation and ideological manipulation and genetic monkeying."

"I wish I could follow this ridiculous line of chatter," Bork snapped savagely. "But I'm afraid I'm wasting your time and mine. Please excuse me."

Sighing, Gambrell said, "You just don't listen to me, do you?"

"I've been listening. What's so important about this *uniqueness* of these people, that must be preserved at all costs?"

Instead of asking, Gambrell crisply said, "Close your right eye, Bork. You're right-handed, aren't you?"

"Yes, but—"

"*Close your right eye.* There. Suddenly you lose depth perception, notice? Your eyes function stereoscopically; knock out one point of focus and you see things two-dimensionally. Well, *we* see things two-dimensionally, Bork, all of us. The whole galaxy does. We see things through the eyes of oxygen-breathing carbon entities, and we distort everything to fit that orientation.

"The Mellidani could be our second eye. If we leave them alone, free to look at events and phenomena in their own special alien unique way, they can provide that other point of focus for us. We have to preserve this thing they have: if we let the Federation destroy it by lumping them into the vast all-devouring amoeba of confederate existence, we may never find another race quite so alien, just as we can never regenerate a blinded eye. *That's* why we poisoned their minds against you. *That's* why we got here first and made sure they would never join the Federation. And they won't."

Angrily, Bork said, "They will! This is ridiculous!"

Gambrell shrugged. "Go ahead, then. Speak ye to the Mellidani, and see how far you get. This isn't an ordinary race you're dealing with. Incidentally, the Mellidani Leader has been listening to this whole conversation over a private circuit."

That was the final gesture of contempt. Bork surged to the door, rage clotting his throat, and stalked out of Gambrell's office wordlessly. Federation dead, indeed! Point of focus! The Federation would absorb the Mellidani, no doubt of it. They *would!*

He reached ground level and found his aides. "Let's get back to the ship," Bork ordered brusquely. "I want to speak to the Mellidani again. The Earthmen haven't beaten us yet."

They drove through the clinging yellow-green fog to the slim needle that was the Federation ship. As they drove, Bork cast frantically about in his mind for some argument that was new, that was not cliché-riddled and timeworn. And no answers presented themselves.

He felt panic throbbing in his chest. The first dark cracks were starting to appear on the gleaming shield of his self-confidence—and, perhaps, on the greater shield of the Federation's vaunted prestige. The Earthman's words echoed harshly in his mind. *You'll never get Mellidan VII. The Federation is dead. Point of focus. Alien viewpoint. Necessary. Perspective.*

Then eleven thousand years of galactic domination reasserted their hold. Bork grew calm; the Earthman's words were air-filled nonsense, without meaning. Mellidan VII was not yet lost. *Not yet.*

*We'll show them,* he thought fiercely. *We'll show them.* But the old Emissary's heart suddenly was not quite sure they would.

*The golden-furred, three-foot-tall, ursunoid Hokas of the planet Toka resemble live teddy bears, with an unfortunate inability to distinguish between reality and fiction, especially regarding the human children's video adventure program* Tom Bracken of the Space Patrol. *So when Toka's nearby militaristic planet Pornia starts a war of conquest, the Hokas blithely assume that they needn't worry; the Space Patrol will rescue them. It's up to Alexander Jones, the young human ambassador to Toka, to persuade them to organize a more realistic defense than creating an imitation of the video's Space Patrol. Jones finds this more easily said than done, when the Hokas mistake him for a visiting Supreme Coordinator of the Space Patrol. After all, all Hokas know that the Supreme Coordinator is an ineffectual bureaucrat who is to be agreed with and ignored, while they charge forth with enthusiastic derring-do against the reptilian Pornians.*

*Poul Anderson and Gordon Dickson wrote eleven Hoka farces between the 1950s and the 1980s. Anderson later said that he paid his daughter's college tuition with the option money from an animation studio for a Hoka TV cartoon series. Unfortunately, the studio could never sell it to a TV network.*

# In Hoka Signo Vinces

## by Poul Anderson
## and Gordon R. Dickson

"Snort!" snorted Alexander Jones.

"What, dear?" inquired Tanni.

"It's those Pornians," he grumbled from behind the newsfax sheet he was holding, still damp of the subspace receiver. "They've finished building that battleship, and now they're putting her into space."

"How awful!" said Tanni musically.

Alex lowered the newssheet and gazed fondly at her blonde beauty. He could never quite get over the exaltation of being married to her. And when in addition, he-still a very young man, only a few months ago a mere ensign in Survey-was made plenipotentiary, with the rank and pay of an ambassador, it was not even a very believable situation.

So far his duties had been light: to reside here in the coastal city-state, introducing the natives gradually to modern technology, leading them toward the eventual formation of their own world government, and so on. Of course, as the Terrestrial cultural mission expanded their activities and brought more of the planet under his supervision, the work would increase; already there were a fiendish lot of reports to file. And even ambassadorial quarters on a new planet were not quite the ideal home for a recent bride, and the Hokas were—well—a little odd, to say the least. But it could have been a lot worse, too. Mixumaxu was fairly civilized, and had a delightful climate. The Hokas, far from chafing at their subordinate status, were falling all over themselves to be friendly and helpful and . . . yes, their only fault was that excessive enthusiasm, too much imagination, too much tendency to go hog-wild over any new concept, too little ability to distinguish fiction from fact.

"I think that's terrible," said Tanni indignantly. "You'd think the other planetary governments would get together and stop them."

"What?" asked Alex, jerked back from his musings.

"Those Pornians and their space dreadnaught."

"Oh, that!" said Alex. "Well, you see, the trouble is, after the last war all the civilized races agreed to complete disarmament except for small interplanetary police forces. There's no military to speak of anywhere in the known parts of the galaxy, and the taxpayers wouldn't stand for any. Damn fool thing, too-" Alex started to fume again. "We need some kind of interstellar police to stop fanatic racialists like those Pornians from building weapons. Why, something like this ship could spoil a hundred years of peace and goodwill, start an arms race and wreck the League-" He got to his feet. "Where's the subspace video? I want to see what Earth Headquarters has to say in today's bulletins."

The newsfax was sentfrom a local bureau a mere fifty light-years away; only by straining his ambassadorial salary could Alex afford a receiver for programs sent all the way from Earth.

"I put it on the porch, dear," said Tanni. "That program the Hokas like so much—you know, *Tom Bracken of the Space Patrol*—it was on and they came to see it like they do every day."

Alex frowned at her. "I hope you didn't leave the circuits open, honey," he said. "You know the Hokas aren't supposed to have contact with anything too modern at this stage of their development".

"I locked it on that one channel," she reassured him. "They can only get the children's programs."

Alex sighed with relief and went out and wheeled in the video. The Hokas were just too blinking inventive, among their other faults. He wished Earth Headquarters hadn't been so quick about allowing them limited trade rights. A few unscrupulous traders could start furnishing them with stuff they shouldn't get for the next twenty years.

He tuned the video to EHQ and sat through an hour of official bulletins. But there was nothing of importance. Pornia was so far from Earth that a lethargic government couldn't appreciate the danger. But it was within a few light-years of Toka, and Alex was acutely aware of that fact. This was not the first time he had grumbled about the situation, to his wife or even to some of the Hokas. You'd think the human race's own history would have convinced it that militarism must be nipped in the bud, but—

He sighed, switched off the set, and yawned. Presently he and Tanni turned out the lights and went to bed.

\* \* \*

Alex was just falling off to sleep when there was a small tap on the window. For a moment, he tried drowsily to ignore it, but it came again. "Hist," whispered a Hoka voice through the opening. Alex cursed, swiveled his eyes toward Tanni, and, saw that she was already asleep. He signaled silence to the bear-like face which pressed its damp black nose to the pane. "Just a minute," he murmured. "I'll be right out."

Growling to himself, he dressed clumsily in the dark and went out on the porch. One moon was up, almost full. In its bright glow he could see two Hokas waiting for him.

Surprise brought him up short, and his breath hissed between his teeth. Gone were the floppy boots, peaked hats, and bell-covered motley of the local folk dress. The two that faced him had adorned their portly bodies with gray tunics, tight whipcord riding breeches, Sam Browne belts, jackboots, and goggled metal helmets. And holstered by the side of each was a-

"What are you doing with those," squeaked Alex. His heart tried to climb out of his mouth. "Where'd you get Holman raythrowers?"

They paid no attention. Solemnly, the larger Hoka saluted.

"Coordinator Jones," he said in the English which was rapidly becoming the world language of Toka, "the expedition is ready."

"What expedition?" cried. Alex. "Look here, Buntu—"

"Sir," said the Hoka stiffly, "I am now Captain Jax Bennison of the Space Control, at your service." He clicked his heels and saluted again.

"Great jumping rockets" exclaimed the other Hoka. "Don't tell me the Coordinator didn't recognize you?"

"It's the moonlight, probably," said the first Hoka.

"All clear and on green now, Coordinator?"

"I—I—" stammered Alex.

"Aye, aye" repeated Jax Bennison crisply. "No time to lose, then. We lift gravs at 2330 hours. Follow us, sir."

The Hokas set rapidly off and Alex, his brain spinning, hurried after them. He didn't understand one part of this—but if it ever got back to Earth that he had allowed Holman raythrowers to get into the hands of aborigines—His brow beaded with cold sweat at the thought.

The Hokas led the way down narrow, cobbled streets between high-walled houses. The city was quiet, asleep it seemed, but the guards at the old defensive wall saluted and opened the gates for them. "Good hunting, Patrolmen," said one.

Outside, there was a broad empty field used for the infrequent spaceship landings. In the moonlight, Alex saw that more than a hundred Hokas, uniformed like the two of them, were lined up at attention. But it was on the large shape behind them that his staggering mind focused.

"My courier boat" he wailed. "What have you done to her?" The once sleek shape of the *Tanni Girl* was now hacked, and scarred. Holes had been cut the length of her sides and the muzzles of primitive gunpowder cannon projected beyond the air-seals. Her name had been painted out and the cognomen *Fearless* replaced it; below were the words *Space Patrol Ship Number One* and a large white star.

Alex made three long strides and caught up with Captain Jax Bennison who was saluting an elder Hoka recognizable as a town official. But this one was now dressed in a blue tunic, gold braid, cutlass, and cocked hat. "What's the idea?" barked Alex hysterically. "My ship!"

Jax pointed to the ornate shield with the legend Space Patrol that he wore on his breast, "Sorry, sir," he answered, "but you know the rights of the Patrol. Patrolmen may requisition whatever is needed just by showing their badges."

"Who said so?" raged Alex.

"Tom Bracken of the Space Patrol, sir," said Jax. "He says it every day on the video."

Cocked-Hat saluted in his turn. "We know that you, sir, as Supreme Coordinator, would approve," he said. "Fleet Admiral Ron Bronz at your command, sir."

"The danger is imminent, sir," added the second Hoka. "The Malevonians are obviously preparing their great push, and yet the Patrol Fleet seems to be elsewhere. We could do nothing but organize our own branch of the Patrol to stop the enemy." He clicked his heels. "Executive Officer Lon Meters at your command, sir."

Alex turned wildly to Admiral Ron Bronz. "What are you doing?" he spluttered

"Admiral's inspection before the Patrol embarks," said the old Hoka. His cocked hat slipped down over his muzzle and he raised it with an irritated gesture. "Damn that tailor. Wouldn't surprise me if he was a Malevonian agent." His voice barked out over the waiting ranks of teddy bears. "Ten-SHUN! Inspection will proceed."

Solemnly, he and Captain Jax went down the lines, touching the nose of each spaceman to see that it was cold and moist. Alex groaned.

"All in good health, sir," said the admiral as he returned. "All clear and on green" His cocked hat slipped down again. Alex found it strangely disconcerting to be addressing now a face and now a hat. " "But—but—but—" he stammered.

Lon Meters leaned over and said to Jax Bennison in a clearly audible whisper: "Something wrong with the Coordinator, Captain? You suppose the Malevonians have gotten control of his mind?"

"Of course not," said Jax. "They wouldn't dare. It's just his crusty way. He has a rough exterior but a heart of gold."

Admiral Bronz turned to Alex. "Well sir, the men are ready," he reported. "Would you make a brief but touching speech before they take off?"

A hundred furry countenances turned expectantly to Alex where he stood in the moonlight. He raised a shaky voice: "This nonsense has got to stop!"

"That's right, sir," beamed Captain Jax. "We've got to stop the enemy."

"Go home to your wives and families!" screamed Alex, trying to rouse a sense of domestic duty. "Go home to your fireside brides!"

"Aye," shrilled the admiral. "When peace has come to the galaxy, we shall return to our homes."

"You've got your own work to do—" pleaded Alex.

"Aye! Aye!" The falsetto cheers seemed to shake the city walls. "We've got to stop the foe!"

"Form ranks!" barked Captain Jax. "Forward march!"

A hundred Hokas faced the boat and tramped toward its airlock. A hundred, voices lifted in song:

"*Off we go, into the vacuum yonder,*
*Climbing high, into the black,*
*Shaking out ee-vil with fire and thunder,*
*Blasting down to the attack!*
*All the wo-o-orlds watch us in wonder*
*Till our mi-i-ission is done.*
*We'll ride on high throughout the sky,*
*For nothing can stop Patrol Ship*
*Number One!*"

"You encouraged them marvelously well, sir," said the admiral.

"Stop!" screamed Alex. He raced after the marching Hokas, trying to stem the tide.

"The Coordinator!" yelled Lon Meters in a burst of happiness. "The Coordinator himself has decided to come with us!"

Before Alex could catch his breath, he was caught up in the onward sweep. The press of a hundred solid little bodies forced him into the boat, up a companionway, and onto the bridge. He heard the airlock clang shut behind him. There was no chance to open it again; all passages were jammed tight with shining-eyed Hokas.

Captain Jax strapped himself into the pilot chair while Alex was still gibbering. "Ready to blast," called a voice from the intercom. The engines growled.

"Ready to blast," echoed Captain Jax.

"Stop!" shrieked Alex; recognizing in panic what was about to happen. "Stop, I say!"

Nobody heard him. Captain Jax pulled the drive switch. Since he had not cut in the acceleration compensators, and Alex was not harnessed in place, the human was thrown back against .a bulkhead and smashed into unconsciousness.

* * *

"Are you all right, sir?" .

Fuzzily, with ringing head; Alex struggled back to awareness. Through bleared eyes, he saw that he was alone on the bridge with Jax and Lon. They were bending anxiously over him.

"Here," said Jax, extending a flask. "Have a pull of Old Spaceman."

No matter what name it went under Hoka liquor was potent stuff. Alex felt a measure of strength flow back into him with a gulp. He pulled his lanky frame up against the artificial gravity till he stood more or less erect. Then he glared.

"Sorry, sir," apologized the exec, Lon. "We didn't realize you were too busy planning our strategy to have prepared for takeoff."

Alex clenched his teeth. "Where are we?" he mumbled.

"Sir," replied the captain, "we don't know. After we went through the space warp, we lost orientation." "Huh?" said Alex. "Went through the what?"

"The space warp, sir," explained Lon Meters.

"Oh," said Alex. For a moment the solemnity of the small Hoka was so convincing that he found himself wondering if the four years of astrogation courses he had taken had not perhaps been negligent in not mentioning this phenomenon.

"Well, then," said Captain Jax blandly, "you realize that we must be in a totally unfamiliar part of space. Maybe even in another universe. Observe." He pointed to the viewscreen and the black, starry sky it showed. Alex goggled. Some of the constellations had certainly changed, though not much

The human's brain began to function once more; he could almost feel it sweating. Video programs never mentioned the elaborate mathematics of astrogation, so the Hokas must have assumed that you simply aimed your spaceship where you wanted it to go. Finding themselves unable to locate their position, they had leaped to the conclusion that a space warp—whatever that might be—had thrown them off course.

In fact, once they began taking the Tom Bracken program literally, everything else followed with a relentless kind of logic: The Pornian menace—they must have equated that with these Malevonians who, not content with mere rearmament, were apparently out to conquer the universe. They must have decided that the ostensible human plenipotentiary was really the Supreme Coordinator of the Space Patrol in disguise.

Then they went ahead and organized their Own unit and-and-

Oh, no!

"Where are we headed?" he asked.

"Sir?" said Lon Meters.

"Top secret," snapped Captain Jax quickly. "Exec Meters, close your eyes and put your hands over your ears." The other complied.

"We had this Pornia in mind, sir," resumed the captain. "It seems to be the local center of enemy operations. But now that we're lost-"

"Well-" Alex was slowly recovering his equilibrium. "Never mind. We're first going to have to figure out just where we are."

"That's what I thought we were going to have to do," said Captain Jax. "Exec Meters, you can open your eyes and ears. Do you think you can locate us, sir?"

A vision of the paper work involved in that little chore floated through Alex's head. As if it didn't ache enough already! "I think so," he groaned.

"Excellent, Coordinator," said Captain Jax. "You take over the chart room, and meanwhile the rest of us will maneuver the ship around and look for enemies."

"Oh Lord" said Alex dismally, but there didn't seem to be much he could do about it and even at trans-light velocities, interstellar space is so big that their chances of barging into a star or planet were negligible. As for the boat, these roboticized models all but handled themselves, which was the reason a few semi-trained Hokas had been able to get her underway.

"Of course," said Captain Jax, "The Malevonians may be any place. Perhaps even now we are in the heart of their stronghold. If—"

He was interrupted by a grizzled Hoka in an acid-stained smock who came indignantly into the bridge.

"Sir," he squeaked "you've got to do something about that chief engineer."

"Do what?" asked the captain.

"How should I know?" cried the newcomer, shaking his fists and dancing with rage. "Feed him to the bems. Make him walk the plank. Anything, just so he'll quit bothering me!"

"I don't believe you've met this man, sir," whispered Lon Meters to Alex. "Dr. Zarbovsky, our scientist. Quite mad, of course—but a genius."

"But if he's mad," said Alex; "then why-"

"Every Patrol ship has a mad scientist, sir, as you well know," said Lon firmly. "Tom Bracken's; for instance."

"How can I build a new-type disintegrator if the engineer won't let me have the busbars from the drive unit?" screamed Dr. Zarbovsky. "Answer me that!"

Alex stepped into the breach. "There should be extra busbars in the storeroom," he said diplomatically.

"In the storeroom," murmured Dr. Zarbovsky. "I never thought of that!" He hurried out again.

Jax and Lon looked awestruck at Alex. "What a brain!" breathed the exec.

"He wouldn't be Coordinator if he didn't have one," said Jax proudly.

"I wonder," whispered Lon, "I wonder if he's a mutant?"

"I'm getting out of here!" snarled Alex. He slammed the door behind him. The two Hoka officers looked affectionately in his direction.

"A crusty exterior," said Lon, "but a heart of gold. Eh, Jax?"

"On green, Lon," agreed the captain.

\* \* \*

For the fortieth time, Alex's coffee cup leaped into the air and splashed on the floor as the boat's gravity beams ripped her through another sudden change of direction. Red-eyed from forty-eight hours with little sleep, he slammed his stylus down on the latest sheet of calculations and started to get up.

A burry voice grumbled over the intercom: "Engine rroom to brridge. Chief Engineerr MacTavish speaking. Wha' the hell d'ye think ye're doing? Can ye no keep the ship on a level coorse forr five minutes straight?"

"Sorry, Angus," replied Captain Jax soothingly.

"We're dodging invisible space torpedoes."

Alex slumped back over the chart room desk, burying his face in his hands.

"Oh, no," he moaned. "Oh, no, no, no, no, no."

He lit a cigarette with trembling fingers, thinking that at least this lunatic ride would soon be over. Be brave, he told himself. Chin up and all that sort of thing. Just a few more hours.

Once he had pinpointed the boat in space, it had not been hard to calculate a path to Pornia's sun. Now they were inside the Pornian System, moving at sub-light speed toward the only inhabited planet. The Hokas had naturally been enthusiastically in favor of going there to do battle.

Well, they'd land, and then he'd turn them over to the Pornians who, possessing a military force, could arrest them and return them to Toka. It was a dirty trick for him to play on his little friends, but he had no choice. You just couldn't allow this boatful of ... of permanent children to go batting around the galaxy.

An obbligato of Hoka voices filtered to him over the intercom from the bridge.

"Rough section of space, this, captain."

"Space is like that, Lon. If the space tides don't get you, the radiation madness does. You dodge a meteor only to find yourself trapped in a Sargasso of deadly space weed. And if you manage to battle your way out of that by some miracle, you emerge to find yourself blasting on all jets straight into the middle of the Malevonian fleet."

Alex closed his eyes and hung on to the coffee stained calculation sheets-the data needed to land on Pornia. He thought bitterly that there might be a cupful of cosmic dust between them and the next star, but that was all that could be expected. ...

"Then there's pirates-"

"Like that one bearing down on us now?"

"Don't be jet happy, Lon. No pirate would dare attack a Patrol ship."

"Well, if he isn't a pirate, what's he doing with the skull and crossbones painted on his ship?"

"I don't see any skull and crossbones."

"Well, I can't see the skull either, but look at those red bloody crossbones on that white field."

"Great jumping comets! Lon, you're right! Attention, all gun crews! Attention, all gun crews! Stand by for battle!"

Struck by a sudden horrible suspicion, Alex flicked on the chart room's little viewscreen. Swimming in the nearby void was a long spaceship with a red cross large on its side.

"Stop!" roared Alex. "That's a hospital ship!"

He exploded out of the room and whizzed toward the bridge. Halfway there, he tripped over a small white-smocked figure.

"Damn interference!" squeaked Dr. Zarbovsky. "Can't let a mad scientist alone for a minute." Then recognizing Alex's sprawled form. "Oh, sorry, sir. I was just coming to see you. Where can I get a one farad condenser?"

"Go to the devil," raged Alex, picking himself up.

"But we don't have a devil on this ship," said Dr. Zarbovsky plaintively.

Alex was already running down the corridor. He burst into the bridge and skidded to a halt before the communications board.

"Do you wish to take over, sir?" asked Jax.

"I sure do," gasped Alex.

His fingers danced over the board as he sent a call to the other ship.

The image of a Pornian two meters tall, snake limbed, with a flat green face sticking out of a high gold-braided collar—formed on the screen. "What's up?", it demanded in the English of the spaceways. "Who are you?"

"Never mind that," said Alex impolitely. "Let me speak to your captain."

"Who are you?" repeated the Pornian in a stiff tone. "We are the Pornian Navy's hospital ship *Sudbriggan*. Identify yourself, or else as aliens without passports you are liable to detention."

"Detention?" said Alex blankly. He hadn't realized the arrogance of the new militarist government had gone that far. "You're kidding!"

The Pornian's countenance turned chartreuse with anger. "Do you insult me?" he hissed. "You are under arrest. Stand by to be boarded."

Alex had a spine-chilling vision of himself explaining to Earth Headquarters just how he and a hundred of his wards came to be interned by the government of a notoriously touchy planet.

"Never mind," he said. "I was just about to leave."

Jumping up from the screen, he stepped over to the control panel. He was reaching for the main secondary drive switch when a thunderous explosion rocked the *Fearless*. Alex felt himself hurled to the floor, his nose sideswiping a table on the way down.

He rose, wiping blood from his face, and glared at Captain Jax. "What happened now?" he yelled.

"Why, we opened fire," said the Hoka, pointing to the viewscreen. It showed a portion of the *Fearless*' exterior as well as the open sky. Smoke was whiffing into space from the cannon mouths. "We didn't get the pirate Malevonian, though" he added regretfully. "His force shield must already have been up."

If anybody, anywhere in the cosmos, has invented the legendary force screen, the Astrogation Improvement Authority of the Interbeing League will be very anxious to meet him, her, it, or xu. Alex took another horrified look at the Pornian ship. It was taking off sunward at full acceleration. The clumsy solid cannon balls had done no more than scratch its armored hull, but the captain had evidently had the fright of his life.

The image of an Earth Headquarters Cultural Development Board was replaced in Alex's unhappy mind by the picture of an Interbeing League courtroom and one Alex Jones on trial for armed assault. Since space piracy, being utterly impractical, had never occurred, perhaps the old laws about hanging pirates were still on the books. At the very least, no plenipotentiary who went around shooting up hospital ships: could reasonably expect to keep his position. A certain dignity is demanded in such an office.

Out of the welter of thoughts there was only one that emerged with any clarity. And that was to catch the Pornian before he could officially report what had happened, explain, apologize, and ask him not to file charges.

"Full thrust ahead!" he bellowed, vaulting into the pilot chair and throwing down the grav-drive switch.

The Hokas whooped with joy.

"Trust us, Coordinator!" shouted Captain Jax. "They won't escape!"

—and the *Fearless* took off in pursuit.

* * *

The Lord High Admiral of the Pornian Navy thundered at the shaken, tentacled figure in the screen before him.

"What?"

"Help! Help!" cried the figure. "Hospital ship *Sudbriggan* reporting. There's a Space Patrol ship after me!"

"A what?" cried the Lord High Admiral.

"Space Patrol Ship Number One," choked the figure. It added breathlessly: "They've got a secret weapon."

"What do you mean, Space Patrol ship?" roared the Admiral. "There's no such thing as a Space Patrol."

"There is too!" shrieked the captain of the *Sudbriggan*. The Pornian Navy had not been in existence long enough to become well-grounded in military courtesy.

"And it's gaining."

Ferociously, the Lord High Admiral punched a button. The communications center of the huge dreadnaught answered him.

"Give me a long-range tracer," rapped the Admiral. "Find out what's behind this idiot."

Communications Center obliged.

* * *

"*Fearless* calling *Sudbriggan*," gasped Alexander Jones into an unresponsive screen. "Come in, *Sudbriggan*. Please come in, *Sudbriggan!*"

The set flickered to life with the terrified figure of a Pornian who must be the exec of the hospital ship. He was waving his eye-stalks, too agitated to find English words.

"Get me your captain," said Alex. "I want your captain."

"N-n-no," stammered the officer. "We shall defend our captain to the l-last enlisted man."

"Then your Admiral," said Alex hoarsely. His contorted face looked more ferocious than he knew. "I must see your Admiral right away. This business has got to be stopped!"

"Eek," said the officer.

"I'm doing my best," pleaded Alex, "but if you don't get me through to your Admiral I can't answer for the consequences."

The Pornian paled at this bloodthirsty threat and switched off his receiver.

"Hey!" shouted Alex. "Come back there!"

"Never mind, Coordinator," said Captain Jax. "We're overhauling him."

The *Sudbriggan* was a glinting speck, lost among the stars, but a glance at the radar tracker told Alex that the courier boat was, indeed, gaining on the slower hospital ship. He mopped his brow in some relief. His chance of catching the other vessel in time to mollify its skipper and prevent a report looked pretty good after all. He began turning over in his mind the form his apology would take."

He had assumed that the *Sudbriggan* had taken off in a random sunward direction, and had no idea that the backbone of the Pornian Navy was close at hand. Consequently, the dreadnaught took him completely by surprise.

One minute, the viewscreen gleamed only with stars. Then all at once, looming up and growing with hideous speed, was the titanic figure of the space battleship, gun turrets glimmering ominously in the light of the distant sun.

* * *

"What is this farce?" demanded the Lord High Admiral angrily, looking at the boat in his tracer screen. He could make out the legend Space Patrol Ship Number One on its bow. What was it, and why was so minute a thing hurling itself so viciously upon the great, and invincible super-dreadnaught?

He twined his boneless hands thoughtfully. Something occurred to him. What was it the captain of the *Sudbriggan* had said?

Secret weapon!

"Fire guns!" bawled the suddenly panic-stricken Admiral, clutching the intercom mike. "Fire torpedo! Fire One; fire Two, fire Three! Fire everything! Shoot that ship down before it hits us!"

Gun crews who have looked on their drills as a sort of pleasant exercise, are not at their peak when suddenly ordered without even the preamble of a battle alert to fire their weapons. Such an unexpected command breeds a certain amount of confusion. Nevertheless, they did their best.

Atomic explosions began to blossom about the hurtling *Fearless*, but in the vacuum of space a shell has to make a direct hit to do any significant harm. Therefore the guns gave way to the space torpedoes that leaped out at the enemy, each as big as the courier boat itself.

Now this was unfortunate. The torpedoes were equipped with the latest tracking devices to find their own targets. But it had been assumed that such targets would be destroyers, at the very least, since nothing smaller could possibly menace the new battleship. So simple preventive circuits had also been installed to keep them from homing on each other.

Thus when they reached the *Fearless* and matched velocities and accelerations, they didn't know what to do next. They trailed undecidedly after the Hoka ship, their computers clicking madly. One computer must have gone insane, for that torpedo blew itself up. The rest moved hesitantly toward their own ship.

The Admiral shivered in his quarters, gripping the arms of his chair and praying for a hit and regretting the day he had ever let the Racialist Party leaders talk him into figureheading the Navy. His wife had warned him against it and his wife always knew best. It was all very well strutting around in gold braid; but he might have suspected there would be a catch to it. And sure enough there was.

He might have known there was a real Space Patrol. He might have known a bloodthirsty race like the humans wouldn't really let a peaceful world like his own get away with a little rearming.

"Please," prayed the Admiral, rolling his eye-stalks toward the ceiling of his cabin. "Please. A direct hit. Just one."

\* \* \*

"But I only want to apologize!" yelled Alex into the blank communicator screen, holding frantically onto the board while the *Fearless* rocked to the nearby explosions. "*Sudbriggan*. Dreadnaught. Anybody. It's all a mistake. I just want to apologize, dammit!"

"What's the old man up to?" Lon Meters asked Captain Jax as they both clung to their pilot chairs.

"I can't tell you," replied the captain with a knowing wink. "But I'll give you this much of a hint. Underneath that bluff exterior, the Coordinator's mighty shrewd. Mighty shrewd."

"Oh," said the exec. They nodded understandingly together..

\* \* \*

All good things must come to an end; and the famous Space Patrol-Pornian battle was no exception. Aboard the enormous ship they opened a safety port to admit the fleeing *Sudbriggan*. It flashed inside, but before they could close the port again, the *Fearless*, moving too fast for Alex to stop her in time, had also entered.

If it had not been for the fantastic safety devices inside the dreadnaught, the episode would have ended then and there. But as it was, the absorber fields channeled the terrific kinetic energy of the two vessels into the dreadnaught's accumulators, and they lay inert in the belly of the monster. The port clanged to behind them.

The torpedoes decelerated as their circuits informed them that they were almost upon their mother craft. They milled about in space, their computers gibbering. One torpedo, perhaps equipped with a better-than-average "brain," went up and sniffed at the safety port, wagging its tail rather wistfully.

The *Sudbriggan* had been the first to enter. Its crew boiled from the airlock and scrambled toward the safety of the dreadnaught's interior. A few minutes later, Alex opened the lock of the *Fearless* and stuck his nose out. He jerked it hastily back as ray beams shot past it and splattered on the hull of the Patrol boat. This was too much. After being shanghaied, kept up for two nights to make calculations, threatened with internment and shot at, Alex finally lost his temper. He went storming back to the bridge.

"Give me a raythrower!" he roared.

"Hadn't you better get into a suit first, sir?" asked Lon Meters.

Alex did a double take. All along the main corridor, he could see the Hokas scrambling into things that looked like a cross between a spacesuit and a set of medieval armor. The exec was holding out one tailored more nearly to human proportions.

"What?" said Alex.

"Combat armor, sir," said Captain Jax proudly. "We used the ship's tools and made it out of the spare meteor plating in the hold."

Alex goggled. The labor in fashioning the suits must have been heartbreaking. Even given the ship's machine tools, the collapsed steel of meteor plating was almost unworkable. For a second he wavered between admiration and a desire to blow his top at this latest outrage on his property. Then he remembered the near singe his nose had taken, and began donning the armor without a word.

"Battle ax," said Captain Jax.

"Battle ax," repeated the exec, handing a wicked looking double-bitted weapon to Alex.

"Raythrower," said the captain.

"Raythrower," repeated the exec, offering a gun.

Alex grabbed the Holman with his first real enthusiasm since this trip started. A smile was forming on his lips when he realized that the object was entirely too heavy to be what it appeared to be.

He inspected it. "What's this?" he demanded.

"The raythrower, sir?" Captain Jax looked a little crestfallen. "We had some trouble with them, Coordinator. We sent off our box tops according to orders over the video, but when we got these, they wouldn't shoot."

"Sabotage," supplied Lon Meters.

"Exactly," said the captain. "So we fixed them up to fire regular bullets like the Western shooting irons. You see-"

He pressed the firing button on his imitation Holman and a slug whanged off the low ceiling of the bridge. Alex ducked before remembering that his new clothes were bullet proof He straightened, groaned as he looked at the clumsy weapon, and then, with a sigh, holstered it and clumped his way toward the airlock. At least his present equipment would protect him until he could get to some Pornian officer and explain the case—But his last feeble intentions of legality were destroyed when he led his Hokas into the first corridor branching from the entry port. A barrage of rays from behind a hastily erected wall of office furniture made his armor glow and sparkle. He tingled with the shock of secondary radiation.

Plainly, the aliens weren't going to give him a chance to parley.

"That's enough!" he bellowed in a rage, his voice coming weirdly from the air holes in the top of his helmet. "Let's clean up the whole blinking ship!" And he charged forward like a miniature tank, using the sheer mass of his armor to break through the barricade and send the defenders scooting before him in terror.

"The old man's finally got his dander up," said the exec to the captain.

"Yep," answered. Jax. "That he has. But let me tell you something, boy. Underneath that dander there's a heart of pure, eighteen-carat, solid gold."

The true story of the cleaning up of the Pornian dreadnaught will never be adequately told, for words are insufficient to describe it.

For a century or more, no civilized entity had been seriously threatened by organized violence. On top of this fact was another: that the advanced military minds who designed this battleship would have tut-tutted in horror if they had been asked how the crew was to defend it against a boarding party. With icy politeness they, would have pointed out that boarding vanished with wooden ships, and that no enemy vessel could approach within three thousand kilometers of this giant without being destroyed. Thus few of the crew had hand guns, and fewer still knew how to use them. So everywhere through the huge ship could be seen shrieking herds of tall Pornians fleeing before one or two small armored figures waving battle axes. It was like a host of Frankenstein dolls let loose in an enormous home for old ladies. Such of the crew of the dreadnaught as was not assailed—and after all, a hundred Hokas could reach only a fraction of the total acreage inside—stayed by its posts, shivering and hoping there would be no orders to counter-attack.

To be sure, there was one center of resistance. When the news reached the Admiral that the crew of the Space Patrol boat had effected an entrance, he gathered his personal staff around him on the bridge and resolved to die fighting. His followers unlimbered a mobile disintegrator, trained it on the doorway, and waited.

Meteor plating is good protection against hand guns.

But it is about as useful as wet cardboard against the full power of a mobile disintegrator. Alex, leading a dozen Hokas around a bend in the main corridor, came full upon the bridge. The Pornians let off a panicky, ill-timed bolt which tore a hole through three floors above. Alex beat a hasty retreat, struggling to restrain the Hokas, who were all for rushing the gun.

"Look," he said grimly, when he finally had them settled down, "are Jax and Lon here?"

"Here, Coordinator.".

"On green—-I mean, aye, aye sir."

"Well, look," said Alex. "That mobile unit isn't like a hand gun—that is, it doesn't have a self-contained power source. It gets its energy from a cable run directly to the ship's generators." As a former TISS man, Alex had of course been given training in the Solar Guard. "Now, what I want you to do is hunt around for the central power control room—it ought to be on this level, and pull every switch you find there. One of them should shut off the juice to that mobile."

The two little armored figures nodded their anonymous heads and toddled off down the corridor. Alex and the rest sat down to wait.

"Mighty smart, the old man," said Lon Meters as they trudged along. "Imagine him knowing the way Malevonian ships are put together."

"There isn't much that goes on in the universe that the Coordinator of the Space Patrol doesn't know," replied Jax Bennison complacently. "Why, I imagine nobody will ever know how many spy rays the old man has in places, and how many undercover agents at work."

"Lonely life, though," said Lon sadly. "Can't trust anyone, the old man can't. The, responsibility for the safety of all civilization rests on his shoulders." He paused, then went on: "Which of us do you think he's picked to take his place when his time comes?" They had, by now, explored up and down several halls and looked into a number of luxurious apartments for the top officers of the dreadnaught. Now they came to a small door with a sign stenciled on it in the spatial English.

DANGER
DO NOT ENTER

"Ah-ha," said Lon.

"This'll be it," said Jax. He swung his battle ax at the lock, and the door—being unlocked—bounced open. They stepped inside.

"Yep," said Captain Jax, looking about him with satisfaction at the ranked masses of levers, wheels, buttons, and switches. "This is it, all right. Executive Meters, you take that side and I'll take this."

They started yanking levers.

Coughing, choking, sneezing, and gurgling, the Lord High Admiral of the Pornian Navy sloshed his way forward to surrender.

"My sword, sir," he said with what dignity he could summon up.

Alex accepted it.

"The ship, sir, is yours," coughed the Admiral. Then his official manner broke down. "But if turning on the fire extinguisher sprinklers, the fumigation system, the leak detector smoke system, the emergency radionic-heating system, the emergency refrigeration system, and directing the sewers into the deck-flushing system isn't a dirty way to fight, I'd like to know what is."

Alex ignored his resentment.

"The terms for your surrender are these," he began sternly.

"Yes, sir," said the Admiral in a meek voice.

"Your government will dismantle this dreadnaught and build no more ships of the line."

"Yes, sir," said the Admiral. "I, for one, will be happy to get back to civilian life—"

"You will disband the navy."

"Glad to, sir."

"You will inform Earth Headquarters of your decisions in these matters, but will not specify the reasons or mention this battle. That is classified information."

"Yes, sir."

"And you will inform the Racialist Party on Pornia that the Space Patrol, which owes allegiance to no race or system, but is dedicated to the upholding of law and order throughout the galaxy, takes a dim view of their government and demands another planet-wide election wherein other Pornian parties shall be given a fair chance to run for office."

The Admiral gulped.

"Well—I—yes, sir, I guess I can do that. Under the circumstances."

"Okay, fine," said Alex. Signaling the armored figures around him to follow, he turned on his heel and went back toward the entry port.

When the *Fearless* was finally settled down on her return trip, Alex called the Hokas together and, speaking over the intercom, addressed them all.

"Gentlemen of the Space Patrol," he said crisply, "our mission is accomplished. Well done! But now I must inform you that there will be no more expeditions of the Patrol for an indefinite time."

"None?" asked Captain Jax in a wistful tone.

"None," said Alex, tossing the keys of the control panel in one hand and clamping firmly onto them as they landed back in his palm. "The Space Patrol is being disbanded as of now until such time as another threat to the galaxy brings us forth to scour the evildoer from the stars and the space between the stars." There was a moment's sad quietude. Then the exec, Lon Meters, spoke up. "But what's going to become of you, sir?" he asked sympathetically.

"That," said Alex, unable to disguise a slight quaver in his voice: "is what I am just about to find out."

He waved bravely to the assembled Hoka officers and dismissed them from the bridge and shut the door on them. The new long range subspace communicator which the dreadnaught's technicians had installed for him glowed as his trembling fingers put in a call. While the Hoka at the switchboard in far-off Mixumaxu routed his beam, he licked dry lips and ran a shaky finger under his collar.

The figure of Tanni appeared on the screen. Her arms folded implacably as she recognized him.

"Well," she said, "and just where have you been?"

Weakly, Alexander Jones started to explain.

*What if an intelligent alien was assumed to be only a pet? What if the whole alien species was deliberately disguising themselves as pets and wild animals?*

*The protagonist of "Novice" is Telzey Amberdon, a 15-year-old girl; a genius, maybe, but still a human. But Tick-Tock, her young leonine pet-pal, apparently the only Baluit crest cat of the planet Jontarou still alive, is a most memorable alien ... as are all of the other crest cats that the human settlers of Jontarou don't see. Can Telzey and TT persuade the crest cats to agree to keep in hiding and not kill all the humans until the humans are ready to recognize them as equals?*

# Novice

## by James H. Schmitz

There was, Telzey Amberdon thought, someone besides Tick-Tock and herself in the garden. Not, of course, Aunt Halet, who was in the house waiting for an early visitor to arrive, and not one of the servants. Someone or something else must be concealed among the thickets of magnificently flowering native Jontarou shrubs about Telzey.

She could think of no other way to account for Tick-Tock's spooked behavior—nor, to be honest about it, for the way her own nerves were acting up without visible cause this morning.

Telzey plucked a blade of grass, slipped the end between her lips and chewed it gently, her face puzzled and concerned. She wasn't ordinarily afflicted with nervousness. Fifteen years old, genius level, brown as a berry and not at all bad looking in her sunbriefs, she was the youngest member of one of Orado's most prominent families and a second-year law student at one of the most exclusive schools in the Federation of the Hub. Her physical, mental, and emotional health, she'd always been informed, were excellent. Aunt Halet's frequent cracks about the inherent instability of the genius level could be ignored; Halet's own stability seemed questionable at best.

But none of that made the present odd situation any less disagreeable.

The trouble might have begun, Telzey decided, during the night, within an hour after they arrived from the spaceport at the guest house Halet had rented in Port Nichay for their vacation on Jontarou. Telzey had retired at once to her second-story bedroom with Tick-Tock; but she barely got to sleep before something awakened her again. Turning over, she discovered TT reared up before the window, her forepaws on the sill, big cat-head outlined against the star-hazed night sky, staring fixedly down into the garden.

Telzey, only curious at that point, climbed out of bed and joined TT at the window. There was nothing in particular to be seen, and if the scents and minor night-sounds which came from the garden weren't exactly what they were used to, Jontarou was after all an unfamiliar planet. What else would one expect here?

But Tick-Tock's muscular back felt tense and rigid when Telzey laid her arm across it, and except for an absent-minded dig with her forehead against Telzey's shoulder, TT refused to let her attention be distracted from whatever had absorbed it. Now and then, a low, ominous rumble came from her furry throat, a half-angry, half-questioning sound. Telzey began to feel a little uncomfortable. She managed finally to coax Tick-Tock away from the window, but neither of them slept well the rest of the night. At breakfast, Aunt Halet made one of her typical nasty-sweet remarks.

"You look so fatigued, dear—as if you were under some severe mental strain… which, of course, you might be," Halet added musingly. With her gold-blond hair piled high on her head and her peaches and cream complexion, Halet looked fresh as a daisy herself… a malicious daisy.

"Now wasn't I right in insisting to Jessamine that you needed a vacation away from that terribly intellectual school?" She smiled gently.

"Absolutely," Telzey agreed, restraining the impulse to fling a spoonful of egg yolk at her father's younger sister. Aunt Halet often inspired such impulses, but Telzey had promised her mother to avoid actual battles on the Jontarou trip, if possible. After breakfast, she went out into the back garden with Tick-Tock, who immediately walked into a thicket, camouflaged herself and vanished from sight. It seemed to add up to something. But what?

Telzey strolled about the garden a while, maintaining a pretense of nonchalant interest in Jontarou's flowers and colorful bug life. She experienced the most curious little chills of alarm from time to time, but discovered no signs of a lurking intruder, or of TT either. Then, for half an hour or more, she'd just sat cross-legged in the grass, waiting quietly for Tick-Tock to show up of her own accord. And the big lunkhead hadn't obliged.

Telzey scratched a tanned kneecap, scowling at Port Nichay's park trees beyond the garden wall. It seemed idiotic to feel scared when she couldn't even tell whether there was anything to be scared about! And, aside from that, another unreasonable feeling kept growing stronger by the minute now. This was to the effect that she should be doing some unstated but specific thing…

In fact, that Tick-Tock *wanted* her to do some specific thing!
Completely idiotic!

Abruptly, Telzey closed her eyes, and thought sharply "Tick-Tock?" and waited—suddenly very angry at herself for having given in to her fancies to this extent—for whatever might happen.

She had never really established that she was able to tell, by a kind of symbolic mind-picture method, like a short waking dream, approximately what TT was thinking and feeling. Five years before, when she'd discovered Tick-Tock-an odd-looking and odder-behaved stray kitten then in the woods near the Amberdons' summer home on Orado, Telzey had thought so. But it might never have been more than a colorful play of her imagination, and after she got into law school and grew increasingly absorbed in her studies, she almost forgot the matter again.

Today, perhaps because she was disturbed about Tick-Tock's behavior, the customary response was extraordinarily prompt. The warm glow of sunlight shining through her closed eyelids faded out quickly and was replaced by some inner darkness. In the darkness there appeared then an image of Tick-Tock sitting a little way off beside an open door in an old stone wall, green eyes fixed on Telzey. Telzey got the impression that TT was inviting her to go through the door, and, for some reason, the thought frightened her.

Again, there was an immediate reaction. The scene with Tick-Tock and the door vanished; and Telzey felt she was standing in a pitch-black room, knowing that if she moved even one step forwards, something that was waiting there silently would reach out and grab her.

Naturally, she recoiled... and at once found herself sitting, eyes still closed and the sunlight bathing her lids, on the grass of the guest house garden.

She opened her eyes, looked around. Her heart was thumping rapidly. The experience couldn't have lasted more than four or five seconds, but it had been extremely vivid, a whole, compact little nightmare. None of her earlier experiments at getting into mental communication with TT had been like that.

It served her right, Telzey thought, for trying such a childish stunt at the moment! What she should have done at once was to make a methodical search for the foolish beast—TT was bound to be *somewhere* nearby—locate her behind her camouflage, and hang on to her then until this nonsense in the garden was explained! Talented as Tick-Tock was at blotting herself out, it usually was possible to spot her if one directed one's attention to shadow patterns. Telzey began a surreptitious study of the flowering bushes about her.

Three minutes later, off to her right, where the ground was banked beneath a six-foot step in the garden's terraces, Tick-Tock's outline suddenly caught her eye. Flat on her belly, head lifted above her paws, quite motionless, TT seemed like a transparent wraith stretched out along the terrace, barely discernible even when stared at directly. It was a convincing illusion; but what seemed to be rocks, plant leaves, and sun-splotched earth seen through the wraith-outline was simply the camouflage pattern TT had printed for the moment on her hide. She could have changed it completely in an instant to conform to a different background.

Telzey pointed an accusing finger.

"See you!" she announced, feeling a surge of relief which seemed as unaccountable as the rest of it.

The wraith twitched one ear in acknowledgment, the head outlines shifting as the camouflaged face turned towards Telzey. Then the inwardly uncamouflaged, very substantial looking mouth opened slowly, showing Tick-Tock's red tongue and curved white tusks. The mouth stretched in a wide yawn, snapped shut with a click of meshing teeth, and became indistinguishable again. Next, a pair of camouflaged lids drew back from TT's round, brilliant green eyes. The eyes stared across the lawn at Telzey.

Telzey said irritably, "Quit clowning around, TT!"

The eyes blinked, and Tick-Tock's natural bronze-brown color suddenly flowed over her head, down her neck and across her body into legs and tail. Against the side of the terrace, as if materializing into solidity at that moment, appeared two hundred pounds of supple, rangy, long-tailed cat. Or catlike creature. TT's actual origin had never been established. The best guesses were that what Telzey had found playing around in the woods five years ago was either a biostructural experiment which had got away from a private laboratory on Orado, or some spaceman's lost pet, brought to the capital planet from one of the remote colonies beyond the Hub. On top of TT's head was a large, fluffy pompom of white fur, which might have looked ridiculous on another animal, but didn't on her. Even as a fat kitten, hanging head down from the side of a wall by the broad sucker pads in her paws, TT had possessed enormous dignity.

Telzey studied her, the feeling of relief fading again. Tick-Tock, ordinarily the most restful and composed of companions, definitely was still tensed up about something. That big, lazy yawn a moment ago, the attitude of stretched-out relaxation... all pure sham!

"What *is* eating you?" she asked in exasperation.

The green eyes stared at her, solemn, watchful, seeming for that fleeting instant quite alien. And why, Telzey thought, should the old question of what Tick-Tock really was pass through her mind just now? After her rather alarming rate of growth began to taper off last year, nobody had cared any more.

For a moment, Telzey had the uncanny certainty of having had the answer to this situation almost in her grasp. An answer which appeared to involve the world of Jontarou, Tick-Tock, and of all unlikely factors-Aunt Halet.

She shook her head. TT's impassive green eyes blinked.

Jontarou? The planet lay outside Telzey's sphere of personal interests, but she'd read up on it on the way here from Orado. Among all the worlds of the Hub, Jontarou was *the* paradise for zoologists and sportsmen, a gigantic animal preserve, its continents and seas swarming with magnificent game. Under Federation law, it was being retained deliberately in the primitive state in which it had been discovered. Port Nichay, the only city, actually the only inhabited point on Jontarou, was beautiful and quiet, a pattern of vast but elegantly slender towers, each separated from the others by four or five miles of rolling parkland and interconnected only by the threads of transparent sky-ways. Near the horizon, just visible from the garden, rose the tallest towers of all, the green and gold spires of the Shikaris' Club, a center of Federation affairs and of social activity. From the aircar which brought them across Port Nichay the evening before, Telzey had seen occasional strings of guest houses, similar to the one Halet had rented, nestling along the park slopes.

Nothing very sinister about Port Nichay or green Jontarou, surely!

Halet? That blond, slinky, would-be Machiavelli? What could-?

Telzey's eyes narrowed reflectively. There'd been a minor occurrence-at least, *it* had seemed minor-just before the spaceliner docked last night. A young woman from one of the newscasting services had asked for an interview with the daughter of Federation Councilwoman Jessamine Amberdon. This happened occasionally; and Telzey had no objections until the newscaster's gossipy persistence in inquiring about the "unusual pet" she was bringing to Port Nichay with her began to be annoying. TT might be somewhat unusual, but that was not a matter of general interest; and Telzey said so. Then Halet moved smoothly into the act and held forth on Tick-Tock's appearance, habits, and mysterious antecedents, in considerable detail.

Telzey had assumed that Halet was simply going out of her way to be irritating, as usual. Looking back on the incident, however, it occurred to her that the chatter between her aunt and the newscast woman had sounded oddly stilted—almost like something the two might have rehearsed.

Rehearsed for what purpose? Tick-Tock... Jontarou.

Telzey chewed gently on her lower lip. A vacation on Jontarou for the two of them and TT had been Halet's idea, and Halet had enthused about it so much that Telzey's mother at last talked her into accepting. Halet, Jessamine explained privately to Telzey, had felt they were intruders in the Amberdon family, had bitterly resented Jessamine's political honors and, more recently, Telzey's own emerging promise of brilliance. This invitation was Halet's way of indicating a change of heart. Wouldn't Telzey oblige?

* * *

So Telzey had obliged, though she took very little stock in Halet's change of heart. She wasn't, in fact, putting it past her aunt to have some involved dirty trick up her sleeve with this trip to Jontarou. Halet's mind worked like that.

So far there had been no actual indications of purposeful mischief. But logic did seem to require a connection between the various puzzling events here...

A newscaster's rather forced looking interest in Tick-Tock—Halet could easily have paid for that interview. Then TT's disturbed behavior during their first night in Port Nichay, then Telzey's own formless anxieties and fancies in connection with the guest house garden.

The last remained hard to explain. But Tick-Tock... and Halet... might know something about Jontarou that she didn't know.

Her mind returned to the results of the half-serious attempt she'd made to find out whether there was something Tick-Tock "wanted her to do." An open door? A darkness where somebody waited to grab her if she took even one step forwards? It couldn't have had any significance. Or could it?

So you'd like to try magic, Telzey scoffed at herself. Baby games... How far would you have got at law school if you'd asked TT to help with your problems?

Then why had she been thinking about it again?

She shivered, because an eerie stillness seemed to settle on the garden. From the side of the terrace, TT's green eyes watched her.

Telzey had a feeling of sinking down slowly into a sunlit dream, into something very remote from law school problems.

"Should I go through the door?" she whispered.

The bronze cat-shape raised its head slowly. TT began to purr.

Tick-Tock's name had been derived in kitten-hood from the manner in which she purred-a measured, oscillating sound, shifting from high to low, as comfortable and often as continuous as the unobtrusive pulse of an old clock. It was the first time Telzey realized now, that she'd heard the sound since their arrival on Jontarou. It went on for a dozen seconds or so, and then stopped. Tick-Tock continued to look at her.

It appeared to have been an expression of definite assent...

The dreamlike sensation increased, hazing over Telzey's thoughts. If there was nothing to this mind-communication thing, what harm could symbols do? This time, she wouldn't let them alarm her. And if they did mean something...

She closed her eyes.

The sunglow outside faded instantly. Telzey caught a fleeting picture of the door in the wall, and knew in the same moment that she'd already passed through it.

She was not in the dark room then, but poised, at the edge of a brightness which seemed featureless and without limit, spread out around her with a feeling-tone like "sea" or "sky." But it was an unquiet place, There was a sense of unseen things on all sides watching her and waiting. Was this another form of the dark room-a trap set up in her mind? Telzey's attention did a quick shift. She was seated in the grass again; the sunlight beyond her closed eyelids seemed to shine in quietly through rose-tinted curtains. Cautiously, she let her awareness return to that bright area; and *it* was still there. She had a moment of excited elation. She was controlling this! And why not, she asked herself. These things were happening in *her* mind, after all!

She would find out what they seemed to mean; but she would be in no rush to...

An impression as if, behind her, Tick-Tock had thought, "Now I can help again!"

Then a feeling of being swept swiftly, irresistibly forwards, thrust out and down. The brightness exploded in thundering colors around her. In fright, she made the effort to snap her eyes open, to be back in the garden; but now she couldn't make it work. The colors continued to roar about her, like a confusion of excited, laughing, triumphant voices. Telzey felt caught in the middle of it all, suspended in invisible spider webs. Tick-Tock seemed to be somewhere nearby, looking on. Faithless, treacherous TT!

Telzey's mind made another wrenching effort, and there was a change. She hadn't got back into the garden, but the noisy, swirling colors were gone and she had the feeling of reading a rapidly moving microtape now, though she didn't actually see the tape.

The tape, she realized, was another symbol for what was happening, a symbol easier for her to understand. There were voices, or what might be voices, around her; on the invisible tape she seemed to be reading what they said.

A number of speakers, apparently involved in a fast, hot argument about what to do with her. Impressions flashed past ...

Why waste time with her? It was clear that kitten-talk was all she was capable of! ...Not necessarily; that was a normal first step. Give her a little time! ... But what- exasperatedly-could *such* a small-bite *possibly* know that would be of significant value?

There was a slow, blurred, awkward-seeming interruption. Its content was not comprehensible to Telzey at all, but in some unmistakable manner it was defined as Tick-Tock's thought.

A pause as the circle of speakers stopped to consider whatever TT had thrown into the debate.

Then another impression ... one that sent a shock of fear through Telzey as it rose heavily into her awareness. Its sheer intensity momentarily displaced the tape-reading symbolism. A savage voice seemed to rumble:

"Toss the tender small-bite to *me*"—malevolent crimson eyes fixed on Telzey from somewhere not far away—"and let's be done here!"

Startled, stammering protest from Tick-Tock, accompanied by gusts of laughter from the circle. Great sense of humor these characters had, Telzey thought bitterly. That crimson-eyed thing wasn't joking at all!

More laughter as the circle caught her thought. Then a kind of majority opinion found sudden expression:

"Small-bite *is* learning! No harm to wait—We'll find out quickly—Let's..."

The tape ended; the voices faded; the colors went blank. In whatever jumbled-up form she'd been getting the impressions at that point—Telzey couldn't have begun to describe it—the whole thing suddenly stopped.

She found herself sitting in the grass, shaky, scared, eyes open. Tick-Tock stood beside the terrace, looking at her. An air of hazy unreality still hung about the garden.

She might have flipped! She didn't think so; but it certainly seemed possible! Otherwise... Telzey made an attempt to sort over what had happened.

Something *had* been in the garden! Something had been inside her mind. Something that was at home on Jontarou. There'd been a feeling of perhaps fifty or sixty of these... well, beings. Alarming beings! Reckless, wild, hard... and that red-eyed nightmare! Telzey shuddered.

They'd contacted Tick-Tock first, during the night. TT understood them better than she could. Why? Telzey found no immediate answer.

Then Tick-Tock had tricked her into letting her mind be invaded by these beings. There must have been a very definite reason for that.

She looked over at Tick-Tock. TT looked back. Nothing stirred in Telzey's thoughts. Between *them* there was still no direct communication.

Then how had the beings been able to get through to her? Telzey wrinkled her nose.

Assuming this was real, it seemed clear that the game of symbols she'd made up between herself and TT had provided the opening. Her whole experience just now had been in the form of symbols, translating whatever occurred into something she could consciously grasp.

"Kitten-talk" was how the beings referred to the use of symbols; they seemed contemptuous of it. Never mind, Telzey told herself; they'd agreed she was learning.

The air over the grass appeared to flicker. Again she had the impression of reading words off a quickly moving, not quite visible tape.

"You're being taught and you're learning," was what she seemed to read. "The question was whether you were capable of partial understanding as your friend insisted. Since you were, everything else that can be done will be accomplished very quickly."

A pause, then with a touch of approval, "You're a well-informed mind, small-bite! Odd and with incomprehensibilities, but well-formed-"

One of the beings, and a fairly friendly one-at least not unfriendly. Telzey framed a tentative mental question. "Who are you?"

"You'll know very soon." The flickering ended; she realized she and the question had been dismissed for the moment. She looked over at Tick-Tock again.

"Can't *you* talk to me now, TT?" she asked silently.

A feeling of hesitation.

"Kitten-talk!" was the impression that formed itself with difficulty then. It was awkward, searching; but it came unquestionably from TT. "Still learning, too, Telzey!" TT seemed half anxious, half angry. "We—"

A sharp buzz note reached Telzey's ears, wiping out the groping thought-impression. She jumped a little, glanced down. Her wrist-talker was signaling. For a moment, she seemed poised uncertainly between a world where unseen dangerous-sounding beings referred to one as small-bite and where TT was learning to talk, and the familiar other world where wrist-communicators buzzed periodically in a matter-of-fact manner. Settling back into the more familiar world, she switched on the talker.

"Yes?" she said. Her voice sounded husky.

"Telzey, dear," Halet murmured honey-sweet from the talker, "would you come back into the house, please? The living room—We have a visitor who very much wants to meet you."

Telzey hesitated, eyes narrowing. Halet's visitor wanted to meet *her*?

"Why?" she asked.

"He has something *very* interesting to tell you, dear." The edge of triumphant malice showed for an instant, vanished in murmuring sweetness again. "So please hurry!"

"All right." Telzey stood up. "I'm coming."

"Fine, dear!" The talker went dead.

Telzey switched off the instrument, noticed that Tick-Tock had chosen to disappear meanwhile.

Flipped? She wondered, starting up towards the house. It was clear Aunt Halet had prepared some unpleasant surprise to spring on her, which was hardly more than normal behavior for Halet. The other business? She couldn't be certain of anything there. Leaving out TT's strange actions—which might have a number of causes, after all that entire string of events could have been created inside her head. There was no contradictory evidence so far.

But it could do no harm to take what *seemed* to have happened at face value. Some pretty grim event might be shaping up, in a very real way, around here...

"You reason logically!" The impression now, was of a voice speaking to her, a voice that made no audible sound. It was the same being who'd addressed her a minute or two ago.

The two worlds between which Telzey had felt suspended seemed to glide slowly together and become one.

"I go to Law school," she explained to the being, almost absently.

Amused agreement. "So we heard."

"What do you want of me?" Telzey inquired.

"You'll know soon enough."

"Why not tell me now?" Telzey urged. It seemed about to dismiss her again.

Quick impatience flared at her. "Kitten-pictures! Kitten-thoughts! Kitten-talk! Too slow, too slow! YOUR pictures—too much YOU! Wait till the..."

Circuits close... channels open... Obstructions clear? What *had* it said? There'd been only the blurred image of a finicky, delicate, but perfectly normal technical operation of some kind.

"...Minutes now!" the voice concluded. A pause, then another thought tossed carelessly at her. "This is more important to you, small-bite, than to *us!*" The voice impression ended as sharply as if a communicator had snapped off.'

Not *too* friendly! Telzey walked on towards the house, a new fear growing inside her ... a fear like the awareness of a storm gathered nearby, still quiet-deadly quiet, but ready to break.

"Kitten-pictures!" a voice seemed to jeer distantly, a whispering in the park trees beyond the garden wall.

\* \* \*

Halet's cheeks were lightly pinked and her blue eyes sparkled. She looked downright stunning, which meant to anyone who knew her that the worst side of Halet's nature was champing at the bit again. On uninformed males it had a dazzling effect, however; and Telzey wasn't surprised to find their visitor wearing a trance like expression when she came into the living room. He was a tall, outdoorsy man with a tanned, bony face, a neatly trained black mustache, and a scar down one cheek which would have seemed dashing if it hadn't been for the stupefied look. Beside his chair stood a large, clumsy instrument which might have been some kind of telecamera.

Halet performed introductions. Their visitor was Dr. Droon, a zoologist. He had been tuned in on Telzey's newscast interview on the liner the night before, and wondered whether Telzey would care to discuss Tick-Tock with him.

"Frankly, no," Telzey said.

Dr. Droon came awake and gave Telzey a surprised look.

Halet smiled easily. "My niece doesn't intend to be discourteous, doctor," she explained.

"Of course not," the zoologist agreed doubtfully.

"It's just," Halet went on, "that Telzey is a little, oh, sensitive where Tick-Tock is concerned. In her own way, she's attached to the animal. Aren't you, dear?"

"Yes," Telzey said blandly.

"Well, we hope this isn't going to disturb you too much, dear." Halet glanced significantly at Dr. Droon. "Dr. Droon, you must understand, is simply doing ...well, there is something very important he must tell you now."

Telzey transferred her gaze back to the zoologist. Dr. Droon cleared his throat. "I, ah, understand, Miss Amberdon, that you're unaware of what kind of creature your, ah, Tick-Tock is?"

Telzey started to speak, then checked herself, frowning. She had been about to state that she knew exactly what kind of creature TT was. ...but she didn't, of course!

Or did she? She ...

She scowled absent-mindedly at Dr. Droon, biting her lip.

"Telzey?" Halet prompted gently.

"Huh?" Telzey said. "Oh.. please go on, doctor!" Dr. Droon steepled his fingers. "Well," he said, "she ...your pet ... is, ah, a young crest cat. Nearly full grown now, apparently, and-"

"Why, yes!" Telzey cried.

The zoologist looked at her. "You knew that-"

"Well, not really," Telzey admitted. "Or sort of," she laughed, her cheeks flushed. "This is the most ...go ahead please! Sorry I interrupted." She stared at the wall beyond Dr. Droon with a rapt expression.

The zoologist and Halet exchanged glances. Then Dr. Droon resumed cautiously. The crest cats, he said, were a species native to Jontarou. Their existence had been known for only eight years. The species appeared to have had a somewhat limited range-the Baluit mountains on the opposite side of the huge continent on which Port Nichay had been built...

Telzey barely heard him. A very curious thing was happening. For every sentence Dr. Droon uttered, a dozen other sentences appeared in her awareness. More accurately, it was as if an instantaneous smooth flow of information relevant to whatever he said arose continuously from what might have been almost her own memory, but wasn't. Within a minute or two, she knew more about the crest cats of Jontarou than Dr. Droon could have told her in hours... much more than he'd ever known.

She realized suddenly that he'd stopped talking, that he had asked her a question. "Miss Amberdon?" he repeated now, with a note of uncertainty.

"Yar-rrr-REE!" Telzey told him softly. "I'll drink your blood!"

"Eh?"

Telzey blinked, focused on Dr. Droon, wrenching her mind away from a splendid view of the misty-blue peaks of the Baluit range.

"Sorry," she said briskly. "Just a joke!" She smiled. "Now what were you saying?"

The zoologist looked at her in a rather odd mariner for a moment. "I was inquiring," he said then, "whether you were familiar with the sporting rules established by the various hunting associations of the Hub in connection with the taking of game trophies?"

Telzey shook her head. "No, I never heard of them."

The rules, Dr. Droon explained, laid down the type of equipment... weapons, spotting and tracking instruments, number of assistants, and so forth…a sportsman could legitimately use in the pursuit of any specific type of game. "Before the end of the first year after their discovery," he went on, "the Baluit crest cats had been placed in the ultra-equipment class."

"What's ultra-equipment?" Telzey asked.

"Well," Dr. Droon said thoughtfully, "it doesn't quite involve the use of full battle armor …not quite! And, of course, even with that classification the sporting principle of mutual accessibility must be observed."

"Mutual… oh, I see!" Telzey paused as another wave of silent information rose into her awareness went on, "So the game has to be able to get at the sportsman too, eh?"

"That's correct. Except in the pursuit of various classes of flying animals, a hunter would not, for example, be permitted the use of an aircar other than as a means of simple transportation. Under these conditions, it was soon established that crest cats were being obtained by sportsmen who went after them at a rather consistent one-to-one ratio." Telzey's eyes widened. She'd gathered something similar from her other information source but hadn't quite believed it. "One hunter killed for each cat bagged?" she said.

"That's pretty rough sport, isn't it?"

"Extremely rough sport!" Dr. Droon agreed dryly. "In fact, when the statistics were published, the sporting interest in winning a Baluit cat trophy appears to have suffered a sudden and sharp decline. On the other hand, a more scientific interest in these remarkable animals was created, and many permits for their acquisition by the agents of museums, universities, public and private collections were issued. Sporting rules, of course, do not apply to that activity."

Telzey nodded absently. "I see! *They* used aircars, didn't they? A sort of heavy knockout gun-"

"Aircars, long-range detectors and stunguns are standard equipment in such work," Dr. Droon acknowledged. "Gas and poison are employed, of course, as circumstances dictate. The collectors were relatively successful for a while. And then a curious thing happened. Less than two years after their existence became known, the crest cats of the Baluit range were extinct! The inroads made on their numbers by man cannot begin to account for this, so it must be assumed that a sudden plague wiped them out. At any rate, not another living member of the species has been seen on Jontarou until you landed here with your pet last night."

Telzey sat silent for some seconds. Not because of what he had said, but because the other knowledge was still flowing into her mind. On one very important point *that* was at variance with what the zoologist had stated; and from there a coldly logical pattern was building up. Telzey didn't grasp the pattern in complete detail yet, but what she saw of it stirred her with a half incredulous dread.

She asked, shaping the words carefully but with only a small part of her attention on what she was really saying, "Just what does all that have to do with Tick-Tock, Dr. Droon?"

Dr. Droon glanced at Halet, and returned his gaze to Telzey. Looking very uncomfortable but quite determined, he told her, "Miss Amberdon, there is a Federation law which states that when a species is threatened with extinction, any available survivors must be transferred to the Life Banks of the University League, to insure their indefinite preservation. Under the circumstances, this law applies to, ah, Tick-Tock!"

So that had been Halet's trick. She'd found out about the crest cats, might have put in as much as a few months arranging to make the discovery of TT's origin on Jontarou seem a regrettable mischance—something no one would have foreseen or prevented. In the Life Banks, from what Telzey had heard of them, TT would cease to exist as an individual awareness while scientists tinkered around with the possibilities of reconstructing her species.

Telzey studied her aunt's carefully sympathizing face for an instant, and then asked Dr. Droon, "What about the other crest cats you said were collected before they became extinct here? Wouldn't they be enough for what the Life Banks need?"

He shook his head. "Two immature male specimens are known to exist, and they are at present in the Life Banks. The others that were taken alive at the time have been destroyed... often under nearly disastrous circumstances. They are enormously cunning, enormously savage creatures, Miss Amberdon! The additional fact that they can conceal themselves to the point of being virtually undetectable except by the use of instruments makes them one of the most dangerous animals known. Since the young female which you raised as a pet has remained docile ... so far... you may not really be able to appreciate that." "Perhaps I can," Telzey said. She nodded at the heavy-looking instrument standing beside his chair. "And that's-?"

"It's a life detector combined with a stungun, Miss Amberdon. I have no intention of harming your pet, but we can't take chances with an animal of that type. The gun's charge will knock it unconscious for several minutes-just long enough to let me secure it with paralysis belts."

"You're a collector for the Life Banks, Dr. Droon?"

"That's correct."

"Dr. Droon," Halet remarked, "has obtained a permit from the Planetary Moderator, authorizing him to claim Tick-Tock for the University League and remove her from the planet, dear. So you see there is simply nothing we can do about the matter! Your mother wouldn't like us to attempt to obstruct the law, would she?" Halet paused. "The permit should have your signature, Telzey, but I can sign in your stead if necessary."

That was Halet's way of saying it would do no good to appeal to Jontarou's Planetary Moderator. She'd taken the precaution of getting his assent to the matter first.

"So now if you'll just call Tick-Tock, dear..." Halet went on.

Telzey barely heard the last words. She felt herself stiffening slowly, while the living room almost faded from her sight. Perhaps, in that instant, some additional new circuit had closed in her mind, or some additional new channel had opened, for TT's purpose in tricking her into contact with the reckless, mocking beings outside was suddenly and numbingly clear.

And what it meant immediately was that she'd have to get out of the house without being spotted at it, and go someplace where she could be undisturbed for half an hour.

She realized that Halet and the zoologist were both staring at her.

"Are you ill, dear?"

"No." Telzey stood up. It would be worse than useless to try and tell these two anything! Her face must be pretty white at the moment—she could feel it—but they assumed, of course, that the shock of losing TT had just now sunk in on her in on her. "I'll have to check on that law you mentioned before I sign anything," she told Dr. Droon.

"Why, yes..." He started to get out of his chair. "I'm sure that can be arranged, Miss Amberdon!"

"Don't bother to call the Moderator's office," Telzey shrugged. "I brought my law library along. I'll look it up myself."

She turned to leave the room.

"My niece," Halet explained to Dr. Droon who was beginning to look puzzled, "attends law school. She's always so absorbed in her studies... Telzey?"

"Yes, Halet?" Telzey paused at the door.

"I'm very glad you've decided to be sensible about this, dear. But don't take too long, will you? We don't want to waste Dr. Droon's time."

"It shouldn't take more than five or ten minutes," Telzey told her agreeably. She closed the door behind her, and went directly to her bedroom on the second floor. One of her two valises was still unpacked. She locked the door behind her, opened the unpacked valise, took out a pocket edition law library and sat down at the table with it.

She clicked on the library's view-screen, tapped the clearing and index buttons. Behind the screen, one of the multiple rows of pinhead tapes shifted slightly as the index was flicked into reading position. Half a minute later, she was glancing over the legal section on which Dr. Droon had based his claim. The library confirmed what he had said.

Very neat of Halet, Telzey thought, very nasty... and pretty idiotic! Even a second-year law student could think immediately of two or three ways in which a case like that could have been dragged out in the Federation's courts for a couple of decades before the question of handing Tick-Tock over to the Life Banks became too acute.

Well, Halet simply wasn't really intelligent. And the plot to shanghai TT was hardly even a side issue now.

Telzey snapped the tiny library shut, fastened it to the belt of her sunbriefs and went over to the open window. A two-foot ledge passed beneath the window, leading to the roof of a patio on the right. Fifty yards beyond the patio, the garden ended in a natural-stone wall. Behind it lay one of the big wooded park areas which formed most of the ground level of Port Nichay.

Tick-Tock wasn't in sight. The sound of voices came from ground-floor windows on the left. Halet had brought her maid and chauffeur along; and a chef had showed up in time to make breakfast this morning, as part of the city's guest house service. Telzey took the empty valise to the window, set it on end against the left side of the frame, and let the window slide down until its lower edge rested on the valise. She went back to the house guard-screen panel beside the door, put her finger against the lock button, and pushed.

The sound of voices from the lower floor was cut off as outer doors and windows slid silently shut all about the house. Telzey glanced back at the window. The valise had creaked a little as the guard field drove the frame down on it, but it was supporting the thrust. She returned to the window, wriggled feet foremost through the opening, twisted around and got a footing on the ledge.

A minute later, she was scrambling quietly down a vine covered patio trellis to the ground. Even after they discovered she was gone, the guard screen would keep everybody in the house for some little while. They'd either have to disengage the screen's main mechanisms and start poking around in them, or force open the door to her bedroom and get the lock unset. Either approach would involve confusion, upset tempers, and generally delay any organized pursuit.

Telzey edged around the patio and started towards the wall, keeping close to the side of the house so she couldn't be seen from the windows. The

shrubbery made minor rustling noises as she threaded her way through…
and then there was a different stirring which might have been no more
than a slow, steady current of air moving among the bushes behind her.
She shivered involuntarily but didn't look back.

She came to the wall, stood still, measuring its height, jumped and got
an arm across it, swung up a knee and squirmed up and over. She came
down on her feet with a small thump in the grass on the other side, glanced
back once at the guest house, then crossed a path and went on among the
park trees.

* * *

Within a few hundred yards, it became apparent that she had an
escort. She didn't look around for them, but spread out to right and left like
a skirmish line, keeping abreast with her, occasional shadows slid silently
through patches of open sunlit ground, disappeared again under the
trees. Otherwise, there was hardly anyone in sight. Port Nichay's human
residents appeared to make almost no personal use of the vast parkland
spread out beneath their tower apartments; and its traffic moved over the
airways, visible from the ground only as rainbow-hued ribbons which
bisected the sky between the upper tower levels. An occasional private
aircar went by overhead.

Wisps of thought which were not her own thoughts flicked through
Telzey's mind from moment to moment as the silent line of shadows moved
deeper into the park with her. She realized she was being sized up, judged,
and evaluated again. No more information was coming through; they had
given her as much information as she needed. In the main perhaps, they
were simply curious now. This was the first human mind they'd been able
to make heads or tails of, and that hadn't seemed deaf and silent to their
form of communication. They were taking time out to study it. They'd been
assured she would have something of genuine importance to tell them; and
there was some derision about that. But they were willing to wait a little,
and find out. They were curious and they liked games. At the moment,
Telzey and what she might try to do to change their plans was the game on
which their attention was fixed.

Twelve minutes passed before the talker on Telzey's wrist began to
buzz. It continued to signal off and on for another few minutes, and then
stopped. Back in the guest house they couldn't be sure yet whether she
wasn't simply locked inside her room and refusing to answer them. But
Telzey quickened her pace.

The park's trees gradually became more massive, reached higher above her, stood spaced more widely apart. She passed through the morning shadow of the residential tower nearest the guest house, and emerged from it presently on the shore of a small lake. On the other side of the lake, a number of dappled grazing animals like long-necked, tall horses lifted their heads to watch her. For some seconds they seemed only mildly interested, but then a breeze moved across the lake, crinkling the surface of the water; and as it touched the opposite shore, abrupt panic exploded among the grazers. They wheeled, went flashing away in effortless twenty-foot strides, and were gone among the trees.

Telzey felt a crawling along her spine. It was the first objective indication she'd had of the nature of the company she had brought to the lake, and while it hardly came as a surprise, for a moment her urge was to follow the example of the grazers.

"Tick-Tock?" she whispered, suddenly a little short of breath.

A single up-and-down purring note replied from the bushes on her right. TT was still around, for whatever good that might do. Not too much, Telzey thought, if it came to serious trouble. But the knowledge was somewhat reassuring… and this, meanwhile, appeared to be as far as she needed to get from the guest house. They'd be looking for her by aircar presently, but there was nothing to tell them in which direction to turn first.

She climbed the bank of the lake to a point where she was screened both by thick, green shrubbery and the top of a single immense tree from the sky, sat down by some dry, mossy growth, took the law library from her belt, opened it and placed it in her lap. Vague stirrings indicated that her escort was also settling down in an irregular circle about her; and apprehension shivered on Telzey's skin again. It wasn't that their attitude was hostile; they were simply overawing. And no one could predict what they might do next. Without looking up, she asked a question in her mind.

"Ready?"

Sense of multiple acknowledgment, variously tinged- sardonic; interestedly amused; attentive; doubtful. Impatience quivered through it too, only tentatively held in restraint, and Telzey's forehead was suddenly wet. Some of them seemed on the verge of expressing disapproval with what was being done here-

Her fingers quickly flicked in the index tape, and the stir of feeling about her subsided, their attention captured again for the moment. Her thoughts became to some degree detached, ready to dissect another problem in the familiar ways and present the answers to it. Not a very involved problem essentially, but this time it wasn't a school exercise. Her company waited, withdrawn, silent, aloof once more, while the index blurred, checked, blurred and checked. Within a minute and a half, she had noted a dozen reference symbols. She tapped in another of the pinhead tapes, glanced over a few paragraphs, licked salty sweat from her lip, and said in her thoughts, emphasizing the meaning of each detail of the sentence so that there would be no misunderstanding, "This is the Federation law that applies to the situation which existed originally on this planet..."

Here were no interruptions, no commenting thoughts, no intrusions of any kind, as she went step by step through the section, turned to another one, and another. In perhaps twelve minutes she came to the end of the last one, and stopped. Instantly, argument exploded about her.

Telzey was not involved in the argument; in fact, she could grasp only scraps of it. Either they were excluding her deliberately, or the exchange was too swift, practiced and varied to allow her to keep up. But their vehemence was not encouraging. And was it reasonable to assume that the Federation's laws would have any meaning for minds like these? Telzey snapped the library shut with fingers that had begun to tremble, and placed it on the ground. Then she stiffened. In the sensations washing about her, a special excitement rose suddenly, a surge of almost gleeful wildness that choked away her breath. Awareness followed of a pair of malignant crimson eyes fastened on her, moving steadily closer. A kind of nightmare paralysis seized Telzey—they'd turned her over to that red-eyed horror! She sat still, feeling mouse-sized.

Something came out with a crash from a thicket behind her. Her muscles went tight. But it was TT who rubbed a hard head against her shoulder, took another three stiff legged steps forward and stopped between Telzey and the bushes on their right, back rigid, neck fur erect, tail twisting.

Expectant silence closed in about them. The circle was waiting. In the greenery on the right something made a slow, heavy stir.

TT's lips peeled back from her teeth. Her head swung towards the motion, ears flattening, transformed in a split, snarling demon-mask. A long shriek ripped from her lungs, raw with fury, blood lust and challenge.

The sound died away. For some seconds the tension about them held. Then came a sense of gradual relaxation mingled with a partly amused approval. Telzey was shaking violently. It had been, she was telling herself, an elaborate test ... not of herself, of course, but of TT. And Tick-Tock had passed with honors. That *her* nerves had been half ruined in the process would seem a matter of no consequence to this rugged crew...

She realized next that someone here was addressing her personally.

It took a few moments to steady her jittering thoughts enough to gain a more definite impression than that. This speaker, she discovered then, was a member of the circle of whom she hadn't been aware before. The thought-impressions came hard and cold as iron-a personage who was very evidently in the habit of making major decisions and seeing them carried out. The circle, its moment of sport over, was listening with more than a suggestion of deference. Tick-Tock, far from conciliated, green eyes still blazing, nevertheless was settling down to listen, too.

Telzey began to understand.

Her suggestions, Iron Thoughts informed her, might appear without value to a number of foolish minds here, but *he* intended to see they were given a fair trial. Did he perhaps hear, he inquired next of the circle, throwing in a casual but horridly vivid impression of snapping spines and slashed shaggy throats spouting blood, any objection to that?

Dead stillness all around. There was, definitely, no objection! Tick-Tock began to grin like a pleased kitten.

That point having been settled in an orderly manner now, Iron Thoughts went on coldly to Telzey, what specifically did she propose they should do?

\* \* \*

Halet's long, pearl-gray sports car showed up above the park trees twenty minutes later. Telzey, face turned down towards the open law library in her lap, watched the car from the corner of her eyes. She was in plain view, sitting beside the lake, apparently absorbed in legal research. Tick-Tock, camouflaged among the bushes thirty feet higher up the bank, had spotted the car an instant before she did and announced the fact with a three-second break in her purring. Neither of them made any other move.

The car was approaching the lake but still a good distance off. Its canopy was down, and Telzey could just make out the heads of three people inside. Delquos, Halet's chauffeur, would be flying the vehicle, while Halet and Dr. Droon looked around for her from the sides. Three hundred yards away, the aircar began a turn to the right. Delquos didn't like his employer much; at a guess, he had just spotted Telzey and was trying to warn her off.

Telzey closed the library and put it down, picked up a handful of pebbles and began flicking them idly, one at a time, into the water. The aircar vanished to her left.

Three minutes later, she watched its shadow glide across the surface of the lake towards her. Her heart began to thump almost audibly, but she didn't look up. Tick-Tock's purring continued, on its regular, unhurried note. The car came to a stop almost directly overhead. After a couple of seconds, there was a clicking noise. The purring ended abruptly.

Telzey climbed to her feet as Delquos brought the car down to the bank of the lake. The chauffeur grinned ruefully at her. A side door had been opened, and Halet and Dr. Droon stood behind it. Halet watched Telzey with a small smile while the naturalist put the heavy life-detector-and-stungun device carefully down on the floorboards.

"If you're looking for Tick-Tock," Telzey said, "she isn't here."

Halet just shook her head sorrowfully. "There's no use lying to us, dear! Dr. Droon just stunned her."

They found TT collapsed on her side among the shrubs, wearing her natural color. Her eyes were shut; her chest rose and fell in a slow breathing motion. Dr. Droon, looking rather apologetic, pointed out to Telzey that her pet was in no pain, that the stungun had simply put her comfortably to sleep. He also explained the use of the two sets of webbed paralysis belts which he fastened about TT's legs; The effect of the stun charge would wear off in a few minutes, and contact with the inner surfaces of the energized belts would then keep TT anesthetized and unable to move until the belts were removed. She would, he repeated, be suffering no pain throughout the process.

Telzey didn't comment. She watched Delquos raise TT's limp body above the level of the bushes with a gravity hoist belonging to Dr. Droon, and maneuver her back to the car, the others following. Delquos climbed into the car first, opened the big trunk compartment in the rear. TT was slid inside and the trunk compartment locked.

"Where are you taking her?" Telzey asked sullenly as Delquos lifted the car into the air.

"To the spaceport, dear," Halet said. "Dr. Droon and I both felt it would be better to spare your feelings by not prolonging the matter unnecessarily."

Telzey wrinkled her nose disdainfully, and walked up the aircar to stand behind Delquos' seat. She leaned against the back of the seat for an instant. Her legs felt shaky.

The chauffeur gave her a sober wink from the side. "That's a dirty trick she's played on you, Miss Telzey!" he murmured. "I tried to warn you."

"I know." Telzey took a deep breath. "Look, Delquos, in just a minute something's going to happen! It'll look dangerous, but it won't be. Don't let it get you nervous... right?"

"Huh?" Delquos appeared startled, but kept his voice low. "Just *what's* going to happen?"

"No time to tell you. Remember what I said."

Telzey moved back a few steps from the driver's seat, turned around, said unsteadily, "Halet... Dr. Droon-" Halet had been speaking quietly to Dr. Droon; they both looked up.

"If you don't move, and don't do anything stupid," Telzey said rapidly, "you won't get hurt. If you do... well, I don't know! You see, there's another crest cat in the car. . ." In her mind she added, "Now!"

It was impossible to tell in just what section of the car Iron Thoughts had been lurking. The carpeting near the rear passenger seats seemed to blur for an instant then he was there, camouflage dropped, sitting on the floorboards five feet from the naturalist and Halet.

Halet's mouth opened wide; she tried to scream but fainted instead. Dr. Droon's right hand started out quickly towards the big stungun device beside his seat. Then he checked himself and sat still, ashen-faced.

Telzey didn't blame him for changing his mind. She felt he must be a remarkably brave man to have moved at all. Iron Thoughts, twice as broad across the back as Tick-Tock, twice as massively muscled, looked like a devil-beast even to her. His dark-green marbled hide was crisscrossed with old scar patterns; half his tossing crimson crest appeared to have been ripped away. He reached out now in a fluid, silent motion, hooked a paw under the stungun and flicked upwards. The big instrument rose in an incredibly swift, steep arc eighty feet into the air, various parts flying away from it, before it started curving down towards the treetops below the car. Iron Thoughts lazily swung his head around and looked at Telzey with yellow fire-eyes.

"Miss Telzey! Miss Telzey!" Delquos was muttering behind her. "You're sure it won't..."

Telzey swallowed. At the moment, she felt barely mouse-sized again. "Just relax!" she told Delquos in a shaky voice. "He's really quite t-t-t-tame."

Iron Thoughts produced a harsh but not unamiable chuckle in her mind.

\* \* \*

The pearl-gray sports car, covered now by its streamlining canopy, drifted down presently to a parking platform outside the suite of offices of Jontarou's Planetary Moderator, on the fourteenth floor of the Shikaris' Club Tower. An attendant waved it on into a vacant slot.

Inside the car, Delquos set the brakes, switched off the engine, asked, "Now what?"

"I think," Telzey said reflectively, "we'd better lock you in the trunk compartment with my Aunt and Dr. Droon while I talk to the Moderator."

The chauffeur shrugged. He'd regained most of his aplomb during the unhurried trip across the parklands. Iron Thoughts had done nothing but sit in the center of the car, eyes half shut, looking like instant death enjoying a dignified nap and occasionally emitting a rip sawing noise which might have been either his style of purring or a snore. And Tick-Tock, when Delquos peeled the paralysis belts off her legs at Telzey's direction, had greeted him with her usual reserved affability. What the chauffeur was suffering from at the moment was intense curiosity, which Telzey had done nothing to relieve.

"Just as you say, Miss Telzey," he agreed. "I hate to miss whatever you're going to be doing here, but if you *don't* lock me up now, Miss Halet will figure I was helping you and fire me as soon as you let her out."

Telzey nodded, then cocked her head in the direction of the rear compartment. Faint sounds coming through the door indicated that Halet had regained consciousness and was having hysterics.

"You might tell her," Telzey suggested, "that there'll be a grown-up crest cat sitting outside the compartment door." This wasn't true, but neither Delquos nor Halet could know it. "If there's too much racket before I get back, it's likely to irritate him..."

A minute later, she set both car doors on lock and went outside, wishing she were less informally clothed. Sunbriefs and sandals tended to make her look juvenile.

The parking attendant appeared startled when she approached him with Tick-Tock striding alongside.

"They'll never let you into the offices with that thing, miss," he informed her. "Why, it doesn't even have a collar!"

"Don't worry about it," Telzey told him aloofly.

She dropped a two-credit piece she'd taken from Halet's purse into his hand, and continued on towards the building entrance. The attendant squinted after her, trying unsuccessfully to dispel an odd impression that the big catlike animal with the girl was throwing a double shadow.

The Moderator's chief receptionist also had some doubts about TT, and possibly about the sunbriefs, though she seemed impressed when Telzey's identification tag informed her she was speaking to the daughter of Federation Councilwoman Jessamine Amberdon.

"You feel you can discuss this... emergency... only with the Moderator himself, Miss Amberdon?" she repeated.

"Exactly," Telzey said firmly. A buzzer sounded as she spoke. The receptionist excused herself and picked up an earphone. She listened a moment, said blandly, "Yes... Of course...Yes, I understand," replaced the earphone and stood up, smiling at Telzey.

"Would you come with me, Miss Amberdon?" she said. "I think the Moderator will see you immediately..."

Telzey followed her, chewing thoughtfully at her lip. This was easier than she'd expected—in fact, too easy! Halet's work? Probably. A few comments to the effect of "A highly imaginative child... over excitable," while Halet was arranging to have the Moderator's office authorize Tick-Tock's transfer to the Life Banks, along with the implication that Jessamine Amberdon would appreciate a discreet handling of any disturbance Telzey might create as a result. It was the sort of notion that would appeal to Halet.

\* \* \*

They passed through a series of elegantly equipped offices and hallways, Telzey grasping TT's neck-fur in lieu of a leash, their appearance creating a tactfully restrained wave of surprise among secretaries and clerks. And if somebody here and there was troubled by a fleeting, uncanny impression that not one large beast but two seemed to be trailing the Moderator's visitor down the aisles, no mention was made of what could have been only a momentary visual distortion. Finally, a pair of sliding doors opened ahead, and the receptionist ushered Telzey into a large, cool balcony garden on the shaded side of the great building. A tall, gray-haired man stood up from the desk at which he was working, and bowed to Telzey. The receptionist withdrew again.

"My pleasure, Miss Amberdon," Jontarou's Planetary Moderator said, "Be seated, please." He studied Tick-Tock with more than casual interest while Telzey was settling herself into a chair, added, "And what may I and my office do for you?"

Telzey hesitated. She'd observed his type on Orado in her mother's circle of acquaintances—a senior diplomat, a man not easy to impress. It was a safe bet that he'd had her brought out to his balcony office only to keep her occupied while Halet was quietly informed where the Amberdon problem child was and requested to come over and take charge.

What she had to tell him now would have sounded rather wild even if presented by a presumably responsible adult. She could provide proof, but until the Moderator was already nearly sold on her story, that would be a very unsafe thing to do. Old Iron Thoughts was backing her up, but if it didn't look as if her plans were likely to succeed, he would be willing to ride herd on his devil's pack just so long...

Better start the ball rolling without any preliminaries, Telzey decided. The Moderator's picture of her must be that of a spoiled, neurotic brat in a stew about the threatened loss of a pet animal. He expected her to start arguing with him immediately about Tick-Tock.

She said, "Do you have a personal interest in keeping the Baluit crest cats from becoming extinct?" Surprise flickered in his eyes for an instant. Then he smiled.

"I admit I do, Miss Amberdon," he said pleasantly. "I should like to see the species reestablished. I count myself almost uniquely fortunate in having had the opportunity to bag two of the magnificent brutes before disease wiped them out on the planet."

The last seemed a less than fortunate statement just now. Telzey felt a sharp tingle of alarm, then sensed that in the minds which were drawing the meaning of the Moderator's speech from her mind there had been only a brief stir of interest.

She cleared her throat, said, "The point is that they weren't wiped out by disease."

He considered her quizzically, seemed to wonder what she was trying to lead up to. Telzey gathered her courage, plunged on, "Would you like to hear what did happen?"

"I should be much interested, Miss Amberdon," The Moderator said without change of expression. "But first, if you'll excuse me a moment. . ."

There had been some signal from his desk which Telzey hadn't noticed, because he picked up a small communicator now, said, "Yes?" After a few seconds, he resumed, "That's rather curious, isn't it? ... Yes, I'd try that ... No, that shouldn't be necessary ... Yes, please do. Thank you."

He replaced the communicator, his face very sober; then, his eyes flicking for an instant to TT, he drew one of the upper desk drawers open a few inches, and turned back to Telzey.

"Now, Miss Amberdon," he said affably, "you were about to say? About these crest cats ..."

Telzey swallowed. She hadn't heard the other side of the conversation, but she could guess what it had been about. His office had called the guest house, had been told by Halet's maid that Halet, the chauffeur and Dr. Droon were out looking for Miss Telzey and her pet. The Moderator's office had then checked on the sports car's communication number and attempted to call it. And, of course, there had been no response.

To the Moderator, considering what Halet would have told him, it must add up to the grim possibility that the young lunatic he was talking to had let her three-quarters-grown crest cat slaughter her aunt and the two men when they caught up with her! The office would be notifying the police now to conduct an immediate search for the missing aircar.

143

When it would occur to them to look for it on the Moderator's parking terrace was something Telzey couldn't know. But if Halet and Dr. Droon were released before the Moderator accepted her own version of what had occurred, and the two reported the presence of wild crest cats in Port Nichay, there would be almost no possibility of keeping the situation under control. Somebody was bound to make some idiotic move, and the fat would be in the fire...

Two things might be in her favor. The Moderator seemed to have the sort of steady nerve one would expect in a man who had bagged two Baluit crest cats. The partly opened desk drawer beside him must have a gun in it; apparently he considered that a sufficient precaution against an attack by TT. He wasn't likely to react in a panicky manner. And the mere fact that he suspected Telzey of homicidal tendencies would make him give the closest attention to what she said. Whether he believed her then was another matter, of course.

Slightly encouraged, Telzey began to talk. It did sound like a thoroughly wild story, but the Moderator listened with an appearance of intent interest. When she had told him as much as she felt he could be expected to swallow for a start, he said musingly, "So they weren't wiped out- they went into hiding! Do I understand you to say they did it to avoid being hunted?"

Telzey chewed her lip frowningly before replying. "There's something about that part I don't quite get," she admitted. "Of course I don't quite get either why you'd want to go hunting ...twice ... for something that's just as likely to bag you instead!"

"Well, those are, ah, merely the statistical odds," the Moderator explained. "If one has enough confidence, you see-"

"I don't really. But the crest cats seem to have felt the same way— at first. They were getting around one hunter for every cat that got shot. Humans were the most exciting game they'd ever run into."

"But then that ended, and the humans started picking them out with stunguns from aircars where they couldn't be got at, and hauling them off while they were helpless. After it had gone on for a while, they decided to keep out of sight."

"But they're still around . . . thousands and thousands of them! Another thing nobody's known about them is that they weren't only in the Baluit mountains. There were crest cats scattered all through the big forests along the other side of the continent."

"Very interesting," the Moderator commented. "Very interesting, indeed!" He glanced towards the communicator, and then returned his gaze to Telzey, drumming his fingers lightly on the desk top.

She could tell nothing at all from his expression now, but she guessed he was thinking hard. There was supposed to be no native intelligent life in the legal sense on Jontarou, and she had been careful to say nothing so far to make the Baluit cats look like more than rather exceptionally intelligent animals. The next rather large question should be how she'd come by such information.

If the Moderator asked her that, Telzey thought, she could feel she'd made a beginning at getting him to buy the whole story.

"Well," he said abruptly, "if the crest cats are not extinct or threatened with extinction, the Life Banks obviously have no claim on your pet." He smiled confidingly at her. "And that's the reason you're here, isn't it?"

"Well, no," Telzey began, dismayed. "I-"

"Oh, it's quite all right, Miss Amberdon! I'll simply rescind the permit which was issued for the purpose. You need feel no further concern about that." He paused. "Now, just one question … do you happen to know where your aunt is at present?"

Telzey had a dead, sinking feeling. So he hadn't believed a word she said. He'd been stalling her along until the aircar could be found.

She took a deep breath. "You'd better listen to the rest of it."

"Why, is there more?" the Moderator asked politely.

"Yes. The important part! The kind of creatures they are, they wouldn't go into hiding indefinitely just because someone was after them."

Was there a flicker of something beyond watchfulness in his expression? "What would they do, Miss Amberdon?" he asked quietly.

"If they couldn't get at the men in the aircars and couldn't communicate with them"—the flicker again—"they'd start looking for the place the men came from, wouldn't they? It might take them some years to work their way across the continent and locate us here in Port Nichay. But supposing they did it finally and a few thousand of them are sitting around in the parks down there right now? They could come up the side of these towers as easily as they go up the side of a mountain. And supposing they'd decided that the only way to handle the problem was to clean out the human beings in Port Nichay?"

The Moderator stared at her in silence a few seconds. "You're saying," he observed then, "that they're rational beings-above the Critical I.Q. level."

"Well," Telzey said, "legally they're rational. I checked on that. About as rational as we are, I suppose."

"Would you mind telling me now how you happen to know this?"

"They told me," Telzey said.

He was silent again, studying her face. "You mentioned, Miss Amberdon that they have been unable to communicate with other human beings. This suggests then that you are a xenotelepath ..."

"I am?" Telzey hadn't heard the term before. "If it means that I can tell what the cats are thinking, and they can tell what I'm thinking, I guess that's the word for it." She considered him, decided she had him almost on the ropes, went on quickly.

"I looked up the laws, and told them they could conclude a treaty with the Federation which would establish them as an Affiliated Species... and that would settle everything the way they would want it settled, without trouble. Some of them believed me. They decided to wait until I could talk to you. If it works out, fine! If it doesn't"-she felt her voice falter for an instant-"they're going to cut loose fast!"

The Moderator seemed undisturbed. "What am I supposed to do?"

"I told them you'd contact the Council of the Federation on Orado."

"Contact the Council?" he repeated coolly. "With no more proof for this story than your word Miss Amberdon?" Telzey felt a quick, angry stirring begin about her, felt her face whiten.

"All right," she said. "I'll give you proof! I'll have to now. But that'll be it. Once they've tipped their hand all the way, you'll have about thirty seconds left to make the right move. I hope you remember that!"

He cleared his throat. "I—"

"NOW!" Telzey said.

Along the walls of the balcony garden, beside the ornamental flower stands, against the edges of the rock pool, the crest cats appeared. Perhaps thirty of them, none quite as physically impressive as Iron Thoughts who stood closest to the Moderator; but none very far from it. Motionless as rocks, frightening as gargoyles, they waited, eyes glowing with hellish excitement

"This is *their* council, you see," Telzey heard herself saying.

The Moderator's face had also paled. But he was, after all, an old hunter and a senior diplomat. He took an unhurried look around the circle, said quietly, "Accept my profound apologies for doubting you, Miss Amberdon!" and reached for the desk communicator.

Iron Thoughts swung his demon head in Telzey's direction. For an instant, she picked up the mental impression of a fierce yellow eye closing in an approving wink.

"... An open transmitter line to Orado," the Moderator was saying into the communicator. "The Council. And snap it up! Some very important visitors are waiting ..."

The offices of Jontarou's Planetary Moderator became an extremely busy and interesting area then. Quite two hours passed before it occurred to anyone to ask Telzey again whether she knew where her aunt was at present.

Telzey smote her forehead.

"Forgot all about that!" she admitted, fishing the sports car's keys out of the pocket of her sunbriefs. "They're out on the parking platform..."

\* \* \*

The preliminary treaty arrangements between the Federation of the Hub and the new Affiliated Species of the Planet of Jontarou were formally ratified two weeks later, the ceremony taking place on Jontarou, in the Champagne Hall of the Shikaris' Club.

Telzey was able to follow the event only by news viewer in her ship-cabin, she and Halet being on the return trip to Orado by then. She wasn't too interested in the treaty's details-they conformed almost exactly to what she had read out to Iron Thoughts and his co-chiefs and companions in the park. It was the smooth bridging of the wide language gap between the contracting parties by a row of interpreting machines and a handful of human xenotelepaths which held her attention.

As she switched off the viewer, Halet came wandering in from the adjoining cabin.

"I was watching it, too!" Halet observed. She smiled. "I was hoping to see dear Tick-Tock."

Telzey looked over at her. "Well, TT would hardly be likely to show up in Port Nichay," she said. "She's having too good a time now finding out what life in the Baluit range is like."

"I suppose so," Halet agreed doubtfully, sitting down on a hassock. "But I'm glad she promised to get in touch with us again in a few years. I'll miss her."

Telzey regarded her aunt with a reflective frown. Halet meant it quite sincerely, of course; she had undergone a profound change of heart during the past two weeks. But Telzey wasn't without some doubts about the actual value of a change of heart brought on by telepathic means. The learning process the crest cats had started in her mind appeared to have continued automatically several days longer than her rugged teachers had really intended; and Telzey had reason to believe that by the end of that time she'd developed associated latent abilities of which the crest cats had never heard. She'd barely begun to get it all sorted out yet, but... as an example... she'd found it remarkably easy to turn Halet's more obnoxious attitudes virtually upside down. It had taken her a couple of days to get the hang of her aunt's personal symbolism, but after that there had been no problem.

She was reasonably certain she'd broken no laws so far, though the sections in the law library covering the use and abuse of psionic abilities were veiled in such intricate and downright obscuring phrasing—deliberately, Telzey suspected—that it was really difficult to say what they did mean. But even aside from that, there were a number of arguments in favor of exercising great caution.

Jessamine, for one thing, was bound to start worrying about her sister-in-law's health if Halet turned up on Orado in her present state of mind, even though it would make for a far more agreeable atmosphere in the Amberdon household.

"Halet," Telzey inquired mentally, "do you remember what an all-out stinker you used to be?"

"Of course, dear," Halet said aloud. "I can hardly wait to tell dear Jessamine how much I regret the many times I…"

"Well," Telzey went on, still verbalizing it silently, "I think you'd really enjoy life more if you were, let's say, about halfway between your old nasty self and the sort of sickening-good kind you are now."

"Why, Telzey!" Halet cried out with dopey amiability. "What a delightful idea!"'

"Let's try it," Telzey said.

There was silence in the cabin for some twenty minutes then while she went painstakingly about remolding a number of Halet's character traits for the second time. She still felt some misgiving about it; but if it became necessary, she probably could always restore the old Halet *in toto*.

These, she told herself, definitely were powers one should treat with respect! Better rattle through law school first; then, with that out of the way, she could start hunting around to see who in the Federation was qualified to instruct a genius-level novice in the proper handling of psionics…

*Elizabeth McCoy began writing about the feline centauroid Kintarans with "Leaping Lizards" in PawPrints Fanzine #1, Winter 1994, followed by five more stories to PawPrints Fanzine #7, Spring 1998, and one in Fantastic Furry Stories #2, October 2001. She reprinted the seven as individual Kindle editions in June 2011 and has written new Kintaran stories since then.*

*Originally the Kintarans were planetbound. Kintara's discovery by humans and other species led to the Kintarans' determination to become a spacegoing species themselves. A frequent theme is how the Kintarans must struggle against their biology and their four-legged physiques to fit into an interstellar civilization designed for two-leggers. McCoy has recently begun featuring the Mmsar, another species that sometimes appear as supporting characters, in their own stories.*

*In previous stories, the sisters Klarin-yal and Coli-nFaran acquired their own spaceship, the* Choosaraf, *and started a new clan with Klarin as captain and Coli as ship's doctor. It is now almost a decade later, and the* Choosaraf's *crew has grown. Klarin and Coli have both become mothers, and their children have become the protagonists of the stories.*

*"What Really Counts" is a reminder that aliens can be really* alien, *and not just furry humans.*

# What Really Matters

## *Elizabeth McCoy*

Nervously, Kinahran M'Choosaraf stepped over the threshold, into her mother's cabin. She had to exert all her seven-year-old strength of will to keep from sidling around like a keesol, but she didn't want the adults to laugh at her. It was dim in Coli-nfarin's quarters, so Kinahran's slit-pupiled blue eyes were wide, adjusting. Her high-set ears flicked around, funneling in the least little sounds from the various parts of the room, while she could feel her nose quivering with the strange smells. Her mouth gaped open just a little to taste the air.

It was certainly full of strangeness: her mother and aunt, of course, and a faint scent of her next-elder brother, and some of the other adults; most strange were the damp scents, of wet fur, not-quite-blood, and the tinge of true-blood.

Coli-nfarin herself was curled on her mattress, surrounded by pillows and even some blankets. She was lying on her lower side, but her upper torso was propped up on even more pillows. Her sister, Wahn Klarin-yal, was sitting alertly half a body-length away. Kinahran made herself stop being skittish, forcing her ears to prick forwards and stay there. In her mother's arms, there was a tiny fur-bundle—an armful for small and delicate Coli, but still seeming absurdly little to Kinahran.

Coli smiled tiredly at her daughter and moved her arms so that Kinahran could get a better view of the little deaf-blind thaso who nursed vigorously. Kinahran took in the sight, from tuftless-tailtip, past tiny-perfect rear paws, flexing forepaws and itty-bitty hands that kneaded Coli's breast, to the crumpled little ears on top.

Indignantly, Kinahran said, "White!"

There was laughter from her mother, her aunt, and her brother behind her. Golden-eyed Daaral-fara recovered enough to speak first. "What did you expect, Mother? All it will take is sending a holo to Rarroriah, and you'll have the complete set of us."

This sent Coli into giggles again, and she flicked her ears and nodded helpessly until the thaso got dislodged and started squeaking. Kinahran had the feeling that she'd become the butt of a joke, and her tail lashed as she looked around. Her glance happened on her aunt Klarin-yal, who had become sober, and Kinahran hastily sat down on her tail, pinning it between her hind feet and under both forepaws (rumpling the tail-tuft) while she washed her right hand and ear. It wasn't good to show aggression in a new mother's den. It could get you ear-notched, even if you were that mother's third-born child.

Klarin-yal apparently took pity on Kinahran's confusion—either that, or she just wanted to defuse the brawl that Kinahran intended to start with her brother, as soon as they were out of the room. "Darral's first words were, 'Oh, another white one.'" The Wahn's voice went flat on the quote, and Kinahran had to stuff her fingers in her mouth to keep from giggling madly at the imitation.

Darral-fara sneezed. "I've run the projections, though." He waggled the display pad he was holding, attracting Kinahran's attention with the movement. "Instead of the full-body white spotting gene that we two and Rarroriah have, the new thaso has a faulty color-gene. Rather than having her—she's a girl, if you hadn't noted—her fur-color *suppressed* by the white-spot, she doesn't have any fur-color at all. Or skin color, or eye-color."

Kinahran's head got a little stuffed-feeling, imagining a Kintaran with transparent eyes and skin . . . "Eeeewwwg! We'll be able to see her *brain* when she opens her eyes?"

This sent all the adults into fits again. Kinahran was *definitely* going to bite Darral's tail later, even if she *was* seven Terran-years old and over half-way to adult herself. Smugly, her brother corrected, "Nih, not clear, colorless. We *will* be able to see her blood more clearly, and since that's all the color that will come to her eyes, they'll look red or pink or something. The human word for it is 'ahl-ba-niss-em,' for the condition, and 'ahl-ba-no' for the product."

For the two new human-words, Kinahran almost forgave him. "But you said no color," she protested a little. "Red and white are colors." They always had been in the crèche, at least. She had crayons with those colors on them, even if Detchal kept stealing the red.

"Sometimes they're colors, but not always. Especially in genetics." Darral-fara said. He turned to Coli-nfarin a bit deferentially, as befitted her son and also a sub-ranking doctor. "I ran the genetic scans, mother—your genes and ova are fine, despite the thaso's little mutation. It must have been an isolated cosmic-ray bumping the genes, or maybe something on the sire's side."

"Well, if she's otherwise healthy, then there's no problem," Coli said with tired satisfaction. She wriggled down in the pillows a little, and glanced over one shoulder to where Klarin-yal sat. The large brown tabby flicked her red leather-stitched ears forwards and carefully padded over to slide her upper body partway under Coli's upper body. The little black-and-white purred loudly, snugged against her fraternal twin sister.

"All right," Wahn Klarin-yal said quietly, "off with you two. Your mother needs to rest."

Quietly, Daaral-fara and Kinahran left the room, Kinahran looking over her shoulder wistfully at the sister-twins. She'd never been able to do that with either music-holo star Rarroriah or gengineer Daaral-fara. Thinking of Daaral made her realize that she still intended to swat him, so she looked around. Coli's second-born son had vanished himself. "Oh, hairballs," Kinahran swore, as she stalked off to her room in the keesol-section of the ship.

* * *

Satisfyingly enough, the next morning in the crèche, everyone was curious as *anything* about the new thaso, and Kinahran was able to draw out the process of revelation—and catch Leln Dazran and Ta-Pera in the "transparent eyes" trap. Kurah-ral, however, started to correct them and Kinahran had to interrupt to use all the fancy words that her brother had.

Detchal, predictably, said, "White is too a color. It's an *icky* color!"

Kinahran turned on him with her ears folded, as did every other keesol in the crèche who had spots of white fur. Kurah-ral, with an immaculate white "cap" over her head and ears and white paws on her otherwise brown-tabby body, pointed out coldly, "You have a white chin, brother."

Detchal, equally predictably, said, "Nih! Is not! White is icky."

Leln Dazran sensibly took some of the best clutch-toys and put them in a cabinet, out of the way.

The utterly unsurprising escalation between Klarin-yal's fraternal twins was halted by the arrival of K'rava. K'rava was the ship's Negotiator—he was a trade expert, a diplomat, and arbitrator of disputes if the parties involved couldn't settle it themselves. He was also one of the main crèche-keepers on the clan-ship. Without pausing, he detoured between the two siblings and grabbed an ear in each hand, spinning them off in opposite directions.

The smallest keesolt watched the intervention with huge, impressed eyes. Kinahran and Teecoli watched K'rava with big, mooning eyes. K'rava's name meant "Like a purr," and his voice indeed was. He was a beautiful pale cream and apricot tabby, with the most lovely rich-gold eyes. His tailtuft was always immaculate, if cut a little short, along with his mane, so that it would fit into vac-suits when he left the ship.

Every female keesol on the *Choosaraf* above the age of six had a crush on K'rava that was nearly as big as the clanship itself. They examined each other for eye-color and fur-color that might signify that he'd sired one of them, and couldn't decide if they'd die if they were his daughters, or die if they weren't. They *didn't* examine their brothers for those signs, though— they *knew* they'd die if an annoying brother turned out to be K'rava's son.

Kinahran herself, despite her white fur and blue eyes, was considered a good candidate for a blood kinship, since it had been her mother, the tiny Coli-nfarin, who had recruited K'rava from his grounder-clan on Kintara—rescuing the young male from a life of squalor and obscurity, and placing him in the *Choosaraf* crèche where he could be properly admired. Kinahran pointed out, either desperately or sadly, that it couldn't be. K'rava was helping her with her language lessons (to the envy of everyone who hadn't wanted to learn languages until *after* Kinahran started), and they were both really good at it—and everyone knew that parents and children just weren't good at the same things.

*Though,* Kinahran thought as K'rava herded the younger keesolt and older, apprentice-age keesolt into two groups, *Daaral-fara **does** kind of take after mother, being a genetic engineer when she's a doctor. It's both biology stuff, and medical stuff. But Rarroriah went ground-side to sing and dance and play music . . . And I'm not a Negotiator! I want to be a comm-officer!*

About then, the first of the adults showed up, for it was Official Apprenticing Day, when Kinahran and most of her friends would choose what they wanted to study for serious, rather than the flitting around and tours that they'd done since they could be trusted around tech.

N'chee was the main engineer, and he had a selection of other technicians with him—those who had apprenticed first with thrusters, or warp drives, or the powerplant, or lifesupport. Keesolt ears went forward and tails went up. "Me! Me! Me!" many of them chirruped, waving hands and forepaws, restrained from dashing forward only by the knowledge that undisciplined keesolt would not be allowed in Engineering at all.

N'chee chuckled and waded into the crowd and started tugging ears and shoulders, picking out volunteers and thrusting them to his entourage. Kurah-ral, who *wasn't* volunteering, was also picked. Her yellow-green eyes were surprised, and she swiveled her white ears around. "But I didn't volunteer?" she said, very quietly, as they passed Kinahran.

The Wahn-of-Engineering ruffled her head-fur gently and licked the white cap of her mane. "You're to be given a *thorough* tour of every major system on the ship, to find where you like best. Wahn's orders."

Kurah-ral made a face. "Oh. *Mother.*" Her tailtip lashed, but she went away meekly enough.

The next Kintaran, who went in just after N'chee and the others left, was from Medical. Though Coli-nfarin, Wahn-of-Medical, was still with her thaso, there were other doctors on the ship. A youngish male with striking black whorls on his gray sides, the medic looked at the various volunteers and finally settled on Ta-Pera and Leln Dazran—probably, Kinahran thought, because they were both small.

After Medical came Pilots and Scouts, which sucked up most of the other keesolt, including Teecoli, to the Pilots. Then Security, Kroygharl and a couple others, and Sensors and Comm, N'balplar, came in at the same time. Kinahran made her way to the tail-less gray tabby, her own white plume up happily. The old electronics expert had the best stories (all different!) about how he'd lost his tail, and since Kinahran didn't want to be a Negotiator or trade expert—or, she shuddered to even think, *ship-Wahn!*—comm officer would be the only other position where she could show off her command of languages.

Of the remaining keesolt, Ravehcroy was already settling down next to K'rava—*she* was going to be an apprentice Negotiator, and she told everyone else in the crèche that several times a day—while Detchal wavered between going with the band of would-be gunners and security personnel, and looking at K'rava and N'balplar.

Suddenly, Detchal bolted towards N'balplar. "Wanna be comm-designer!" he blurted out, ignoring Kinahran's flattened ears. "Wanna make pretty comm-stuff!"

N'balplar put his ears forward and blinked. "If you insist, Detchal. Don't you think you'd have more fun with Kroygharl, learning how to shoot things?"

Looking desperate, Detchal explained, "*Everybody* wants to shoot things! And Ravehcroy talk-talks, and K'rava'll make us *babysit!*"

"Well," N'balplar sighed, "you can always change your mind tomorrow. That's what apprentice-year is for."

Kinahran glared, flat-eared, at her cousin as the trio left the crèche-room. Detchal licked his shoulder spotless and ignored her. She told herself that he'd give up when he saw how hard comm-work was.

* * *

Some eighty days later, both Kinahran and Detchal were doing comm-work—at opposite ends of the room, most of the time. The only good thing that had come of Detchal's comm apprenticeship, Kinahran thought, was that he'd stopped trying to hit her when N'balplar wasn't looking. The tailess crewkint was very, *very* good at knowing what was going on behind his back, and he cuffed Detchal whenever Detchal tried to pick on Kinahran. Of course, he cuffed Kinahran if she tried to bite Detchal's tail, too, but Kinahran's desire to do that was slowly fading.

Simply, and plainly to everyone but Detchal, Kinahran was better with the comm gear than Detchal was. She was busy learning the basics—small repairs, tricks of operation to boost range or signal quality, the standards for the major races in the sector—while Detchal obviously saw himself as a visionary. Left to himself, he tried to take comm gear apart like a new-weaned keesol, and put it back together uniquely.

Ten days before, Kinahran had managed to rig an open channel on one of the hand-comms in N'balplar's workroom, broadcasting to an ear-button in her own white ear, and overheard N'balplar talking to Wahn Klarin-yal, Detchal's mother, and Kroygharl, Klarin-yal's eldest son.

The comm officer had said, "He's enthusiastic enough, I suppose—but none of what he does works! Not even a little. He overheats components, trying to feed more power through them, crosses wires . . . By the time he's through, half of his toy has to be scrapped and reworked before it can be used again. Kroygharl, can't you *draft* him?"

Kinahran had heard the burly gray-and-white sigh, scraping claws absently against the floor. "He knows I'm blood kin. Even if he liked Security work, I don't think he'd let it show."

Wahn Klarin-yal had added sourly, "I think all this tech has gone to some people's brains—back when all Kintarans were grounders, you could have as many hunters as you needed. N'eetha was what you made of what you did, not trying to avoid the profession of everyone else in existence. He's probably running ahead of what he knows because Kinahran loves doing the basics and he's trying to out-n'eetha her."

To Kinahran's disappointment, she couldn't see N'balplar's response, and he hadn't continued to talk about her. "Well, I suppose I can bring in one of my immediate heir-technicians, and trade time with that one, instructing each of the keesolt individually. Maybe if he's forced to learn the basics, he will."

"And maybe," Wahn Klarin-yal had said, "we should just encourage him to join a hunter-ship and go shoot at Kaa on the borders. He'll draw the looks like his sire did, pretty lad, but I don't think he's got the brains for a clanship post."

Kinahran had been very proud of her eavesdropping, though—even more proud than the time, years ago, that she'd tattled on Detchal pushing Leln Dazran off cargo-crates. In that case, she'd had to explain that she wasn't tattling on the people *playing* in the cargo bay, away from the crèche-keeper's view, but on *Detchal*, for being a bully and making Leln Dazran cry. It had been nearly thirty days before Ta-Pera and Teecoli had forgiven her, since they'd gotten in trouble for sneaking out.

In this case, though, no one had found Kinahran out, and she hadn't gotten into trouble, and it had worked perfectly. Sometimes when she thought of it, she couldn't help but chase her tail and bite her toes gleefully. And she took care to work very, very diligently on the basics of comm-ops. She'd get to comm-design eventually.

\* \* \*

A few ten-days after that, the clanship got to Lellona—a Sparrial-discovered world with a few Sparrials on it, but basically uninhabited due to lack of mineral resources. It had thick jungles and flat plains, and mountain ranges poking up here and there for no reason that Kinahran could see, though Teecoli's mother, Scout Rallabree, tried to explain it to all of the keesolt in the crèche.

Kinahran, Teecoli, Kurah-ral, and Leln Dazran put their heads together in the back of the room. "I read about it when I was doing that tenday with K'rava," Kurah-ral whispered. "It's called a 'sti-kkkh' or 'srrhikh' or something."

"'Strri-ghk'?" Kinahran hazarded a guess. "With the letters ess, tee, rrr, eye, khay, and eee?" Kintarans had had no standardized written language of their own when humans had found their planet. Many human words—and their alphabet—had been adopted into Trade Kintaran. If there weren't any weird alterations in the text Kurah-ral'd read, she could spell it out.

Kurah-ral made squiggly patterns on the floor with her finger, thoughtfully. "Khih, 'strrighk.' It's where everyone refuses to work until they're given something they want."

Teecoli twitched her beautifully-plumed tortoiseshell tail, caught between her hind-legs to keep it from betraying their conspiracy. "Don't they get in trouble?"

Kurah-ral shrugged, both forepaws on her own tailtip. "If we don't ask for much, maybe they'll humor us more."

Kinahran wasn't sure, but she kept quiet, blue eyes darting to the holo on the wall, showing those delightful plains, those mysterious jungles . . .

Leln Dazran held his shining black tail in both his hands, washing it thoughtfully. "What if we offer to help?"

"Help?" the three females chorused quietly, all eyes suddenly on the younger boy.

"Help," he repeated. "We're here to pick up stuff—some plants and animals with medicinal properties, pretty pets and flowers, and any interesting rocks we can find."

"How'd you know that?" Kurah-ral hissed at him, her ears going a little flat. "Mother didn't say anything about that to me!"

Leln Dazran crouched down submissively. "They were talking about it some in Medical—Ta-Pera knows about that—and Ravehcroy said that K'rava was telling her about how it's good to trade things you just find, instead of only running cargos for other people. She said that was harder than just talking to people."

"So," Kurah-ral mused, gnawing at the idea and one finger. "We go on apprentice-strighk, and then offer to help gather stuff—chase animals and pick plants and rocks. And in exchange for this, we get what? More work?"

Teecoli washed both hands at once. "We offer to help half-days, and then we get to run around groundside the rest of the day!"

"Might work," Kinahran allowed.

Kurah-ral flicked her white ears. "We'll do it," she said decisively.

*  *  *

By the next day, nearly all the other keesolt had been coaxed or bullied into going along with the strighk. They crowded into the crèche-room, trying not to step on the younger keesolt, and shoved Ravehcroy to the front.

The black and white apprentice Negotiator looked petrified, staring into her teacher's face.

K'rava looked amused and curious. Gently, he told Ravehcroy, "All right, you're obviously supposed to negotiate something. Now, take a deep breath and let yourself be calm. Even if it's something you're not sure you approve of, it's not your idea—it's someone else's. Fur smoothing down?"

Ravehcroy nodded, took another deep breath, and washed her mane back into place. Then she looked calmly at K'rava again. "Negotiator K'rava, we, the *Choosaraf* apprentices, think it is shameful and mean that we are denied the chance to play on the planet Lellona, which Scout Rallabree has said is as safe as Kintara. Because of this horrendous privation, we will refuse to do our apprentice-jobs until we are given shore-leave on Lellona." She stopped abruptly and wrapped her tail around her forepaws decisively, to show it was K'rava's turn.

K'rava nodded. "The words are a little unpolished, but the delivery is good," he said. Then, "You understand that this is a clanship, and even the keesolt are needed to do some things to ensure that we are all fed and housed and provided with the things that make life worth living." He gestured at some of the clutch-toys the more nervous keesolt were holding. "Perhaps some of you could go downside, helping the adults?"

"We are all participating in the strighk, and so we all want a chance to go downside and play, but we might do some hunting or gathering after we've been able to run and climb as we please." Impressively, Ravehcroy didn't have to put a paw on her tailtip to keep it from twitching with excitement. Her back-fur rippled a little, though.

K'rava looked thoughtful. "All of you, and you'll help three-quarters of the day, before you run off to play."

"Half the day, with play-times before and after," Ravehcroy shot back, both her ears—one black, the other white—pricked forward.

"Half the day, and help before, playing after. I think I can sell that to Wahn Klarin-yal, without getting you all in trouble for asking too much." K'rava added, in the face of Ravehcroy's confusion, "A good Negotiator knows her wahn's moods, and what she will and won't accept in a deal. If you're not sure, you'll have to ask her."

Ravehcroy ducked her head a little, then turned over her shoulder to look at Kurah-ral. The Wahn's daughter looked thoughtful, then nodded. Ravehcroy looked back to her mentor. "Khih, we will end the strighk now, and go back to what we're supposed to be doing. If the negotiation holds, we will not go back to strighk."

K'rava chuckled and bowed his own head, acknowledging the bargain.

As the keesolt left the room, hurrying to their various mentors, K'rava strode into their midst, wrapping a hand around Kurah-ral's shoulder before she could escape. Kinahran's curiosity over-rode her good sense, and she sidled closer from behind the pair. "You know," he murmured, "Wahn Klarin-yal was intending to do the half-day thing in the first place, as a surprise. Except she'd intended that there would be a day of play at the start, before putting you keesolt to work."

Kurah-ral's ears and tail went down in horror, but she rallied with, "Then someone should have leaked it to us. We did the best we could with the data we had."

"'We'?" he asked. "Who else devised this plan? Who got the others to cooperate?"

"I had help!" the tabby protested. Then her ears drooped again. "But I was the one who decided when the plan was done."

The Negotiator chuckled again. "Wahn-of-Keesolt, eh? Not bad, for a first try. You'll do better next time, but I'd advise you try a little data-gathering *before* you go on 'strrike,' khih?"

Ears going a little up, Kurah-ral nodded, and K'rava gave her a gentle shove towards the door. Then he turned, nearly tripping over Kinahran as she tried to get herself out of the way. She froze as K'rava looked down at her with his huge golden eyes. "Next time," he said, "you volunteer to gather information for your keesol-Wahn. Communications, Sensors, and Security are all starting places for one who gathers data quietly."

With that enigmatic comment, he went back to where the youngest keesolt were babbling questions.

Kinahran skittered out of the room, and finally decided that K'rava had implied she'd be a good spy. She looked herself over, thinking disgustedly, *Not with all this white fur, I wouldn't be. I stick out like a supernova.*

\* \* \*

Further negotiations between K'rava (now with Wahn Klarin-yal looming behind him) and Ravehcroy (with Kurah-ral and the other main conspirators clustered behind her) netted every keesolt a half-day of freedom on the first day, *before* they had to start giving the adults a hand. They could choose their groups, and would be accompanied by at least one adult.

With much discussion, the keesolt decided to group off by terrain they wanted to deal with first—plains, mountains, or jungle, or some combination thereof.

Kinahran cleverly picked a spot that had all three, in the hopes that she could get some running, climbing, and pretty-rock finding in at the same time. Happily, her mother decided the location would be worth putting a temporary base at, so whoever chose that spot would have it longer than the first half-day.

For adults, they got Pilot Lelocha, Scout Rallabree, Coli-nfarin (and thaso), K'rava, and Lelocha's gray-furred son, Dazaterl, who was eleven Terran years old, and a junior Security member. He said that he'd rather be called 'Terl, since it was shorter.

For keesolt, it was Kinahran, Kurah-ral, Detchal, Leln Dazran, and Lineelin, a gray and white Security apprentice two years older than

Kinahran, who only showed up after finding out 'Terl was with that group. Kinahran would have preferred Teecoli or Ta-Pera, so there wouldn't be so many boys, but consoled herself that it meant less of them to sigh after K'rava.

The first half-day was wonderful. The gravity was just 1.12 gees, a little lighter than ship-grav, but not enough to make everyone clumsy, and the air was only a little thin. Half the time, they didn't need the little breather-masks they'd been given. Kinahran's thaso sister had a tiny one that she wore whenever she wasn't nursing, though.

They even started their work early, walking through the beginnings of jungle and picking flowers or interesting plants to take back to Coli-nfarin for testing. Rallabree made them wear gloves to do that, but that was only sensible—and it let them dig up roots without getting their fur dirty.

'Terl and Lineelin caught some little merfah-like things, except they had purple-brown fur and green-brown scales both, and nasty sharp teeth that got buried in the boys' gloves. Kinahran was impressed—especially by 'Terl, who was a bit short and stocky, but a very pretty gray all over. Kurah-ral was impressed too, but she insisted that Kinahran help her catch live things as well. They managed to get one animal, like a fast, vividly dark-green Terran-turtle with a long brown tail, and found a dozen of the furry lizards sunning themselves on a fallen log, but Detchal came and spoiled their hopes by thundering up and trying to grab a handful. He got one, but the rest scattered, and it turned out he'd broken his.

Coli said that broken ones were all right, since they could be killed and dissected, but Kinahran knew her mother was just humoring Detchal, and hissed, "Oh, great, now he's going to start breaking *everything*," to Kurah-ral.

Finally, after it had gotten dark—even for night-sighted Kintarans, since there was no moon for this planet—they were called back to the shuttle for a meal.

Detchal piped up, "Is the fur-merfah I caught edible? Does it taste good? Can I eat it?"

Coli smiled and juggled her white thaso around to nurse her on the other side. "Not really, I don't think it would, and nih. However, I think I found some interesting biochemistry in it that might make a soothing ointment, with a little tinkering. They have little poison glands in their mouths, which would make you itch for a day or so, but if it's heated..." She went off into descriptions that nobody but maybe Leln Dazran understood.

After the meal, Rallabree and K'rava explained that they wanted a group to go into the nearby foothills and look for rocks. Since they hadn't played in the foothills yet, all the keesolt volunteered. Rallabree nodded. "All right. I'll stay behind, with 'Terl—another group of keesolt are going to be coming here and hunting for more plants and animals, and I want something a little more systematic this time."

"And if you want something done," Terl quoted, "gotta do it yourself."

Kinahran sighed, which was unwise because Detchal noticed, and teased her about it for nearly an hour after they were supposed to be asleep in the shuttle's cargo-bay. It took Lineelin threatening to bite him to shut him up.

\* \* \*

The next morning saw K'rava and the keesolt in the sun-warmed foothills, industriously picking up rocks to see if they were pretty, and scanning them to see if they were useful. Gray-backed, white-bellied Lineelin was the best at that, even better than K'rava, though Leln Dazran came close. Lineelin also lived up to his name—"Here-There"—by somehow being in six different places at once. Kinahran would show him a rock, then shift her gaze to pick up another, and suddenly he'd be over by Kurah-ral, and the next moment he was beside Leln Dazran, and the moment after that he was threatening to whap Detchal for trying to steal one of the pretty rocks in Kinahran's pile.

It was enough to make one dizzy, above and beyond how high they'd gotten.

K'rava, who'd been a crèche-keeper for *ages*, just meandered around slowly, keeping an eye on everyone and picking up the occasional rock. He was the one who noticed Lineelin's perch—a dead, stunted tree that gave access to a small cliff hollow he was scanning—was about to fall.

With a snarl and a beautiful spring, the Negotiator landed almost in the middle of the tree and grabbed Lineelin, throwing the boy towards the main part of the cliff. Then he tried to jump, but the shock had torn the tree's roots out entirely, and K'rava vanished down the steep incline in a shower of dirt and rocks and tree, scrabbling indignantly and yowling.

Lineelin was almost caught in the rockslide as well, but Kinahran and Leln Dazran managed to grab his arm and fluffed-out tail and drag him to safety.

Kurah-ral was already skittering down the path they'd climbed, her own tabby tail as fat as a foreleg. After a second trying to decide if the new ground was stable, Kinahran bounded after her cousin, and the other keesolt followed.

It was a long way down before they discovered where K'rava had fetched up. Fortunately, not much seemed to have fallen on top of him, though he was lying very still in a pile of rock and dirt and bushes. He didn't respond to their calls, either. Kinahran stifled a wail of dismay with both hands over her mouth and nose, and saw Kurah-ral's white ears going down and nose start to run just a little.

Leln Dazran nervously tested the pile of rock and dirt with an ebony forepaw, then started easing himself onto it. "Don't make any noise," he said. "Or jump around. It's flat here, but we don't want to set anything off above us!"

"I think that's snow-avalanches," Lineelin said dubiously—but quietly. He edged onto the dirt-pile as well, just in grabbing range of Leln Dazran's black tail.

Detchal was starting to follow, when Kurah-ral grabbed him by his tabby tail. "You stay!" she hissed. "You're a fat-footed klutz! Kinahran, you go with them! I'll keep fat-foot here from doing anything dumb."

Detchal hissed at his sister-twin and tried to bat at her. Kurah-ral hissed back, "No noise! No jumping!"

The fraternal twins were still exchanging insults as Kinahran carefully followed the two boys. Skittishly, she stayed a body-length away as Leln Dazran got to K'rava and began checking for pulse. Lineelin pattered carefully around the area, testing the stability, then motioned for Kinahran to come a little closer.

She didn't like it when she did. K'rava was sprawled on the mess, his beautiful cream-and-apricot fur covered in dirt—and blood in his mane. Worst of all, one of his forelegs seemed to have developed an extra elbow, and the other forepaw was bent very wrong. It made her forelegs and hands hurt just looking, and she squeaked, covering her eyes and crouching.

Kurah-ral hissed something loudly. Leln Dazran called back quietly, "No, he's alive. But his forelegs are both broken, and something hit him on the head, and I'm scared to move him because I don't know if his spine is hurt!"

Kurah-ral spat. "Then use your scanner, idiot!"

Leln Dazran flinched a little, but dug out his scanner and started fiddling with it. After a while, frowning mightily, he said, "I *think* I've got it set right, and it looks like his spine is okay . . ."

Kurah-ral looked up at the steep incline that K'rava'd come down. "Well, we can't leave him there."

With a sigh, Leln Dazran flicked his ears in assent. "I know." He looked up at Lineelin and Kinahran. "Come on, help me straighten him out a little, *carefully*. Then we can pull him to the path in a straight line."

Kinahran shuddered at the thought of having to touch one of K'rava's broken legs, or his bloody head, but she helped with his hind-legs. Lineelin, to her gratification, looked nearly as nervous. Leln Dazran's tail was bottled

163

up, like everyone else's, but the rest of him didn't look scared at all, except a little when his pupils went wide.

Finally, they had their Negotiator dragged back to the path, and Leln Dazran started plundering their small first aid kits. "He's breathing good, and has a good pulse," the little black-furred keesol explained. "So I want to get some kind of splint on his legs before I try giving him any Quickheal. At the least, I hafta set them straight, or they might quick-heal crooked."

Kurah-ral nodded and directed everybody else to hunt for straight sticks. Detchal, released from her damp-palmed grip, washed his tail indignantly for several seconds, then set off into the mess to pull branches off the tree that had carried K'rava down. Kinahran and Kurah-ral found another tree, and used their pocket knives and claws to wrest some limbs off it.

Leln Dazran's ears went back dubiously as he looked at the various offerings, but he selected a few from each pile and started using bandages from their first aid kits to tie the splints in position.

Lineelin was already washing K'rava's blood-and-dirt matted mane, spitting out dirt and scrubbing his tongue off with the back of a hand every few licks. Kinahran would have helped, but there really wasn't enough room.

Kurah-ral was washing her own fur. She looked up. "Kinahran, where's a comm?"

Detchal pointed to a bit of cracked plastic in the rockfall. "K'rava's got busted."

"I've got one," Kinahran volunteered, digging in a belt-pouch. "It's not very long-range—it's only fit to talk from one end of the clanship to the other—but I could probably get through to the shuttle if I worked real hard at it."

"Do it," Kurah-ral ordered, and Kinahran sat down to try.

It didn't work—instead of picking up the shuttle's identification transponder, Kinahran was just getting noise. She was about to try to send something anyway, when she realized what that noise pattern was. She'd never seen it before in real life, but she'd read about it in some of the textbooks. "Kurah-ral," she quavered. "I can't pick up the shuttle. Someone's *jamming* it!"

"Jamming it?" Lineelin asked quietly.

"Jamming!" Detchal said scornfully, overriding the Security apprentice's question. "You just mean you can't get through!"

"Well, *you* try!" Kinahran spat back, shoving the comm at him.

Lineelin intercepted it, backing up to keep it out of the other boy's hands. "Show me the pattern, Kinahran."

She went over and did so. He peered at it. "Khiiih . . . I think that's a jamming-static pattern, all right."

Detchal snarled and grabbed the comm. "You're both crazy. Who would want to jam the shuttle?" He started pushing buttons, near randomly. "I'll try to broadcas—"

Kurah-ral hit the comm out of his hand. "Nih! You'll do no such thing," she hissed. "Kinahran's Communications, and Lineelin's Security. If they both say it's jamming, I'll believe them! And only pirates would want to jam a clanship!"

Everyone shuddered, though Detchal tried not to show it. "I'm Comm too," he protested.

Slyly, Kinahran corrected, "Comm-*design*—you skipped ahead in the textbooks, so I'd be left behind, and even if you could build a comm, I don't think you can read 'em as well as I can."

Detchal fluffed his fur and growled at Kinahran, but didn't claim to be k'eetha by knowing everything she did.

Kurah-ral took her personal transponder off from around her forepaw, where she'd tied it. "We have to get rid of our tracking transponders. If the shuttle's being jammed, then they can't trace us by them, and the people doing the jamming might be able to." As everyone else—even a reluctant Detchal—shed their transponders, Kurah-ral continued, "We'll bury them in the rockslide a little, and then we'll take K'rava to a better hiding place, and cover up the tracks, and . . . and decide what to do next then."

Lineelin took the transponders and went back to the rockfall pile, wedging them in various places amidst the rock and dirt, while Kinahran retrieved her comm.

Biting at his black tail-tuft, Leln Dazran felt along K'rava's spine. "I'm pretty sure nothing's broken there," the apprentice medic said, "but we still want to keep him as straight as possible."

They wound up giving K'rava the Quickheal and waiting five nervous minutes for it to take effect. Lineelin scouted a little way down the trail, and sprinted back saying there was a side-trail that went around a bend and under an old, old rockfall-arch. It wasn't a cave, to confuse sensors for real, but it was better than being out in the open.

Then they carefully got K'rava on top of Kurah-ral, Lineelin, and Kinahran—with Detchal and Leln Dazran holding the Negotiator's upper torso straight—and the three keesolt started walking semi-sideways down the path. It was slow, heavy going that they couldn't have done in full grav, and they left a lot of footprints. But they got to the quasi-cave Lineelin had found. He slithered out from under K'rava and checked the place out a bit better, shoving at the rocks to see if they'd hold. Then he came and wriggled back under the adult and they went in.

Leln Dazran took Kurah-ral's belt pouch and emptied it out to make a flat pillow for K'rava's cheek. Then he used her little flashlight to peer into his patient's eyes. "Concussion," he said, finally. "I don't think he's going to wake up for a while."

Kinahran and Lineelan looked at Kurah-ral. The Wahn's daughter was brushing the dirt off her white-socked forepaws, getting ready to wash them. "I guess we'll have to send someone to see if the shuttle's still there," she sighed.

"I think we should hole up here and ambush any pirates who come for us!" Detchal countered.

Kurah-ral glared at him, breather mask dangling around her neck but washing forgotten. Her ears were back. "You've been watching too many holovids! We need to find out if the shuttle's still there, and if it is, we can get an adult! Coli-nfarin's a doctor; she can help K'rava! Then we can worry about who's doing the jamming. Who knows—maybe it's one of the other keesolt, playing with the shuttle transponder!"

"You think you're the Wahn, don't you?" Detchal snarled as he pushed down his breather mask, lashing his tail. "I'm her keesol too, just like Kroygharl!"

"But your plan is *stupid*!" Kurah-ral spat back at him.

Kinahran thought that Detchal's plan was dumb too, but she didn't say anything. She backed away, towards K'rava and Leln Dazran. Lineelin looked at the siblings and backed away as well, to behind Kurah-ral. Everyone's tail was lashing, even Leln Dazran's.

"Tooth and claw, brother?" Kurah-ral hissed softly. "We're not barbarians anymore. We use cunning. No one's standing behind you. If you win, the others will drive you out."

Detchal glanced in the direction of K'rava and the other two keesolt. Kinahran folded her arms and stared back at him, ears pressed down. She felt Leln Dazran's tail thumping against hers as they tangled in mid-lash.

Detchal looked back at his sister, ears folded down tightly. He snarled, crouched, seemed to hesitate a moment.

"Give it *up*, brother!" Kurah-ral told him.

He sprang at her, and there was a sudden yowling and spitting, with brown-tabby fur flying everywhere. Kinahran and Leln Dazran put themselves between the brawl and K'rava, and so did Lineelin, after a moment.

The security apprentice looked at Kinahran. "I've got a mini-stunner," he said breathlessly. "I could try hitting him with it."

166

Kinahran shook her head. "You might hit Kurah, and then we'd have to gang up on Detchal to make him not be stupid. You can risk it if he starts winning, maybe."

Lineelin let his mouth hang open into a hunter's grin, watching the tangle of fraternal twins. "Kurah's been apprenticing in the basics of everything on the ship—that includes Security and unarmed combat. Kroygharl's been teaching her personally."

Kinahran's blue eyes went wide. She blinked at him, then turned back to the fight.

It lasted long enough that she was starting to get worried, but suddenly Kurah-ral did something weird and twisty with her body, and she was in the air while Detchal was flailing around on his back, and then she was landing on his upper torso with all four paws.

Kinahran could hear Detchal's explosive WHOOF as his lungs got compressed by his sister's full weight. She winced, wondering if this meant he'd have broken ribs for Leln Dazran to have to bind up somehow.

Kurah-ral sprang off and to one side, letting Detchal cough and struggle for breath. One of her white ears was ripped nearly in half down the middle, and there were clawmarks all over her, including one that went down her cheek, just missing an eye, and bled freely. Kinahran was appalled. That had been a *serious* challenge, not their usual keesolt-spat.

Lineelin moved to Kurah-ral's right hand, mini-stunner produced from wherever he'd had it stashed, aimed at Detchal. Leln Dazran hovered with a first aid kit in his black hands, yellow eyes fixed on the horrible tear in the Wahn-daughter's ear.

"Yield, Detchal," Kurah-ral panted. "I could have torn your throat out then. You can feel the scratches."

Kinahran looked, and saw that while his ears were only a little notched, there were three bleeding scratches along the side of his neck—not deep enough to kill, but Kurah-ral'd obviously had the chance. Kinahran gulped, feeling her nose going white with shock. That had been a *serious* serious challenge, and Kurah-ral had maybe considered making it to the death, even if she wasn't even quite Kinahran's age!

"Fine," Detchal gasped. "We do it . . . your way . . . Get ourselves all killed!" He rolled all the way onto his stomach and panted, not trying to get up.

Kurah-ral turned away and ducked her head so that Leln Dazran could hold the pieces of her ear together and put a plastiskin patch on the inside. She said, "Lineelin and Kinahran will go to see what's with the shuttle. The three of us will stay here with K'rava and deal with whatever happens. I'll do sentry-things, I think. If we're not here when you two get back, well . . ." She thought a moment. "We'll have to meet somewhere."

Lineelin suggested, "That big rock at the bottom of the pile, the one we thought looked like the spot on Ravehcroy's back. At sunset."

Kurah-ral nodded. "Khih. That's good. That's where any of us will meet, if we're separated."

Kinahran swallowed and added, "If there's somebody bad there, then what about the stream in the woods, somewhere before the little waterfall? We can start and walk upstream till we get there, and nobody could watch all of it, right?"

Lineelin nodded at her, and they both looked to Kurah-ral for confirmation. She nodded, and looked wistfully at Lineelin's mini-stunner. "I don't suppose you've got two of those?"

He looked at it thoughtfully himself. "You take it—you've got to defend K'rava, and we can just run away." He handed it over. "Come on, Kinahran—it's going to be a long walk, and I want to mess your fur up."

Kinahran sighed and muttered, "I just *knew* that was going to happen . . ."

*   *   *

On the way down, Lineelin grabbed up dirt, mud and moss, rubbing it into Kinahran's fur and mane. When they started getting real plants, he broke off those and streaked their sap on her as well, following it with more dirt. Kinahran couldn't help herself. Her nose started running, and she whimpered, "Nih, nih! It's nasty-dirty! Oh, my fur, my fur! My n'eetha white fur!"

Cruelly, Lineelin said, "It's not n'eetha on the *Choosaraf*. Your brothers and sister are all white too."

"It'll be n'eetha when I leave the *Choosaraf*, to go start my own clanship," she retorted.

He looked startled at her. "You're going to do that?"

"Maybe." She looked at him and sniveled again. "It's not fair! Why don't you have to get *your* white fur dirty?"

He looked at his white legs and chest, and crossed his eyes trying to regard the white that went up his chin a little. "I forgot," he muttered, starting to streak gunk onto himself. Kinahran helped him. Enthusiastically.

*   *   *

After they were camouflaged, they stalked into the edges of the jungle, rather than going through the plains. It took longer, but they were able to hide better. When they were within looking-distance, Lineelin had them climb a tree.

It was a good choice. Once they'd gotten high up, they could see the shuttle. Lelocha and Coli-nfarin were sitting in front of it, with Coli's white thaso in a basket on her back. Another adult was there as well, but there were five or six gray tabbies on the ship, so they weren't sure which it was. As they watched, 'Terl and Rallabree and another two adults came into view with several of the keesolt—Kinahran spotted Ta-Pera and Teecoli, as well as some keesolt who were closer to 'Terl's age than hers.

Distressingly, a couple of bipeds were in the group, at the rear. They were hard to make out at first, since they were wearing camo-outfits designed to take advantage of the floral coloration on the planet. Kinahran squinted, and thought the bipeds might have bulges like sidearms, and maybe one had a rifle slung on its back?

Lineelin was squinting too. "Camo-faced," he muttered. "No way to tell if they're Halloth or Human. No tails, though."

"What if they're natives?" Kinahran said breathlessly.

"This place was surveyed by Sparrials—they'd have scented natives, betcha." He broke off, peering at the group around the shuttle.

The keesolt, with drooping tails and ears, were getting herded into the shuttle, with some of the adults (including Lelocha) following. The tabby, Rallabree, and Coli-nfarin stayed, forming a small half-circle around one of the bipeds, staying about a meter away from him. The other biped had faded back towards the trees, and it was harder to see that one.

There was some talking, that even their keen Kintaran ears couldn't decipher; Rallabree made annoyed gestures, the alien made some hand gestures back, and finally Rallabree and the tabby sat back, ears folded and arms crossed. Their tails lashed.

Coli-nfarin stepped forward, till she could have reached out and touched the biped. Her ears were mostly up, and only the tip of her tail twitched. Eventually, the biped made some reply, and turned away with a beckoning motion.

As it walked towards the other one and the treeline, Coli-nfarin followed, thaso still on her back. Rallabree and the tabby went into the shuttle. A moment later, the second biped appears—sans rifle—and went into the shuttle too.

As they watched, the shuttle turned on its flying lights and took off, heading for orbit.

"Hostages?" Kinahran squeaked. "They took my mother and baby sister for hostages?"

Lineelin's ears were flat down against his head. "Maybe. I can't think why else we'd have seen what we saw. I just wish I knew what race that was—I'd feel a little better if it had been Humans."

"We've got to rescue my mother and sister!"

"We've got to get back to Kurah-ral and the others, and find some place to hide K'rava. Even if these people don't have scanners of their own, they'll be able to use the *Choosaraf*'s now. Your mother looked like she was insisting on going along, so I don't think she's in instant danger."

Nose running, Kinahran meekly followed the security apprentice down the tree, and they made their way back to the hiding place. They could move a bit faster now, since they knew the path they'd taken.

As they got closer, Lineelin sent Kinahran on ahead while he tried to erase their tracks, wrapping a bundle of grass around his tail as well as taking clumps of brush in his hands. Forgetfully, Kinahran tried to wash her shoulder, but had to spit several times to get the nasty camo-tastes out of her mouth. She loped ahead.

She wanted to run up to Kurah-ral and yowl, *It's pirates, it's pirates! They've got my mother!* But she thought about what K'rava had said to her the other day, about getting *information*, and about the lessons N'balplar had taught, to make sure his apprentice comm officer wouldn't exaggerate wrong . . .

She rushed into the little hollow and looked around. Leln Dazran was crouched to one side, over K'rava's still-unconscious form, and cried, "Kinahran!" Detchal stalked from the other corner, sulkily.

A moment later, Kurah-ral came slithering down through a crack in the tumbled boulders that Kinahran hadn't seen before. "Lucky I was on watch," she said. "Or you might have gotten jumped on."

Detchal sniffed at Kinahran's fur. "*Yuck!*"

Kinahran snorted and barely kept herself from trying to wash. She scratched between her shoulder blades with a hindfoot instead. "Lineelin's coming, after he gets rid of our tracks. We climbed a tree and saw the shuttle—the other group of keesolt got here, and I guess their shuttle just dropped them off, 'cause there was only ours. But they weren't alone—there were a couple of bipeds in camo with them, and I think they made everyone get on the shuttle and go away, with one of the bipeds on board. The other one went off somewhere we couldn't see, into the jungle, with—with my mother and baby sister!" Her nose started running, and she swiped at it, which made it worse since the dirt and gunk on her fur burned and stank.

"Did anybody look hurt?" Kurah-ral asked.

Kinahran blinked, and tried to think. "Niiihhhhh," she finally said. "Nobody limping, no burned fur. But the aliens were walking behind everybody else, so maybe they could have shot them. I think I saw sidearm holsters, and I'm pretty sure one had a rifle on his back."

"But," added Lineelin as he showed up, "nobody had weapons drawn. So while I can't think what else could be happening, they don't act *quite* like pirates."

"They're just trying to trick us!" Detchal stated. "We gotta go catch one and take his weapons and shoot them all!"

Kurah-ral twitched her ear, flinching away from the torn one. "They might be homesteaders," she said doubtfully. "If they hadn't filed a claim, or filed it so recently that we didn't know about it, then we might be trespassing on their colony-world."

"What about their clanship?" Leln Dazran asked. He was still crouched over his patient, occasionally washing K'rava's cheek or shoulder. If K'rava stayed unconscious much longer, Kinahran thought, the Negotiator was going to be seriously damp around the edges.

Kurah-ral suggested, "They could have been dropped off here, or their ship might be making a trip back somewhere to get more people. They might have been worried about *us*, if they're just colonists. There are Kintaran pirates."

Detchal sneered. "You're just looking for some excuse not to do anything! You wanna sit here and let them catch us all and sell us to *Kaa*!"

Kurah-ral hissed at her brother; almost involuntarily, he edged backwards a little with his tail trying to curl against his body. Kinahran was impressed, and hoped this behavior persisted when they were back on the ship. *If we ever get back on the ship*, she thought, nose starting to run again.

Kurah-ral was giving instructions again. "Lineelin, find some place where you can watch the rockfall our transponders are in. The rest of us are going to have to get K'rava somewhere further from there."

Lineelin nodded. "I'd say the jungle, but I don't think we've got the time for that if they've got access to *Choosaraf* shuttles now. You'd probably do better scouting along in all these boulders, and see if you can find a real cave. And ditch all the power-cell stuff somewhere, 'cause their radscanners could pick it up."

Kurah-ral nodded bleakly. "You get started. We'll find somewhere else and if you can't find us, then we'll meet either at the rock or stream, 'bout an hour past sunset."

Lineelin gave a final nod and turned away, loping out of their hiding place with his grass-covered tail dragging across his tracks.

* * *

Though they looked hard, they didn't find much better than another old boulder-fall, with openings on both sides. Kinahran followed a pseudo-path that led from the back of the 'fall, and put their power-cell driven equipment in various nooks and crannies along it, hoping that it would be less noticeable to scanners than if it were all in one place.

Then she went back to wait, and scratch her itchy, filthy fur and lick her pawpads and palms—the only parts of her that she could bear to taste.

They all had ration-bars in their belt-pouches, like good little spacer-keesolt, and the growling in their stomachs finally prompted them to gnaw at the pseudo-meat things. Detchal finished one of his first and tossed the wrapper away. Kurah-ral almost did the same, but then looked at the wrapper in her hand. She stuffed the plastic back into her belt-pouch. "Somebody get Detchal's—if we have to move again, we don't want to let them know we were here. If anything, we might want these to lay a false trail."

With an admiring look, Leln Dazran went to retrieve the tossed trash. Kinahran wouldn't have tossed her wrapper so casually anyway, since she was using it to hold her food—her hands, even palm-washed, were nothing she wanted touching what she ate.

Afterwards, they passed around the canteens that Coli-nfarin had insisted they carry. (K'rava's had cracked, and Detchal'd drunk all his water even before the accident.) Kinahran was glad her mother had been worried about dehydrated keesolt.

Kurah-ral was still looking thoughtful and upset, despite the food and water. Finally, she said, "We have to plan what to do if we're found."

"We fight!" Detchal said. "We fight and kill them, or die glorious deaths!"

"Ugh," said Kinahran. "You're not *serious*, are you?"

He washed his shoulder, which she took to mean he wasn't sure himself.

Kurah-ral shook her head. "No. We don't do that. If they've tracked us down, then they'll be armed and ready for a bunch of keesolt. If they find us . . . If they find us, we try to run away and escape."

Leln Dazran snuffled. "But what about K'rava?"

A grating, beautiful voice said, "What *about* K'rava?" The Negotiator opened one eye and twitched.

"Oh! K'rava!" Leln Dazran cried. "Don't move! Your spine may be hurt!"

"I think all of me hurts," he muttered, subsiding while Leln Dazran helped him drink a little from a canteen. "What happened?"

They explained, mostly all at once until Kurah-ral whapped everyone else across the ears. ". . . and we don't know if they're pirates or not," she finished.

"Ahhhh." K'rava closed his pain-haunted gold eyes again. (Kinahran sighed, wishing they had more Quickheal.) He said, "You can't take the chance. You're right, keesol-Wahn. If they come, you must run. But try to take Kinahran's comm with you—then, if they are not pirates, I can contact you. I think I know enough of the *Choosaraf* family tongue to tell what is going on without them knowing exactly what I say."

Kurah-ral thought about that, then flicked her un-harmed ear in assent. She hadn't mentioned her brawl with her brother.

"Oh, don't go back to sleep," Kinahran said as K'rava's breathing started to even out again.

Leln Dazran pulled up one of the Negotiator's eyelids. "I think he's unconscious. But his pupils are reacting better to the light, I think, so I guess that's okay."

"Ohhhhhh." Kinahran bit at a forepaw pad.

*       *       *

It was full dark by the time they heard something, on the trail below them. Kurah-ral looked from Kinahran to Leln Dazran, and waved Kinahran forward, handing her the ministunner—the one bit of powered equipment they'd kept.

Kinahran hunt-crept out of their shelter, close to the wall, and low to the ground. They'd been sitting in dark shadows, so even the starlight was bright to her eyes. Not as bright as it could be, but . . . She shifted her breather-mask down and caught a whiff of scent—acrid, paint-like stuff—and saw people moving along the trail. There were a few more gravel-scuffing noises.

Kinahran edged back into hiding. "'S bipeds," she said. "Camo-painted, maybe. Smells bad. Can't tell species. Looks like they're on our trail, though."

Kurah-ral's white ears folded down. "Then we've got to get away." She looked at K'rava, and Kinahran heard the Wahn's daughter snuffle a little.

"We can fight," Detchal hissed. "How many were there?"

"Urrrr . . . Five, six maybe?"

"If we get the drop on them . . ." Detchal purred.

Kurah-ral lashed her tail. "We only have one stunner!"

Leln Dazran said, "We might be able to get their weapons. I could hide in that niche, and try to grab one if somebody else caused a distraction."

Kinahran said apologetically, "I know running is smart, but I don't want to leave K'rava like this."

Kurah-ral's tail drooped in defeat. "Nih, me neither. Kinahran, you go get your comm, and hide up there —" she pointed to a place they'd seen earlier, that took a jump only a Kintaran could do easily. "We'll set up an ambush. Run away if it looks like we've all been shot or captured."

Kinahran nodded and handed the ministunner back, then skulked up the trail.

The jump was scarier in the darkness, especially since she had to make it quiet. The crunch of dirt and stone under her claws sounded awfully loud to her nervously rotating ears. Waiting was even harder. Finally, she saw one of the bipeds discover the tumble of boulders. It crept in, saying something quietly.

There was a sound of a stunner, a yowl that sounded like "idiot!", and some scrabbling. Two more bipeds dashed in after the first, and there were more stunner-sounds, louder this time. Then there was scrabbling again and two shapes came racing out of the rockfall, up-trail. Starlight gleamed on Kurah-ral's white ears and mane as she followed her brother's flight.

Kinahran backed away from the edge of her perch as the two made the leap. Detchal went pelting away down the other side, but Kurah-ral paused long enough to say, "Dazran's stunned. Come on!"

The trio raced away, into the night.

\* \* \*

After a long time running, they came to a stop, panting in great lungfuls of the thin air. Detchal's breather mask looked like it had a crack, but was probably still concentrating the oxy in the air for him.

Kinahran tried to slow her breathing, holding her mask tightly over her nose and mouth. When she wasn't feeling so dizzy anymore, she asked, "So what *happened??*"

Kurah-ral kept a wary eye on her brother as she explained, "One came in, talking in Human-speak. I'm not sure what it said, because Detchal jumped at it and tried to use the ministunner on it. Then some more came, and were about to shoot at Detchal, and I think Leln Dazran made a grab for one of the drawn weapons. There was some stunner-fire, and Detchal ran, and I couldn't see anything of Leln Dazran, so he was probably stunned." She took in a deep, ragged breath, nose glistening wet in the starlight with her repressed sobs. "And K'rava was still unconscious, of course."

Detchal took his mask off and started washing his shoulder. "We're better off without the thaso," he stated.

Kinahran laid her ears back. "The 'thaso' was our only medic," she pointed out. "Now we've just got us, and Lineelin, if he hasn't gotten caught. At least he can probably hit what he aims at with his stunner."

Detchal lifted an arm to try and get at his elbow. Kurah-ral's white and patched ears went down. "He dropped it," she stated flatly.

"He *what?*" Kinahran let her own ears go back and down. "Idiot!"

Detchal snarled at both of them.

Kurah-ral levered herself up. "We don't have time to deal with all that. We're supposed to meet up with Lineelin now. Detchal, you take the rock. Kinahran and I will go by the stream. We'll find him quicker that way."

Kinahran nodded. "And I can mess up *your* white fur, Kurah!"

The Wahn's daughter looked at Kinahran with her pale ears folded tightly back. "You've been *waiting* to do that, haven't you?"

Detchal had gotten up and padded off. *Almost* out of earshot, his mutter drifted back. "I *said* white was an icky color!"

\* \* \*

Lineelin wasn't at the stream. Kinahran and the newly-dirtied Kurah-ral crept up to the waterfall, filled Kurah-ral's empty canteen, and then slunk back down, sniffing the breeze carefully.

"We said rock first," Kinahran pointed out.

"Khih, but I was hoping that it would be too open. We've wasted enough time here. Let's go see if the aliens caught Detchal."

*I hope they did*, Kinaran thought, but didn't say it. Instead, she asked, "You said one talked Human? Do you remember any of what it said?"

Her friend rotated her ears back and frowned. "Nih, not really. Maybe something like, 'halloh,' but Detchal jumped it too quickly for it to say more."

"Figures."

\* \* \*

They skulked towards the rock, lying flat whenever they could and doing little hunt-creeps, with their bellies brushing the ground, and even their hands silently pattering against the dirt like the six-legged bloodfangs did on Kintara. They worked their way downwind, and carefully pulled aside breather-masks to taste the air.

Detchal, as dusty and tired as either of them, was obviously there. After a moment, Kinahran could make out his tabby mottling next to the boulder. For a moment, she couldn't smell Lineelin, but then she caught some of the nasty-sap scent from a breeze across her nose, at an angle that wouldn't have gotten her subtle odors anyway.

"I can't scent Lineelin," Kurah-ral muttered.

"I can—smells like dirt-stuff."

"Oh, great, maybe he's cyber-augmented or something." The other girl flicked her tail once, and led the way towards the rock.

When they were almost there, Lineelin stepped out of a shadow and put his forepaw on Kinahran's tail. She gave the tiniest of squeaks, and Kurah-ral paused to glance back.

Lineelin said, "Good, you covered your white. I was hoping you'd think of that."

"*I* thought of it," Kinahran grumbled, twisting back to take her tail in her hands and yank it out from under the security apprentice's foot.

"Whatever. Let's get somewhere less open. I think those aliens have night-goggles."

*   *   *

Lineelin led them fairly deep into the jungle, until they came across a fallen tree—a huge one, that had torn up enough ground around its roots that they could creep in and curl around each other.

"We can't stay like this long," Lineelin muttered. "It's good visual cover, but we're prime targets for a stun-rifle, all packed together like this. Now, this is what I saw—about ten, maybe twelve bipeds showed up at the bottom of the cliff, where we stashed the transponders. They dug them up, along with K'rava's broken comm, and started scanning around. They're scan-happy, and I don't think they noticed our trail then.

"Half of them went walking back down, the other half stayed around and were calling in Human-tongue. Stuff like, 'Keesolt, come out! You're not in trouble! Was someone hurt? Can we talk to Karravha? We want to help you!' And they couldn't even pronounce K'rava's name right. Then they started calling *our* names—but they weren't getting them very right, either. Finally, they started talking to themselves, and *they* walked away, down the path.

"I hung around, then started looking for a way to get on the trail again without risking them spotting me or being able to bracket me between them. That's when I spotted the other group, six, I think, heading up the trail. I shadowed them for a little bit, but couldn't find any good places to hide except in a tree where I could see the base of the trail.

"When they showed up with Leln Dazran all limp and being carried, I got worried, but the rest of you weren't there. Then I heard an aircar go by overhead, and I figured that they were going to airlift K'rava out or something. So I hung around in the tree until it was pretty clear the rest of the squad wasn't coming back by foot, and then I figured I'd check out the rock first, found Detchal, you two showed up, and now we're here."

Kinahran stuffed her fingers in her mouth, then spat them out again as she tasted dirt and sap, shaking her head to try and dislodge the nasty flavors. "I hope Leln Dazran's all right," she whimpered.

Detchal snorted, but Lineelin overrode whatever snide comment the other boy was about to make. "They were carrying him pretty careful—maybe they hit him with Morphazine. Detchal said you lot tried to fight, and even one of us keesolt weighs 'bout as much as the average biped."

Kurah-ral sighed. "I hope you're right. I don't like that they wouldn't have tried to calm him down and talk to him, though." She snuffled quietly. "Oh, I want an adult."

"They're all on the ship," Detchal muttered darkly, eyeing his sister with his ears back.

"Mother isn't," Kinahran pointed out, picking dead roots out of her mane. "The aliens—Human, maybe—have her, and my thaso sister."

Kurah-ral washed her palms rapidly. "If we keep skulking around here, we're going to get caught. Without K'rava, we've got a lot less to lose by trying to sneak up and find out what's going on."

Detchal snapped at her wounded ear, but she jerked out of range. He growled, "Sneak up, find out, pfft! We have to make an *attack*! Something bold, daring, unexpected! We need to get Aunt Coli out of their clutches!"

"You're crazy," Kurah-ral muttered. "If we start by fighting with them, we only find out that they fight when attacked. If we sneak up and listen, then we can hear what they talk about and maybe get some clues if they're pirates or people who have a right to be here."

"Coward," Detchal snarled.

"Idiot," his sister hissed back.

Lineelin reared up on his hind legs and batted at each of them with his forepaws. "We can always do both," he pointed out once he had their attention.

The fraternal twins flicked their ears, but settled back down. Kinahran let her breath trickle out of her. They didn't have time for dominance-spats anymore, especially when Kurah-ral felt guilty for letting K'rava and Leln Dazran be captured.

Sulkily, Detchal asked, "You got a plan, *Se-cur-i-ty?*"

Lineelin hunter-grinned at him. "I got *two* plans, comm designer. One for you, and one for me. Kurah and Kinahran get to decide which they want to do for themselves, but I think we need at least one each."

Kurah-ral tilted her head, ears to the sides for a little while, then put her ears forward. "Okay, Security. Talk."

"Well, when I was spending all that boring time in the tree, I did a lot of thinking . . ."

* * *

"Here's the perimeter," Lineelin murmured. Kinahran slid to a stop behind him and hoped that Kurah-ral was less scared than she.

Kurah-ral had the comm, and was going to broadcast with it, as a distraction. When the aliens homed in on her, Detchal was going to try to jump them while Kurah-ral abandoned the comm and either helped Detchal or hid herself, whichever seemed most useful.

Meanwhile, Lineelin and Kinahran were going to creep up and spy on the alien camp.

"It has to be within walking distance," the security apprentice had said. "And walking distance for *bipeds*, probably Humans. In this gravity, they won't want that to be far."

Detchal had wanted to know what was wrong with the grav, but they'd ignored him. Lineelin'd explained he thought he could find the alien camp, and Kinahran had instantly volunteered to go with him, saying, "I know lots of languages, Human and Halloth and Mmsar and all, and my *mother* is there!"

Now Kinahran was wondering if she'd made the wrong choice. Surely Kurah-ral was more graceful than she, better able to keep up with the determined Lineelin.

"How come you're so good?" she whimpered softly as he sniffed around for the acrid camo-paint smell.

"I dunno," he muttered back absently. "Maybe it's genetics."

"Your mother's in Security?"

"Nih, she's in with the Scouts. I think maybe my sire's in Security. My ears are set almost the same as Kroygharl's, and he's old enough."

Shyly, Kinahran offered, "My brother could do a gene-sequencing, if you wanted, and you could find out for sure."

"Nih, not for a while. It may be n'eetha to know a sire, but it's not normal. It'd feel icky, 'specially if he didn't want to know about it."

"Oh." He was right—it was strange to think they were cousins directly instead of just clan-cousins, as the matrilineal lines of descent went.

"Maybe when I'm not a keesol anymore. Haaaah, there's the sentry." He hunkered down and Kinahran followed his example, slitting her eyes so they wouldn't reflect starlight, and moving her breathing mask down so she could scent what was happening.

There was indeed a biped patrolling along, several body-lengths away. It was almost as quiet as a Kintaran, but they could catch whiffs of its acrid paint occasionally as it passed upwind of them. Lineelin waited for several seconds after the sentry had gone by, long enough for Kinahran's hindquarters to start trembling in suppressed frustration, before he raised up and led them in a fast hunt-creep straight ahead.

Twice, he paused and carefully stepped over something that Kinahran could barely see until she was nearly nose-to-nose with it—a wire of some kind, set at just above her ankles. She supposed that a biped, who couldn't hunt-creep with eyes and nose just above the ground, would have been more likely to trip over it and make a noise.

Then they halted again, with a camouflaged tent right in front of them. Lineelin's ears went down flat for a moment and his tail twitched in annoyance. But he led Kinahran around it, and they got to a spot where they could scent that they were surrounded by aliens. The pair of Kintarans sniffed deeply.

"Humannn?" Lineelin breathed, almost directly into her ear.

It tickled, and she twitched her ear several times to clear the tickle out while she nodded. The acrid-paint odor was strongest, but the scent of Human did seem to be there. Kinahran felt a little better.

She stayed hunkered while he looked around, trying to spot a good tent to spy on. It was pretty quiet—a little too quiet, really, for the local wildlife seemed to have a good idea where the alien camp was, and weren't hanging around—which was good for Kintaran ears to sift through the wind-sounds for voices.

A familiar murmur drew her attention, and she patted Lineelin's nearest hindpaw, pointing at one of the larger tents. When he brought his head around, she breathed, "Mother!" into his ear and watched while he twitched that ear and nodded. He led the way again, heading towards the downwind tent and oozing past all the others (and their set-up lines) that were in the way.

They'd almost gotten close enough to make out words—there seemed to be an alien in the tent with Coli-nfarin—when he froze again. Kinahran froze too, and watched as a biped sentry loomed out from behind a tree. It started heading their way. She felt her tail try to bottle up, even with all the gunk rubbed into it. She looked to see where Lineelin was, but realized that he'd crept off somewhere while she was trying not to panic.

The alien didn't seem to be aware of her, so she just stayed frozen and prayed for protection by the spirits of her foremothers—Pilot Ch'ichat, Shaman Neeri, and all the others whose names had been forgotten in the days before spaceflight.

It almost worked. Though the sentry didn't turn away, it did seem to be about to go right past her. Until it stepped on her tail. She couldn't help the tiniest squeak of pain and protest, nor the reflexive twitch as she tried to tuck it against her body as she obviously should have done earlier.

The biped looked down at her looking up at it, with a moment of almost equal shock, she thought. Then it moved a hand to get at something in its belt. It didn't make it. It didn't even finish the beginnings of its verbal alert. Over a hundred Human pounds of security apprentice leapt from darkness and slammed the biped to the ground.

*That*, unfortunately, made some noise, since it thrashed around and gasped, like Detchal had done when Kurah-ral landed on him. Lineelin jerked the rifle off the sentry's back and shoved it at Kinahran. "Here! Get your mother!" He stayed sitting on the biped's back, almost calmly looting its belt of pistol-weapon and a knife.

Kinahran grabbed the rifle, managed to sort out which way to point it, and raced to the tent-entry, bursting into its bright interior with practically no plan whatsoever.

There was a Human in a chair-thing right in front of her—he didn't have the face-paint of the others, though his clothes were still camo, and she could see his brown-tan skin and the brown of his hair. She scented her mother and the white thaso strongly as well, but ignored that to aim her weapon at the Human. The red targeting-laser dot jittered a circle on his chest like a chase-toy and the light seemed to dim and flare as her pupils went narrow and wide with agitation.

"Yooo let m'mara gho!" Kinahran demanded, blanking on the Human words for "my mother" at the last instant and using Kintaran instead.

"Kinahran!" she heard from one side, but her hunt-focus kept her from looking at anything but down her rifle. She absently realized it was a laser-rifle, not a stun-rifle. The dot jittered back and forth.

The Human slowly raised his hands, away from the belt he wore and the holster attached to it. "You're . . . Moonfur?" he asked softly, like a crèche-keeper when a thaso was sleeping.

One part of her mind couldn't blame him for wondering, with her fur all gummed up and dirty like it was. She laid her ears back tighter. "Let m'mara go!" she said again, lashing her tail.

She heard her mother sigh, and say in that same quiet voice, "Generral Embil, I *told* you that jamming would be considerred a pirrate activity. Little Blackfurr told you they thought you might be pirrates, and I a hostage. You should have let us brroadcast."

The man nodded very small. "Apparently. I hadn't thought a group of seven and nine year olds would be so hard to track."

Kinahran's nose was running with frustration. "Mother," she whimpered in Kintaran. "What is going on? Why don't you want to be rescued? Do they have the thaso?"

General Embil leaned to one side a little, with the bouncing dot wavering around his camo'ed chest. "Your safety's still on," he remarked, hands still raised.

Kinahran started to scrabble at the rifle with one hand, but her mother reached out and held her wrist gently. That broke the hunt-concentration enough that she could look at the small doctor. Coli-nfarin had the thaso curled up against her, on a sleeping bag, and was smiling, ears up. "It's all right, my thaso, my keesol, it's all right. They're Human military, playing military games in a high-grav place. It's hide and seek for them, and they don't want the other Human players to know where they are. They showed us valid ID, and they've been polite. It's only this continent they're on."

Kinahran let the laser-rifle droop and licked at her nose. "Not pirates? Not slavers?"

"Nih, they're legit, as far as we can tell." Coli stretched and tried to wash Kinahran's cheek, but made a face and scrubbed at her tongue with one hand.

From outside, there were noises of several stunners, and Lineelin called, "Kinah! What's taking so long? They're onto us, no time!" There was more back and forth with sonic weapons, and some Human voices raised in puzzled shouts, as well as a call of, "We're not gonna hurt you, kid!"

Coli was obviously chewing on a snicker. She looked at General Embil and the Human nodded. In the family dialect, Coli called out, "Lineelin, is that you? Everything's fine. They are not pirates."

Kinahran added, quaveringly, "Mother's okay, and I'm okay, and the thaso's okay. And I guess that means K'rava and Leln Dazran are okay too, 'cause Mother said she'd talked to Leln Dazran."

"Well, tell 'em to quit firing at me an' I'll quit shooting them," he returned belligerently.

Coli touched Kinahran on the shoulder, and she startled a little. Then Kinahran turned to the General and said, "He ssayss he sstopss sshooting them when they sstop sshooting."

The Human blinked, much like a Kintaran. He had put his hands on the arms of his fabric-stool again. He called out, "Cease-fire! Let the kid come into the tent so he knows his friends are all right!"

"He took down Lighthart and Wu!" came an indignant female voice.

Kinahran watched the Human's brow-fur go up, but the General just replied, "Let him come in anyway. We'll have more stunner-practice drills later."

Lineelin came sidling into the tent shortly after, backing partway in before turning and covering the General with his stun-pistol. He was limping on one hind-leg, just a little, so maybe they'd stunned him there. Seen in artificial light, his fur looked a real mess—grimy, sticking out at all angles, with twigs and things caught in it, especially in the parts that'd used to be white. Kinahran wrinkled her nose and laid her ears back in revulsion, then realized that her whole body probably looked like that.

His own pupils were flaring and contracting, trying to reach the point between near-terror and normal light-requirements. He glanced at Kinahran, still holding the rifle though its muzzle was resting on the ground. Then he looked at Coli and the thaso, and back at General Embil. Finally, the security apprentice lowered his stunner (which had been keeping a red targeting dot squarely on the middle of the Human's chest, with hardly any jittering at all) and came out of his defensive crouch.

"You might have broadcast something," he complained in Kintaran.

Coli burst out with the chortles she'd had clamped in her teeth. Kinahran translated to the General, "Herre-therre ssayss you could have brroadcasst ssomething!"

The man harumphed. "I didn't know that a couple of pre-teens could sneak into the camp without getting stunned . . ."

While Kinahran translated the harder words to Lineelin, who was a little too agitated to remember all his lessons in Human, Coli replied, still giggling, "They arre not prre-teen for Kintaran childrren, Generral. They arre closerr to a Human child at twelve orr fifteen. And we arre meant to be hunterrs."

"And I'm security!" Lineelin added, after he'd gotten the gist of all that. Kinahran translated it, and then asked, "But wherre iss, wherre arre Kurah-ral and Fat-toess?"

"Fat-toes?" the General echoed quietly, then shook his head. "Hold on . . ." He tilted his head in a way that Kinahran associated with implant communicators and subvocalization. "If you mean the little diversion pair, I've had a report that my people stunned one, and are trying to talk another out of a tree without getting hit by falling tree-branches. I suppose it can't get much noisier, so if someone could please persuade the last one that everything's all right?"

Coli looked at Kinahran. "Moonfurr, you arre the comm experrt herre. Can you worrk a Human comm?"

Kinahran narrowed her eyes at the General. "May-be," she said in Human. "I'd need to ssee it."

He rolled his eyes and pulled out a comm from a belt-pouch, punching something into it. "It's set to the right frequency. You just need to talk."

She flicked her ears at him and made sure it was on. "You talk first, mother," she said, handing it to Coli.

Then she translated some more for Lineelin while Coli talked Kurah-ral down from the tree.

". . . and apparently you stunned two of them," Kinahran whispered while Coli at last returned the comm to the Human. "You're a good shot!"

"Aw, it was easy," he said, licking a palm proudly. "I was able to smell their paint, and hear 'em shooting at me—hardly had to do more than poke the stunner 'round the tree! But I don't think they were taking me very seriously. They should have tried to flank me, but they didn't. I think they didn't expect I'd be so good." He leaned over and licked Kinahran's shoulder absently, then started spitting and scraping at his tongue.

Her nose began running again, and she wailed in Human, "I want a baaaaaath!"

\* \* \*

When the shuttle came to pick them up the next day, the reunion was almost everything that Kinahran could hope for. Clean and white again, she sat with the other keesol around K'rava's stretcher. The Negotiator, with Coli-nfarin in close attendance, was alert, and there were light, high-tech splints on his broken forelegs. Both the adults had let the children know that while the Human military folk were less than pleased by all the trouble that had been caused, the clan was highly amused. "And," Coli had added, "General Embil says it will do his group good to know that a few alien keesol were able to penetrate their security perimeter. He said it will make them sneakier in the long run."

The General was also there, and when the shuttle landed, he stepped forward to greet Wahn Klarin-yal personally and talk about apologies and restraint and diplomacy things like a Negotiator. Kinahran didn't notice much, keeping close to her mother so she didn't get trampled. Kurah-ral and Detchal were hanging back (Kurah-ral's ear was still patched, and whenever anybody asked her about it, she just stared back coolly), waiting for their mother to finish talking, but the others' parents had shown up—Leln Dazran's sire, Detts Dazran, was washing the boy all over, while Lineelin chattered happily to his mother.

Kinahran wasn't terribly surprised when Kroygharl came out of the shuttle and took possession of Kurah-ral and Detchal, him being their half-brother and all. He also washed Lineelin's ears once, apparently approving.

Kinahran *was* a little startled, though, when *her* brother showed up! Daaral-fara headed towards them—ruffled Kinahran's mane in passing, exchanged licks with their mother, and then he . . . he turned to K'rava and said, "Sire . . . I was worried about you."

The Negotiator smiled at Kinahran's brother. "I was worried about us all, for a little there. So she finally told you?"

"Nih, I did the gene-sequencing myself, last year."

K'rava chuckled. "And only now you say. Why am I not surprised? N'eetha you may be, but you do keep your secrets."

Kinahran just gaped, looking between her *brother*, her annoying *brother*, and the beautiful K'rava. Her ears drooped as she realized that their eyes were the exact same shade of gold, and their ears were tipped at the same angle, and their noses were close . . . She saw that Kurah-ral and Detchal were standing near enough to have heard, and their eyes were big, their ears pricked forward.

"Moooootherrrrrr," she wailed, burying her face in Coli's shoulder. All their adventures, rescuing K'rava, dealing with the maybe-pirates-who-weren't-after-all, getting her *fur* all disgusting—all for *nothing*! The adventure-tales wouldn't last five minutes in the face of the knowledge that Kinahran's BROTHER was the son of K'rava! Now everyone was going to be sighing over *Daaral-fara* and talking about how wonderful he was, and Kinahran just wasn't going to be able to *stand* it!

"Is something wrong, keesol?" K'rava asked, looking bemused.

Kinahran could only look at his lovely golden eyes, wonder what her own genes might show, and snivel at him, ignominy snatched from triumph. "I . . ." she quavered. "I am *not* going to be a spy," she said finally. "It gets my fur all messy."

Then she stalked off.

Behind her, she heard her brother—her suddenly-famous brother—ask, "What was that all about?"

She flattened her ears so she couldn't hear any answers and ran, bumping into Lineelin.

He grabbed her shoulders and washed her ear himself. "See what I mean about knowing sires?" he asked quietly. "Takes all the fun out of life."

She glared with her ears folded, then repented with a sulky "Yeah," pulling her ears upright. If she were nice to her maybe-bloodkin Lineelin, maybe he could get her an introduction to 'Terl, who really *was* a very pretty gray all over.

# Glossary

**Halloth**—Not a Kintaran word; the race-name for a humanoid, mammalian alien-race using haemocyanin in their blood; their coloration spans from indigo to aqua.

**Kaa**—Not a Kintaran word. Kaa are a snake-like reptilian race: raiders, slavers, and pirates (technically "privateers" of the Kaa Empire) at the fringes of "civilized space." They eat sapient species—including other Kaa. To Kintarans, they smell *delicious*.

**Keesol**—child. Plural: *keesolt*.

**K'ee'tha**—Also spelled K'eetha. The same as, or "baby-same" or "copycat." Connotations of immaturity.

**Khih**—yes or yeah.

**Lomerf**—a falcon- to eagle-sized, warm-blooded, scaled, egg-laying animal with four legs and wings, native to Kintara.

**Mara**—mother

**Merfah**—a rabbit-sized, warm-blooded, scaled, egg-laying, six-legged marsupial, native to Kintara. Yummy to Kintarans.

**M'mrah**—Biological sire. Kintarans are rarely concerned with paternal accuracy.

*Mmsar*—Not a Kintaran word; the race-name for a warm-blooded, reptilian-seeming alien race.

**Mrah**—father-figure, not a biological sire.

**N'ee'tha**—unique; connotations of adulthood and status. Also spelled *N'eetha*.

**Nih**—No, or nope.

**Thaso** or **Thasolis**—baby. Plural: *thasot* or *thasolist*.

**Wahn**—captain, or leader.

# Names

**Ch'ichat**—Roaming Feet, Kinahran's grandmother, deceased.

**Choosaraf**—First-Star, the clanship.

**Coli-nfaran**—Ferncloud. Her name could also be translated as Feathercloud. Kinahran's mother.

**Daaral-fara**—Golden-warm, with a sound-pun on "Sun-warm." Coli-nfaran's second son.

**Dazaterl**—Gray Boy, Lelocha's son, a young security-kint on the *Choosaraf*.

**Detchal**—Fat-Toe, Klarin-yal's youngest son and Kinahran's cousin; a child on the *Choosaraf*.

**Detts Dazran**—Big Blackfur, Leln Dazran's father.

**Kinahran**—Moonfur, Coli-nfaran's eldest daughter, and third child.

**Klarin-yal**—no translation; Captain of the *Choosaraf*, and Kinahran's aunt.

**K'rava**—Like-a-purr, the *Choosaraf*'s Negotiator, and part-time babysitter.

**Kroygharl**—Noise-mouth, Klarin-yal's firstborn son, chief of Security.

**Kurah-ral**—Pink-head. (Probably referring to appearance as a newborn.) Klarin-yal's youngest daughter, a child on the *Choosaraf*.

**Leln Dazran**—Little Blackfur, a child on the *Choosaraf*. His father is Detts Dazran.

**Lelocha**—Skinny-hand, or Dainty-foot. A pilot, and one of the many part-time babysitters on the *Choosaraf*.

**Lineelin**—Here-there, a security-apprenticed child on the *Choosaraf*.

**N'balplar**—Without-a-Tail, the *Choosaraf*'s main sensor officer, also in charge of communications gear.

**N'Chee**—To Roam Far, the *Choosaraf*'s chief engineer.

**Neeri**—No translation in Trade Kintaran; possible implication of doing something differently. Kinahran's great-grandmother, deceased.

**Rallabree**—No translation in Trade Kintaran; possible implications of "standing while moving," such as a pilot with a neural implant might do. A Scout/pilot on the *Choosaraf* and Teecoli's mother.

**Rarroriah**—Brave-white, or Courageous White. Coli's firstborn son.

**Ravehcroy**—Purrs-Loudly, a child on the *Choosaraf*.

**Ta-Pera**—Blue-stripe, a child on the *Choosaraf*.

**Teecoli**—Tortoiseshell Feather, daughter of Rallabree. A child on the *Choosaraf*.

A team of three space explorers—two humans and a bipedal, red-furred caprine Parjan—in a galactic future in which all of the species are equal (so far), come to a planet that they name Paradise. The native Paradisers are furry, looking roughly like large bipedal, split-tailed fennecs, but so what? There are 1,745 intelligent species in known space, and most of them are more furry-looking than the humans, with fur, tails, claws, and muzzles; and they all get along. The Paradisers, however, are rare hermaphrodites.

The space explorers, led by Sovil Sartun, a human Zulu, are welcomed as gods, and asked to resolve a political dilemma of the Paradisers that is leading toward civil war. SciControl's policy is to not get involved in native disputes, especially with unknown species. But the Paradisers seem friendly, and it is flattering to be taken as a god. What harm can it do?

Will the Paradisers' hermaphroditic nature make a significant difference?

# Kings and Vagabonds

## *by Cairyn*

"Furry again", Galzaan Brakh sighed. "Now, could anybody please explain to me why it seems to be totally impossible to find a nice colony of pretty hairless tailless humanoid girls anywhere!"

"They probably hide when they see your scout probes coming", Sovil Sartun mumbled. He tried to focus on the far-range instruments. "Now, could you please feed the AI some biological data?"

He could understand Brakh's frustration. Three centuries of cheap science fiction had built a certain image in the collective mind of human folklore: Man was the most important species in space, and every worthy foe or good friend in the universe was at least humanoid. Well, some bony ridges along the nose or forehead, or a greenish complexion, or a finger more or less was acceptable, but any race that deviated from the common standard was either supposed to be exotic decoration, or especially nasty enemy, or dumb slave of the humanoid masters. Masked as equal ally, of course. Even with the boom of completely computer-generated motion pictures, the public still was fed pictures of glorious humans battling evil cat-people.

Of course, that was back when people still had time to put motion pictures together. Or watch movies. Or operate computers just for fun. The movie industry was somehow a secondary consideration in the time after the Global Shock, on a planet with half its land mass either desert, or radioactive, or biohazardous. Mankind was still trying to gather the shards, when the first Alliance scout vessels landed.

They did help with the ecological recovery, and they brought a technology with them that finally allowed the scattered survivors a decent life. But they shattered forever the image of Man as the center of the cosmos, and they proved all the science fiction trash wrong. There were no human-shaped aliens out there, no scantily-clad space girls, no dark-robed sinister Emperors.

Oh, the majority of the known one thousand seven hundred forty-five intelligent life forms had two arms and two legs and a head, being humanoid in some sense of the word. Almost ninety percent were carbon based, adapted to an environment similar to Earth before the Global Shock. But they had fur. And a tail. And claws. And a muzzle. And they looked generally very much like the enemy humans had fought in movies for centuries.

To add insult to injury, they were technologically advanced, more civilized and annoyingly helpful. Mankind immediately split into two fractions: those who accepted the aliens—the furry—as they were, and those that built up a grudge in their hearts for being forced to accept the charity of otherworldlers, or at least watched the development of Earth's culture with a growing dissatisfaction.

Man was no longer the center of anything. Copernicus, Galilei, Newton, Einstein, Shou Wong and Clanbourne-Maxell had successively and gradually moved mankind out of the focus of things, showing it its true place somewhere among many other species in a somewhat remote spiral arm of the galaxy. But many humans did not want to share, and the Anti-Fur Faction (AFF) represented a much stronger political movement than most people were ready to admit.

There were others, however. Those who admired the furry. Those who went to the stars.

Sovil Sartun was one of them, a descendant of twenty generations of space travelers. Only a few years after the discovery of Earth by the Alliance, hundreds of thousands of humans left their homeworld, settling somewhere in space where they felt more welcome than in the increasingly hostile climate of Earth. They prospered there, and became the part of humanity accepted and liked by the furry. The Diaspora—Mankind scattered throughout the vastness of space. They were the token humans that made the Alliance forget that there was another humanity out there, a hostile, brooding humanity on a reclusive backwater planet called Earth.

Sovil Sartun was a Zulu. At least that was the part of his heritage he chose to concentrate on—like most spacers, he was the result of five hundred years of interracial marriage. He was tall, muscular, in peak condition—the very image of a fierce warrior.

To his chagrin, his complexion was not a handsome deep black but just a muddy light tan, and his eyes showed traces of the Asian part of his lineage. But he couldn't do anything about his genes, and thus he concentrated on shaping his body and mind into the very image of the invincible Spaceman, an endeavor he had been more successful in than anyone had believed possible. His mental powers, his nerves of steel and his ability to empathize had made him the leader of the First Contact Team 10 of the small expedition.

Galzaan Brakh, on the other hand, was his exact counterpart. He was of Earth, and although he was not xenophobic, and curious enough to venture into the big unknown, he carried around the heritage of a world where mankind still lingered in the very center of the universe, where the old prejudices were cherished and welcomed. Brakh was white, middle-sized, not exactly handsome, dark-haired and a few pounds above normal weight.

But while he was rather ordinary to look at, he possessed a feverish mind, an eidetic memory and a strong will. He was one of the chosen few who still understood the complex symbolism of artificial intelligences (a rather flattering term for the ultra-fast abstract data processors) and were able to answer the three fundamental questions of computer science: How do I get the damn thing to do what I want? Why didn't the damn thing do what I wanted it to do? and Whom can I blame for the damn thing's crooked programming?

Brakh's human-centrism and nonfur chauvinism were a constant source of secret (and not-so-secret) annoyance for the third and final crew member, Cherenofalyje Racthurianna—Cherac for her friends (and everyone else who was unable to pronounce her name). Cherac was a Parjan, one of the furry. Her goatlike appearance had been the target of Brakh's jokes in the beginning, but when the novelty wore off, the tech specialist turned towards more rewarding topics.

However, even Sartun sometimes felt at odds with Cherac. It was easy to close one's eyes and to imagine the Parjan as human, just for the sound of her voice—she could imitate any accent with uncanny precision, and she had a pleasing soft and dark baritone. But on turning around or opening one's eyes, looking at her...

Parjan had a long snout with slits for nostrils, not even remotely cute. Other Furries had fuzzy round heads and a distinct 'stop' on their muzzles. Humans responded to them because the Furries met their instinctual baby pattern. Parjan did not belong to those species. Coarse fur covered all of their body. Four sizeable horns grew from their foreheads, and the ears were in continuous twitching motion.

And the fur was bright red... with yellow facial patterns and black spots on hands and feet.

There were people who claimed Parjan looked like devils.

Sartun knew better. Cherac was social, helpful, sometimes even funny. There was nothing devilish in her character.

Only when he turned around suddenly, and stared into two horizontal pupils in alien eyes, he wondered… Humans depended so much on appearances, and even more on their own prejudices and their self-created mythology. If even he, born and bred under foreign stars, had difficulties accepting a furry as she was, just because of his own centuries-old images of half-forgotten nightmares, then how could he expect humanity to ever acquire a seat among the furry as equal species?

There was too much fear involved. Too many misunderstandings. People were seeing too often what they wanted or expected to see, instead of what was there.

All that blindness…

\* \* \*

The little, wedge-shaped translight spacecraft *Hadaga-14* approached the planet in free fall. The scout probes were sending data, continuously updating the AI core. Thirty minutes to critical distance; thirty minutes until Sovil Sartun had to make a decision.

There were no energetic emissions anywhere, no sign of space travel, no spacecraft anywhere in the planetary system (at least not in the primary rotational plane).

Once again, Sartun stared at the image an earlier scout probe had transmitted. It was a spaceship, standing on something like a landing field. There was no spaceport in view, just a flat square of barren earth. No living beings in sight either. And the image was not exactly crystal clear. But it was a ship, and where there was a ship, there had to be spacefaring intelligences.

The image had been taken during a routine surveillance mission, by an unmanned deep space probe. Those probes were sent out regularly. The galaxy was big, and there were hundreds of worlds to explore; too many to send manned ships to. The probe AI's results decided whether a world was worth the trouble or not.

However, sometimes the results were ambiguous. On the world in question, the probe had not found any sign of a technologically advanced civilization, yet sent home an image of a spaceship. Settlers who had fallen back into primitivity? Remains of stranded traders? Leftovers from a first contact situation that had turned bad? Without a team on the scene, the researchers' curiosity would never be satisfied.

Obviously, that curiosity was strong enough to make SciControl—the Diaspora's science branch—send out the *Hadaga-14* all the way. If there were signs of advanced space travel out here, SciControl wanted to make a first contact.

Twenty-five minutes. If they hadn't found the spaceship until then, or any other proof that the local culture had already been contaminated by advanced intelligences, they were required to stay in a far orbit. Primitive societies were not to be tampered with; a big hands off for research teams. The Fourth Rule of Protection.

Not to mention that primitives did not offer much of interest for SciControl; 'not worth our time', as one high-ranking officer had put it. Sovil Sartun did not like that attitude; to him, it looked as if the only thing the Diaspora was searching for was new weapons technology. That was an unsettling thought; the last thing the Zulu wanted the Diaspora to become was another outpost of human hatred and warmongering.

Yet he had never found the strength to leave SciControl's deep space research. It was what he was born for.

Twenty minutes.

"Coherent data available", the AI announced. The tiny short range scout probes, only some centimeters in diameter and cloaked in invisibility fields, had collected enough data for the AI to assemble—and, hopefully, to make sense of. Almost undetectable, especially by primitive life forms, they could gather their information up close, spying on the private life of this world's inhabitants. About nine hundred of the minispies had been released two days ago, on first approach.

It was an effective method of acquiring the language, customs, habits, and social structure, even biological data. It was also pretty intrusive, as Sartun sometimes thought: not everyone might like a little flying spy in the privacy of his bedroom.

*What they don't know...*

But it was not what *they* knew. It was what the researchers knew.

Maybe it was efficient. But every time Sartun ordered the probes to be released, he got a queasy feeling in his stomach. One of those days, he just knew, they would discover a secret this way... a secret that had better stayed buried. Oh, then they would be sorry.

But it had never happened... yet...

Sartun sighed and forced his mind to return to the task at hand. "Give me a short overview."

The AI complied and presented images and data. For several minutes, they just studied the screens.

"That is not a spacefaring civilization", Cherac summed up. It was rather obvious. The natives had a civilization, more advanced than they had thought at first sight, but it was still far, far below high tech—even below industrial level, in a way.

But there was the ship. Sartun hit the stop button. One of the minispies had passed by the artifact, and sent some more images.

"So it wasn't just a mislaid file", Galzaan Brakh stated. "I almost thought the probes got mixed up. Look at that!" He pointed at some detail on the hull. "No corrosion, no weathering. The rain has not even washed the entry burns away. I guess the thing has been there no longer than, hey, a few months at best."

"The landing field is clean as well. No weeds." Cherac switched her pointy tail from side to side. "I'd say those natives have pretty regular contact with space truckers."

"With *what?*" Brakh grunted. "I wish you'd not talk in Parjan terms."

"Never mind." Cherac did not sigh, but her lips and nostrils always betrayed her true emotion.

"So, it's decided", Sartun concluded. "We can make first contact. The Diaspora has found another promising world."

"Profitable is the term here, I think." Brakh shook his hair violently. "Although I doubt we'll find much of worth."

Something still bothered Sovil Sartun. "AI, can you zoom in on those border markings?" He pointed at some poles that lined the landing field. They were out of focus and rather far away. Irregularly shaped conical things topped the markings. Sartun could not see what it was. Without any native around, it was hard to guess sizes.

Of course, even when zoomed the image stayed blurry and inconclusive. A pity; the intelligence of the spy probes left a lot to be desired. They just followed a preset path, without curiosity or some sense of judgement. Nine times out of ten, they missed the truly interesting points.

Sartun had a hunch that this was not an example of the rare tenth time.

\* \* \*

They aligned their course and went into low orbit around the planet, still gathering data while going through the information they already had.

Sartun gave the biological data a quick glance. Furry, as Brakh had stated initially: Yet another species that did not lose its body hair in the course of evolution, and retained a protruding muzzle. And a tail. That pattern seemed, indeed, more common throughout the universe than the evolutionary path that had made humans lose almost every hair on their body, and made their jaw recede over the generations, and had robbed them of their tails.

As far as Sovil Sartun knew, the Clanbourne-Maxell theorem explained why certain development patterns appeared with such a high probability, and why carbon-based oxygen-breathing lifeforms were dominant in this sector of the galaxy. It was much too mathematical for his taste, though; hyperfractal geometries and subspace meta-attractors were made for people like Galzaan Brakh, not for him.

The initial images, some of them still from the first probe that had prodded SciControl's curiosity, showed the natives only in blurry stills. One meter sixty tall on the average, two-legged, mostly humanoid. The arms were a bit longer than a Terran's, the chest had a barrel-like appearance, with a protruding chest bone.

SciControl classified the natives as species FG-22a. An artless name for a slender and graceful race, as the more recent scans showed. Brakh's probes had made some motion shots, sewn together by the AI in computer simulations to form movement patterns.

The feet of the natives resembled hands; maybe they had descended from tree mammals. Three fingers, plus thumbs, with four joints on both fingers and toes, made hands and feet appear slim and long.

A desert fox head with big plushy ears, a pointed muzzle and big, expressive eyes contrasted the tail arrangement: the tail was otterish with a broad base and conical form, but it split at half length into two separate ends that could be used as a prehensile organ.

Sensors indicated that the fur was soft and dense. A white, inverted zebra-like pattern covered the black pelt.

Species FG-22a possessed a lion's mane, running down across the back almost to the tail base. It did not cover the front side of the neck or the chest, but hair tufts grew on the shoulders, like a general's epaulettes. Those tufts were artificially colored by the natives, depending on their social status.

They wore little clothing, mostly functional, belts and loincloths, but there was a lot of jewelry around—earrings, necklaces, intricate pearl hairnets.

The most interesting fact was hidden from plain view, but of course the probes had scanned the natives' anatomy thoroughly. They were hermaphrodites, male and female at the same time, and fully functional in both roles. As a result, their society knew no stronger or weaker sex, and individual status was not based on gender but on social standing, guild membership, and personal influence.

Sartun tried to study the files on social behavior Cherac was preparing. Family life, well, that should be interesting... The natives knew some kind of relationship between two people, but there was a wide range of variation. In some, one individual dominated the other; in others, the partners were of equal standing.

They didn't have enough data to make extrapolations on long-term relationships. The customs of the natives included some kind of marriage. But who raised the children, and was that a role that was determined early on, or rather flexible? A pity they wouldn't stay long enough to do some real research, but a first contact did not include a permanent base on that world.

"Have you read the interesting parts yet?" Cherac asked. She peeked over Sartun's shoulder. "Oh, I see. Curious, isn't it? There are not many herm races around."

"Animal life is also two-gendered", the Zulu remarked.

"Oh phooey, who cares for the local fauna..." The Parjan blinked mischievously. "I say we should socialize a bit."

"Do we have enough data already?" Sartun frowned. A first contact with not enough preparation was a difficult thing.

"Don't tell me you want to stay in orbit even longer..." Cherac made a long face, something she was pretty adept in. "They are not hostile or xenophobic. They know spacers already. And they have some kind of planetary government, so we can talk directly to the head of state."

Galzaan Brakh looked up from his holomonitors. "Planetary government? Impossible; not with that kind of tech. Look at that; they are using ox carts! A planetary government needs some kind of communication system, and logistics. The highest form of technology I have spotted is a steam engine. What about mass media? What about public transportation?"

"Well, but they have sorcerers", Cherac claimed.

"They have... what?"

The Parjan shrugged, a gesture learned from the humans she was surrounded by. "They call it sorcerers. I'd rather use the term 'mutants'. Individuals with paranormal abilities. Telekinesis and teleportation. They form a guild of their own, and serve the king of Paradise both as messengers and transportation."

Sartun slowly shook his head. "I see you have named that world already."

"Your mythology, not mine", Cherac countered. "But it fits: a friendly planet. Green and lush, and not even spoiled by its growing civilization.

Have a look at the cities: not crammed like most pre-tech towns, but spacey, open and harmonic."

"I admit that the steam engines are pretty advanced—if you can say that of steam engines. Good mechanics too, employing wind and water power. Efficient." Coming from Brakh, that was high praise.

"On the other hand, Paradise has a strict guild system", Cherac stated. "The individual is restricted by a lot of customs and traditions. Rigid laws, and a rather static society. There are no wars, but some violence on the individual scale. I'm not sure what to make of it."

Sartun looked at the front screen, showing the planet in blue and green glory. Paradise… a dream of a lost innocent age. He wondered whether the world was aptly named. Most paradises showed their dark sides sooner or later.

Well, they would find out. That was what they were here for.

* * *

Spy probes had their limits. They could provide their translators with enough data to make communication possible by just observing and listening. But for a more thorough understanding of that world and culture, a direct contact was necessary. SciControl had established a protocol that favored an early personal meeting with the natives. It avoided misinterpretations.

After only a few hours of collecting data, Sovil Sartun decided to advance to the next level.

They had found out how the Paradisers called their planet and themselves, but since it was only another variation of 'the world' and 'the people' in the local dialect, Sartun decided to stick with 'Paradise'. Maybe it was only nostalgia, but he liked the ring of the name.

The *Hadaga-14* approached the landing field. It was the obvious choice for touchdown. Explorers could land about anywhere, including swamp ground or dense forests, but since the Paradisers had prepared this place, they would expect visitors from space to land here. Sartun wanted to meet their expectations as far as possible. It made first contact much easier.

There were Paradiser guards around who went off to alert the local authority as soon as they spotted the spacecraft. Sartun went down smoothly and slowly, giving them time to get comfortable with the notion of alien visitors.

He was surprised by the fast reaction. No sooner had the ship cut the engines, as a group of Paradisers materialized out of nothing at the edge of the landing field. One moment the spot was empty, the next moment at least twenty natives stood there.

Teleportation. Well, that should make things interesting for SciControl. As primitive as Paradise seemed, there was much more to find here than on any other backwater world Sartun had ever seen.

With abilities like that, the Paradisers might even make allies for the Diaspora.

"Hurry up", Sartun demanded. "They are already here!" He pulled the light protective spacesuit out of the closet; no way he would go out without an LPS to guard his hide. There were no compatible bacteria around, and the air was breathable, but that did not justify taking risks. The Zulu hurried to don the suit; the Paradisers were almost knocking at the door already.

"Uh, Sovil…", Cherac began.

"Not now. Tell me later, please." The sudden rush made Sartun nervous. Protocol. Finding the right words. First contacts were not a trivial matter. He had taken part in other first contacts before, but never one that happened so fast. Normally, the natives had to be wooed and coaxed before they even dared to show their faces.

Not here, though. The Paradisers were pretty confident, to the brink of boldness. They had assembled in front of the airlock before Sartun could open it, and waited.

Closing the LPS, the Zulu punched the buttons that opened the outer doors of the airlock. Cherac, in full gear, touched his shoulder. "Sovil, I think you should really know…"

"Tell me later, I said." Her insistence made Sartun a little grumpy. Didn't he have enough to think of?

They stepped out of the ship, into the light. The first thing Sartun saw was the tight row of Paradisers, watching his every move. The second thing was the row of poles lining the landing field. He had forgotten about them, and now got the first clear look at the conical things that adorned the stakes.

They were heads. Severed heads, belonging to some unfortunate reptilian beings. Some of them still stuck in space helmets. Those were no Paradisers. And it explained why the spaceship that had gotten their attention in the first place was still sitting here, without a crew, untouched.

The crew was not in any shape to fly.

Cherac cleared her throat. Sartun turned around.

"Tried to tell you", she said apologetically.

\* \* \*

"Are you good gods or evil gods?"

Sovil Sartun blinked. The translator worked, simultaneously recording speech and replaying it with only the small delay necessary to evaluate the words in context.

"Are you good gods?" the Paradiser repeated. "Or are you evil gods?" The natives had formed a circle around the newcomers, curious and fearless, although wary. Their leader was one of the tallest Paradisers they had seen yet, but even he had to tilt back his head to look at Sovil Sartun. He wore the most clothing too, scarves and bandannas and fluttering rags, and an impressive assortment of jewelry. In his hand he held a long ceremonial staff with iron mountings.

"We are no gods", Sartun started, "we are space-travelers. We come from a different world..." They had to know the concept already... or at least that was what he had thought. If they had killed the previous visitors instead of making contact, they might still be oblivious to the realities of space travel.

"Don't try to deceive me, god", the Paradiser interrupted him. "You fly in a god's ship, you wear god's clothing, and you look different from us. Thus, you are gods. The only question that matters is, are you good gods or evil gods?" The furry made a grand gesture with his hand. "If you are good gods, you arrive at a most convenient time. We will welcome you with a celebration. If you are evil gods, though..." He pointed at the row of staked heads with his staff. "Those gods were evil. They came with their god's ship to take slaves and to drown our world in fire. They did not know about our sorcerers, though."

"We come in peace and friendship", Sartun claimed. He did not like the thought of pronouncing himself a god, but he was aware that he could not dissuade them from the notion right now, so he decided to skirt the matter. Later on they could still talk about space travel and otherworldly civilizations. Right now, the most important part was not to annoy them. First impressions had to be favorable.

Especially when their unfortunate predecessors had become some sort of grisly decoration.

The Paradiser made some gesture with his ears, maybe the local form of nodding, and announced: "They are good gods!"

The other natives started to cheer. The translator, though, caught another remark from the leader, obviously not meant for the 'gods', but the delicate machinery translated faithfully. "...they better be... if they know what's good for them!"

Sartun began to suspect that these people had a very special attitude towards gods.

\* \* \*

They did not have to wait long for the celebration. Flower-adorned, elephant-like animals dragged two-story carts towards the landing field. The lower stories were open at the sides and laid out with rich cushions. Sartun recognized that the carts were technically as advanced as he could imagine without high-tech: generous spring suspension, rubber tires, two steering axles and brakes on all wheels proved that the cartmakers here knew their craft. The Paradisers urged the newly-appointed gods to enter.

The landing field was not far away from the planet's capital, the king's throne. The Paradisers did not use teleportation again, but relied on the animals to get them to the city.

The Paradiser who had greeted them first introduced himself as Lavandil, King of the World, Judge of All Life. He had residences all over Paradise—his sorcerers could carry him anyplace he was needed within a heartbeat—, but due to its significance, the landing field had been built at the site of the main palace.

This soothed Sartun somewhat. If the Paradisers attached such importance to the landing field, then the 'evil gods' were not the normal kind of visitors here.

"I put all my duties on hold, though", the King explained. "The arrival of gods is always more important than any kind of local struggle. The whole day is dedicated to you."

Soon, they had passed the outer city limits. More and more Paradisers assembled, ran with the carts, lined the streets. After a short time, thousands of natives celebrated an instant festival around the procession. Paradisers stood on the streets, peeked out of the windows, some had even climbed the roofs—a useless effort, because the second story of the carts was blocking the view at the gods anyway. Parents held their children high so they could catch a glimpse of the gods.

"We are very pleased." Sartun tried to imitate a local gesture of respect by slapping his hand against his chest. "We would like to learn more about you—and about the evil gods as well."

"There is a sorcerer waiting at the palace to explain everything to you. Just ask him whatever you want to know." The King nodded gravely; nodding here emphasized the meaning of a spoken phrase.

Apparently, the Paradisers were not very surprised. Everything—the landing field, the lack of fear, the preparations, the festival—showed that the arrival of gods was not uncommon.

Lavandil pointed at the crowd. "Show yourself to the public; people will want to see you in all god's glory."

Sovil Sartun, Cherac and Galzaan Brakh leaned out of the cart and waved, smiling but not showing their teeth (which might be interpreted as a threat).

Sartun wondered whether the Paradisers were naive enough to let themselves be exploited by space merchants, or whether they could meet otherworldlers as equals. Then he remembered the severed heads on the spikes and shuddered. The 'magic' of the Paradisers seemed strong enough, and they didn't like to get trampled on.

The serpentine path led up a vast hill crowned by the residence of the King. The castle was enormous; it covered an area of several square kilometers, and the central towers seemed to be more than two hundred meters high. Multiple walls surrounded the central buildings in concentric rings, but many organic looking outbuildings and wings spread over the area, covering not only the ground between, but also growing up the walls, lining the walkways, huddling against the giant ancient blocks. Little palaces, adorned with towers and gargoyles; bridges that spanned small lakes and meadows in graceful arcs.

The architects had left a lot of free space between the buildings: parks and stone gardens, flower beds and rivers mimicked the surrounding landscape. The whole area seemed to be built employing the principles of a Japanese garden, displaying all the important elements close together in a harmonic way, where every new look, every new position presented something hitherto unseen to the spectator.

Then the carts reached the innermost ring and the central palace. Parabolic arcs soared into the skies, terraced towers pointed at the sun. The roofs were covered with living grass, here and there fusing with balconies or even gardens. The style reminded Sartun of ancient East Indian temples. Here and there remains of old defense installments could be seen, but they were obviously no longer functional.

Even the inner rooms proved that the Paradisers regarded nature as an important architectonic factor. Water plays and lots of green places were integrated everywhere in the building.

The city had been beautiful as well, but only one building there had been as rich as the palace, showing an equal grandezza and boldness: a lonely tower at the other end of the town. Sartun asked Lavandil what that tower had been.

"The tower?" The King nodded and slapped the ground with both tail ends. "The residency of the Da'danji! Yes, he-she is the reason why your coming is appreciated so much. The next regular visit is not scheduled for many more months. And I fear..." He made a grunting sound that could be interpreted as a sigh. "I fear either me or Shedunje will get mad, or we start a war against each other. None of us wants to wait any longer. The Interpreters of the Law cannot come to a satisfying conclusion, and even the High Sages of the City Karacate are divided in the matter. The gods alone may decide whom he-she belongs to."

The translation 'he-she' was obviously a combination of 'he' and 'she' that was meant to reflect the double gender of the Paradisers. Sartun could only guess why the translator didn't use 'it' instead, but maybe the AI thought 'it' would imply some kind of neutrum—and the Paradisers were of *both* sexes instead of *none*. Since hermaphrodite species were rather uncommon even among the furry, there were no general appropriate translations available, only obscure local terms which were no better in the context.

He had to wait some more for answers to his questions. That was one of the problems in first contacts: every answer immediately raised more questions, until a complete analysis of the society had been done. Until then, curiosity had to wait. The most pressing matters had to be answered first.

They were led into a hall where a sorcerer, clad in white wrappings, almost looking like an underdressed mummy, lectured them on this world's history and some details on society. He tried to make it interesting, but the three visitors quickly learned that he was not doing this for the first time. The sorcerer had been speaking in front of gods before.

In fact, alien space travelers were rather common; at least once a year a merchant ship visited Paradise. The King had signed several trade agreements with five or six different species. They delivered high-quality ores to Paradise so the natives were not forced to carry on extensive mining operations ("that is bad for the fur"), as well as prefabricated metals and special medicinal drugs tailored to the Paradisian organism. As payment, the Paradisers offered all kinds of natural products and exotic handicraft that was sold as luxury items on the traders' homeworlds.

No Paradiser had ever left his-her planet. Some were interested to go, but the rigid society forbid them to accompany the gods. The space travelers would have been glad to take them along—especially the sorcerers, since telekinetic abilities were rather scarce throughout this sector.

Sartun guessed that the trading species were completely unknown to the Diaspora as well as to the Alliance, or else there would have been *some* information on Paradise in the database. Probably, those aliens had their homeworlds and bases in the far sectors, facing away from Alliance space. Paradise was quite a way off every known stellar route, but now that they had learned about those other 'gods', it might become the joining point for new trade connections with unknown species.

"We do hope to join the ranks of the gods one day", the sorcerer explained, "but we believe that this time will not come for a thousand years."

The Zulu wasn't too sure about that; other societies had undergone even more dramatic changes in shorter periods. But the Paradisers liked to think in huge time spans.

He wasn't able to discuss the matter with his colleagues: Lavandil urged them on to the feast. It took some convincing until the King understood that they could not eat the local food. The proteins were too different to digest, and other substances in the food might even prove poisonous. They were already running around without helmet, breathing the Paradisian air. Eating the local food would challenge fate… and it was forbidden by regulations anyway.

Lavandil pointed out that other spacers had actually eaten with the King, but Sartun could only guess about *their* metabolism. They might have entered a region of space where the Clanbourne-Maxell theorem favored a different kind of evolution. He didn't want to insult the king, but there were security limits after all.

The Paradisers didn't take offense in the end, and ate heartily while the gods chewed dried emergency rations. Dances, instrumental music and songs provided the entertainment on the celebration. Some of the music was even bearable for human ears—although Cherac with her finer ears cringed all the time.

It was a loud and long feast. Sartun was glad when the King decided they had celebrated enough. Servants led the gods to their assigned quarters, spacious rooms with elaborate design, soft carpets, many mosaics on the walls and large bathrooms attached.

They didn't have beds though. On Paradise, people slept curled up in big piles of cushions.

Sartun shook his pillows violently, expecting some parasites to crawl out of them—a local variant of fleas or bedbugs maybe. He had some experience with primitive accommodations. But he was surprised. The Paradisers were a clean people, and their hygienic standards were well advanced, far more than their technical level. They had running water and a sewer system, public baths, even sewage purification plants (however low-tech). The stench of middle-age cities, often present in primitive cultures, was absent here.

Sartun kept his LPS on, nevertheless. Its systems would protect him from nasty surprises. The suit was not very comfortable to sleep in, but the Zulu fell asleep before he even managed to take notes on the many questions he still had.

* * *

A soft sound in the *very* early morning startled him. The LPS had already reacted and fired up a protective force field around him. But the nighttime visitor was no assassin who wanted to spill a god's blood, but the King himself.

"God Sovil Sartun, I ask for your advice", the ruler whispered. "The Invisibles have heard my plea by sending you. Gods' wisdom may decide what mere people's law can no longer provide."

Sartun deactivated the force field and got up. He followed the King through the silent palace, up to the central towers, until they had reached an open, grass-covered platform high over the city. Lavandil settled down on the ground. A fresh breeze blew, ruffling his fur and mane.

Sartun sat down beside him. There was only a low, frail-looking rail protecting him from a fall. They were at least a hundred and fifty meters high, not counting the hill itself. The view was gorgeous.

The Zulu was not worried though. The LPS possessed antigrav capability; it could easily carry two persons. It was not recommended to use the flight aggregates while making contact with people who had not yet discovered flight themselves, but an emergency surely justified that breach of protocol. Besides, the Paradisers were hard to surprise anyway.

"Now, King Lavandil, what is it you desire?" He tried to sound formal and polite, but noncommittal. Hopefully, the translator was able to recreate the subtle undertones as well. "Do you have difficulties with evil gods?"

"Difficulties?" Lavandil responded, a bit irritated. "The gods are the same as always. They seldomly change. We have been talking to them for at least two hundred years now, and aside from occasional unpleasant encounters with evil gods, we had never any trouble with them. I guess for gods time has not the same meaning as it has for us.

But desire, yes, desire it is. I am talking of the Da'danji. Shedunje desires him-her as well. And tradition grants him-her the right to court him-her, if so he-she decides. But I am the King, and even if I would not be involved personally, it would still be a loss of face to lose the Da'danji to Shedunje."

Desire? A marriage conflict? A social and political matter? That was not what Sartun had expected. Some more mundane problem, something that could be solved scientifically. But no, it was just like his luck to stumble into a personal conflict between the very king and… whom?

"Who is Shedunje, anyway?"

"Umm, yes, I keep forgetting that you don't know about us... The other gods would know. He-she is the master of storytellers, a bard, a wordsmith, a singer. A vagabond, in the terms of the ancestors. He-she is the antipole of the ruler. While I am the lord over the world, he-she thrones over legends, stories and ballads.

I own everything, according to tradition. He-she owns nothing in the same tradition. Everybody provides him-her with a meal or gives him-her shelter for the night, and more. But he-she is forbidden to accumulate wealth; his-her possessions are only what he-she can carry with him-her."

Sartun lost patience with the translator's weird wording. That 'he-she' and 'him-her' sounded as if the King got the hiccups.

Lavandil and Shedunje seemed to occupy a male role, or at least something close enough. So, the Da'danji played the female in this relationship. Sartun commanded the translator to use the appropriate pronouns.

Lavandil hadn't noticed the quick exchange between the space traveler and his computer (or if he had, he chose to ignore it). He stared at the first light of the coming dawn, lost in thought. "His power... his power is immense though. Is there any greater force than in the dreams of the people? And he rules over them. He forms their desires, he quenches their thirst for knowledge and laughter with a single word. He plays with their emotions, singing a tune of happiness or dejection, working his magic on every soul, until his spell holds the smallest children and the eldest crones in its thrall."

The King leaned on the rail. "If someone asked me who of us has the greater power, I couldn't honestly answer. Kings and vagabonds, there is no greater difference than that. And yet we are alike in a way."

Sartun studied the King intensely and tried to keep his otherworldly objectivity. "And who is the Da'danji?"

Sighing, the King let himself fall back into the grass. "The Da'danji! She is the prettiest flower in the world. A red rose among white roses. So beautiful! Slender as a willow. Fur, silky and tender like the touch of an evening's breeze. A voice like gold and honey.

She resides in the Tower of Morning, amidst numerous servants and guards. Once a day she strolls through the city and delights the people with her presence. I saw her there, I admired her for hours from afar. Before that, the problem was academic; I might even have given her to Shedunje, just to keep the peace. But when my eyes fell on her, I knew that I must have her. It is the tradition, anyway: she is destined to become mine..."

Fallen in love. Was there any older story in the book? Two men and one woman (not counting the fact that the men were women as well, and the woman a man). Sartun swallowed hard. The gods were supposed to solve the problem, to decide... was that the core of the problem?

"Shedunje desires her as well. Tradition gives him the right. He has a rightful claim as well." The King turned around and pointed his tail straight into the air, the ears flattened. "And there is no Da'danji in this generation anymore, except her. That is the difficulty."

"In this generation?"

The King peeked at the god who knew so little of this world. He started to tell a tale of past millennia, events that had happened so many generations ago—and of which the sorcerer had not spoken during their lessons on the previous day. Slowly Sartun started to get a grasp of the whole messy situation.

Once, there had been a perfect woman (or a perfect man), called the Da'danji; a mythical figure like Helena of Troy. In that time, long before the sorcerers emerged and the planet was united, three kings started a war for her attention, ravaging their countries and laying waste to the bountiful land, until famine and poverty subdued the population.

In a society where everybody could fall in love with anybody else, where everyone could relate to burning desire, there was no calming voice; reason was not in high demand in those times, and the war went on until the three kings were dead.

Their sons however would continue the war when they grew up. As long as the Da'danji lived, she was a reason for war: not so much as a woman any more, but as a symbol of the kings' eternal competition.

Thus, the Da'danji had to find a way to solve the conflict. She had seen countries die; she was determined to end the wars once and for all.

So she promised each of the three sons of the three deceased kings a daughter of hers, of the same beauty, just as desirable as she was; every daughter her exact image, every daughter alike. If those kings-to-be had the same wife, essentially, there would be no war anymore. The Da'danji would have broken into the rulers' single-mindedness, and they could finally concentrate on prosperity instead of the dreadful conflict.

To achieve her goals, she cloned herself. Being male and female in one person, she could be mother and father at the same time. (Lavandil did not tell how she did it, technically, and he probably didn't know anything about genetic recombination, so Sartun would look it up later on. The main point was that it worked, apparently.) That had been some taboo in Paradise society, still was indeed, but the Da'danji was special... she was the one who got away with breaking it.

Every son of the dead kings got one of the Da'danji's 'copied' daughters as a mate, as soon as every one of them was old enough to be married away. There was a celebration for three joinings in three kingdoms, and finally, peace came over the land like a new, welcomed season.

Sartun wondered if forging a lasting peace was actually as easy as this, or if Lavandil had left out a major part of the story.

A fourth child—the last of the clones—was chosen to continue the tradition, generation after generation. For centuries, each newest Da'danji cloned herself and gave her daughters to the great leaders of the planet, to ensure a lasting peace. The influence of the Da'danji became obvious after a short time; none of the leaders was willing to wage war on a country whose ruler had the sister of his wife as a wife himself. And if he was, his wife had enough influence to talk him out of his disturbing ideas.

The downside was that kingdoms could no longer be hereditary. The sons could not marry women that were genetically identical with their mothers. Future kings were appointed by a powerful council, selected from the ranks of the nobles. Lavandil did not talk much about the change that reformed the face of society in the following centuries, but that was a clear understatement. To Sartun, it sounded like a thorough upheaval.

Then again, maybe it was not so much of a downside at all…

Society changed, and the role of the kings changed as well. With the coming of the sorcerers—a topic that had been ridden to death the day before by their prolific sorcerer-teacher—and the unification of the planet, two poles emerged, replacing the rule of the tribal kings of old: the King and the Vagabond, a lord of the mundane and a master of dreams. From that day on, the Da'danji had only three children, one for the King, one for the Vagabond, and one to continue the line, all of them called by the same name. In this generation though the old Da'danji had died after giving birth to only two children, and since the youngest had to serve the continuation of the genetic line, there was only one daughter left for both Lavandil and Shedunje.

Sartun wondered what the Da'danji herself might think about her role and position. She seemed more a slave of circumstance, caught in a situation that had been written in stone a long time ago. The Da'danjis had been bartered away for political reasons since the first bearer of that name. Lavandil seemed to have fallen in love (as much as human concepts could be applied at all), but was this true as well for Shedunje or the Da'danji herself? And for how long exactly would this infatuation endure before giving way to the political realities?

The sun rose above the horizon, and the first rose fingers of dawn touched the Tower of the Da'danji. Silver plates flared up in red light.

Lavandil stood enraptured, his back fur standing on edge, staring across the town. His expression betrayed his longing for the unknown beauty.

Or was it rather a longing for the unattainable ideal he saw in the Da'danji, for the traditional, generation-old myth of a being who, in reality, possibly fell short of his imagination?

*Lovestruck*, Sartun thought. *Hopeless.*

\* \* \*

The sorcerer who had introduced them to the land's history the day before—his name was Hayim—took them on a sightseeing tour through the palace the very next day. The 'gods' learned about the government structures and the bureaucracy, and finally visited the School of Kings where possible future rulers were trained for the office they might inherit later.

"Inherit" was not quite the concept though. The regency could not be inherited from the father; none of the kingly pupils were blood-relatives of Lavandil. That seemed only sensible, after all, the Da'danji was the promised wife for generation after generation, and with the traditional concept of inheritance, the son of the King would have had to marry someone who was in every respect the very image of his mother.

"Oedipus would be delighted", Cherac murmured at the thought. She was well acquainted with Terran mythology and history.

Only those children deemed intelligent and strong in character were chosen for the School of Kings, and from their ranks, the Council and the teachers would finally select the future monarch. The others were still eligible for high offices all over the planet, but only one could become King for life. Since a thousand years this principle had proven its worth, and it mirrored its opposite in society: bards and storytellers as well selected their master from a host of capable candidates, not simply appointing someone whose sole merit was to be the son of someone special.

Sartun had long lost track of the usage of male and female attributes in this hermaphroditic society. Cherac had pointed out to him that the Da'danji could as well take on the male role in her predestined association with the King. Dominance seemed to be one of the original Da'danji's character traits anyway; who but a dominant spirit could have devised a plan that used his own offspring as a tool for power?

For this was what things looked like: The Da'danji lived on in her children, as a perfect genetic copy. Her character, her nature, her body. And since she brought up and educated her daughters as well, she could pass all of her ambitions to them, all of her plans. Every inhabitant of this world died and was forgotten except her, his genes lost in the vast pool of the general populace. But not the Da'danji. She was eternal in the sense of the word. The tribal leaders changed as well as the modern rulers. The leaders of society were transformed and refined. But the sisterhood of the Da'danji always sat at the centers of power.

Only slowly and with Cherac's help Sartun began to realize that the Da'danji might be everything else but a victim of the self-created tradition. She was tradition itself. And tradition was the source of her power.

Only the gods, standing outside of society, were able to recognize the truth. It was no coincidence that the tribes forgot their wars after their leaders got a Da'danji as partner. It was the sisterhood's own influence. Sartun got a queasy feeling in his stomach. What they did here—had been asked to do—could have repercussions upon the future of Paradise.

\* \* \*

After lunch (more ceremonial than the previous day's feast, and just as frustrating for the space travelers) Hayim offered to introduce them to Shedunje. They crossed town in some kind of two-wheeled rickshaws, drawn by teams of Paradisers who set a brisk pace. The two-story carts were obviously too cumbersome and slow for quick trips; besides, there were limitations on the use of animal-drawn vehicles within the town's borders for hygienic reasons.

Shedunje might not own anything, but his residence was far from humble. He dwelled in a suite in the largest hotel in town, with a beautiful view and most friendly service. Food and beverages of all kind were free for him. The hotel owner treated his guest with utmost kindness; small wonder, since the presence of Shedunje the Vagabond increased his own status tenfold.

But it certainly didn't look as if Shedunje abused his position. He worked tirelessly. Stacks of closely written pages filled his work desk. Again and again his instruments sounded, and three times a day he performed in public places and sung ballads or recited epic poems.

"You have to hone your skills all the time, like a knife, or they will get blunt", he said apologetically. "What may I do for the gods? Oh, I guess you are here to inquire in the matter of the Da'danji, aren't you? The King has sent you as mediators."

Sartun involuntarily had to admire the beauty of Shedunje, so different from the masculine appearance of Lavandil. The ruler stuck out from the androgynous Paradisers through his distinctly male demeanor, tall and powerful, as if born for the role of King. King, not Queen. Sartun hadn't used the male attribute initially for nothing.

Shedunje was a different case altogether. He was as much female as he was male. Slender, sinewy, erect, with a dreamy expression and bottomless dark eyes. His fur pattern was irregular; other than with the other Paradisers they had seen, the white stripes on his coat formed cryptic, letter-like glyphs. The King wore ceremonial scarves and capes, Shedunje showed off his body as if he wanted to underline that he owned nothing— and more, that all the public had a right on him, could own him.

Even based on the standards of the Diaspora (if not Terra), Shedunje was an enchanting creature with fluid moves, catlike and proud. Independent. Responding to no one, dependent on nothing, yet serving all Paradisers.

Sartun understood why Lavandil had said he didn't know who of them both wielded the greater power. The Vagabond was a king.

"The ruler did not send us, but he made clear that he'd appreciate our advice."

"Very interesting." Shedunje jumped to sit on a table. "And what is the advice of the gods?"

"We cannot come to a conclusion", Cherac responded, "without having a clear picture of the situation."

Shedunje folded his long-fingered hands in front of his muzzle. "The gods are not to judge the affairs of this world. Love alone decides. Maybe fate determined that only one Da'danji should exist in this age, so the King and I would have to concentrate on our true feelings instead of taking for granted that we would both possess the most beautiful woman in the world." The translator used the word 'woman', still faithful to Sovil Sartun's earlier command, interpreting the Paradisian language the best way an AI could.

"I think we should take a good look at the most beautiful woman in the world", Sartun suggested. "I think it is pretty strange that the ever-changing whim of fashion should have no effect on the sense of beauty here. In the Diaspora, not even two human-settled worlds can agree on what beauty is."

"The Da'danji is what beauty is. She is the source of all beauty, and the mirror that reflects all things beautiful. Her gait is the model we all follow. Her voice is the melody we sing. Her goal is perfection, and that makes her the ideal we all try to achieve. I don't think Lavandil is even able to appreciate her."

Love? For Sartun, love and ideals seemed to be incompatible—or at least hard to combine principles. Shedunje seemed to adore an abstract portrait instead of a living being.

"Did you ever try to talk to Lavandil?" Galzaan Brakh demanded to know.

The bard threw his tail over a shoulder and let the two tips swing. "Of course not. Kings and vagabonds never meet. I have never been inside of the palace, and the King never attends my performances. That is the tradition, so he won't be enchanted by my words. I regret this tradition, though; I am sure even the King would hold a good ballad in high regard."

"Then, we will have to undermine tradition a bit." Sartun felt that the King and the Vagabond needed to talk to each other in person, urgently, instead of quarreling from afar. "You will come to the palace, and we will invite the Da'danji to this meeting as well. We gods do not want to be involved in this matter. As you said, we are not to judge the affairs of this world. Only you three are able to work it out. Maybe the Da'danji has already chosen one of you, and you just don't know about it."

Shedunje let his teeth click, a gesture Sartun could not interpret without the help of the data collection. The translator didn't offer advice. "A wise decision", the bard declared. "Wiser than I expected it from the gods." It might have been irony.

Only when they were already well on their way to the Tower of Morning, Sartun realized that, despite all his good intentions, he had finally claimed the attribute 'god' for himself—taking on a responsibility he might not be able to fulfill.

*   *   *

If Shedunje was a mysterious beauty, the Da'danji was bright as the sun. Her fur was almost white, with only thin black stripes on her back. The perfect symmetry of her limbs added to the feminine delicacy of her build. She did not color the tufts of hair on her shoulders, like most Paradisers did. Loosely combed, maybe even carefully arranged, her long fur flew down her back. The body fur seemed soft as down, catching the light of the countless lamps that lit the room.

The Da'danji had nothing left to chance: the reception, the ornate chamber, the elevated platform from where she looked down on the gods. Heavy fragrance filled the room. Smoke rose from some vessels. The bright cheerful colors of the tapestries and the furnishings underlined the white of the Da'danji. Servants with palm fronds stirred the air.

"Gods, I see", the Da'danji said. "Interesting. Among all the powers of the Ancient Beginning, the gods are supposed to be the most powerful. Some claim that there are worlds where only gods live." It was not a question, and Sovil Sartun didn't bother to reply. "You know, I would have liked to see a god's ship from the inside for once. When I was little, I used to watch the gods coming and going, but my guardians never let me meet them in person. I guess this is Kings' business only... but still, I always was fascinated with the gods. Unfortunately, the evil gods' ship does not open for us." She lay stretched out in a big heap of pillows, but since she rested on the elevated pedestal, the team had to look up to her. Every move she made seemed calculatedly impressive. And the tales she related were... selected.

"We have come to make a proposal." Sartun took a deep breath. The heavy scent in the chamber threatened to give him a headache, but he could hardly close and seal the LPS without being rude. "The King Lavandil and the Vagabond Shedunje would like to meet you in the palace. They are eager to discuss the question whose wife you will be, as your tradition demands." He wondered briefly what word the translator had used for 'wife'—then, whether the Da'danji listened at all. She mustered him with sleepy eyes.

Although the display was apparently meant to be seductive, Sartun saw a predator hiding behind the façade. The Da'danji pulled the strings from here, lurking, waiting for the right moment to strike. Until now, Sovil Sartun had been unsure whether his original interpretation of the role of the Da'danji was correct—the Da'danji as the victim of a powerful tradition that formed her life for her—or rather Cherac's opinion that the Da'danji was a force behind the scenes, the hidden factor in the interplay of the authorities on Paradise. But now there could be no doubt. The Da'danji did not behave at all like a slave of fate, a dutiful servant of ancient laws.

She was the lord here, the mistress who played her cards even against the gods.

"The power of the gods is without equal", she finally stated, as if he had never spoken a word. "Godfire raining down onto the world. Gods' ships that penetrate the eternal black void beyond Paradise. Invisible genies, carrying around gods through the air, as if they possess bird's wings. Oh, I know a lot about the way of the gods." She sat, letting her legs swing over the edge of the pedestal. "I know what you are thinking—do we not have sorcerers at our beckon who can step from one side of the world to the other through a mere thought? Sorcerers who have defeated evil gods again and again, and thus must be just as powerful as the gods themselves? But I think—no, I know for sure—that there are sorcerers among the gods as well, and beyond them the Kings of the gods. For them, Paradise must be like a pebble in the ocean, insignificant and small. I wish... I wish I could see the worlds of the gods with mine own eyes, and look up to the thrones of the Kings of gods."

She swung down from the platform and accompanied Sartun on his strange, low-legged stool; the preferred kind of seat here. "Tradition forbids it. But yet, I know that somehow, some day, my dreams will come true." Her hand touched his face, soft fur stroking his cheek, and suddenly Sartun was glad that the head was the only part of his body not covered by the LPS. He was accustomed to being close to nonhumans—in fact, it was hard to live in the Diaspora and not come very close to a furry or two—but no one had ever shown this kind of directness, this degree of aggression.

The Da'danji drew back her hand, as if surprised by her own boldness, then leaned lasciviously against Sartun's body. "I will accept your proposal. But I have to prepare a bit. Let me get dressed for the occasion. I hope I will meet you again in the residency of our beloved King." She stood, then quickly strode—no, *danced*—towards a door, disappearing in a whiff of perfume and cloudy fluff. The first contact team stared at the door, perplexed.

Sartun was unable to move. Hell. The ambitions of the Da'danji were even more dangerous than he and Cherac had anticipated. She didn't want a bard. She didn't want a king.

She wanted a god.

"Hey", Cherac whispered in his ear. "Hope you don't forget: She's a man!"

\* \* \*

"Do you still know what you are doing?" Galzaan Brakh pouted.

"I think I know." Sovil Sartun shrugged, not really convinced.

"What we are doing is not covered by any SciControl guideline."

"It's not forbidden either. The Laws of Protection do not apply. If you want to put it that way, this civilization is already contaminated."

They had met in the palace chamber Sartun had been assigned as a sleeping room. For the moment, the King was occupied with preparing the festival, and didn't show any interest in the gods any more. Hayim the sorcerer had offered some more lessons on Paradise history and culture, but the team couldn't concentrate on science right now. Sartun had an uneasy feeling in his stomach, and having Brakh and Cherac criticize him didn't help at all.

"That is no reason to make it even worse", Cherac stated. "Every world has the right to solve its problems on its own. Make its own mistakes. Find its own way."

"What did we do? We just offered a meeting. They could have thought of that themselves." Sartun felt defensive about the whole affair. Was it so wrong to give advice? Advice that had been asked for.

Well, if one knew next to nothing about the planet, and assumed the role of gods...

"Shedunje said it is against tradition that King and Vagabond ever meet. You are breaking their tradition—and usually there are at least *a few* reasons a tradition is formed." Brakh violently shook his head. "I am not convinced."

"You'd rather have them marching directly into a war? You heard Hayim; in the old days Paradise was a battlefield for the favor of the Da'danji! I will certainly not watch them massacre each other."

"Noble, noble", Cherac hissed. "Even if it would be their decision? Besides, I have not seen any hints of a war. You are just playing the great Spaceman again! Mister Solve All Universal Problems! Your ego will get us into a mess."

"That is not true!" Sartun tried to defend himself. But he knew that Cherac was correct, at least partly. They had no right to interfere. When the King had asked him, he should have declined all responsibility. At least common sense and simple morale dictated to remain passive.

The law might not require non-interference. But Paradise defeated all the rules in the book anyway. Normally, a pre-tech world would have been off-limits for them, but others had made first contact here for whom, apparently, the laws were less strict (assuming of course that the nameless spacemen who made this contact had acted in accordance with their laws, not as pirates or freebooters). A non-industrial planet that stood his own against spacefaring civilizations—Sartun could not remember any similar case. Strong telepaths and telekinets serving in a society that was more feudal than anything else...

Were they the reason he had acted rashly? The possibility that SciControl might lure a few of them into service? But he had never been convinced of SciControl's methods; certainly his subconscious would not betray him this way. He was a man of reason! Or at least that was how he had seen himself until now.

"I didn't do it for myself", he concluded lamely, knowing it was not true the moment he had said it.

"Whatever." Cherac did not even bother to question his statement, looking right through him. "You made your move. I just hope that no catastrophe will follow."

\* \* \*

But the festival already threatened to become just that: a catastrophe. Lavandil showed off his power with a parade of armored guards, and Shedunje commented on the marching troops with scorching irony. The feast was a lot bigger than the one Lavandil had arranged for the gods, louder and faster and more colorful. The message was obvious. But Shedunje shamed the King by singing love ballads all night long with a voice like silver bells, not even making use of the orchestra Lavandil had assembled.

Lavandil dressed up in splendor, with gold jewelry and fine silks. Shedunje only wore a loincloth and a yellow scarf wound around his arm. The rivals mustered each other all the time, as if they wanted to challenge the other to a duel to the death. Which may not have been so far from the truth, except that Paradise did not know a dueling tradition.

Sartun watched the event worriedly. He realized that some of the guests had left already, fleeing the hostile atmosphere. While the King and the Vagabond tried not to show their weaknesses and to put their virtues on display, they failed to impress anyone, especially the Da'danji, who hardly took notice of both. She was coldly observing them like a scientist might observe lizards performing a genetically programmed mating dance.

The Zulu had to agree with Galzaan Brakh: there was a reason for the tradition that King and Vagabond should never meet. However competent they were in their respective field, however dedicated and knowledgeable: in their competition, they made fools of themselves.

It took them quite a while to notice, though. The Da'danji showed only condescension for their attempts to impress her, to woo her, to prove their never-ending love to her. She had only eyes for the gods. She was a bit more subtle than in her Tower of Morning here, hiding her approach, biding her time. But to Sartun, her ultimate goal was perfectly clear. Even Cherac seemed not to be safe from her advances.

King and Vagabond resigned more and more, realizing the fruitlessness of their efforts. The farther the evening went, the less resolute their display became, a show no more to wake the interest of the Da'danji in them, but just to confirm they were too stubborn to give up. Their disappointment was obvious. The rules of tradition meant nothing to the Da'danji; the perfect woman was the one who had broken them in the first place. And neither Lavandil nor Shedunje could see any of their romantic ideas realize in the actual person they had met.

The festival became a drunken brawl between some guests in the early hours of morning. Guards stormed in, removing the combatants, messing up the hall in the process. The King had stopped caring; he performed sword dances for the few guests who were still sober enough to appreciate the entertainment. The musicians had gone to sleep or were raiding the kitchen for a morsel or two. Shedunje drew pictures of light and shadow on sheets of paper that had been stained by beer. Two old men (maybe retired sorcerers of the court) watched him, offering critique but apparently too far gone to make sense. The Vagabond did not mind, ignoring the nuisance.

The rivals did not quarrel any more. Maybe Lavandil and Shedunje knew that the Da'danji would not get her gods—they could not fail to notice her scheming, after all, they were the only ones still sober at this event—but what did it matter any more whose wife she would become then? If it was not romance, if it was not love... it became a matter of tradition only, and the tradition had become hollow, stale and empty.

Finally, Cherac and Galzaan Brakh fled to their rooms, locking them from the inside. Sartun left the festival as well, climbing up the stairs to the viewing platform the King had shown him to catch the morning breeze.

The King was already there. He stared across the city at the Tower of Morning, half hidden in darkness. Two silver moons shone, near their setting hour.

"God Sovil Sartun, I knew you would come here."

"I am sorry. I expected something different from this meeting." He felt guilty for his meddling. After he had met the Da'danji, he should have realized that her interests lay elsewhere. He had accepted robbing Lavandil and Shedunje of their illusionary love. In retrospect, the outcome was obvious. But something had driven him to interfere; maybe only the urge to set things right. To fill out the spaceman's role that he had chosen. Sartun was about to lose some illusions about himself as well.

"Me too, god Sovil Sartun. She was... so different from the time when I first met her. Today, she was cold. Unfriendly. And she had eyes for you only."

"I... did notice."

"Why? Pray tell, what does a god have that I don't have? You don't wear a fur, as far as I can see, and you don't have tails; your heads are almost bald; you cannot eat the most delicious food we prepare, and you are forced to wear clothing no Paradiser could breathe in. I do not mean to be rude, but... How is it possible that she loves such as you?"

"Love?" Sartun laughed coarsely, a sound that surprised Lavandil. "The one thing she loves is power, power that comes with the gods, power no King and no Vagabond can give to her."

Lavandil fell silent for a while. "Will my love ever be fulfilled? The longing of the morning, the desperation of the night? My heart breaks, and no one is there to fill the void." He seemed to have difficulties to say goodbye to his fantasies.

"You are not in love with a person", Sartun stated. "You love an ideal. An image you painted yourself with little resemblance to the true Da'danji. But she is not what you see in her. She is real… a Paradiser like you. She has her faults, sure… and currently, her interest may be focused on gods… but we will leave soon, and then the Da'danji will choose one of you."

*For the one that promised her the most power*, he thought, but didn't say it aloud. The King was intelligent enough to draw his own conclusions—provided that love, or what he took for it, did not blind his reason. Politics was the keyword here. The sooner he realized that, the better for him.

"And Shedunje as well is different from what I thought", Lavandil continued. "He is the greatest bard I ever had the pleasure to meet. His wit is sharp as a knife. His voice is like silk and silver. At his side, I appear as a blundering fool. Even when you are gone and the blaze of the gods' power will no longer overshadow my rule, how shall I compete with him?"

"He is just a Vagabond", Sartun remarked, and regretted his words immediately. The King looked at him, the ears strangely flat.

"Yes. And more. An impressive person. My dreams seem to turn against me, and nothing remains as it seemed. A day that has seen the most remarkable changes. Would you be so kind and summon Shedunje for me? I'd like to speak to him."

Turning around, Sartun could not help but to smile. The King had just sent a god on an errand. Very interesting. The concept of gods here was obviously a bit different from what Sartun was used to.

But now everything would work out. Once the two combatants had talked, and the Da'danji realized she could not impress the alien 'gods', the old rules of tradition would once again surface—maybe everything would go its usual path the next day already.

The festival had died off, the guests were gone. Sartun looked around, and finally had a servant lead him to the room that had been prepared for Shedunje's stay.

The bard did not sleep. He paced up and down, humming sad notes.

"The King wishes to speak to you", Sartun told him.

"Oh? So he wants to savor his triumph?"

"Triumph?" The Zulu remembered the King's words somehow differently.

"He is the ruler of this world. Glory. Splendor. Magnificence. In all the years I spent traveling the world, I have never experienced such opulence. I am at a loss for words, and that is something I do not experience very often. Now I learn what it means to be King. There is a power in his words I do not command. I conjure up dreams without substance, while he builds an empire. And beyond his Kingness..." His tail swung back and forth in sorrow, his ears twitched. "He is tall, strong, muscular, an athlete. At his side, I appear as a thin dwarf. He commands the power of the ancient lords, the generals of lore. In a play of myths, I would cast him the hero. The great characters from the days of old follow him in his shadow. Someone like the Da'danji yearns for him. I do know that she adores the powerful; my world can never be hers." The disappointment showed clearly in his face; Sartun didn't need a translator to interpret the bard's expression. "I should write a ballad about him, although I would be the comic relief in a tale like that." He, as well as the King, had loved an ideal. Maybe different from the King, but still an image that had proven wrong. An illusion had died. And he found it just as difficult to let go of his dreams.

Sartun could not fight his curiosity. Instead of just telling Shedunje where to find the King, he showed him the way upstairs to the tower platform. The King waited patiently. Although Sartun had needed more than half an hour for the way and the search for Shedunje, it seemed as if Lavandil hadn't lifted a paw.

The two rivals looked at each other. Sartun could sense how much strength this meeting demanded of them. Finally, the King brought himself to speak. "I am sorry, bard. I was a childish fool today."

Shedunje made an averting gesture. "Someone who has the courage to call himself a fool has found a knowledge that raises him above the level of the other fools. And aren't we all fools, each one in his own way?"

From there on, the talk seemed to go well enough. Sartun wanted to listen, ignored by both King and Vagabond, but the way the translator worked demanded a high level of concentration of its user, constantly checking interpreting levels and logic arrays, and the Zulu was much too tired to do that. Soon only fragments of words drifted at Sartun's ears.

He was not worried, though. Lavandil and Shedunje seemed to be intelligent people. They appeared quite able to work out a solution that would both serve the tradition and their own interests. Together they might even be able to convince the Da'danji to give up her power game (although Lavandil was probably the one who would win her over; he ruled the world after all).

The sun rose and bathed the city in golden light. Sartun blinked. The King and the Vagabond still talked, apparently about a lot of things that weighed heavily on their minds. The Empire. The gods. The world. About the future and the past. About their hopes and dreams.

Finally, Sovil Sartun fell asleep, the long day taking its toll.

* * *

He awoke stiff and not very well rested, but his conscience was clean. In the end, he had not failed the Paradisers in his god role. Shedunje and Lavandil were gone, the day well advanced. The city was too far down and away to hear the bustle and hustle, but Sartun saw tiny Paradisers crawling through the streets like ants.

He wondered to what conclusion the two had come. Shedunje's ideals were more abstract, his vision of the future filled with reflections of myths. During the festival, Sartun had learned to know the bard as a character of the extremes. His demands were high, and his shattered hopes must fill him with desperation. He would probably turn his back on the Da'danji, now that she had proven to be more… worldly than expected.

Lavandil on the other hand had mastered the School of Kings, learning the harsh truths of life. He knew about the differences between ideals and reality, and in his position, he would certainly be adept in overcoming personal disappointments for the greater good of Paradise. His chances to tame the beautiful, but clever and greedy Da'danji were pretty good. He might even find happiness of some sort with his future wife.

Stiff-legged, he stumbled down the ten million stairs of the tower. Cherac and Brakh were already awake, having apparently slept longer and deeper than him. Sartun dutifully reported the events.

"Let's hope they got sensible", Cherac murmured while they were on their way to the royal suite. "You didn't look at the foot of the tower, just to make sure they didn't throw each other over the rail?" Sartun hoped she was joking, but with Parjan, one could never know.

Hayim the sorcerer sat in front of the suite portal. His expression was impossible to interpret. "The wisdom of the gods often generates strange results", he said.

"Did Shedunje and Lavandil come to an agreement?" Sartun demanded to know.

"Yes", the mutant replied slowly. "One could say that."

For a moment, Sartun feared the worst. Had the King executed the bard to get rid of the rival? But Hayim continued: "The Da'danji has left for the Tower of Morning one hour ago. I tried to convince her that the gods are not willing to take her along on their endless journey. I am afraid there is nothing she desires more."

"My impression exactly", Sartun murmured.

"Hey, admit it: she impressed you a lot!" Cherac chuckled behind him.

Hayim opened the wings of the portal. "The King has commanded that you are welcome anytime. Please do not expect a formal audience."

In the center of the rich hall a pit filled with pillows served as a bed, the lair of the King. Lavandil himself was half buried under ornate blankets. He looked quite contented. So, he was the victor in the quarrel. Sartun had expected as much.

"I bid you a good day, King Lavandil", the Zulu said. "I hope all things have turned out to everyone's satisfaction?"

A second shape dug out from under the pillows. "It couldn't be better", Shedunje claimed. "We have made important discoveries, and found insights unheard of."

Sartun blinked. Then he blinked again. Shedunje? He considered breaking out into hysterical laughter, but chose to stay calm in the interest of the mission.

Of course; it made sense. Every Paradiser could take on a male or female role as he or she pleased. Shedunje had switched roles. Or maybe Sartun had just tried to see male and female roles when there were none, because the true structure of the social behavior of species FG-22a was beyond his understanding. There were no males and females on this world, never had been. He had made a grave mistake when he had ordered the translator to address some Paradisers as men, others as women.

The bard had admired the King's virtues. The King had adored the bard's grace. Both had more in common than they could have known, forever separated by tradition. Both had been disillusioned by their meeting with the Da'danji. Maybe they had found in each other more of their ideals than in the white-furred beauty they had believed to love.

The Zulu heard Cherac giggle behind him. She found the situation funnier than Sartun himself.

King and Vagabond left their bed. "I hope you will stay for the ceremony", Lavandil asked. "You are, after all, the source of our newly found happiness." Against his will Sartun had to admit that the two made a nice couple. After a millennium of separation, the two poles of Paradise society finally found together. Many things would change.

Maybe the family line of the Da'danji would expire in this generation.

He sighed. Massive intervention in planetary affairs without SciControl consent. Sartun had failed to think about every possible outcome of his meddling, had relied too much on instinct. Well-meaning but not thinking. Not thinking at all.

The result might be to the satisfaction of the involved powers, but who knew what would become of this society in the long run? Even if he hadn't actually broken the rules, this report would not look well in his files. Embarrassing. Cherac was right; he had done it for himself, for his image.

Not thinking…

He would have to work hard both to make good his slip, and to get himself under control. Before some error like this would lead to disaster.

"The wise advice of the gods has turned our fate to the better", Shedunje declared beaming all over his-her face. "Maybe your infinite wisdom can assist us in one more question. In the center of the province Loghrau…"

"We would love to", Sartun interrupted him-her. "But I am afraid we have to leave. The call of the King of gods has reached us from beyond the clouds. Our help is urgently required elsewhere." He fumbled at his LPS controls, activating the antigravity unit. "Farewell and live in peace and happiness." With high acceleration, he aimed at the next open window, shot out of the room and turned towards the landing field.

Cherac and Brakh followed quickly, hardly taking the time to say goodbye. The Parjan was still giggling. Sartun saw a long, long flight back ahead of them.

The Paradisers looked after them. "Gods", Lavandil sighed. "Who will ever understand what is on their mind?" He-she embraced gently his-her partner.

"One day", Shedunje prophesied, "one day we will understand. Then we will become gods ourselves." The bard touched the King's muzzle lovingly.

Outside, three gods crossed the skies, slim silhouettes against the blazing sun. The natives of Paradise looked after them, cheering, waving.

But the gods never looked back.

*Phyllis Gotlieb wrote six Starcats stories: the novellas "Son of the Morning", "The King's Dogs", "Nebuchadnezzer", and "A Judgment of Dragons" (collected in* A Judgment of Dragons*); and the novels* Emperor, Swords, Pentacles, *and* The Kingdom of the Cats.

*The Galactic Federation is a confederation of species united through ESPers. Its capital is Galactic Federation City on Earth, a city in the tundra under a climate-controlled dome.*

*When the planet Ungruwarkh is discovered, inhabited by cougar-like carnivorous crimson felines who are over-hunting their food supply, membership in the Federation becomes the Big Red Cats' chance for survival. The Federation identifies Prandra as an especially powerful ESPer. She is invited to become Ungruwarkh's ambassador to the Federation, along with her non-ESPer mate Khreng. Some of Galactic Federation City's ambassadors, and the City's human staff, do not trust the fiercely predatory Ungrukhs.*

*Someone starts killing the City's inhabitants, making it look like an Ungrukh is responsible. Prandra and Khreng (with the help of GalFed investigator Duncan Kinnear) must clear themselves.*

*The three Starcats novels are murder mysteries. A Judgment of Dragons (Berkley Books, April 1980) is Prandra and Khreng's book. Emperor, Swords, Pentacles (Ace Books, April 1982) features their daughter Emerald, and her mate Raanung. The Kingdom of the Cats (Ace Books, July 1985) features grand-daughter Bren, with her mate Etrem.*

# The King's Dogs

## by Phyllis Gotlieb

Galactic Federation City on Sol III stands on tundra under a dome; a solar-electrified, water-recycling, self-supporting civil-service city in a civil-service world. Aliens from hundreds of worlds hop, skim, or lurch in tanks along its huge white-flagstone avenues. On its eastern rim the MedPsych Annex is enclosed in force-fields and white-noise walls. The ESPs within love privacy, and so, even more, do the non-ESPs outside.

For half an hour every dawn and dusk two big red cats pace the hexagonal flags around MedPsych. Inevitably they fall into step, consciously break it, fall in and break. Prandra, the ESP of the two, knows that when Khreng has matched her pace their minds are joined, and neither wishes to share one mind all the time. Distant outworld cousins of the leopard, they are leopard-sized, but their color is incongruously harsh against the white stones, among the green boxtrees in cement tubs. Khreng is bright crimson, Prandra as much darker as if his shadow had rested on her. Both are striped with narrow black chevrons peaking at the crown and falling along the flank to the hip, each stripe centered with a thin white line.

Around his neck Khreng wears a medal, a diplomat's gold star. As the senior representative of Ungruwarkh on Sol III he has been made its ambassador. He knows he has been given the honor because Prandra is the ESP, but he does not care; he is the stronger and the tracker; Prandra does not care for any reason. They do not know completely what ambassadors do: they are aware that neither of them is very diplomatic. Prandra wears the ESP's insigne on Sol III, a steel medallion engraved with a lightning bolt wound by a snake. It is sometimes called the Cracked Caduceus and other names; from her point of view it is a dog tag.

Khreng has caught through Prandra a thought in the mind of some passing lover of literature. "What is that about dogs and kings?"

223

"It is a piece of what Solthrees call poetry, like the words of singing, written on a tag by a man named Alexander Pope, who gives a dog to a king:

" '*I am his Highness's dog at Kew; Pray tell me, sir, whose dog are you?*' "

"Is that directed at us?"

"Evidently."

Her mind is savage and morose; he pushes on: "Why does he think of us as dogs? We are not dogs of a king, nor serve any dog of a king."

"It is how their minds work. They put a tag on a creature they consider animal and call it a dog."

:*For God's sake, stop being so damn sensitive. Some idiot was making an absentminded allusion.*: Espinoza, their own ESP guide and counselor, the centuries-old brain-in-a-bottle, is wheeling down the hall to have his nutrient pump adjusted. His mind fades past the walls of a white-room.

Prandra snarls, "Cats *are* sensitive and dogs are hypocrites." She hooks a claw in the chain and stops. Responsibility. If she does not work for GalFed, there will be no cattle or feed-grains for starving Ungrukh.

"That's the price of being Earth-compatible cats," says Khreng.

"It is the price of being a bloody damned ESP."

Khreng leaves the walk and wanders about the lawn, sniffing some fascinating scent. Whose dog are you, Khreng? Prandra continues alone... I am alone here. Espinoza has his own affairs. Khreng is bored. She glances at the evening sky through the dome's roof. She and Khreng prefer dusk because they do not have to wear tinted contacts to dim a sun brighter than their own. She begins to trot, chain jingling. Here, Rover! Here, Rex! Here, Fido! , Good boy! She sneers. The sweat of fear is around her. *The jaws that bite, the claws that catch.* The literary mind, an idling engine, intrudes. Shut up, stupid! A leap, jaws closing on nape, *crunch!* Not here.

The angles of the buildings shift, the sky turns pink, then red as the plains of Ungruwarkh. Their children, Tugrik and Emerald, are growing across the dark emptiness, forgetting Khreng and Prandra. Half-grown now, Emerald mated, pregnant when we reach home? ESP Emerald chained brains to be bottled in the dark globe. Not Emerald! Prandra gallops; no prey in the scant flesh dangling from bickering alien heads. Prandra skims the wall: too late to pass the gates, hurl herself at the dark city. Uncivil servants go to bed early in the short tundra nights.

Red, red sky, buildings elongated like spears, their few windows vanished, the sun is down. The spears are tipped with dying light like blood. ...An opening among the spears: she smells blood. A shadow crouches, nipping at greens. Not Khreng. Big fleshy thing, no mind, only meat. From where? Saliva pools in her jaw, she is ready to rip meat from bone with her rasp tongue.

"Khreng?" Gone, white-roomed; she will save his portion. Drop it at his feet. Here, Khreng the tracker! Dog. Hyena.

Flesh hot in her nostrils; she goes to ground, thickens her haunches, tail lashing, up and out her powered thighs propel, red claws flash, teeth bare—

The shadow-figure turns, rises, is a man, Solthree, eyes wide, hands raised, pale star palms turned out—*Espinoza!*

Screaming:

"Don't—"

\* \* \*

"—pull me into your damned bloody dreams, woman! Hell's blazes!" Khreng's swipe sent her tumbling off the bed. "Hyena! Since when am I a hyena after hunting with you all the years?"

Prandra lay on the floor, tongue hanging out, feet slippery with sweat. She shook her head, stood and shook her whole body. She felt drugged.

"Are you sick?" Khreng touched her nose and forehead with his padded hand. "You don't seem feverish."

"I don't know… am I here?"

"What are you saying? You are in our room."

She lifted her head and looked at the pale walls, the great round velvet bed, the rough flagstone slab. She lay on that, scraped her back and flanks on it. "You thrash about so much I can't sleep half the time," Khreng grumbled, "and when I do you call me names."

Prandra crouched on the stone. "I never have such dreams until we come here. It's not in my mind to call you names. That's filthy."

"Whose mind is it in then?" he snorted.

"There are other ESPs here."

"Their thoughts don't come through these walls. What does Espinoza think if he knows you want to eat him?"

"Lummox!" she roared.

He grinned. "Names?"

"Who wants to eat some old brain?" She sniffed. "In my dreams he is not bottled, he is a man as he sees himself. I do not want to eat people. I am satisfied with the meat we get. Something is giving me terrible dreams!"

"We share the same food."

225

"The kitchens are not white-walled. I know if drugs are put in the food. Something is wrong." She jumped from the stone and began to pace. "Maybe in my mind… from being in a strange place… with all those strange thoughts. Wearing a tag and being called a dog."

"That is from your dream."

"Not only. Who is not afraid of a creature that is thought of as savage here?" She sprawled on the floor, tail snapping like a whip. "It makes my head hurt… maybe we ask for separate rooms… if my, head is sick you should not be joined to it."

He stared her in the eye, so close that their whiskers melded. "That is not sickness, it is foolishness. If you can handle a Qumedon in a strange place hundreds of years back, you can get along here. On Ungruwarkh you know when a mind is sick and you never say maybe."

"How do I know my own mind?"

"Your sister knows hers, when it is unbalanced; she asks for help too— and you give it. Have you forgotten everything? Ungrukh know. Maybe not other ESPs. Whatever is bad here comes from somewhere else: we find out." He licked her neck. "If it is a someone, likely it is happier if we separate and become more vulnerable."

"That seems sensible."

"I am glad you think I am capable of sense."

She bit his ear and hopped onto the bed. He followed and they writhed together in their fierce way. After, they smoothed each other's fur, and Khreng said, "Now maybe you sleep without dreams."

She hissed, "Now I am really awake. I want to go out."

"Better not disturb Espinoza now."

"Later. I want to think first." Before she reached the door he had fallen asleep into a dream of Ungruwarkh and the children. She paused to savor it…

\* \* \*

Down the hall padding in silence past guards in green gold-braided uniforms; she had learned to move so that the hateful chain did not ring; her red eye shine reflected the dimmed ceiling lights. The men on guard thought of jungles. "Here, kitty, kitty," she muttered. Passed Espinoza's door. Not yet.

*Don't*—

Why Espinoza, whom she loved? Why leaping on fleshy animal? Far back in the time-warp she had killed a pig, stunned and butchered it, like any so-called civilized person. Certainly she had lusted after it, but she had eaten its meat out of a bowl, with Khreng. On Ungruwarkh there were no large food animals; she had caught and roasted the diseased fish, like her compatriots. And why were those low-ESP guards fearful? Big red cats are fearsome, but if they mind their business...

Their business is meat—

Stop.

Something was contaminating their minds.

She trotted, galloped, into the darkness. More guards. ESPs are valuable and cause jealousy. No one else was out. Most went to bed early in the short tundra nights ... stop. That was in the dream.

She looked up. The buildings stood in their right shapes and proportions, unblooded. The flags had cooled. She smelled the earth the plants were potted in and the worms that coursed it. The sky was paling slightly in the east. She jumped the ornamental fence of the children's playground and rolled in the sand, climbed the bars, slid the chutes, snaked the winding tubes. The patterned coolness of the metal soothed her. She stretched on the sand and watched the fading eastern stars.

Smelled flesh. Her head rose, she growled softly like an engine idling. The Solthree woman, Nerrta, was watching her, fingers clamped on an arabesque of the fence.

That odd one they considered so beautiful, whose mind was impervious even to the most powerful ESPs. The only Solthree of the kind ever discovered, perhaps the most valuable of her kind. Black eyes, smooth light-brown skin, flowing dark hair, deep red velvet robe. Hands tight on bars, eyes fixed. Seeing what? Glowing coals in the head of red demon? Some transparent mind saw them.

The man Metaxa, tall, heavy, dark-bearded, put a hand on her shoulder. *Get away! Retro me, Satanas!* The literary mind.

*Fool!* Prandra stared him down, saw her red eyes in his. His arms circled the woman to lead her away. Her hands clamped tighter. He pried them off finger by finger.

Fear.

Not only of savage cats, but of/for—

:*Get out! Get out!*:

It was he who insisted on broadcasting to the universe. "Calm yourself, man. You are creating your own fears."

The woman let herself be drawn back. She moved oddly, bent legs placing one foot before the other with flattened soles.

Prandra leaped, cleared the fence in a red arc that blended with the shadows.

Metaxa, the man of immeasurable wealth, explored alien cultures and collected artifacts. The woman, Nema, like the Qumedon, was a mystery to Prandra, who was not—and might never be—powerful enough to esp her. Metaxa was incomprehensible culturally: he collected facts and objects for their own sake.

Espinoza at end of patience: *Because they're pleasing to look at! You've just been too busy surviving to make or look at things for pleasure. You've done extremely well at tool-making for a people without opposable thumbs, and if you had the kind of climate that snowed you into a hut or holed you into a cave half the year, you'd have been inventing games and artifacts as well.*:

"We have games—"

:*Good*—:

"But things are things."

:—*Good!*:

"We are only savage and ignorant to you."

:*No! Get it straight! You're not savage because you don't kill from ignorance. Your ESP has prevented that. Otherwise you might have become like many primitive tribes. That, and your intelligence, have turned you off the branch that sacrifices to gods. Add the survival crisis that makes you value lives, and you've got an advanced ethical system. Plus complicated tool-making abilities: that gives you a culture. You've still got sore spots because your tribes compete instead of cooperating. You and Khreng have got to change that. All you need now is to understand and enjoy what's pleasing.*:

"Why should we gather things we don't need?"

:*You don't have to! Just understand those who do!*:

"Why?"

:*Never mind. Just turn up my oxygen before you go.*:

\*   \*   \*

But who could understand Metaxa? The collector of things, of snatches of poems (about dogs and claws) from books, had found a child in the kitchen corner of a slum (community of poor people with few implements, like the village of Kostopol in the time-warp)—and what was he doing there? (:*Going slumming*,: says Espinoza tartly, losing Prandra.) Filthy neglected child who could not move or talk because of behavioral blockage originating in the brain (called autism). Feeding and excreting in silence, broken sometime by an hour's screaming, and beaten for it.

Metaxa had taken her away and given his life to her, leaving wife, children, mistress (subsidiary mate). Had fed, clothed, tended her, found specialists to teach her to walk, use her hands, signal her needs, though she never spoke. Metaxa had polished her like a jewel. An ESP doctor had discovered her powerful faculty.

And why?

\* \* \*

"Hello, Espinoza."

:*Go to the window and watch the dawn for me.*:

Through the dome's struts the sun was rising out of a delicate lavender veil. :*That is beautiful.*:

She grinned. "If you say so."

:*One more and one less.*: The sun reflected a star from the dark bowl of his own dome. After a moment he said, :*Posthypnotic suggestion.*:

"Ah... you *are* first class, Espinoza."

:*If I were class-one, maybe I'd know who did it, and why. But there is something going on—you'd have figured it out yourself in a while.*:

"The dreams make me afraid. Fear cramps reason."

:*I can't move... and I'm tired. That cramps it too...*:

The room was tiny, the window took one wall. Nothing was there but Espinoza's globe on its stand, pump humming. Prandra contorted herself to lie down around him. "I am ignorant. Please help."

:*You need a class-one.*:

Though Espinoza was class-two, she had on his testimony been granted pro-tem second-class ESP status as soon as she arrived. But she and Khreng had come not to be classified but to learn food farming; in Terraform sector the embryos were developing, to be frozen for shipping. She was waiting in Med-Psych because she was an ESP, and she expected to be ratified at GalFed Central on the way back to Ungruwarkh. "The number ones are odd here."

:*Everyone is odd here. It's a backwater.*:

"You want very much to be here when we are away."

:*I always do when I'm away, and vice versa.*:

"Espinoza... is this ugly thing reaching you?"

:*I don't know...* :

"Wyaerl and the Lyhhrt are odd to me because they're from other worlds. Sheedy is a wasted old man, and the woman doesn't behave like a Solthree."

:*Metaxa's the funny one. I'd say he was some kind of fake if I didn't know his mind.*:

"But who will help, Espinoza?"

229

:Nudnik, I'll think about it! Go get some sleep. You've probably had your share of dreams for the night. Leave the door open. All I get to hear is stupid thoughts, but they're better than nothing.:

"I stay with you."

:And break your bones trying to sleep like that? Go on, get out already!:

But there was powerful affection beneath the thought, and in her mind she touched her nose to the cheek of the man-image, long gone, who had lived and walked beneath the sun.

\* \* \*

Khreng sighed. "Now I am ready for breakfast, I suppose you want to sleep."

"Yes. Go eat. Now I know how I get the dreams but not who does it, or why."

"So I am right after all."

"Right. Fill your belly and don't say I don't listen to you." She flung herself on the wide bed and dropped into velvet sleep.

\* \* \*

*Espinoza is dead.*

More dreams! She writhed, her claws flashed, her tail whipped.

"Pull in your claws, woman. It is no dream."

*Grief...* Khreng was licking her face, shuddering. A drop of sweat from his nose-tip, his only tear fell on her eyelid.

She leaped up, electrified. "Espinoza!" she howled. Through the open doorway shivers ran down the halls. *Cracked shell spilling brains and liquids! ESPINOZA!*

"Be quiet! They take him away." Khreng flung himself on her, pinned her down before she reached the door.

*Espinoza...?*

\* \* \*

"You were the last to see him alive."

MedPsych's director, Madame Yamashita, sat on a plain chair in the Committee Room: a small woman in a simple dark blue coverall with the insigne, on its breast; her hair was gathered at the back of her neck by a gold-and-enamel clasp. The rest of the committee were faceless to Prandra; she recognized a few vaguely as Earache, Slipped-Disk, and Six-Toes.

She said quietly, "You read me, Madame. I am not shielding." The pillars of her legs quivered, but she would not lie down to stop them.

Yamashita, a stolid and competent class-two, flushed slightly. "This is an inquiry, not a trial, Prandra. I know you are full of grief and anger."

"I regret expressing them so violently."

The director chose to miss the edge. "You discussed with Espinoza your troubled dreams and the possibility that they were induced by some outside agency."

"You know this."

"Please repeat it for our reports."

"Espinoza and I discuss the weather while he ESPS my problem, he says my dreams are perhaps engineered by post-hypnotic suggestion. I reply: If so, can you help? He promises to think about it and tells me to go sleep. I tell him I stay with him, he says no. I leave—and he is killed." Her voice trailed into a rasp.

"There were no witnesses to this conversation."

"What for? It is private business. He asks me to leave the door open when I go."

"When he was found, the door was closed."

"I presume murderers do not leave doors open."

"Why didn't you ask help from someone in authority?"

"I am fearful after having a terrible dream, and I have no friends in authority."

Yamashita clasped and unclasped her hands. "Don't you consider anyone else here your friend?"

Prandra said patiently, "Madame, I am a stranger and ignorant. I know Khreng is my friend, and Espinoza. I esp no one uninvited because it is not courteous, and perhaps I miss gestures that are offered in friendship."

They faced each other in perfect awareness: Khreng and Prandra had been treated correctly, even generously, but not with friendship. The faint frown-line between the director's brows indicated that she was wondering why; it seemed the wrongness of the atmosphere had spread like a malign growth.

The pale brown hands steepled their fingertips. "Last night you were seen behaving strangely in the children's park."

"That is not strange for Ungrukh. We exercise the way children do here, but not for long, because we tire quickly." Get to the point, woman!

She did. "Espinoza was killed between four and six in the morning. There is no way of identifying the hour more exactly... he could have been killed either before or after you went to the park."

Prandra's fur rose. "The guards—"

"Those at the outer doors report you left at four thirty and returned at five fifteen. Metaxa clocked you at five. The guards in quarters don't recall seeing you at all... they have probably been tampered with in some way."

Prandra felt caught in the hideous dream. "I am glad you are not accusing me of anything," she hissed.

"Be assured we are not. We are trying to lay down the basis for a full-scale inquiry. It is on record that while you were in the Qumedon time-warp, you used hypnosis to—"

Prandra, claw hooked in chain, was on the point of ripping it from her neck and flinging it across the room. Then she stopped and thought... What *can* I do, Espinoza?

*Eisenkop! Use your head for a change!*

She inhaled deeply. Unhooked the claw from the chain and crouched down. Slapped the floor with the whole length of her tail.

Committee jumped.

She slapped the floor again. "Madame, I am ignorant of many things on this world, particularly the numbers of various articles of diplomatic relations among the worlds of Galactic Federation which state that since Khreng and I constitute an embassy, we do not need to answer the kind of questions you ask unless put by an authorized GalFed committee." She stopped for breath. The sentence was sweet in her mouth. "Your inquiry in this area is extra-legal, your committee unconstitutional, and I have the right to ask for advice from the legal department of GalFed. You strike from the record all exchanges following my account of what happens, and—and you leave me alone to be sad for the death of a friend I love." She rose and loped toward the door. Someone jumped to press the button and let her through. Committee was afraid she might claw down the wall.

*       *       *

Khreng was pacing the halls. "What now? Are we in the firepot?"

"Yes. While I am in there I have the feeling that something/somebody is counting on me to jump up and attack them. Is that crazy?"

"Why ask me? If it is true, it is damned strange, and if it is not, it is still damned strange."

"And that is pretty damned helpful."

"What else do you want? If the feeling comes from some particular person you tell me; and if you don't say so you feel it in everyone. It cannot exist by itself in the air." They were passing Espinoza's room with its bored guard, and Prandra shuddered. Khreng stopped. "Air," he said.

"There cannot be any scent left after all this time."

"Everybody and his brother is going in and out all morning so I can't get near, but ventilators are not as bad as wind for carrying scent away and maybe something is left."

"No one's allowed in here," the guard said.

"I don't want in," said Khreng. "Only to smell around, if you allow the expression. If you move down the hall in order not to overload my nose, you may keep your gun aimed at me in case I break any rule or law."

The guard wrinkled his forehead, shrugged, and moved back, gun in the crook of his arm. Khreng inhaled deeply at the base of the door, raised his head, then his body, bracing himself by the forelimbs. "Don't expect much. Khreng the fearless tracker does it better on Ungruwarkh."

"Any fool knows that," said Prandra sadly.

"We still must do all we can, woman." Sniff. "Here you are, and Yamashita—I see her this morning—some Lyhhrt, they hardly smell, and—"

"Hurry up!" the guard snapped. "If anybody finds you here, I'll be in trouble."

Khreng calmly lowered his head until his nose was buried in the carpeting. "A scale from Wyaerl, all those guards, very confusing... that one, Sheedy, is always pinching—"

The guard snorted. "He tries it with all of them. If he wasn't a blind old fool, he'd get a few punches."

"—that woman, Nema, and... myself, of course—"

He sneezed. "Carpet fluff, and..."

Prandra finished for him. "And what is left of Espinoza."

"Tracked on somebody's shoes—"

"Which are now in some waste disposal."

"For God's sake, are you training to be a hunting dog or something?"

The guard found four savage red cats' eyes fixed on him. He swallowed. "I'm sorry! I didn't mean to insult you!" His fair skin was now hotly flushed. "It just popped into my mind."

"Maybe you ask yourself where it comes from," Khreng said quietly.

\* \* \*

"Half the people in this place are visitors of Espinoza," said Prandra.

"All likely with good excuses." Ahead, an apartment door opened and a wisp of vapor escaped from it, followed by Wyaerl. Water and air tanks strapped to his back, he took his walk at high noon.

Wyaerl was not a telepath; he could only have been described as an inside man. He had a sense for the insides of things, and his people were used for surgery, metallurgy, mining, life- and physical sciences. Sky-blue in color, he was shaped like an elongated pancake, two meters long; though his translucence made him look like jelly, he was tough as saddle leather. His rear half was a huge muscular foot that propelled him in the manner of a snail. His front end projected forty or fifty tendrils with specialized uses: light and sound sensors, because he had no eyes or ears; prehensile digits; tools that split into almost invisible ends to explore earth or porous stone.

When he sensed the Ungrukh, he extended his foot to brace himself and raised his front end. His tendrils quivered. Across his half-meter expanse of belly was a slit opening into a pouch that held his generative organs, both male and female, and his feeding and excreting processes. Normally shy, like his species, he rarely invited esping, and breathed through slits in his back; the only way he could speak was to extend his feeding tube, suck air, and expel it in an excruciating squeak.

Khreng and Prandra stopped. The breathing tube came out, sucked air like wind in a chimney. "What is, troubling you," said Wyaerl, "is something, inside something."

"Do you know what that is?" Prandra asked.

"No." Wyaerl withdrew the tube, flopped down with a thud, and pushed off in a cloud of his planet's ammoniac atmosphere.

"That is a very deep thought," Khreng said. "Everything is inside something."

"He goes to a lot of trouble to tell us," said Prandra. "Maybe he helps."

"Maybe something else helps…"

They glared at each other. "Say it, big man. You think I am too hard on Yamashita."

"I know she is an arrogant woman who deserves it, but—"

They chorused, "She is also somewhat afraid and unsure—"

Khreng huffed, "It is your thought in your head. You make her look bad, and among her people that is a great dishonor. She is only trying to do her work properly."

"I'm aware of it. To get us out of the stewpot, I must apologize." She growled, "And you know how good I am at doing that."

"Then have your meal and think it over."

"No. I do it first; otherwise I throw up."

"Damnation, your stomach is iron like your head! Your dinner spoils."

"Ha. It is cold from their food-boxes. You breathe on it and bring it to body heat." She grinned. "Meat tastes much better that way."

\* \* \*

But she did not go at once to Yamashita's door; there were words to prepare. She trotted the white hexagons, eyes slitted against the glare of noon because she had not bothered about her contacts. It was hard to concentrate on apologizing (humbling oneself) with her mind still full of grief and fury.

Espinoza had wanted to die. But, as she had once done, he said: *It is always better to be alive today…* He had given her a gesture, his mental shrug, and she had given him the words. *Espinoza!*

Think of Yamashita… She crouched on a patch of warm earth by the playground fence watching the children on the seesaws and slide. A little carousel tinkled faintly. Some of the children belonged to employees, a few were proto-ESPs. One good second-class, possibly higher, a couple of lower unknown quantities. Two or three of them looked delicious. She nestled chin on paws and thought of Yamashita.

"Hey, there's that cat!"

"I can see it, dummy."

Children at the fence, staring.

Madame Yamashita, I come to tell you it is not my intention—

A handful of sand fell on her back.

She opened one eye and met the stares of the children. Mischief. Pull kitty's tail. The skin of her back rippled and shook it off. She was too warm and lazy to move.

—to hurt or embarrass you; I am deeply sorry to offend you. I only try to make clear—

Another fistful of sand.

At her eyes! She dug her head beneath her forearms, stunned by the mind-kaleidoscope of their fury.

"Aah, that's not enough! Get some gravel out of the pots, there!" Children outside the playground encircling her. Stones rained, one at her closed eye with stabbing pain.

On Ungruwarkh she had survived ambushes. She sent feelers to their heads: puppets, bewildered. Some of them enjoyed stoning an animal, some did not care, some hated it: none knew why they had chosen that moment to do it. And there was a kind of shield between them and the adults; no one had noticed.

Prandra had several choices, some disastrous. First she used most of her strength to break the shield; then, well battered, she took the line of least resistance. As the stones rained down she rolled over on her back, exposing her belly with paws in the air, tail limp, eyes closed, neck crooked at an impossible angle, with jaws gaping and tongue hanging slack. She looked like a horridly dead cat.

Guards began shouting, parents screaming, the hail diminished and stopped.

"Prandra!" Arms pulled at her. "Are you all right? Prandra!"

She opened her eyes slowly and straightened her head. Guards, clerks, one or two Lyhhrt in their curious little gold boxes on wheels. She moistened her mouth with her tongue and rolled over. Parents shaking and yelling at the children, slapping some of them. Good. "I am all right."

"My God, your eye's bleeding, we've got to—"

"Leave it. I attend to it myself." She pulled free and shook herself vigorously, not caring where the dust landed, then headed back toward the residence.

Damned good piece of acting, if I say so.

Her eye hurt badly, she was both exhilarated and furious. She would apologize and go home to Ungruwarkh. Fight and starve. Damned Solthrees, pretending to be civilized. Food and wisdom you get here, says Espinoza. Where are they, you dead fool?

At the residence doorway she sensed a significant presence and looked up. A tall man was leaning there, arms folded, ankles crossed. One of committee! Six-Toes. His name was Kinnear. "I am on my way to apologize to Madame Yamashita," she said. "That must please you."

He said, "That eye's swelling shut. I'll send you a medtech."

"Thank you."

As she passed, he said out of the corner of his mouth, "Quite a good act you put on."

"I say so myself," she purred.

* * *

Prandra's rage almost negated the sense of obligation, but she wanted Yamashita to see her in this condition. She knew that was a shameful idea, but she could not control it.

She buzzed Yamashita's door and waited. No answer. The at-home light was on, she buzzed again, paced up and down, tried once more. Nothing.

She esped; a guard came trotting. "What happened to your eye?"

"Never mind. Madame Yamashita does not answer."

"Maybe she's sick. She gets headaches. I'll have somebody call in."

At the end they had to bring techs to remove the door.

Yamashita was sprawled across her bed wrapped in a brocaded kimono. Her hair was loose, the little gold-and-enamel clasp on the floor. Her face was almost beautiful in repose and her hair fine and silky; a thick tress lay across her throat but did not hide the deep claw slashes that sliced her arteries, nor the river of blood that flowed over the bed.

Prandra's belly convulsed, she gasped and choked. She let two guards lead her back to the room where Khreng waited, presently a medtech rolled in to inject her swollen eyelids and bathe her eye with drops to shrink the distended vessels.

* * *

She raged. "If I go earlier I save her!"

"Now you are irrational," Khreng snorted. "How does an apology save her life?"

"Don't you see? It is like with Espinoza. How can I prove I do not kill her first and then go out to put on an act with the children? Even Kinnear knows it is an act."

"According to your memory, and it does not fail as long as I know you, Kinnear also knows it is an act of self-defense. You are too hurt and angry to think straight."

"That is true."

"And you tell him you intend to apologize."

"That can seem a misdirection... and these claw slashes..." She shivered.

"That is not your style," he said dryly. "Any fool knows no serious cat kills like that."

"There is no shortage of fools here."

"Wait and see. One way or another we get out of this... take out our ship..." He grinned. "At the worst a good bleach and a job in the circus. Here is fresh food. Now eat."

Day and night passed, and morning to the zenith. Prandra slept most of the time. Khreng watched over her, saw the swelling of her eye go down, called the medtech for a shot to calm her tossing; when she quieted and began to murmur the names of their children he lay beside her and slept.

"We go home." She was pacing. Round and round, tail slapping the walls. Her eye was better except for the odd dart of pain.

Khreng sprawled on the bed. "You are making me dizzy. We see what they have to say. There is no choice."

"They likely tell us to get legal advice in a hurry. I use my hurry some other way."

"And that makes the enemy very happy."

"What enemy? There is no substance, scent, thought-track. Nothing to hunt." The door chimed.

"Come in!" Prandra roared. Khreng tsked and pushed the button. Kinnear came in and leaned against the wall in his characteristic pose, arms folded, ankles crossed. He was very tall, with a bland oval face, thinning blond hair; broad shoulders tapered down to a wedge-shaped body. He had the small-pupiled blue eyes that are as good as an ESP shield for hiding thought.

Khreng said, "Excuse me, I don't know your name."

"I'm the one Prandra calls Six-Toes."

"His name is Kinnear." Prandra dropped to the floor, sulking.

"I am polydactylic," Kinnear said. "I had the extras removed from my hands; they weren't pretty. Most Solthree ESPs have some kind of abnormality."

Khreng shifted from the bed to the stone. "Sit."

"In a moment. I haven't apologized for letting Prandra be hurt."

"What's the difference? Espinoza and Yamashita are dead." Prandra blinked. "In committee you are open minded, so I know you have six toes. I am not, except for evidence, so how do you know I call you that?"

Kinnear coughed. "I have a habit of esping uninvited. I'm head of Security."

"Ah," said Prandra. "And still they are dead. Now I suppose you come to read us our rights."

"In a sense. The autopsy's been done." He smiled grimly. "And here comes Wyaerl now."

Wyaerl appeared with his inchworm step, air tank hissing furiously, food-pipe extruded. "I, hurried." Kinnear extended his hand. Wyaerl bent his top half and with one tentacle dropped something into the open palm. Kinnear nodded. "Iron," said Wyaerl. "Not steel, it broke, with force."

"Look." In Kinnear's hand was a metal fragment shaped into the perfect replica of an Ungrukh claw. "From the wound."

Khreng grunted. "Who makes it?"

"We don't know yet."

"Then you are no further ahead," said Prandra. "It appears someone wishes to place suspicion on us again, or else make it seem as if the Lyhhrt are trying it because they do so much metal work."

Kinnear said, "*Suspicion* on the Lyhhrt? How do you know they aren't guilty?"

"Aah! Lyhhrt? Those little lumps of that stuff—"

"Protoplasm."

"—who make their working shells so fancy in precious metals so others do not look down on them? Do they make a claw in plain iron without all their stars and flowers?"

"But in this case—"

"Find me one. No Lyhhrt here would do that!"

On the surface of his sorrow for Yamashita he was amused and a little condescending. "Can you esp a Lyhhrt?"

"Of course, but who needs to? You have only to look at them and it is clear as your day."

"You can esp Lyhhrt, ha? Then if it's not you or the Lyhhrt, where would you begin, Prandra?"

"Kinnear, I don't know or care. Khreng and I are leaving. If you believe we are in the clear, we rather starve on Ungruwarkh than stay here another day."

Kinnear flushed with embarrassment. "Um... one of your ship's engines has been blown up."

Khreng said, "Blown up..."

"A charge of explosive," Wyaerl piped. Prandra was staring at Kinnear.

"We've put extra guards around your supplies and equipment," he said. "Two weeks of repairs."

"That helps." Are you sure you don't do that yourself to keep us here, Head Security Man?

His flush darkened; he said quietly, "I'm glad you didn't say that aloud."

Unrepentant, Pranda said, "No apologies yet. But you make sure you stay alive, Kinnear."

He laughed. "Did you know that only a class-one can esp a Lyhhrt?"

"Yes, but who cares?"

"I do. While you're waiting, why don't you take your class-one exam and you can have it ratified at GalFed Central?"

"From what examiners? Old raveled Sheedy, or the Weird Lady?"

He said coolly, "We also have the Lyhhrt, and I'm a good enough class-two to sit on the Board..." He paused. "And... if you don't mind another brain-in-a-bottle, Madame Chatterjee is really first class."

"Are all those on your staff?"

"Some of the Lyhhrt are here on their own business, like Wyaerl... what about it?"

Prandra considered. "Khreng, if I agree to this, do you tell me I have a swollen head?"

"Do you need to be told?"

Kinnear said, "You don't shield well enough yet, Prandra, and you'll need training. Chatterjee does that, and she can stick a pin in you."

"I worry about stones, not pins." She kept her eyes on Kinnear but was careful not to esp him. "You seem to trust us, Kinnear. Are you immune to psychological poison?"

"No... I've had dreams too. But what reason could you have had for killing Espinoza? He was the person you loved most on this world."

"He is tired and longing for death."

"You always knew that about him. You had a thousand chances to kill him and make it look like an accident—"

"After which we are esped and found out—"

"—or even in genuine kindness if you had a simpler morality."

"Savage morality," Khreng growled.

"Yes, our—let us say, enemies, try to make us seem savage and untrustworthy. We are expected to be accused of killing Espinoza and Yamashita—like wild beasts. I am to get insulted and jump on committee, and rip up little children at play. Somebody thinks we have not much control."

"But if they want to get rid of you"—Kinnear scratched his head—"and then blow up your ship..."

"Nobody tries to kill us yet, Kinnear," said Prandra. "It seems somebody wants us to leave—*but not on our own ship!*"

"Somebody wants you for something..."

"Yes. Isn't that interesting. And no one knows what." She cocked her head. "Yesterday I think you are esp-ing me from the time I leave Committee until I meet those playful children..."

"I certainly never expected—"

"I don't mean that. During that time Yamashita is murdered."

"I know." He licked his lips. "I was fifty meters away from her and somebody shielded so well I never caught a hint of it. Same with the ship. And I'm stuck. I'm short of staff and I have to sit in as head of committee too... God, I wish we had Chatterjee on this, but she's so damn shy about that bottle she'll hardly ever come out of her room."

"How long?"

"Nearly two hundred years."

"Very nice for her." Prandra's sigh, like Espinoza's, was in the shape of a tear.

"If I don't get this cleared up in a hurry, I'll be kicked out, we may not get our MedPsych division funded... everything happening... nobody will come into this kind of danger, especially with children." He stared at the metal fragment. "I'm going to trust you. I must, I need help. With my kind of funds I just don't have that many class-ones to—"

"Play around with," Khreng said, basso profundo.

Prandra having declared she would turn truly savage if she did not get out, the Ungrukh took their walk at noon. The sun sparkled through the dome, the flagstones were hot. After ten silent minutes, Prandra turned off the path, and Khreng hissed, "Oh, no! Not the playground! What do you think you are doing, woman?"

"Something is not good there."

"And you make it better and get beat up again?" He hooked a claw in her chain.

"Don't stop me, Khreng." Knowing better, he let go.

There was an oppressive air about the playground, and the children went through their games in a lackluster way; in the spirits of some, Prandra sensed a dusting of guilt. "Nine are sorry they hurt me, and four think it is too bad they do not hurt me more. Ha." She grinned. "There is no shortage of bent ones on Sol Three." Since staff was rarely Outworld, all the children were Solthrees.

"See those guards?" Khreng said. "The guns in their hands are not stunners."

"Is it forbidden for a big cat to play with a small child, since yesterday it is the other way around?" She pushed open the gate. Khreng, willy-nilly, followed; the guards shifted their weapons. Prandra paid no attention; she trotted to the silent carousel, pulled the switch, and jumped to the back of a yellow-maned lion. "Come on, Khreng, take a ride with me."

"You are crazy." He found a zebra.

Kinnear's mind broke through her calm. :For God's sake, Prandra, watch it!:

:Keep trusting, Kinnear.:

Round and round they went, bodies undulating to the rhythm of the music. Khreng grumbled, "What do you think you are doing?"

"Enjoying myself."

The nervous parents at the gate were joined by doctors, clerks on lunch hour with sandwiches and coffee-bulbs; a couple of Lyhhrt in wheeled runabouts, two or three more gleaming in engraved workshells with multiple joints and stilt legs. Blind Sheedy with coffee dripping down his zipsuit as usual, one hand on the shoulder of his exasperated eye-guard. And even blank Nema, with Metaxa. "What a marvel," said Prandra. "Maybe we are born for the circus."

"Shut up," Khreng said.

"Tcha! It is you who talk of a circus." She jumped off; Khreng stopped the machine. She rolled in the sand, stood and shook herself; if the air had been less humid, the atmosphere might have matched that of the more habitable places of Ungruwarkh on one of its better days.

But she did not like the guilt on these spirits.

She began trotting in a circle, shoulder to shoulder with Khreng; the children backed away in a larger circle around them. She stopped short before one sullen boy about twelve. "You like dogs better than cats, hah?"

"Yes." ESP-in-training who liked, or thought he liked, to stone animals.

:*I don't bite children, baby.*: His mouth turned down at the corners, and she laughed. "Dogs lick your face and fetch sticks." She snorted. "Dogs play dead." With a twist she flung herself into her dead-cat position; then sprang up on hind legs. "Cats can play tricks too, and yesterday I play one on you!"

She dropped to fours and circled slowly, abreast with Khreng. The children were small statues of perplexity and suspicion. "I am not badly hurt, so you don't have to feel guilty"—a breath of her mind blew dust from them, and the air lightened,—"but my eye is sore, and next time you think first when you feel like throwing stones at anyone!" She found a girl of seven or eight, an ESP small for her age, but brash, and young enough to play the games of little children. "You like a cat-back ride?"

The child twisted her fingers and stuck her tongue in her cheek. "Uh-huh."

Prandra's voice deepened. "Do you mean yes?"

"Yes, ma'am."

"Ask your mother."

The child drew a line in the dust with her toe: "She says all right."

Prandra crouched and the child bestrode her! "Not the chain. Hold the hair at the sides of my neck where it starts getting longer. Khreng gives rides too." Khreng said nothing, but the stretch of his nostrils expressed a lot. He accepted a squirming body.

Round and round in tandem spiral... Now, love you know how it is on our world Ungruwarkh with our children.

Red lava plains, pale sun, a nip in the air; one tongue of flame from a volcano in the north; Firemaster speaking from one of his many mouths; out of caves and fissures cats join, running until there is a tribe, an odd good-humored one, for each cat is ridden by a cub, thrilled/joyful/half-scared, little claws deep in the fur prickling the backs they ride on, patches of feverish heat between little body and big one, minds always open for the marauders over the hills...

"What the hell do they think they're doing? What are you letting them do?"

The Ungrukh stopped.

"Go on! Go on!" the cubs-children cried.

"In a moment, children."

Metaxa, red-faced, shoving against watchers toward the gate. Nema, still as a mannequin, hands on the bars.

"Playing with those animals!" Metaxa's mouth was a screaming cave. "Why don't you let them roll in the snake pit at the zoo?" His face burned with sweat.

Prandra watched, satisfied. She read confusion and anger in Metaxa, and did not know what to make of them, but if nothing at all had happened, she would have been deeply disappointed. Metaxa still yelling, "Don't you underst—"

Guards to either side grabbed him in mid-word, and Kinnear stepped up to him deliberately. "Are those your children, Metaxa?"

Metaxa's mouth clamped shut. He shook loose of the guards, barreled his way back through the bewildered onlookers, and dragged Nema from the fence more roughly than he had done on that evening. She did not even blink.

The little girl yanked at Prandra's fur. "More!" Prandra wrapped her prehensile tail around the thin waist and set her on the ground firmly. "Everyone has a turn."

Finally they lay on their backs with the smallest children crawling over them like ants, rubbing their faces in the soft belly-fur and shrieking with laughter. Prandra plucked them off gently, one by one. "Enough now. Big pussycats get tired fast."

"Can we do it again tomorrow?"

"Yes, tomorrow." The children went back to maps and lessons, and the adults, somewhat bemused, followed. Sheedy was laughing and shaking his head; it had been a circus to him. The Lyhhrt skimmed or stilted away.

\* \* \*

"All right, you've defused a lot of fear and hostility, and that exhibition was very pleasing—except for Metaxa," Kinnear said. "Now, Honorables, what were you trying to prove?"

"We are fishing, and there is a pull on the line," said Prandra. "Also," Khreng said, "now we make ourselves nice kitty-cats, we are pushing. Killer is less apt to try blaming us and more likely to attack us instead of someone else."

"That's a fine improvement," Kinnear said. "Where does it leave me?"

"Blameless. We take care of ourselves."

"But how can Metaxa's blowup be a pull on your line?"

Khreng and his nose knew what to make of that: "Of all who go to Espinoza's door around the time he is killed—Prandra, Wyaerl, Yamashita,

Nema, guards and all, there is no trace of Metaxa. Although he keeps himself very clean, there is no one I know who smells stronger—and there is no skin-flake, oil droplet, atom of sweat... he is never seen apart from Nema, and she is hardly capable of blowing her own nose without him. Today he is a very frightened and angry man. Isn't that strange?"

\* \* \*

:*Why do you always speak in the present tense?*: Madame Chatterjee asked.

"Yesterday is before my birth and tomorrow is after my death," said Prandra. "That is what Ungrukh feel and how they speak." The blue glasstex globe on its stand, the tiny room, were exactly like Espinoza's. "May we keep the door open? I am tired of whitewalls."

:*I understand what you feel about the present. But I concentrate better with a closed door.*:

Prandra sighed, a low rumble. *And hallucinate better.*

:*That too,*: said Chatterjee.

The bottled brains—they were called converted, and called themselves bottled—spent much time alone, of necessity; they hallucinated much, because of lack of sensory afference, and learned to control it rigidly, to keep their minds in order. Chatterjee was sufficiently down-to-earth. She had died of mutant cholera at thirty-six, and maintained her self-image at that age: a small, wiry woman with beautiful black eyes and graceful brows; hair beginning to gray.

"I don't mean to offend you," Prandra said.

:*You don't, except to make me jealous of your freedom, as every embodied person does.*: Image of a wry smile. :*It is not that good a motive for murder. I am not a superb shielder, nor a strong hypnotizer.*:

Prandra, shocked, said, "You are far ahead of me, Madame."

:*I intend to stay that way.*: She asked abruptly, :*Where is there a white, yellow, and blue ball?*:

"In the seal-pool at the zoo."

:*You did not break my shield then.*:

Prandra grinned. "No, I remember seeing it when I am there." She added, "Calcutta has many green trees, though there is still much poverty."

:*Good. Now you try... green... ah... why do you call your daughter Emerald, which is a green jewel in the English language, when your people are red?*:

"Ha. Khreng hears it when he visits GalFed Central, and he likes the sound. Perhaps it is the beginning of an appreciation of Art in us Ungrukh."

Chatterjee permitted herself a smile-thought, and Prandra couched in the narrow space. "Madame, I think we can like each other, if you permit. And I learn as well as I can. But people are being killed, and I must find out why, and what the killer wants of Khreng and me. Can you help?"

Slowly: :*Oh, I am very willing to like you…*: and shrinking.

"I understand, Madame. Espinoza also spends over two hundred years in a bottle, and does not care at the end. One day I too howl for death in my bottle and there is nobody to hear. Nobody so kind to smash it, as even I cannot bring myself to do. From the bottle it is dangerous to think of flesh and bone; food, sleep, sex, running in the open air. Even drinking cold water when you are thirsty. Espinoza is lucky. Yamashita is lucky it is too late to save her brain. So you stay in this room, and teach ignorant people like me to do useful work—but you must also have to answer a lot of stupid questions, and you do not come out where the people are alive with their love and hate and anger—and I think that is narrowing and wasteful." She rose beside the door, but could not bring herself to open it, and stood there, head and tail hanging.

:*I know.*: The mind-touch was light as a peacock's feather. :*You spoke harshly to Yamashita and did not apologize. I have not been aware for so many years without understating. What you don't understand is that even as an embodied person I was almost as retiring as I am today, and I regret it, but it is too late for me to change very much. I do want to help, not only by teaching you. I will gladly do whatever is necessary, but you can help me to work at my best by bringing me your thoughts and feelings as you brought them to Espinoza… I don't believe—I don't believe you will come to love me as much as you did Espinoza, but I am your friend, yours and Khreng's. Agreed?*:

"Yes, Madame," Prandra whispered. "Agreed."

\* \* \*

"Wyaerl, Kinnear asks me to help him in his investigations. May I question you?"

"Yes," Wyaerl piped. "You, may, esp." He withdrew his tube and flopped to the carpet like a relieved flapjack.

"Why do you come here?"

:*On our world we have colonies of squatters from many places trading in illegal drugs and also farming and processing them from plant matter disturbing our economy ecology and morale which GalFed can't do much about because they don't extradite and because a good number are Solthrees especially some rare impervious types who cannot be esped I came here for help of which little is forthcoming there is no one suitable and we have spent too much credit already so I am going home soon with my disappointment is that enough?:*

"It's certainly comprehensive. Can I ask you one more question without insult?"

*:Go ahead I know you don't intend to insult my humble self.:*

"You go to visit Espinoza some time before or after he is killed—"

*:No no without insult I assure you that is not so though there were many times I consulted Espinoza he was most agreeable that was one time I did not you may esp as much as you please.:*

"Thank you, I know you are not lying," said Prandra.

"I am sorry for Kinnear," Khreng said.

"Are you sure there is a trace of…"

"Old woman, I know I find a fresh undried scale with Wyaerl's personal scent and his planet's atmosphere on it. In Espinoza's doorway. If it is a plant it carries the planter's scent. That is it." Prandra patted his forehead. "You are the authority. I accept."

"Who is there?" asked the speaking-tube.

"Prandra."

The door opened; Metaxa was drawn about the eyes, but the beard hid the rest of his broad high-colored face. He held a glass with a bent tube in it. "What do you want?" His control was brittle.

"I am allowed to ask questions, and you are permitted not to answer."

"Otherwise," he said coolly, "you will esp." He had pushed his sleeves up the arms and unzipped the suit halfway down the chest; gray hair burst from the opening and on his forearms. The hair of his beard was thick and lively brown; she wondered briefly if he colored it, and answered no. It was not himself he decorated with jewels or perfumes; his personal smell was strong, even to her unauthoritative nose.

"No, Metaxa. Sometimes you push your thoughts at me. I don't care for that, because I don't esp without permission, except to defend myself. That is Kinnear's business."

"And you're working for him…" He shrugged.

"Come in, read all you like. I'm not hiding anything." Metaxa and Nema had an apartment of several rooms; the walls were covered with hangings, reliefs, pictures, the floors crammed with furniture and figurines and things Prandra did not recognize, but she did not want to risk knocking them over. She tucked in her tail and crouched near the door.

Nema was sitting in a chair by the window dressed in one of her beautiful gowns, a blue shimmer. She was twenty-two years old, mature in body and with the face of a sleeping infant. Metaxa sat down beside her and offered the tube to her mouth. She sipped once, blinked, raised a fist and swung with great power. Glass and tube bounced against the wall splashing and fell to the carpet.

Metaxa's face was expressionless as hers. He rubbed his arm, picked up the glass and tube and put them on a table. Prandra's skin prickled.

Nema's hands folded themselves in her lap and Metaxa turned to Prandra. "What do you want?" he asked again.

"Does the lady Nema go anywhere without you, or you without her?"

"No. We're always together, all the time." His forehead was wet; he did not wipe it. "Why?"

"It is the kind of question Kinnear asks. We try to help."

His eyes were shrewd. "I think it's the kind of question an Ungrukh asks. Kinnear would want to know where we were at the time of the murders."

"If Kinnear wishes to know that, he asks."

"He already has... Madame." His voice lingered on irony. "I'll tell you and save you trouble. When Espinoza was killed, we were asleep here together, and when Yamashita was killed, we were having lunch here together. Are you satisfied?"

"No, Metaxa. Can you prove you are not drugged or hypnotized either time? That is the kind of question an Ungrukh asks. I am grateful for your cooperation."

"You surprise me. Anything else?"

Before she could answer, Nema stood up and headed for the door as if she were blind to the body in her way. Prandra scrambled to avoid tripping her, and Metaxa jumped to open the door before she crashed into it. Then he took her by the elbow and let her lead him where she would.

Prandra slipped out and watched them down the hall. Nema went blindly in her curious stilted walk. Metaxa glanced back once, but said nothing.

*Pray tell me, sir whose dog are you?* Prandra scratched at her neck where the chain rubbed it. All at once her fur stood on end and her legs trembled.

A pinhole had opened momentarily in Metaxa's mind, exploding volcanic fury: a firestorm of fear, despair, disgust—and hatred for the woman, Nema. Khreng came round a corner, sniffing, and stopped beside her. "Tune down, or they receive you on Ungruwarkh."

She was shaking. "I can't help it."

"What do you expect from a man with a ring in his nose?"

"I never try to put one in yours," she snarled. "What do you smell here?"

"Metaxa, Prandra, Nema, guards, Lyhhrt."

"Why Lyhhrt? They are not around all day."

"Ask them."

"They don't talk to class-twos."

"Then ask Kinnear."

\* \* \*

"They don't talk to me, either," said Kinnear. I'm a class-two, remember? They think in a way it's impossible to grasp unless you're a very powerful ESP. You must have picked up thoughts from them. What were they?"

"Yes, no, and maybe," Prandra said. "And some garble about Cosmic Thought."

"There you are. I had Sheedy question them and they say they weren't anywhere near Espinoza—or Yamashita."

Khreng growled, "Everybody is at Espinoza's door, and nobody is. Maybe my nose is playing tricks."

"No, but somebody is, and I don't pretend to understand." He pleated his hands. "Right now it's Metaxa I'm worried about. He's a walking hornet's nest."

"He's unconscious of it," Prandra said, "or he doesn't stay with her."

"I've never figured why he does. He's very proud, he's what used to be called a self-made man. Worked in a dockyard, at the beginning, earned everything he has, and learned everything he knows, by himself."

"Yes," said Prandra. "The literary mind. And now we work for GalFed, we are dogs of the king, hah?"

"Don't put on any stupid act for me. Now that's opened up, he's going to blow—at you or Nema. You saw all the stuff crammed in his place. That's the Art. He's also got weapons collections. I don't have authority to confiscate them, and if I did, he'd find more—and bring in his lawyers too."

"I doubt Nema lets him hurt her."

"Then we'll give you some guns."

Khreng guffawed. "Without thumbs, Kinnear? First you spend a month learning to build up the grips so we can hold them, and days teaching us to use them, then we fall all over our feet and shoot our tails off carrying them? Knives are better."

"Carry knives."

"Kinnear, we are good with knives," Prandra said, "but we also play with little children. Even if I am attacked once, we still look pretty odd if we seem to need knives to defend ourselves from them. The kind we use best are in our heads and hands, and we leave it that way."

:Still your old self, Prandra,: said Chatterjee. :You may need weapons.:

"I am not shy about using a knife if I need one. We still don't know whom to fight. Our ship is ready in ten days and we are not staying longer."

:*When do you want to set the exam, then?*:

"In eight days, if you believe I am ready. Otherwise I take it at Central. I still have a lot to learn."

:*You can begin today by picking a lost memory out of my unconscious— within the bounds of good taste.*:

"That is not what I have in mind."

:*What I have in mind is my stock-in-trade, and you have agreed to learn.*:

Prandra sighed and shut her eyes so tightly, the bristles above them stood straight up. "The brass table from Benares... the one passed down through generations in your family, you plan to give it..." Her voice trailed off and she twitched in embarrassment.

:*I said unconscious, not suppressed!*: Chatterjee's thoughts could sting like arrows.

"I admit I have no tact," Prandra muttered. "Begin again."

:*No. I promised it to my daughter, but she refused to see me after I was bottled. Not for many years. She came when she was nearly as old as I. I gave it to her.*: Her mind went blank. She asked vaguely, :*What was I saying? ... Prandra, you are blocking me! Tell me at once!*:

It seemed to Prandra that the pump had speeded up and the glass bubble might burst. "Do you really wish to keep a painful memory?"

:*If I avoided painful thoughts, I could not be much of a teacher.*:

"The brass table."

:*Good. If you hadn't told me, there would have been no exam.*:

"Why? Because I block better than you?"

Grim smile-thought. :*Because a pupil shows courtesy— even to a humbled instructor.*:

"I am learning."

:*Have you always been able to block?*:

"On Ungruwarkh we call it netting, because it is like catching the best fish out of a school of diseased ones—and our fish are terrible. That is why I am here." Prandra grinned. "Madame, there are many things I can do that I don't know the right names for, or can't control properly. I am grateful to learn how to use them."

:*Before we are through you, will teach me to block as well as you do. Now tell me the problem.*:

"Khreng's sense of smell is not evidence to the Iaw but it is to me. It tells us everyone is everywhere, and nobody admits to being anywhere. Even Wyaerl, who is as innocent as the morning dew, says he is nowhere near Espinoza on the night of death, and we know he is. Now—"

*:Prandra, you tell me.:*

"Ah, that is a block... but what matter in Wyaerl's head is so dangerous that it must be fished out?"

*:Perhaps... Wyaerl wondered if he could bring up to Espinoza the possibility you would agree to stop at his world on the way to Ungruwarkh, to help with his trouble. He didn't feel he knew you well enough then to ask you personally, and he was even shy of asking Espinoza—But you seem to have impressed him.:*

"I can tell you he is not all that shy when you get to know him, but I find nothing of that in Espinoza. I began to see past that block: it is not desired for us to become too friendly with anyone here, or leave too early—and our engine is blown up. Ha."

*:What else?:*

"The Lyhhrt are also among those who are not at Espinoza's door—they say."

*:Two of them, Administration and Liaison, I've known well for several years; they work hard and deal honestly. The other three are visitors, and they have never seemed hostile. I don't intrude on their privacy, and they leave me with mine.:*

"They seem close to Nema."

*:No, they scarcely go near her. She's not really a staff member. More of a showpiece, because her mind is so much like theirs. She cannot communicate very well with anyone.:*

"Kinnear considers you much more valuable."

*:I am not jealous.:*

Prandra laughed. "There's no need to be jealous of that one."

Chatterjee said, *:I am beginning to look forward to that exam. What kind of illusion form are you planning?:*

Prandra shrugged. "I'm not sure. I'm not a person with many illusions." She raised her hand to the door button.

*:Prandra... :*

She waited.

*:I don't know much—not even where the danger lies—but it is enough to make me afraid. It was probably meant that you be captured and used for some purpose, on the premise that you were savage and ignorant, even though intelligent. Now you are stronger and have learned much more. Perhaps too much.:*

"I know. Now we are on the edge of finding out, I think... and we are meant to be killed."

*:I feel responsible.:*

"For what? Our feelings for Espinoza? And our curiosity? No. For helping me out of my ignorance? Kinnear suggests this training and I accept. I am responsible. For Khreng as well."

\* \* \*

Two big red cats trotted the grounds in the evening light, followed by two armed guards ordered by Kinnear and mounted on foot-controlled mopeds. "There is nothing like a good run in fresh recycled air and escorted by guards to make one feel alive and carefree," said Prandra.

"As long as they keep behind. I am tired of smelling them."

They passed the zoo's reptile house. "There's a scent for you," Prandra said.

"Better than our fish." Khreng paused by the tiger's cage, where the great beast lay snoring. "Over three hundred kilos, my guess. Khreng times three. I wonder what it is like to be that one." The tiger opened one eye and closed it again. "I think I keep on being Khreng."

Prandra laughed. "A nice toy for children." She stopped at the playground fence.

"No more bloody damned carousel rides!"

"Don't get excited... look: over there is where I see Nema and Metaxa the night Espinoza dies. My nose is not yours, but... if we close our eyes... smell: Nema, Metaxa, fear of/for—what? Her/him/ them/it..."

Khreng opened his eyes. "It?"

"Yes. Let's go back." She seemed depressed.

\* \* \*

Khreng rubbed his back on the stone slab and sat up. "What in Firemaster's name is the matter?"

She bit off a loose claw scale. "I believe... if we do not come here, Espinoza and Yamashita are still living."

"Maybe. And Ungruwarkh is dead as a stone."

"The tribes fight over what we have to bring them, and many die."

"Not necessarily. If so, they are better to die for hope than from starvation. What else?"

"Why ask?"

"I am with you all these years and I don't know you? When you twist your head twenty degrees clockwise, there is something you are afraid to tell me."

She sniffed.

"Are you afraid I am frightened, or angry?"

She whispered at last, "I am afraid we die."

"That's how you save me?" He stood in a swift angry movement. "Woman, you better tell me pretty damn fast. I am a fine figure of a man on my world if I step down alone from the ship and tell everyone Prandra is dead because I am ignorant!"

"I always know you are vain," she hissed.

"I am vain enough to believe we are equals and can take this risk together as we always do."

"I am afraid others may be killed. That is part of why my head IS twenty degrees clockwise... everyone knows everything and nobody admits knowing anything."

"That is a contradiction. You are afraid they may be killed and then they are all liars and conspirators."

"I don't mean that. They have information they are unconscious of, and we are ignorant. If they become conscious, they are dead."

"Killer cannot murder all of MedPsych."

"There is no need. (One) when we are not here, nothing is upset; (two) we arrive and Killer finds some use for us; (three) Killer finds us too hard to handle and becomes enraged and frustrated; so he (four) kills us and returns to (one); leaving what is not conscious, unconscious."

"(One-a)," said Khreng sarcastically, "only having to explain two big dead red cats."

"Not if they die by accident or foolish mistake."

"And you have in mind?"

"We lack that carefully hidden information but—I want to get back to our people, on our ship. Forget the exam. If we stay under guard until we leave, we are safe."

He hacked with laughter. "Do we sit safe in that village long ago and let the Qumedon kill the Rabbi and his people? Whether the test means anything or not, you spend the rest of our days hurting your spirit because you let Espinoza's murderer go free."

"If we move, we risk other lives."

"Whose are you counting?"

"The helpless ones who suspect, like Chatterjee, perhaps Sheedy."

"Why don't we ask them about risks?" He opened the locker tossed a knife-harness to Pranda, and buckled on his own. "This is not the first time I play the fool for you."

She sighed. "The trouble is, we are not playing with fools."

"What is the use of the game, otherwise?"

Prandra slid Chatterjee's door open a crack.

:*Yes, Prandra?*:

"Madame, Khreng wants to sleep in front of your door tonight. Do you object?"

:*Of course not. In India I was always very fond of cats.*: She added with deeper irony, :*Good hunting.*:

"She takes the chance," said Prandra. Khreng crouched at the door, a heraldic beast. He did not intend to sleep.

"I've never seen anything like that before," said the guard.

"Make sure you don't miss anything else." Prandra ambled down the hall. The chain jangled, the scabbard bobbed against her side. She wrenched at the chain until it broke and let it drop. Not only because she hated the Cracked Caduceus: in a fight it might choke her. She stared at the medallion lying on the carpet and remembered the little gold-and-enamel clasp near Yamashita's bed. She went on, pushing her mind against the tangle of occurrence and evidence.

*Metaxa goes everywhere with Nema; Nema always carries trace of Lyhhrt. There is something about that shield I break in the playground that smells like Lyhhrt. But—*

*No Lyhhrt here would do that,* says Prandra.

*They scarcely go near her,* says Chatterjee.

*Then what have they created: Nema, Metaxa, Lyhhrt? Something inside,* says Wyaerl. *A structure forms and while it is building, pieces are taken away. Stupid Nema; Metaxa's love/hate/anger; courteous Lyhhrt...*

One room open and empty: Sheedy, the one she had not questioned— she quickened around a corner and... blink, the guards were gone.

Behind another door, silent screaming: *Leave me alone! Help! please don't!*

She stopped cold. Ambush?

She whacked that flimsy door off its mooring with one shoulder and flattened it with a terrific crack on the tiled floor of a laundry room. Sheedy, gagged with a pillowcase, was being pummeled by four of the guards.

Her breath went out in a burst of mingled relief and disgust. She roared. The attackers had left their guns behind. They jumped, gaped and fled, whimpering, clawing at each other to get out. She ripped off the gag. Sheedy coughed and flailed his arms. "What? What ? ... Prandra?"

"Yes," she drawled. "None other."

He fell to his knees and began to sob. "Prandra, I can't see."

She took one of his hands and guided it to her neck. He clutched her around the throat with both arms. "You saved my life!"

"That shoulder is a bit sore, Sheedy. Get up. You are not hurt, only your pride."

He dragged his sleeve across his nose. "I have no pride."

"Find some." She stood on hind legs and hauled him up. "Hold my arm, look through my eyes. I take you to your room."

He whimpered, "You despise me."

"I don't despise you. I need you." Sheedy *was* first class when he wasn't drunk or chasing the boys who hated him. It was his self-hatred she couldn't stand.

"Oh, now I see! I see! Cat's eyes, beautiful strength and graceful... everything bright, so strange... marvelous, Prandra, oh—"

"And very hard walking hind-legged. Come on, Sheedy. I lend you my eyes another time."

\* \* \*

Khreng waited. He did not know what he was waiting for. On Ungruwarkh he knew what was to be hunted, Prandra knew approximately where it was, and he found the way to it. Simplicity itself. Why am I sitting here like a stupid lump of a dog? If I wait long enough I get fleas. He blinked, and the hall began to spin. He blinked again, the hall spun faster. He thrashed against the engulfing dizziness, but his head was being dragged down and down until it thudded to the floor. In the center of a black vortex a tiger's eye flared briefly and died.

\* \* \*

Sheedy's room was unlit, but bright enough for Prandra's eyes. Sheedy gulped whiskey, still marveling at seeing through the eyes of a cat. His hand trembled on the bottle's neck, his lip quivered at the glass's edge. "Tremendous, gorgeous, cat's eyes. I should get a cat."

"There is a nice big one in a cage out there. Sheedy, put down the whiskey for a minute, and I don't mean inside your gut. I want to talk."

"Talk away, talk away, long dark nights—hah?—meant for talk, all day I talk, Khagodi, Xirifri, Yefni, every lizard, serpent, thing with gills, talk-talk, nights I get nothing but cats, whiskey talks, says good things to the old gut—"

"Now it's time for Nema, Metaxa, Lyhhrt, Sheedy—"

He belched.

:*Sheedy!*: Ah, what a wretch! How she could have grabbed him by the neck and shaken him, broken him, scooped his brain by the roots, picked it for nits, and smeared it on the wall!

"That's right," he giggled. "Brains on the wall. Living sculpture. Freeze it and give it to Metaxa." He choked and coughed.

She slumped. He was doing everything possible to shy away from the knowledge that might kill. And she had no right to push further. But.

:*I have no pride.*:

:*Do you not, Sheedy? You let me look?*:

:*Look away, Big Mama, you look. You find it, I'll buy you a drink. You and this flabby old bastard.*:

She startled. Like the bottled ESPs, Sheedy also had a vivid self-image but this one stood back and observed. He was a strong, supple young man with ugly contempt for the sagging flesh that imprisoned him; he took unceasing and demonic revenge on it. This was not quite a separated personality of the multiple type—Prandra had met just one in her life— but it was the self that hated Sheedy.

Sheedy babbled on, gruesome nonsense of cats' eyes and mashed brains. Prandra addressed Other: :*Young one, if you are so clever, give me information I need that does not get you into trouble.*:

:*I don't care who gets into trouble. Least of all him. Anyone who's stupid enough to let glaucoma blind him without having it treated deserves trouble.*:

:*If foolishness is a sin, we are all in hell before we start. He sees enough of himself. You are claiming superiority you do not yet show.*:

Sullenly, :*What do you want?*:

:*Data on Lyhhrt you gather and file for Kinnear. I have his permission.*:

:*That's a whole world you're talking about.*:

:*I don't need the whole world. You esp what I want, I boil it down. You know how, it's your specialty.*:

\* \* \*

Faint noise made Khreng raise his head. He thought he might have had some kind of blackout, for he had no sensation of waking. He noticed vaguely that the ceiling lights were out in the hall, then caught the scents both perfumed and personal, of Nema, and the suggestion of Lyhhrt that always came with her. He padded down the hall, following. She seemed to be moving ahead. If she turned she might see him, but he was the tracker, and silent, so silent he could not have been heard among thorns. Even the guards did not see him because he was so silent, for they did not stir.

There was an open door with a blue creature standing in it and waving tendrils furiously, piping, "Don't—" but that slow one could not catch him. He heard a thump behind, did not turn because what was ahead was so important. What was so important he barely saw, a flicker, a shimmer. And always the scent.

Guards turned to statues by enchantment.

His mind was a dark cone; at its small end a tiny Prandra roared and reached for him. Ridiculous. She knew he was the tracker... across the lobby through open doors into darkness, past the guard mounted on moped staring at nothing, no swerve toward the infants' park... scent always steady and faint moonlight on the shimmer...

Pausing at iron gate and snicking of bolt... vanishes—

Hot and rank hit him a blow. Green eye shine lanced his brain.

HA HA HA, says voice from the sky, POOR KHRENG IDIOT KHRENG GOES CRAZY WITH VANITY HE WANTS TO PLAY WITH—

*Tiger!*

He awoke, shook darkness from his head skittered back growling.

Tiger on four feet waved its tail gently, stepped softly across the cage, and with one paw pushed open the creaking gate.

And roared. The air split.

\* \* \*

Prandra relaxed, began to luxuriate in the flow of information.

*—:not just formless masses of protoplasm, they have complicated nervous systems and muscles of thin fiber. They need food and water to reproduce, but if they're stranded without, they grow skins, shells, scales, whatever they need to wait for good conditions. They reproduce by fission, not often, they're nearly immortal. Before reproducing, a group will fuse to exchange genetic material, hardly any two have the same genes. On Lyhhrr they lie about by thousands with joined pseudopods, like the ends of nerve-cells, in marshes and lakes, on hills under seas, thinking Cosmic Thoughts; don't ask what those are, would have been doing it for millennia, more if GalFed hadn't discovered them, shown them how to use the false limbs to build true bodies. They chose metal, I don't know why, probably body chemistry. Once they got separate bodies they became individuals, maybe not such a good idea. They work well enough for GalFed, but it's hard for them to communicate. Superb artistry in those workshells, maybe afraid people won't respect them because they don't look like much...*

*:More? The sticky part, private but not classified. Two of them were posted here eight years ago, Administration and Liaison. Liaison had been important*

*at GalFed Central but got to be a nuisance because he began insisting that workshells were too clumsy for minds with so much power, ought to be controlling animals, insensate lifeforms, instead. GalFed hit the roof in whatever they call their Intergalactic S.P.C.A., as well as Human Rights Div. Who knows what'll turn out to be sensate? Sent him out of the way rather than squash him. The shuttle crashed here. Admin was unhurt. Liaison disappeared except for his empty workshell. Theory was he'd crawled somewhere, wounded, then died and dissolved. After a while Admin asked to be allowed to fission to carry out the work of both. That took three years because it's a long way to Lyhhrr. Three years more, and Admin-Laison asked for more staff and these three showed up. I suspect an investigating committee .That's all.:*

:*Investigating, after eight years?*:

:*I said it's a long way. Give the old fart my regards.*:

Young Sheedy's image collapsed on itself and folded away.

"I've been enjoying our conversation, Prandra," Sheedy said over a hiccup, "but it's time for some serious drinking, and—"

"I am enjoying a conversation with young Sheedy."

"Glad to hear it. He's quite an interesting fellow."

"He has a tough mind. Both of you together make one good man... Sheedy, why not let up on the bottle a little?"

He snickered. "I'm hardly likely to get any in the bottle, am I?"

Tiger shrieked.

Sheedy knocked over bottle and glass. "What was that? My God, the power's off, no white-walls!"

Prandra slammed the T-screen's buttons without raising a flicker.

"The door won't open! I'm locked in!"

Prandra pushed the manual release, and dragged open the heavy door. "You can get out. Take my advice and lock yourself in." She bounded down the hall.

KhrengKhrengKhreng? Khreng and Tiger! She found the blue lump, Wyaerl, forced herself to stop. Flattened, great welt across his back. His bottles had been wrenched out; she replaced the tubes in their slits, clumsily, because she was not wearing finger-prostheses for fine-muscle work.

"Badly hurt?" She smelled Metaxa.

:*Temporary paralysis, nerves pinched by swelling, and:*— his mind was remarkably clear— :*inside something—is at the zoo... :*

Not only. She picked up Khreng's thought-track now. Nema and Lyhhrt. Nema plus Lyhhrt.

She broadcast to all quarters. *Chatterjee, give your head. Sheedy, put down your fear and help! Lyhhrt, are you hiding when you know the lost one is an insane killer?* Two of them now, and one in Tiger.

In the darkness and without white-walls, Prandra felt as if she were out in space in a lattice of stars, each star a soul with its flickering intelligence: Kinnear, committee, guards, Chatterjee, Sheedy, Lyhhrt—asleep hypnotized, fearful, cold as stars seemed from their distances and on the edge of the universe Khreng facing *Tiger*.

Khreng did not deceive himself. Compared to a tiger he was a runt. He backed up, roaring. Tiger advanced, silent now, jaws open, stub teeth between the fangs a steel gate.

Khreng, crouching, dared not reach for his knife. Tiger's jaws wanted a grip on a limb, tail or throat. He saved his breath, wrapped the long tail around his loins. Claws reached, Khreng snaked under, Tiger reached out again, and raked his side. Most terrible was that part of his self-adored Tiger, gold under the moon and black flame stripes leaping up his flanks. Ungrukh in the volcanic zones had once worshiped a Great Cat until the Prophet of Firemaster had risen in their tribes. Blazing green eyes. O Great Cat!

His pads slipped in driblets of his own blood, his side stung. He was half stunned, could not even smell the beast, an immortal engine, gold and flame rippling. It leaped.

Prandra howled.

Jolted, Khreng ducked beneath the belly. "Away! Get away!"

"There is a Lyhhrt alive in that beast!"

Tiger paused and turned toward her.

"Save yourself, I sacrifice to the Cat for you!"

"Idiot!"

Tiger was bent on killing its challenger, the cat; Lyhhrt Six, on murdering Prandra. Nema, harboring his fission-brother, Lyhhrt Seven, lay in bed, smiling; Metaxa in forced sleep beside her, face twisted in a hideous grin.

The eyes, turned away from the moon, had darkened. Prandra regarded them: she did not worship the spirit of Cat. She had conceived, brought forth in blood, given the teat, cleaned the excretions, and disemboweled the prey; she had burrowed too deep in living matter to respect any ghost. She drew out the knife, wound her tail round its handle and held it against her side. Tiger-Lyhhrt moved forward, gathering speed.

:*Wyaerl! Wyaerl!*:

Whisper of thought: *Beneath the ribs…*

Khreng roared and leaped. Tiger clawed his forehead before he landed, then rose over Prandra, claws out.

:*Chatterjee! Sheedy!*:

They were trying to rouse the others. There was nothing else they could do.

She slewed, twisting, her teeth caught the skin of the throat, jaws came down slamming the crown of her head as Khreng's knife dashed in and out among the stripes of the flank. The beast turned aside, roaring; Prandra rolled out of reach of the claws, fireworks bursting before her eyes from the pain in her head. Khreng's blade slithered under the loose skin blunted itself along the steely ribs. A few red lines ran among the stripes. Tiger did not stop. A claw slashed Khreng between the eyes and he retreated.

Prandra backed away, snarling. Lyhhrt wanted her badly, if Tiger did not. She thought briefly of the shelter of the cage; Tiger wheeled and planted itself before the bars: Lyhhrt reasoning.

Three cats made points of a triangle. Khreng whetted his knife on the flags. Prandra's head was pounding; she shook it, flicking droplets of blood from her brow-hairs.

Ah, but Tiger was beautiful. She shook the beauty away with her blood. Lyhhrt hidden among the vitals. She was tiring; Tiger could eat bullets, and his jaws were as wide as the sky.

She pulled Khreng and herself under her shield. Have I learned at all, Chatterjee? It was not safe there but dark and lonely. She leveled an arrow of thought at Khreng. He tossed her his knife, she clamped her tail round it with the other. One more effort.

She and Khreng charged from two directions, screaming. Tiger-Lyhhrt, intent on Prandra, was not prepared for the fangs driving into the base of its tail, and reared howling. Pranda took a knife in each hand, an awkward maneuver achieved in desperation, and drove them upward hilt deep under both sides of the ribcage.

Lyhhrt died in a silent convulsion.

Light flashed, sound burst: Tiger's eye exploded. The head, falling forever, hammered her to the ground.

She dragged herself from under, gasping.

Kinnear was on the steps, cradling his heavy gun with its lights, sights, triggers, tubes, grips. Any number of people had gathered behind him. She had not heard them coming. She did not care that they had come.

Khreng began to howl. He circled the fallen beast, dripping blood, howling prayers to Firemaster, to the Great Cat, to the gods of the equatorial zones of Ungruwarkh where tides ravaged the sands, begging forgiveness, absolution, vowing repentance.

"Khreng!"

He went around and around, raising hideous voice. She forced herself to stand, planted herself before him, cursing. He swiped her aside. She dropped and let him go.

In a few moments the zookeeper, a little stick limbed black man in pajamas and hastily wound turban, came and shot him with a tranquilizer dart. He made one more round, still howling, and collapsed.

The zookeeper stood scratching in his thick gray beard and looking at the tiger. "He is not badly hurt, your man." He added, almost sorrowfully. "In my native state in India, Tiger is called the dog of the gods, because he does always what they wish."

She raised herself on trembling forelimbs. Kinnear gave his gun to somebody else, crossed the bloodied stones. He bent to pull the knives from the tiger's belly, wiped their blades on his sleeves and held them out to Prandra.

With the last of her strength she grabbed and flung them away into the darkness. "Civilization." She spat. "Take that thing apart until you find the Lyhhrt."

*　*　*

Khreng woke up in a fearful temper. "Zookeepers! Tranquilizer darts!" He screeched outrage. "Haven't they the decency to use a stunner?"

Prandra growled, "Stunner gives you ten days of headache and we need to lift off."

Both had been crammed with antibiotics; a few hairs had been shaved off Khreng; the skintex sprayed on his wounds gave him a couple of sickly pink stripes. The temper was caused by sheer humiliation that he, the rational being, had found himself almost groveling to a foreign god.

"For a groveler you do great fighting, so shut up," Prandra said.

The door buzzed and opened. Kinnear was standing on the doorway with his hands up. "If you feel like throwing things, I'll leave," he said.

"We're not quite that peevish," said Prandra. "What I feel like, is a fool. I say Lyhhrt have nothing to do with the murders, and I am completely mistaken; I know I must not take risks, and I behave irresponsibly and risk lives; then I cause the death of an insane person and an innocent beast, and that is horrible."

"I suppose that's the truth from your point of view. But we did find the Lyhhrt; Wyaerl would be dead if you hadn't replaced his air and water: now he just has a big bruise; most of us are grateful that many things we couldn't grasp before are becoming clear—and there is one Lyhhrt who is not guilty who would like to speak to you, if you're willing."

"We're willing," Khreng said. "Don't pay attention to the old woman's grumbling. Without that shot of yours we are still fighting Tiger, if not Lyhhrt."

"Listen who is talking," Prandra snorted. "The rational man!"

Kinnear laughed. "I'd better send him in right away."

\* \* \*

The Lyhhrt, who appeared in his most magnificent workshell was one of Admin-Laison; in near Solthree form, he was wearing all of Lyhhrr's art in precious metals and inset jewels. He was taller than Kinnear, and his shell's head was shaped something like one of the primitive masks on Metaxa's wall. Prandra remembered her conversation with Espinoza, and his pleasure in seeing the morning sun even through her alien eyes. And then the ashy bleakness of the planet where Ungrukh struggled and fought. Primitive.

Admin-Laison's mind opened to welcome Khreng and herself, and she glimpsed a planet, swirling in marsh and fog, that was even more dispiriting than her own: its crawling lives had been taught by others not only to create their magnificent gleam and brilliance, but painfully to speak to the peoples of the Galaxy. Inside some part of the cold metal was a slug like being who deeply admired the grace and beauty of the Ungrukh.

:So much so, unfortunately, that some of us wished to make workshells of you.:

"We are honored to speak with you, don't blame yourself," Prandra said. "There are so many questions to ask I don't know where to begin."

:At the beginning,: said the Lyhhrt; he was very literal-minded. :Our former Liaison was so powerful, even we could not esp him. He called our shells clumsy and did his best to convince us that others considered them pretentious and ridiculous.:

"Then he is certainly mad," Prandra said, half blinded by the reflected light of the creature, whose people were called the Shining Ones by many weaker ESPs.

:An unfortunate combination of genetic material—particularly since he is a killer. But he is a genius—and in that other respect he is quite right, when we must go about on wheels or walk in such a graceless manner.:

"Like Nema," Prandra whispered.

The Lyhhrt hesitated. :Yes... at first he tried to control animals—wild or domestic insensate beings on several worlds—by telepathy; he found this unsatisfactory; when he decided that he must work from within, he was declared a menace to Lyhhrr and our organization in GalFed and sent with what we

261

*felt was a qualified guard to what we believed was a safe post—here. We were horribly mistaken. I-brother are culpable and will of course resign.:*

"I think Kinnear prefers not," said Prandra. "You better stay. I say once already if fools are sinners we're all in hell."

*:There... were... other curious deaths here before you came.:*

"I'm not surprised. It is why you ask help. So your rebel gets inside..."

*:In Nema—we suspected that—and he sent a fission—twin to the tiger, because he admired strength and savagery—:*

"And stupidity."

*:No. He was aware those others were hardly more satisfactory than metals. He was waiting for someone like you.:*

Khreng, reading through Prandra, shivered and tried to suppress the involuntary memory of a case of intestinal flukes for which he had been treated with hearty doses of emetic.

Lyhhrt had little sense of humor and could not smile, but they did their best. *:No, not exactly. We are not—what Solthrees call Protean—not shape-changers: one could not crawl into things, like a worm. Once inside, our man extended pseudoaxons and hooked them into the host spinal cord. To get inside—:* He sprung open a little drawer in his belly and held out a small steel object shaped like a flattened egg. It split, a dozen tiny knives were packed inside. *:We are superb surgeons and dissectors, and we leave no scars. This came from our brother in the tiger.:*

"And the false claw is made, I presume, by Nema-Lyhhrt," said Prandra. "It is interesting that the genius who despises metalwork cannot do it very well. And what do you do about Nema?"

*:Guard her, and report the case to GalFed Central. We are certain, but Khreng's sense of smell is not evidence against Nema, and you were forced to kill fission-brother to save your lives... Before I—we go it must be said it is good to speak at ease and at length with an Outworlder, as you know we rarely can.:*

"Thank you—particularly since I'm still class-two.:

*:It is unfortunate that the situation remains essentially the same.:*

"I hope not," said Prandra.


"Prandra, it's no use throwing yourself around," said Kinnear. "You and Khreng are going to stay under guard, just like Nema and Metaxa, until you lift off out of here—only, unlike them, you're staying together so you can scratch each other's eyes out."

"In my dreams I tell Espinoza I am too stupid to trap his killer!"

"And what does Espinoza say to you?"

"He tells me he is content and... I must remember Yamashita, who is so much worse off, and—and—"

"Espinoza is a wise man even in your dreams," Kinnear said gently.

Prandra was not to be put off. "You tell Metaxa everything?"

"We told him what we suspected."

"And he is angry?"

"Angry enough that we decided to put Nema in a room of her own, with Lyhhrt guarding her— and a nurse to take care of her. If he did try to attack her... well, he might find himself putting a gun to his own head."

"I think he is angry at us."

"No, he's angry at having been taken. At first he thought we were accusing him of murder, but we all believe she did the work. He knocked down Wyaerl, we fished that out of his mind, but he was obviously under hypnosis, and no one will charge him. It shocked him enough so that he began to put things together, realize how he'd been chosen to be her guardian, from the start."

"So he goes free..."

"Eventually. We haven't discussed that with him yet. We want him under surveillance, but we don't want all his lawyers. If we can put up a case, he'll be a witness— but he'll go free. It's strange that in spite of everything he knows and feels in one part of his mind, the part she controlled doesn't hate her: it still believes he chose her as a collector's piece. He'll go into a rage, and end in tears."

"She goes free too," Prandra growled.

"The body with the useless brain will go someplace where it'll be taken care of. The criminal—I'm sure the Lyhhrt will keep after that one if it takes thirty years. I gather that any evildoer who disrupts the Cosmic Thought keeps the world at one remove from God—and whatever that is, it's a deadly sin."

"In thirty years I may be a live brain but I am a dead cat." She scratched her nose with the tip of her tongue. "You think Metaxa tries to free her?"

Surprised, Kinnear said, "How can he?"

"You think she can't find a way, with opportunity? And all her power? Especially when *he* is going free? Nema is two: infant and Lyhhrt. We know about her. But Metaxa is three: love, hate, and doubt. We know about him too: he is malleable. Those three parts can be turned off and on; she does not have to be the only one who pulls switches."

Kinnear let out his breath in a long whish. "You've just beaten my head in with the unthinkable."

"It is not forbidden to think about it, surely."

"I will. Believe me, I will."

"Good. You find your cat friends helpful... but Kinnear, remember one thing. No harm. I am just speaking of Khreng and myself. No harm. Ungrukh have ideas about sin too."

\* \* \*

GalFed's ESP examinations are open to the public in order to dispel the ESP mystique; they are rarely well attended: the exam to a non-ESP is as kriegspiel to a non-chess player.

Prandra, at one end of the Committee Room, with Khreng dozing beside her, looked half asleep. She was crouched on the rough flagstone brought in for her by an earth-mover; she did not want to grow too comfortable. She was sulky as always before some difficult task; she would be worse later. Her half-closed eyes skimmed her audience: armed guards, curious clerks, a couple of outworld ESPs she did not remember having met. Wyaerl, a blue rug with a purple welt; Chatterjee, reflecting the window on her dark globe; Sheedy, looking as if the light hurt his eyes. Metaxa was openly yawning; he had been allowed to come because he had not much else to do.

Kinnear, somber and a bit nervous, sat with the rest of the committee, a conglomeration of faces. The Lyhhrt were the surprise, all five in a golden row: they had considered the occasion important enough to come in force, leaving Nema attended by three crack shots in a portable white-wall cage. Prandra was the day's star and could esp as she pleased, but she caught nothing from the Lyhhrt. Committee was backache, triplicate reports, and thank-God-it's-nearly-over, get-rid-of-these-damn-cats-and-back-to-normal.

Yes.

The door closed. The silence lengthened.

"Are we ready?" Kinnear asked.

:*Yes.*: said Chatterjee. Prandra grunted.

"This is an examination for ESP class-one status of the candidate Prandra, daughter of Tengura of Ungruwarkh, Galactic Catalogue Feldfar five-five-three Anax Two. Candidate was previously attested class-two by this committee on evidence of Sector-Liaison Diego Espinoza. Examiner: Sita Chatterjee. Begin."

:*Forms obligatory,*: said Chatterjee. :*Search, collate, shield, lock, block and break.*:

An hour of silence punctuated by aborted snores from Khreng. Metaxa got up and left halfway through, and the guard who followed him seemed grateful.

Prandra was tempted to make slips, out of mischief and impatience. Damned savage trouble-making cats, hah? Respect and affection for Chatterjee stopped her. She picked thought-trains tossed from ESP to ESP, set them in order, flicked them back, sometimes with force just short of headache-making, until Sheedy winced. She took pity and subdued herself. She needed all her control. Set up shields and blocks and withstood battering against them, drove herself against the shields and blocks of others.

Played childish games with adults and wished she were back on Ungruwarkh, where life was simpler.

\* \* \*

Metaxa had been allowed to keep his guns and the obsolete projectiles they used; his guards wore metal- and explosives-detectors. There was one half-forgotten weapon hidden and unnoticed behind the wine racks in his refrigerator, a more modern version of the zookeeper's tranquilizer gun, made of plastics and tiny enough to be palmed. He had carried it in earlier years through the dark places where he made his deals. It was not lethal, he was no murderer, but it was just as effective as the stunner and far less harmful. Its crystal darts had lain preserved in the cold place where they could not sublimate, and were good for a day of body heat. He did not need a day.

The corridors were almost deserted. He paused at a door. "I want to use the washroom."

"Your own place is up one floor. Can't you wait?"

"No."

The guard shrugged and followed him in. As he was turning to shut the door, Metaxa touched him lightly beneath the ear with the little muzzle and pressed a stud.

"Hey..." The man staggered and within three seconds fell. Metaxa came out alone and slipped into the next doorway, an elevator.

\* \* \*

The white-wall cage was a collection of wire-mesh panels fastened to a platform with runners, and blocking Nema's door. The men inside were sleepy and hot from crowding. There was no one else in the corridor. Seeing Metaxa alone, one of them, through a yawn, said, "Where's your guard?"

"He had to use the washroom."

They did not react; they could not esp him, and as usual were a bit stupefied from boredom. He stopped before the cage. "Couldn't ... couldn't you just let me look at her?"

"No, sir. We have orders."

"Just to look, please?" He flattened a hand against the mesh, in appeal. "Please?"

"Mr. Metaxa, I'm warning you, get away from here!" The man grasped his weapon tighter, unwilling to raise it before wealth and power. "You know you're not supposed to be—hey, what are you do—"

Metaxa slid the panel aside, touched him under the jaw, and shoved.

He fell against the others so hard they were too crowded to aim their guns, and Metaxa had them. He closed the cage and pushed it aside gently, careful not to trip up the wire that carried the current. Slid Nema's door open. The nurse by the doorway, holstered and armed, was weaving something useful with complicated bobbins and spindles. He put her to sleep before she had time to look up. Seven darts left. He did not think he would need more. The door closed.

"Darling?" Nema in a chair, blank as always, hands folded. Always when he saw her, everything changed. "Didn't you think I'd come for you?" She looked at him.

"Nema!" He came forward, hands reaching for hers.

"My skimmer's still on the roof, I've been watching with the telescope and the port way is hardly guarded—"

She sat up suddenly, incisively, pushed his hands away and signed with her own in the language he had taught her: *To the apartment.*

"But, darling, why? I've put out the guards, we can get away now, from here." Once again he tried to take her hands and she pushed them aside.

*To the apartment.*

He shrugged, helplessly. "You know I always do what you want. But that's so danger—"

She stood, put a hand on his mouth. Grasped him by the wrist and pulled him across the room, to the door.

He was forced to put out one more guard they ran into rounding a corner. A burly one who thrashed and kicked even with the dart in him, and Metaxa had to use another. He began to sweat.

* * *

Forms ended. There was a wearied pause. Prandra nestled her chin into her forelimbs, whisked the tip of her tail back and forth, tick-tock.

:*Forms-optional,*: said Chatterjee. :*Category: illusion.*:

If the other part of the examination had bored her, this one Prandra had been dreading. What was demanded was the creation of an original illusion by mass hypnosis, of a person, place, time, situation, real or imaginary. She was aware that she was not imaginative or original enough to impress an audience of sophisticated ESPs. She came from a long line of realists: she was one of the few people on Ungruwarkh who had never seen the "plains-companion," the hallucinatory cat-companion which often accompanied lonely travelers over the vast barrens, and her own great-grand-mother had made a career of convincing the tribes that the phenomenon was psychological rather than supernatural. She had not been helped by researching the examination records of earlier candidates, who had produced marvels. She could extrapolate, reproduce, modify. What could she show here? A sunny day on Ungruwarkh? She had done that for the children and it was worthy of children. Her experiences in the time-warp? She had given those, in exhausted detail, to historians and exobiologists. She could bring Sita Chatterjee embodied in her finest sari woven with peacocks on gold, a perfect eye blazing in each tail-feather... or Yamashita... too painful. Espinoza?

Oh, Espinoza...

:*Do you want a recess?*: Chatterjee asked.

"No..."

Khreng raised his tail and let it fall. Prandra swallowed and stood up on fours. "Madame Chatterjee, members of Invigilating Committee, and audience..."

\* \* \*

"What are you doing?" Metaxa, perplexed, stood watching in the kitchen doorway.

Although Nema could not take care of herself instinctively, like normal Solthree humans, she could use her hands to perform other actions—everything, perhaps, a Lyhhrt might do in a workshell. *I am preparing this for you.* She had run a half liter of water into an ice bucket, found a small metal box, taken out several vials of crystals, shaken them into the water, swirled them to dissolve.

She took the bucket into the living room, in her even mechanical walk, and set it on a table beside the couch. He followed, a man in a dream. She faced him, slipped the gown from her shoulders till she was bared to the waist. Her mouth formed the shape a primitive sculptor might have created and called a smile.

Metaxa had never felt sexual desire for her, perhaps never had been allowed to. "What is it?" he whispered. Her breasts trembled with pulses. She pulled down his zip and peeled the cloth from one shoulder and arm till he showed a forequarter of gray hair and aging flesh that might have been the record of years in a foreign service. His arm moved as if it were submerged in water. "Don't... can't you see the danger? What—" His fingers groped, in slow motion, for the sleeve.

*Leave it.* She moved back, still with the terrible alien smile. The pale skin below her ribs quivered and rippled. She motioned toward the couch and he sat, slowly. She pushed down his shoulders until he was reclining. Then she took a small metal case from her pocket, opened it, removed a tiny blade and set it lengthwise into his flesh below the seventh rib.

He was too numb now for shock or horror. He stared at it, watched a drop of blood gather and run down his skin.

She picked up the bucket and held it at her waist; in her own abdomen an opening appeared, a few centimeters long, a drop of blood gathered and ran, a tiny blade pushed out, slowly, came clear, fell into the folds of her dress. A tentacle emerged, a pseudopod, like the tongue-tip from a mouth; inside the skin something writhed struggling among layers of muscle.

Metaxa did not know how long it took. In the time he knew it was an eternity until the creature freed itself and slid into the basin: a Lyhhrt, half normal size. A newborn, newly divided Lyhhrt-brother enveloped in the crinkled transparent membrane of fission.

"Dearest, I know... I understand..." There seemed to be a thickness in his speech. "You're making sure... we'll be together... always... wherever I go..." He could not tell whether he was babbling wildly or muttering to himself. Inside his head, a person struggled and screamed.

And the Lyhhrt was not ugly, better looking than an octopus or starfish. It was translucent pink, the size of a hand, and looked more like a flower; its five true limbs were rounded at the ends like petals, and on its back there was a star pattern of deep red spots. Underneath was a tiny pulsing heart, and just below the surface veins, nerves and muscles extended. It was a brain with limbs, a fearful intelligence. It lay placidly in the water, absorbing nutrients into its birth membrane, welling and gathering strength. Nema's wound closed, a little blood crusted on its lower lip.

"Always together," Metaxa babbled, "A part of you in me..."

The Lyhhrt grew, absorbed half the liquid, reached three quarters of the way toward adulthood. Nema knelt beside the couch and offered the bowl, like a priestess. Offered Metaxa to the bowl. The Lyhhrt stirred; its envelope was smooth, the skin beneath would grow to match. It extended the tip of one limb into a thin tentacle and hooked it over the edge of the bucket on its way toward the blade embedded in Metaxa's flesh.

Metaxa shuddered, pulling on his strength. Sat up cautiously, not to disturb the knife, drew on saliva and swallowed before he got words out:

"Did you really think you could?"

\* \* \*

"... although I believe I qualify as a class-one ESP," Prandra said, "I have no ability to produce the illusions you expect in these examinations. I create only what I see or know. I am also affected by what happens here. I cannot show you imaginary rainbows or fireworks when people are murdered and I want justice. Therefore I set myself the humbler task I consider most useful, of—can you show yourself, please, Kinnear?"

Heads turned. Kinnear stood up, hands knotted white. His image wavered, rippled, reformed... darkened. Blond hair and blue eyes turned brown; his face grew ruddy, beard lengthened and thickened. And he was Metaxa.

"Thank you for your help, Metaxa. Members of the audience, for my illusion I set myself the task of convincing you from the time you come into this room that Metaxa is Kinnear and Kinnear is Metaxa." She added dryly, "Convincing the murderer is, of course, the work of the Lyhhrt."

\* \* \*

Still-life: the man on the couch, Nema, the bowl with its reaching Lyhhrt.

The man's outline wavered, his face and hair paled, his beard dissolved... and he said much more sharply, "Administration-my-brother, do you witness?" He looked straight into Nema's eyes, wondering if Killer could see through those blank dark disks, and what he saw.

:Yes, Kinnear. I witness and will so testify.: Over Kinnear's shoulder spidery metal limbs unfolded themselves and hooked, pulling up the small steel workshell of Lyhhrr's official Administrator, who had accomplished two marvels of his own: speaking to Kinnear for the first time, after lying crowded and uncomfortable against hot flesh for two hours.

"Thank God," said Kinnear; his face and chest were running with cold sweat. But the gun was in his hand; while Admin scuttled to drop the lid of a cloisonné vase over the bucket, he shot three darts into Nema's neck.

Admin grabbed the bucket as Nema jumped up in a convulsive whirl, gave a single shriek and crumpled. Kinnear addressed that T-screen. "All right, Comm-Unit, cut the video and ring committee. And Admin—will you get this goddamn knife out of me before I split open?"

A Lyhhrt could not laugh. But it tried. *:Take it out yourself, Kinnear. It is barely cutting your skin.:*

In the Committee Room the T-screen buzzer sounded, and everyone jumped.

\* \* \*

The door slammed open. Metaxa rushed into his apartment and stopped short. "You said she wouldn't be hurt!"

"She wasn't hurt" said Kinnear, and sighed. "No harm. She got three darts—a tranquilizer for her, and two to paralyze the Lyhhrt, they won't have any effect on her. We made up four of them."

Metaxa fell to his knees beside Nema. She lay curled up, her breath came in whimpers. Her gown was tangled about her waist; he pulled the bodice up over her back and breast, the skirt over the plastic covering of her diaper. The look on his face was something to turn away from.

Kinnear, drained, raised his eyes to the red shape in the doorway. It was Khreng, planted square, the whack of his tail keeping all comers at bay.

"Where's Prandra? What's happened?"

"Nothing," Khreng said. "She is gone back to quarters to sleep, what do you think? She leaves a message: Tell Kinnear he is a brave man."

"Brave? Anything and everything could have gone wrong. I was half crazy with fear."

"That has nothing to do with bravery! I think," Khreng considered for two seconds, "you are maybe even as brave as I am."

Ambling back to quarters, Khreng paused at the open door of the deserted examination room, where a blaze of reflected light caught his eye. One chair was still taken by an empty workshell, brought by the four Lyhhrt to sit in while its usual inhabitant was occupied elsewhere.

\* \* \*

*:Well, Prandra, are you satisfied with your status?:* Chatterjee asked.

"It is good to be class-one," Prandra said quietly. "It remains to be seen whether I become first class."

*:Yamashita would also have been your friend one day, if...:*

"I know. Now I know we have friends here, and we can say good-bye to Espinoza, through you."

A committee had formed in the lobby of Administration-Quarters: Kinnear, Sheedy, two Lyhhrt, and Chatterjee. Wyaerl, bubbling quietly, was there too because he was leaving for his world with Khreng and Prandra. Khreng wrestled the chain of the gold star over his head, untangling it from ears and whiskers. "Kinnear, I thank you for the use of this beautiful artifact, but a gold star does not make me a big man on Ungruwarkh."

"I'll want to know how you're getting on," Kinnear said. He seemed to be trying to find something else to say, and failing.

:*We will get on beautifully!*: Wyaerl's mission had succeeded and he was filled with happiness. :*Although you may find it somewhat boring on my poor world*—:

"Good!"

:—*where we hunt the eggs of the plaak or lie about at the edge of the waters and sleep*—:

"That's exactly what we like to do," said Prandra.

:—*and occasionally the drug-runners have a fight and kill each other, but otherwise*—:

"Your world is the marvel of creation!" Khreng rumbled. "It is on the way home to ours."

*However exotic aliens may be, they usually have a fixed form. Not Esen-alit-Quar, the "Blue Blob" in Czerneda's Web Shifters series. The long-lived Esen usually mimics "a slight young girl" when disguised as a Human, although she can become anything she wants. Esen has appeared in five Web Shifters stories: the three novels* Beholder's Eye *(DAW Books, October 1998),* Changing Vision *(August 2000), and* Hidden in Sight *(April 2003); and two anthology short stories, "She's Such a Nasty Morsel" in* Women of War, *and "A Touch of Blue" in* Heroes in Hiding.

*"A Touch of Blue", the most recently published, is set early in the series when Esen is still living with her web-kin in Ersh's greenhouse on Picco's Moon. Esen's "sister" Lesy wants her to help enter an art show on the private space station of Portula Colony, an artists' group, disguised as two of the three-eyed, five-armed Dokeci. Esen is dubious—is one species' excrement really another species' art?—but the Dokeci consider it valuable enough to be worth stealing ...*

# A Touch of Blue:
# A Web Shifters Story

## by Julie E. Czerneda

Ersh, Senior Assimilator and center of my personal universe, had firm ideas about what I should do with my time. These ideas doubtless stemmed from my being the most Recent of my kind and, to be honest, an unprecedented accident, but I hardly viewed them as fair. After all, was it my fault I'd been born instead of properly budded from Ersh's flesh as the rest of our Web?

I plopped another seedling into its pot and straightened it morosely. One such idea was this morning drudgery in the greenhouse.

My education was another.

Ersh had decided I was to receive the wealth of knowledge gained by our kind of the biology and cultures of more ephemeral races only after she herself had sorted that knowledge through her own flesh. *Doubtless leaving out the good bits.*

My toes snapped the seedling at the stem. I hastily shoved the remaining piece deeper into the soil. It might not wilt until after I'd left. Despite centuries of practice, I wasn't good with plants.

*I wasn't good with anything.*

I sighed heavily, my tail sliding between my legs. Enjoying the melancholy, I sighed again.

"Esen."

I straightened in haste, the movement sending the tray of transplanted seedlings flying off the table in a spectacular spray of dirt, tiny green stems, and pots—pots that shattered noisily on impact with the stone floor. Well, except for the one that arced through the air all the way to the wall, which produced more of a smash and slither.

"Esen-alit-Quar!"

*At least she wouldn't notice the broken seedling,* I consoled myself as I warily turned to face Ersh.

I was Esen-alit-Quar when in trouble, Esen for short, Es in a hurry or between friends, not that I felt warmed by friendship at this moment. Ersh's massive crystalline Tumbler-self had an ominous tilt forward. I tried to unobtrusively tilt backwards—not easy in my current form, that of the canid-like Lanivarian. This was my birth shape, the one I preferred for the value of its useful hands and still the easiest for me to hold.

For we were Web-beings, creatures of energy and matter and transitions between, able to spend some of our mass to bind our remaining molecules in a different, memorized form until choosing to release and return to the flawless teardrop of blue that was our heritage.

I was still working on that part.

"Hi Esen." A dark eye peered around the side of Ersh.

My jaw dropped in a grin. "Lesy! Welcome home!"

My web-kin didn't come out any further. I wasn't surprised. We were six in the known universe: Ersh, Skalet, Mixs, Ansky - my birth mother, Lesy, and myself. Lesy and I shared one other characteristic. We both did our utmost to avoid facing Ersh when she was annoyed.

Ersh herself, likely taking my grin and greeting as signs I wasn't suitably grief-stricken about her dying seedlings—which wasn't entirely true, since being the one who'd have to clean up and repot fresh ones all afternoon, I felt significant anguish at my fate—chimed a note of distinct temper. Lesy's eye disappeared.

I spread my arms in appeasement, which helped hide pots. "You wanted me, Ersh?" this brightly, with a deliberate lift of my ears.

"Not on any level," she muttered, but not loudly enough to expect a reply. She did expect me to hear, being fully aware of the capabilities of my current ears. In more normal tones, "Lesy does. You're going with her, Youngest."

I blinked. "Going where?"

The immense greenhouse was the deepest portion of Ersh's house, that house a series of rooms quarried into the side of a cliff almost as old as she. The cliff was part of Picco's Moon, a world of rock and rock-based life, its surface stained by the lurid orange and purple reflection of Picco except during Eclipse. Lesy didn't come here unless summoned by Ersh; she kept to her windowless room when here, other than occasional conquests of the kitchen. She wouldn't go outside unless forced by Ersh.

Why? Because Picco's exact shade of orange, as she frequently reminded everyone but Ersh, drained her creativity.

As creativity was something Ersh insisted I avoid at all costs, I judged Lesy's claim as another concept I'd be taught when I was older. *If that ever happened.* Though I suspected this one fell within the category of what Skalet called "Lesy's idiotic prattle."

We were the closest of kin, together forming the Web of Ersh. *Didn't mean we were always kind to one another.*

"Go where?" I repeated, ears heading back down. A kitchen summons was likeliest. Lesy could clean up after herself. Well, she could, but rarely did. I'd take refuge in planting if necessary.

I hated wet paws.

One, then three dark eyes, each the size of my clenched fist, peered at me from behind the crystal form of Ersh, reflecting in gleaming facets until there might have been thirty. The glowing green ring encircling each signaled unusual excitement. Or a fever. Lesy's middle-aged Dokeci-self was prone to stress-related illness if she persisted in using it within significant gravity. Which she did. "Dokeci-Na, Youngest! The western continent. I'm holding my first exhibit in the capital!"

"Pardon?" Our kind might possess perfect recall; that didn't mean we couldn't confuse one another. Portula Colony was Lesy's preferred home. I'd been there before: a quiet, self-contained environment inhabited by, at most, forty self-absorbed artists. It wasn't Picco's Moon, but the next best thing for a young web-being of uncertain parentage—so Ersh had proclaimed. *Boring.* Though there was, I recalled fondly, a remarkable pool. But Dokeci-Na?

An entire planet teeming with life—life that had evolved there? Life that wasn't rock?

*There would be restaurants,* I thought, charmed beyond reason. I tipped a questioning ear towards Ersh, hardly daring to believe my good fortune.

"After you finish here," Ersh said with remarkable restraint, considering, "pack and be ready. The shuttle's on its way. I need not remind you of the Prime Laws or what I expect from your behavior off world, Youngest."

"No, Ersh." Her expectations consisted of my staying out of sight and out of mind, which basically translated into "don't talk to ephemerals." One day I would, *if I lived that long.* Right now, I wasn't trained for such interaction. Wouldn't be a problem; Dokecians didn't believe anyone my age could hold a conversation.

But if behaving meant I'd get my first-ever visit to a world without opinionated crystal?

My tail swung wildly, knocking the surviving pots to the floor.

"Esen-alit-Quar!"

*  *  *

I possessed Lesy's memories of Portula Colony—those Ersh deemed fit for me to have, anyway. A private space station, it lay within view of the famous Jeopardy Nebula, said view the source of inspiration for the colony's artistically-minded population. Portula was the place Lesy currently favored when not on a mission for our Web. Since she went on fewer missions than any of the web-kin but me—for no reason Ersh deemed fit for me to know—Lesy had had time to become well established within her isolated home. We were to head there first, to finalize the shipping of her art, then accompany that art to Dokeci-Na.

The closer our transport drew to Portula Colony, however, the more worried Lesy became. *And not about her art.*

"You're sure you can maintain this form on the planet, Youngest?"

This being the fourteenth time she'd lifted the top of my crate and peered within to inquire, I wrapped my arms over my face and wiggled the now-black fingerlike tips at her.

"Don't do that!" she gasped. "That's—it's not done. Do you hear me, Esen-alit-Quar? That's very rude!"

If Lesy was trying to sound like Ersh, I didn't have the tubal pumps to tell her how infinitely far from the mark her soft, anxious complaint registered. I did lower my arms and sent an apologetic ripple of pink through my skin. "Sorry, Lesy," I added aloud, though Dokecians relied more on appearance.

Hers? More flustered than ever, judging by the welts rising over her round face. "Don't call me that!"

We were alone and she'd used my birth name first, but I'd learned over a century ago never to correct my elders. *Where they could hear me, at any rate.* "I'm sorry, Riosolesy-ki." My name in this form, Ses-ki, lacked respectful prefixes, a prejudice against callow youth I'd noticed crossed species' boundaries. "Are we there yet?" I tried to shift position.

"Don't do that!"

I was truly trying to behave, but this was one too many "don'ts." *Especially before we'd even arrived.* "You try sitting on—what am I sitting on?" My box, while padded on all sides, held more than over-compressed Esen. Lesy had slipped in a few packages at the last minute. None, she assured me, edible, or I'd have been rid of them during the preceding hours.

"Those are art supplies. Important secret art supplies."

I squirmed. "They feel like rocks."

The welts acquired a mottled red. A frown. "You peeked!"

276

"I sat," I corrected, shifting again. The Dokeci form consisted of a round head with a handsome rubbery beak and those three massive eyes. The head sat on a thick neck from which the five long flexible arms sprang like a collar above a pair of sturdy hips. The rest of the body was a boneless abdomen that swung like a pendulum between the triple-jointed legs. Mine, though compact and firm, now had distinct sore points. This form wasn't designed for sitting, let alone being pressed against rocks, artistic or otherwise. "Can't I come out?"

"We're almost there," my web-kin promised, slamming the lid down.

I put my arms over my face and wiggled my fingertips.

* * *

Free at last. *In more ways than one.* I stretched my arms, after carefully checking the placement of fragile objects, kicked myself from the floor, and let myself drift back down in a slow spin. Not quite null-gee, but close enough for fun. Portula's operators balanced the physiological preference of older Dokeci with the practicality of keeping paint on brushes and out of the air scrubbers. The Dokeci were a species who lost significant musculature with age; to make it worse, their abdomens enlarged and sagged towards the floor. By the middle of their lifespan they depended on the strong limbs of younger kin.

Those, like Lesy, who wanted to remain independently active had a choice of donning support devices—none, she confided, in the least fashionable—or cheat by living on low gravity stations like Portula. Personally, I'd have abandoned the form by her age, not that she'd asked my opinion. I'd noticed that about my Elders before now.

Spin done, I poked around Lesy's quarters. Nothing had changed. The pillows, carpet, and cupboards of supplies were in my memories along with the way to the station galley, its menu, short cuts to the common areas—including that remarkable pool—and, for some reason, the completely unremarkable aft shipping hold.

*Where I didn't plan to waste my time.* "Will we have time to use the pool?" I asked.

Lesy's topmost eye sent me a vague, preoccupied glance, the rest of her attention on the packages of rocks she was removing from my crate. "Yes, yes. Let me put these away first."

"I'll help." I bounded towards the crate, abdomen swinging.

Unfortunately, it was somewhat more difficult than I'd anticipated to lose all that wonderful momentum.

I crashed into both crate and web-kin.

We fell together in a slow motion grapple of writhing arms and packages, packages that spilled out over the lovely finger-knotted carpets, packages that cooperatively rolled free of their wrappings to expose the deep glitter of gemstones.

I extricated myself from Lesy, whose skin flickered with alarmed pseudo lightning and rising splotches of violet. "Sorry," I said. *Already a habit.* I picked up the nearest stone, being helpful, only to stare at what I held in disbelief.

"Pretty, isn't it?"

Pretty was an understatement. The gem had a fiery inner glow that could come from only one source. *Biology.* "This," I scowled, "isn't a rock." It was a Tumbler excretion.

*Or worse*—I dropped it and wiped my fingertip vigorously on the carpet, the rest of my arms stretched as far away as possible. "It's not one of—"

"Waste not, want not."

Smuggling excretions was the only persistent non-Tumbler enterprise on Picco's Moon, an enterprise involving clandestine landings and distressingly noisy responses by those who claimed to be in charge—not that Tumblers noticed either, considering soft-fleshed beings to be, at best, implausible. Ersh herself took precautions to discourage prospectors, licensed or otherwise; namely she sent me out every few nights to collect any deposits made by wandering neighbors—not to mention the piles from those who visited Ersh for those month-long chimings over rare salts. I'd almost filled a deep cleft in the cliff over the years.

Ersh's own? Suffice to say I'd never asked nor wanted to know, and viewed that ignorance as one of the bright spots of my short existence.

I rose from the floor, my own skin flaring with outrage. "You've been stealing from Ersh!?"

"There's no need to raise your voice." Lesy somehow managed to pout adorably without lips. "She lets me take the prettiest. For my creations. You know how highly Ersh values my art."

I was beginning to get the idea. Elder or not, Lesy was a worse liar than I was.

As for her art? I remembered innumerable lectures from Ersh. I wasn't to ask about Lesy's creations, or Lesy's dreams for that matter. When either topic arouse during our rare meals together, those decidedly unweblike aspects of our web-kin's nature made Skalet twitch, Mixs grumble, and Ansky offer more food.

While they made me curious. And, I realized abruptly, Ersh wasn't here. That she'd inevitably find out wasn't something I need worry about now.

*A great many of my decisions were made on that basis.*

"What do you do with them?" I asked, unable to stop myself.

Her skin ridged and developed a faint flush of pink. "They're part of my newest creation. An entirely new art. Would you like to try? I'll teach you. What a wonderful idea, Esen!"

*Where had* that *come from?* My epidermis did its best to turn inside out. "Try?" I echoed weakly. "I really don't think we have time for—this isn't—"

Lesy was ignoring me. I was used to that. But what she was doing while ignoring me offered sufficient novelty that I closed my mouth and watched with all eyes.

Two hands opened cupboard doors, while the other three reached in to pull out, with blinding speed—Lesy could move when motivated—a bucket, several narrow white tubes, an assortment of hammers and pointed tools, and, last and requiring all five hands, what appeared to be a large nondescript mold of, yes, it was a face.

Ersh's face, to be exact. Even as a Dokecian of considerable age, features reversed and made of puce-toned plas, I'd know that expression anywhere. Lesy might have thrown molten plas over the Senior Assimilator while she was mid-argument with me.

Lesy must have mistaken my stunned silence for approval, for her blush deepened and she thrust the face mold at me. "Beautiful, isn't it? It's the very same image they used in the 44th Dynasty coins. Not the same, really. Bigger." This with small spots of worry. Her arms twisted, rotating Ersh's frozen scowl. "Too big? It's 155% life-size. I like big eyes, but one never knows—"

"'Coins?'" I echoed.

"Some shields did survive, a statue or two. Coins were the main—you should know this."

"A certain person doesn't," I said testily, "share everything with me." While it was quite reasonable Ersh had lived within Dokeci society in a time known only through the earliest—that I did know—remains yet uncovered by that species' archaeologists, it went against everything I knew that the center of our Web, the being who ruled caution above all, *who insisted I travel in a crate* ... that she'd be ... "She was famous?"

"Infamous," Lesy giggled. "Legendary. Teganersha-Ki rose to power on the severed arms of her enemies. United the western continent against the east and north. Brought in plumbing."

The plumbing I could believe. Ersh regularly cited the hallmarks of a successful technological society. Sanitation was top on her list. "Does—" There was no safe way to ask, so I went for blunt. "Does she know about this?" I flailed a finger at the face.

Lesy faded to a smooth, nonplussed beige.

While I flushed abashed purple. *Of course Ersh knew.* There were no secrets from the sharing of memories held within our flesh. Well, there were plenty of secrets within Ersh's flesh, but only because she alone had the ability to pick and choose what to include per bite.

The rest of us? Doomed to reveal every memorized instant of our lives. However dull or personally mortifying.

I stared at Ersh's reversed face—presumably shortly to be coated in pulverized Ersh excretion with the result sold to the locals for use as pots or doorstops—and felt an unexpected twinge.

*How often did we disappoint her?*

\* \* \*

As a Web-being, I had intimate access to the aesthetics of all more ephemeral species my kind had yet explored. That didn't mean I knew good art from bad—just how to fake it in the appropriate company. At the moment, I would have gladly traded all the memories in my flesh for a clue how to tell the three glittering heads on the shelf apart.

"Don't you want to take yours home, Youngest?" Lesy's skin was beginning to spot.

I tried not to look obvious as I examined the results of our labors. The molding process had reminded me of putting soil into pots, though wetter. The final finishing—that had been more challenging. Lesy's instructions consisted of "follow your dreams" as she herself used all five arms to quickly glue bits from a box to Ersh's thunderous face at seeming random. While singing, which I hadn't attempted.

Glue I could and did. *Not that I'd anything to follow.* Only Lesy claimed to remember dreams. The rest of us? Memories lasted, intact and detailed; whatever might visit our sleeping minds did not. After first learning of ephemeral nightmares, I'd decided that was fine with me.

Without guidance—and to be honest, some coordination issues with five arms—an embarrassing number of my small bits were also glued to carpet and furnishings. Lesy forgave my lack of control once I'd helped pull off the pieces somehow glued to her skin. All three busts now stared back at me, looking as if they'd rolled down a garbage heap after dunking themselves in syrup. The leftmost one had only one eye exposed, giving it

Julie E. Czerneda

a baleful look. The centermost was blinded by strings of cheap plas beads. The right—I looked away, hoping in vain Ersh wouldn't taste the memory of her heads.

"Shouldn't I leave it here, Lesy?" I suggested. "This is a place of artists." *I had no shame.*

She almost glowed. "We'll do better than that. We'll put your first work of art on exhibit with mine!" Her arms swept up the leftmost lump as if it were precious. "I'm proud of you, Es."

*Which made no sense.* We had no possessions. There were no physical manifestations of a Web culture. We were, that was all. Was this Lesy's difference? A compulsion to make things without purpose or value?

*Then what were dreams?*

My troubling thoughts might have manifested in stripes on my skin for all my web-kin noticed. After tucking all three heads into a fresh shipping crate with great care—a procedure which required privacy for no reason I could imagine, but I was used to climbing into cupboards on command—Lesy grabbed the nearest of my arms. "I'll show you the rest." She towed me towards the door with frightening enthusiasm, her abdomen bouncing up and down. "My best work is in aft shipping already." She halted our forward motion with a quick grab by two arms at a convenient handhold. "I think it's my best. Oh dear. What if it isn't? And where are you going?"

I'd have thought it obvious, since she'd let go of me in order to grab said handholds. I thus sailed onward, arms flailing as if that would help, tumbling in midair until the lower part of my anatomy met the corridor wall with a *smack* and I slid, slowly, to the floor. "Who knows?" I muttered.

"Know? I can't. Can I know my best?" Lesy could fuss without pause for breath. She hurried forward and took my arm again, hauling me to my feet. "Cureceo-ki says it's my best work. He'd know, wouldn't he?"

I blinked at her, something three eyes did quite well. "Who is Cureceo-ki?"

"You remember, Ses-ki!"

"No one told me," I stressed the second last word. In this alien environment, no web-being would be more specific. *Or ought to be,* I thought, worried by Lesy's now-distraught posture. Upset, a Dokeci's forward-facing arms became rigid and unusable, aimed outward to fend off trouble. Which was me, in this instance. As she continued to hold onto me with an arm over her hip, the rest were fending off my abdomen. "Who is she?" I asked more gently. The pronoun was the accepted neutral, since the species had an astounding variety of reproductive forms. It took birth or an autopsy, Ersh had told me, to sort out who was pregnant.

"'He,'" Lesy insisted, either knowing more than I did about the individual in question—*presumably*—or imposing her own pronoun—*likely*. Since my arrival, those in the "family-way" made her uncomfortable, Skalet admitting the same reaction. "The museum's curator. Cureceo-ki personally arranged the exhibit." Her third eye widened, its aim somewhere behind me. "Oh dear." The surface of her skin wrinkled, the crevices lime-green. "He looks upset. Hush."

"Greetings, Riosolesy-ki," the approaching Dokecian said, ignoring me. His skin was lumpy and dark, arms almost stiff. *Not a happy being.* "What's the delay? We've been waiting for the rest of the shipment."

Compared to Ersh's ability to obliterate my existence when preoccupied, this corpulent and aging being was an amateur. However, he did have species-mores on his side. Dokeci my age were considered little more than obstacles to traffic. So I did my best to be inconspicuous, though I'd have preferred to bristle. With aquamarine highlights. *And a pithy comment or two.*

"Why the haste, Curator?" Lesy surprised me by protesting. "I've yet to pick which cloak I'll wear to the gala. You did promise a gala for the opening of my exhibit."

*Trust personal adornment to stiffen her arms.* Lesy loved anything she could add to her form's sake. Otherwise, in any form, her reaction to conflict was distress and flight. None of us, not even Ersh, would speak harshly to her. Unlike this curator.

So different was Lesy from our siblings, so frail and uncertain, that I often wondered if Ersh had somehow robbed her at birth—if birth was what you called sorting which parts of your own flesh would leave you and become opinionated.

*Or had Ersh chosen to discard with Lesy's flesh every shred of weakness from her own?*

Some curiosities I knew better than to pursue.

"Some haste would be useful, my lovely Riosolesy-ki. There are precautions to be taken—much to complete!" Cureceo-ki's tone eased only slightly, but he held out a gracious arm, eye rings aglow. "I will take care of everything while you prepare yourself. I merely need—" His lower two eyes seemed to search Lesy for something. Sure enough, he asked sharply: "The rest of the supplies—for the demonstration. Where are they! Don't tell me you forgot them!"

If I'd been Lanivarian, my lip would have curled over a fang, rude or not. My fingers itched to wiggle at him.

But Lesy's skin swelled into a glorious mottling of amber and ultraviolet. *Triumph?* "We've created three new works for the exhibit! The crate's waiting in my room. You will take care of them, won't you?"

"But ..." I'd never seen a Dokeci completely pale before. *Not attractive.* "What about the supplies?" Cureceo-ki squeaked. "Don't tell me you rui— used them all?"

"I don't think so." Lesy took a moment to think deeply. I could have answered for her; under the circumstances, I couldn't imagine why. "Why yes. There's quite a few left."

The curator's skin flushed with smooth whorls of elated rose. "With more of your exquisite art, Riosolesy-ki. How splendid! Splendid. Come now, you must rest and prepare yourself while we finish our tasks. Your audience awaits."

I kept my third eye locked on the curator. Dokeci vision was extraordinary, quite reasonable in a species that relied on the morphing of skin to provide emotional context, though such cues could mislead, depending on the intentions and skill of the owner of that skin. Dokeci dialects were laced with wisdoms such as "wrinkles don't lie" and "never buy from a smoothie."

Needless to say, by this point, I didn't trust a patch of Cureceo-ki's hide.

\* \* \*

"You should try on your cloak for the gala, Ses-ki. We won't have access to the wardrobe bags in transit, I'm quite sure. Space travel is so inconvenient. I've always thought so. Did I mention the gala?"

*With every other breath.* "We know mine fits," I reminded her. "Are you sure we shouldn't go down to shipping and check on your work?"

"You may be fine." The pout was back. "I'm still in turmoil. Turmoil!"

I relented. What Lesy didn't mention was that whatever cloak she wore would have to hide the supports her more mature Dokeci-self would need on the planet. Here, on the station, she could enjoy swirling the fabric around. Her arms swept up the next option, a green gauzy mass that resembled a "cloak" only by virtue of being wrapped first about her neck. It gave her a striking resemblance to an overripe seed pod.

Cureceo-ki had taken the crates, including the one with Ersh's heads. If his arms were tighter around the crate containing the remaining excretions, that wasn't my business. Ephemeral greed, as Ersh would say, was their curse, not ours.

The door chime sounded. Lesy swirled her way to it, clearly thrilled to show her cloak to someone of better taste than her Youngest web-kin. But it was only a delivery. She turned back into the room, arms wrapped around a bouquet of flowers and a slim twisted bottle filled with a copper liquid. "Look, Ses-ki! Welcoming gifts from the gallery!"

"You haven't left yet," I pointed out.

Lesy ignored this, busy pouring the liquid into two glasses. She looked at me, her skin mottled pink, then returned the liquid from one of the glasses to the bottle. "When you're older," she clucked at me. She took a sip. "Wonderful vintage."

As I was at least 400 years more vintage than any living Dokeci, I opened my mouth to complain.

The glass slipped from Lesy's finger. She let out a surprised moan and her skin went flaccid, its color draining away. She slumped to the floor, the gauzy green cloak settling around her.

I desperately firmed my hold on my Dokeci-form as Lesy abandoned hers, cycling to that perfect teardrop of blue, her surface glistening with drops of moisture. *Poison.*

There wasn't much time. The Prime Law. *Never reveal web-form to aliens.* I lunged for the bouquet of flowers and tossed them at her. The leaves, stems, and flowers touched and became her, their living matter assimilated into web-mass. *It should be enough.*

It was. She was back as Riosolesy-ki, sprawled on top of her gauzy cloak, a copper stain spreading from the dropped glass.

I waited expectantly.

She didn't move.

*Not good.* It was impossible to poison a web-being—our instinct to cycle was too quick for that. When Lesy returned to her Dokeci-self, her memory would have rebuilt everything about her forms' sake, not unmetabolized drugs. A web-being remembered broken bone, not any painkiller still in her blood.

My tubal pumps were protesting. I eased closer, careful to avoid the stain, and poked Lesy firmly in the abdomen. *Nothing.* I laid the first portion of one arm over her skin. Warmth, overlapped pulses, a rise and fall that signaled respiration.

I moved away, far away, finally huddling in the furthest corner from my web-kin's unconscious self.

I was alone.

I'd never been alone before.

*How was I to know what to do?*

\* \* \*

Portula Colony was a cluster of spheres, the centermost and largest containing both gravity generators and living quarters, the outer being studios and communal space. The pool, with its view of the nebula, was to one end. To the other was a slowly growing tangle of warehouse pods. Most were for Lesy's previous creations—she was, if nothing else, productive. I shuddered at the image of corridors jammed with junk-coated Ersh heads.

But I had other concerns. Lesy was still unconscious. There was nothing to eat in her room. *Panic made me hungry.* Help for her and food for me could be summoned. There was also a criminal curator to be caught, preferably in the act.

All of which would be easy—for an adult. There was a com panel - visual, given Dokeci self-expression. There were neighbors. Probably five-armed station security patrolling the outer corridors, eyes vigilant.

*And there was me, alone, trapped by this form.* Young Dokeci became clever mimics before developing an understanding of language. Lesy's "idiotic prattle" just about covered it. No adult on this station could believe a word I said. The sudden inexplicable appearance of a non-Dokecian on Portula would likely be noticed.

*Ersh would not approve.*

That left me one alternative. I went to the art supply cupboards. "I'll show you non-verbal," I muttered to myself, pulling out supplies.

\* \* \*

"My work's been stolen?? Are you sure?"

I could only gaze, mute, at my web-kin. I'd never seen Lesy happier.

I wasn't alone. The station manager rumpled in confused distress. "You authorized the shipping request, Riosolesy-ki," she repeated, as if this might help, "but the destination wasn't the gallery on Dokeci-Na. I'm deeply sorry, Riosolesy-ki. The entire affair appears to have been a hoax. The gallery hasn't—there's no exhibition of your work scheduled. Cureceo-ki falsified her credentials. You were sedated." A neat sidestep around "nearly murdered," I decided. "Altogether an elaborate, well-planned theft, I fear. Portula Station will of course pursue a full investigation."

"Oh, I couldn't possibly press charges." Lesy sparkled. "No need for an investigation. They loved my work. They had to have it. What artist could want more?"

I felt sorry for the perplexed station manager as Lesy almost pushed her out the door.

There was something less happy about my web-kin as she looked at me. "You've done it now, haven't you?" In a low voice. "I can't hide what happened."

"What do you think happened?" I asked innocently.

"You called for medics, security personnel. Set the station on alert! She'll have to know. She will know. This will be bad, Ses-ki." Lesy sank on a cushion, her skin mottled with distress, only to bounce up again. "What—?" She reached underneath and pulled out the head of the infamous Teganersha-Ki. "This isn't mine," she announced. She plucked at the gauzy green fabric covering most of the face "This is. What have you done to my cloak, Ses-ki?"

I took the head and put it over mine. "Help! Help! This is Riosolesy-ki. I think I've been poi—poi—poisoned!! Ahhhhhharggghhhhhh." My voice echoed within the cavity, coming out deeper and nicely desperate. I pulled off the head and grinned.

"That's—" One of the things I loved most about Lesy was her laugh in any form. Now, she dropped on her abdomen and rocked back and forth, her beaked mouthparts clicking together in a blur, her skin rising in welts of purple that drew the same response from my own.

Ersh might not like being imitated, but she'd have to admit I'd followed her rules.

*Well, she didn't have to admit anything, but there could be a volume reduction in the inevitable lecture.*

Once we'd both calmed, Lesy sighed. "My only regret, Youngest, is we won't be going to Dokeci-Na. I know you were counting on it. I'm sorry."

I shrugged with all five arms. "There's the pool."

Lesy smiled. "Wonderful idea. Just what we need. Let's go!" She surged to her feet.

*It felt odd to feel the Elder.* "What about your art?" Cureceo-ki might have been after Tumbler excretions, but the end result was the same. All of Lesy's "best"—or at least her newest—work was gone. "What if it's never found?"

My Web-kin lifted her arms and spun around. "I will always have it in my tubal pumps." *Which made no sense.* Then she stopped and winked her uppermost eye at me. "Besides, each piece is marked. Long after the current owners pass into dust, I'll be able to find everyone."

"How?"

"My creations are part of me; I am part of them."

*Was this more idiotic prattle?*

Looking at my triumphant, ever-mysterious web-kin, I wondered suddenly if any of us took her as seriously as we should. "What do you mean?" I asked.

Lesy winked again. "A touch of blue, Youngest. That's all. Signed work is more precious, don't you think? Now, shall we go?"

I followed my Elder to the pool.

But I kept wondering ...

*Where was the first Ersh-head I'd made?*

*And why hadn't I seen blue paint in Lesy's cupboards?*

*Finally, here are the traditional furries of furry fiction. Are they bioengineered? Is the story set in a fantasy world in which everyone just happens to be a furry? Don't worry it too much -- just relax and enjoy the story.*

# Fly the Friendly Skies

## *by Bryan Feir*

The golden-brown feline stood at the front of the cabin in her tight blue uniform, finishing off the pre-flight spiel. "Please keep your seat belts fastened at all times while in your seat. Once we achieve our suborbital trajectory, effective gravity will be considerably lower than you are used to. If this causes you any discomfort, please summon one of the flight attendants. Also, airsickness bags are available underneath the armrest of your seat."

She gave a professional smile as she looked down over the cabin; it was smaller than usual for an aircraft, and all the seats were first class ones that could be folded back like small beds. "We thank you for joining us on this inaugural flight of the new Starliner suborbital flight, which should take us to Tokyo in just under three hours. We hope you have a pleasant flight."

She began to walk down the aisle towards the rear of the plane, the tight skirt constraining her movements. Noticing a shift out of the corner of her eye, she swayed off to the side just enough to avoid a groping paw from the wolf sitting near the front; she continued down the aisle without giving any sign that anything had happened.

Reaching the back of the cabin, she pulled on the curtain that separated the galley area from the main aisle, and only then let herself relax.

Standing in the galley were two other flight attendants, a deer and a vixen, both wearing the same tailored uniforms. The deer gave the feline a bit of a smirk. "So, Jen, what's the verdict?"

Jen made sure the curtain was latched down, then turned back to face the others. "Whoever chose these uniforms needs to be on the receiving end of a sexual harassment lawsuit. It's hard to walk in these tiny skirts."

The deer laughed, "But we're 'reliving the glory days of air travel.' Or so all the ads say."

"In that only people who are seriously rich can afford it, sure." Jen leaned over and rubbed her paws over her legs. "And whoever thought to put us in stockings, anyway?"

"They don't bother me any."

The feline snorted. "Cervines don't have the fine fur underlayer to interfere with anything too tight."

"And the person in charge of the uniforms is a horse. They don't either."

The vixen finally looked up from where she was shaping her claws with a file. "At least the skirt being tight at least means it won't be trying to float up when we hit the top of the flight path in free-fall."

The deer chuckled. "Tammy has a point… for once." As the vixen stuck her long tongue out, the deer added, "So, what's the crowd like?"

Jen leaned back against a support pad on the wall, and started wrapping the safety harness around herself. "Mostly ordinary first-class types. Seats 2-C and 4-D were drunk before boarding, so keep some extra sickness bags handy. The wolf in seat 2-C has wandering paws. 3-D and 3-F are a mouse family with a child of about two years; that's the only child on board. The little Pekingese in 6-A looks annoyed about something, and may take it out on anyone who happens to be too close. There are at least two obvious reporters in there, so hopefully everybody will be smart enough to not to cause too much of a ruckus."

The vixen hmmmed, nodded, then tucked her little file down into a pocket before she began to buckle herself in as well. "So what's the plan for the first drink run?"

Jen brushed her hair back behind her to pin it back against the wall. "We'll park the cart on the left side of row 2 to block the wandering wolf; I'll be at the front, you can be at the back to coo over the mice for a bit. Daisy, if you could handle the calls for the first pass? We'll switch for the meal run, Daisy handles the cart with me and Tammy sits on call."

The deer finished buckling herself down. "Fine by me. I've got just one thing to be thankful for, myself."

Tammy looked back at her across the galley area. "What's that?"

"Nobody's getting food until *after* we pass free-fall."

Jen chuckled as the engine noise rose, nearly drowning out her words of "Amen to that."

# About the Authors

<u>Ken Pick</u>

Ken Pick (1955-current) is a greymuzzle computer programmer and polymath from Southern California who's been keeping a low profile in the furry community since the 1980s. Cursed with a hyperactive imagination (among other things) he writes (among many-many other things) in an attempt to reproduce the classic s-f magazine fiction he read in the Seventies.

Originally written for an anthology of Catholic SF, "Mask of the Ferret" is the first "episode" of a projected novel centering around ferret "bad girl" Jill Noir and Vatican "operative" Fr. Heidler -- not so much space opera as living their lives in a space-opera universe. Jill herself was inspired by a fursuit at the first Further Confusion masquerade in January 1999.

<u>Alan Loewen</u>

Craig Alan Loewen (1954-current) was born in Easthampton, New York; the product of a long line of German Mennonite farmers on his father's side and a long line of Episcopalian whalers and fishermen on his mother's side.

Loewen became an avid reader in his early years. His favorite novels will always be H. G. Wells' *The War of the Worlds* along with Jules Verne's *Journey to the Center of the Earth*. Loewen knows that his writing did not originate in a vacuum, and acknowledges he stands on the shoulders of such giants as C. S. Lewis, H. P. Lovecraft, Alan Garner, Robert Holdstock, and many others.

Loewen's stories come from a plethora of experience in working as a factory worker, inner-city security guard, park ranger, youth worker, radio personality, stage actor, stage and parlor magician, an ordained member of the clergy, computer salesman, counselor for mood disorders, life coach, and a host of other vocations.

Loewen presently lives in Gettysburg, Pennsylvania. Married and with three sons, he shares his home with a Sheltie, three cats, a sun conure lovingly dubbed "The Death Chicken," and way too many rabbits.

## L. Sprague de Camp

L(yon) Sprague de Camp (1907-2000) was a popular and prolific s-f author throughout most of the 20th century. He specialized in humorous s-f & fantasy, such as "Nothing in the Rules" (1939) about a small-town swimming contest in which a mermaid is entered. (She gets drunk on the chlorine in the pool.) Many of his stories featured anthropomorphized aliens and animals; notably the four "Johnny Black" stories (1938-1940) about an experimentally intelligent black bear, one of first appearances in s-f of an "uplifted" animal. He and Fritz Leiber coined the phrase "sword & sorcery", and he edited the first s&s anthology in 1963.

De Camp's story here, "The Inspector's Teeth", is from his *Viagens Interplanetarias* series of light space operas, which Donald A. Wollheim dubbed "sword & planets" s-f in parodic imitation of Leiber & de Camp's s&s.

## Robert Sheckley

Robert Sheckley (1928-2005) was known mainly for wryly humorous and satiric s-f short stories, many about mishaps of overconfident humans among newly-discovered interstellar aliens, particularly from the early 1950s through the late 1970s. He was one of the first writers of television s-f, authoring several scripts for *Captain Video and His Video Rangers* (1949-1955). His short stories have been adapted into episodes of anthology s-f radio and TV programs from the U.S. to the U.S.S.R. His short story "Seventh Victim" (*Galaxy Science Fiction*, April 1953), expanded and filmed as the 1965 Italian/French movie *The Tenth Victim*, was the first of many futuristic government-authorized televised "murder contest" novels and feature films, such as the Japanese *Battle Royale* and the American *The Hunger Games*.

## Robert Silverberg

Robert Silverberg (1935-current) began writing s-f in his early teens. He had one novel published in 1955 while in college, and 49 short stories, novelettes and novellas in 1956, many in collaboration with Randall

Garrett. Most were space operas, but in the mid-1960s he began writing more literary s-f, winning many Hugo and Nebula awards. He currently has 49 individual s-f novels, several s-f novel series such as *Majipoor* (27 novels), 56 short fiction collections, 66 edited individual anthologies; several anthology series such as *Alpha* (nine volumes), *New Dimensions* (12 volumes), and *Universe* (three volumes); and over 150 s-f book reviews. His non-fiction books, many under pseudonyms, include numerous biographies, works on Egyptology, archaeology, and other subjects, and such histories as *The Stolen Election: Hayes vs. Tilden, 1876*. And this is only a partial list. He promptly joined the discussion on furry fandom's *Flayrah* of one of his s-f novels.

### Poul Anderson

Poul Anderson (1926-2001) met Gordon Dickson while both were college students in Minneapolis, and became lifelong friends. Aside from collaborating on the Hoka stories, they led separate careers as s-f novelists and short story writers, specializing in both humorous and dramatic adventure plots.

Anderson's notable heroes include the interstellar trader-team of the flamboyant merchant-prince Nicholas van Rijn (loosely based upon Denmark's King Christian IV) and his agents, the human David Falkayn and his alien partners, the catlike Chee Lan and the huge dinosaurlike Adzel. Several of Anderson's stories feature "normal" but intelligent animals, including his 1954 novel *Brain Wave*, and his "Operation" fantasies with the werewolf-witch detective team of Steve and Virginia Matuchek and Ginny's smart-ass cat familiar Svartalf. Many readers noted extremely strong plot parallels between Anderson's novelette "Call Me Joe" (*Astounding Science Fiction*, April 1957) and James Cameron's motion picture *Avatar* (20th Century Fox, December 2009).

### Gordon R. Dickson

Gordon R. Dickson (1923-2001) was best-known for the interstellar space-mercenary Dorsai dramatic stories, and the *Dragon Knight* fantasies featuring Jim Eckert, a modern American whose mind is trapped in the body of the fantasy-world dragon Gorbash. (Nine novels; Dickson was writing a tenth when he died.)

Both Anderson and Dickson were Guests of Honor of the annual World Science Fiction Conventions, and both won Hugo and Nebula awards. Dickson's short story "St. Dragon and the George" (*The Magazine*

About the Authors

*of Fantasy & Science Fiction*, September 1957, expanded into the novel *The Dragon and the George* (Doubleday, July 1976), was purchased by the producers Arthur Rankin Jr. and Jules Bass and used for its plot for their August 1982 Rankin/Bass Productions' animated feature *The Flight of Dragons*, nominally based upon the story-less picture book by Peter Dickinson.

## James H. Schmitz

James H. Schmitz (1911-1981) specialized in light space opera featuring strong female characters fighting for personal equality. His stories were usually set in the Federation of the Hub, a future galactic civilization of the fourth millennium dominated by humans, but with intelligent aliens. His best-known characters were the older secret agent Trigger Argee, and the younger Telzey Amberdon. "Novice" (*Analog Science Fiction -> Science Fact*, June 1962) is the first of 13 Telzey Amberdon stories (many with her partnering with Trigger Argee), set when she is a mid-adolescent whom nobody takes seriously. None of the humans, anyway...

## Elizabeth McCoy

Elizabeth McCoy (1971-current) is a writer with Steve Jackson Games in the role-playing game industry. In 1995 she and her husband Walter Millikan wrote the GURPS supplement, *GURPS Illuminati University*; the codification of the online campaign, winner of the 1992 Origins Award for Best Roleplaying Supplement. In 1993 she, Millikan, and Steve Jackson won a lawsuit against the U.S. Secret Service for illegally seizing the company's computers and electronic information in 1990; an event that led to the creation of the Electronic Frontier Foundation. The names Kintara and several others in McCoy's stories are derived from planets and creatures in Steve Jackson Games, and are used with permission.

She writes, "Elizabeth McCoy has been writing about Kintarans for many years now, with stories appearing in the magazine *PawPrints Fanzine*, as well as in Sofawolf Press' anthology *Best In Show*. (Those stories, and a couple others set in that universe, are now available as ebooks at most ebook-sellers; there's a list at elizabethmccoy.dreamwidth.org.) She lives in the Frozen Wastelands of New Hampshire with a spouse, child, and cats. She thanks everyone who has enjoyed her stories, hopes you liked this one, and is very awkward talking about herself in the third person. ...look, a shiny thing! *runs away*"

## Cairyn

Cairyn's real name is Ronald W. Klemp (1964-current). His full fursona is Cairyn Playful Otter. He was born in Northern Germany and became acquainted early on with science fiction and fantasy literature. Despite these leanings he chose computer science as his professional career, the starving poet firmly in mind.

He is one of the first German furry fans, since the early '90s, and is one of the main staffers of EuroFurence; the European furry convention usually held in Germany. He is also one of the more prominent European furry authors with several short stories, best-known for his novel *Khiray of the River*, serialized online during the 1990s and published in both German and English since then. "Kings and Vagabonds" was first self-published in English in his fanzine *Storyfur Prime*.

## Phyllis Gotlieb

Phyllis Gotlieb (1926-2009) was one of the first s-f authors proud to be known as a Canadian. She was as well-known for poetry as for her fiction. Her first s-f short story was "A Grain of Manhood" in *Fantastic Science Fiction Stories*, September 1959. Her first s-f novel, *Sunburst* (Fawcett Gold Medal Books, December 1964), was the inspiration for the Sunburst Award for Canadian Literature of the Fantastic, presented to a Canadian author annually since 2001. *The Canadian Encyclopedia* says, "Her other fantasy novels include the bestselling Starcats trilogy: *A Judgment of Dragons* (1980), featuring two cat protagonists, *Emperor, Swords, Pentacles* (1982) and *The Kingdom of the Cats* (1985). *A Judgment of Dragons* won the inaugural Aurora Award for best Canadian Science Fiction and Fantasy Novel." "The King's Dogs" was the second story in *A Judgment of Dragons*, actually a fixup of the first four Starcats novellas.

## Julie E. Czerneda

Canadian Julie E. Czerneda (1955-current) has been writing s-f since 1997. Her novel *In the Company of Others* (DAW Books, June 2001) won Canada's Prix Aurora Award. She has three Web Shifters books featuring the shape-shifter Esen-alit-Quar. She has also edited 15 anthologies of s-f & fantasy. She says that she "transformed her love and knowledge of biology into science fiction novels published by DAW Books NY, including

## About the Authors

*The Clan Chronicles, Web Shifters,* and *Species Imperative* (to be re-released as a 10th anniversary omnibus in 2014) series, and [the standalone] *In The Company of Others.* Her work has received international acclaim, multiple awards, and best-selling status. Her latest, *A Turn of Light* (DAW Books, March 2013), marks her debut in fantasy, and it's huge, with toads and a dragon. Julie's next release will be *A Play of Shadow* (November 2014), sequel to *Turn.* After that, it's s-f again, first *Reunification,* then a joyful return to Esen. For more about Julie's work, please visit <u>www.czerneda.com</u>.

<u>Bryan Feir</u>

Bryan Feir (1968-current) was born in Prince George, B.C., Canada. He has been reading s-f and comics since the mid-70s, attending s-f cons since the mid-80s, and active in the furry fandom since just before FurryMUCK started in 1990. He has been writing prose and poetry off and on since 1980 or so, joined the Furthest North Crew Amateur Press Alliance in 1995 and the Megamorphics APA in 1997, then became the production manager for the Furthest North Crew in 1997. He works as an embedded systems programmer, and does writing, bookbinding, and latchhooking on the side.

# About the Artist

Roz Gibson

Roz Gibson (1963-current) is a graduate of the California Institute of the Arts character animation program (BA 1989). She has been doing animation, freelance illustration and comics for over two decades. While her best known works are the Jack Salem comics, she has also done numerous other projects, including art director for the long-running furry artist fanzine *Huzzah*, work for Antarctic Press, Radio Comix, and collaborations with webcomic artist David Hopkins. She lives in the Los Angeles area with a husband and four cats. Most of her recent art can be found on her FurAffinity gallery: http://www.furaffinity.net/user/rgibson/

# About the Editor

<u>Fred Patten</u>

Fred Patten (1940-current) joined the Los Angeles Science Fantasy Society in 1960 while in college, and has been an active s-f & fantasy fan ever since. He began writing for and publishing fanzines in 1961 (see http://www.zinewiki.com/Salamander), and has written over a thousand reviews of anthropomorphic literature since 1962, irregularly for s-f fanzines in the 1960s, 1970s, and 1980s; for *Yarf!* from 1990 to 2003, for *Claw & Quill* in 2004-2005, for *Anthro* from 2005 to 2008, for *Renard's Menagerie* in 2008, and for *Flayrah* since 2011. He founded the Ursa Major Awards and has been on its administrative Anthropomorphic Literature and Arts Association since 2001. He is a member of the Furry Writers' Guild and the Furry Hall of Fame. He also co-founded Japanese anime fandom in 1977 and wrote regularly about anime and manga for over 25 years. He was awarded the Comic-Con's Inkpot Award in 1980 for helping to introduce anime to America. A stroke in 2005 has left him partly paralyzed and bedridden, from which he carries on his fanac via a MacBook Pro laptop.

# About the Publisher

<u>FurPlanet Productions</u>

FurPlanet is a small press publisher serving the niche market that is furry fiction. We sell furry-themed books and comics published by us and most major publishers in the community. If you can't get to a furry convention where we are selling in the dealers room, visit *www.FurPlanet. com* to shop online.

www.ingramcontent.com/pod-product-compliance
Lightning Source LLC
Chambersburg PA
CBHW071859020726
47502CB00003B/811